APOLLO

Bosnian Chronicle

Ivo Andrić

Translated from the Serbo-Croat
by Celia Hawkesworth
in collaboration with Bogdan Rakić

APOLLO

Apollo Librarian | Michael Schmidt || Series Editor | Neil Belton
Text Design | Lindsay Nash || Artwork | Jessie Price

www.apollo-classics.com | www.headofzeus.com

First published in the Serbo-Croat language with the title *Travnička
Hronika* in 1945.

First published in Great Britain in 1992 as *The Days of the Consuls* by
Forest Books.

This paperback edition published in the United Kingdom in 2016
by Apollo, an imprint of Head of Zeus Ltd.

1 3 5 7 9 10 8 6 4 2

A CIP catalogue record for this book is available
from the British Library.

ISBN (PB) 9781784971120

Typeset by Adrian McLaughlin
Printed and bound in Denmark by Nørhaven

Head of Zeus Ltd
Clerkenwell House
45–47 Clerkenwell Green
London EC1R OHT

For Bogdan, Svetlana and Nikola the Third

The Bridge Over the Drina is probably Ivo Andrić's best-known work but *Bosnian Chronicle* is his best.

For much of its existence the Ottoman Empire was a more tolerant entity than its Christian counterparts across Europe. And yet faced with the pressures of European commercial expansion and technological innovation, the Empire's highly codified social structures began to buckle. As they did, the conservatism of the Ottoman elites, especially in places on the imperial periphery like Bosnia and Hercegovina, became ever more entrenched.

Andrić's remarkable examination of a society unable to grasp the profundity of the rapid changes taking place on its borders is exquisitely poetic, especially as rendered in Celia Hawkesworth's elegant translation. Andrić paints an intricate portrait of rivalries, suspicions and fears between and within the rich variety of Bosnian communities – Muslim, Jewish and Christian – as seen across a span of seven years by a young French consul who arrives in the remote north Bosnian town of Travnik at the height of Napoleonic power.

With an uncanny eye for historical detail, Andrić unveils the fearful dynamics, both domestic and foreign, that would eventually condemn the Ottoman Empire to extinction and Bosnia and Hercegovina to a painful cycle of poverty, underdevelopment and violence, which in some eyes justified its epithet in the local language as the *tamni vilayet* or Dark Region. Yet despite the despair inherent in almost every page of this book, Andrić's descriptive prowess made this one of the most elevating reading experiences I can recall. An absolute gem.

Misha Glenny, 2016

Introduction

*B*osnian Chronicle was completed in Bucharest while the Second World War tore Europe apart. It was in Bosnia that the starting gun for the First World War was fired in 1914, some of the cruelest action of the Second World War occurred, and the bloodiest European war of the late twentieth century was fought. Such events are foreshadowed in Ivo Andrić's turbulent pages which draw the jagged fault line between cultures and religions at the beginning of the previous century. West meets east in distrust and misunderstanding. The Chronicle's events and non-events are prophetic, a sense of drama intensifying, yet deferred. The reader learns no longer to anticipate climaxes, settling instead, alert, into the present of the narrative.

The Ottomans, after conquering Bosnia in the fifteenth century, built mosques and market, improved the roads and modernized the town. When nearby Sarajevo was burned by the Austrians in 1699, Travnik succeeded as administrative centre. For a century and a half, up to 1850, Travnik was the capital from which the governors of Bosnia ruled this province.

Travnik cannot be called a city. In population it was — and is — little more than a modest town. But it was a focal political and commercial centre. Here lived the Vizier, appointed by the Sultan in Istanbul. Here he held his Divan, the assembly that considered or rubber stamped his decisions. Under his arcane aegis rival communities coexisted in tension one with another. The local beys, Muslim men of substance, pursued their affairs, meeting to smoke, drink coffee and set the world to rights in the shade of the old lime tree in the garden of Lutvo's, on the edge of the bazaar. There the *Chronicle* opens just as the Europeans arrive, and there it ends with their departure. Under the same lime tree the same beys smoke and gossip.

Before the Ottomans modernised what became Travnik, there were earlier inhabitants, Christians, Romans. Each culture over-wrote, without erasing, the one that came before. In the midst of the bazaar stood the Yeni Mosque, built on what had been the Church of St Catherine, itself superimposed on a Roman temple, which in turn rested on 'large red blocks of granite, the remains of a far older cult, a former temple of the god Mithras.' Travnik, like other Balkan communities, is an unresolved palimpsest, baffling the Europeans in its volatile complexity.

The inhabitants of nineteenth-century Travnik were suspicious and tolerant in equal degrees. No one was given an easy ride, no one apart from the beys ever felt quite at home. But distrust and hostility were kept within bounds. Emblematic of the situation, displaced and self-effacing, was the small population of Sephardic Jews, expelled from Andalusia over three centuries before, who survived as merchants, craftsmen, beleaguered money-lenders. Viewing the world from the perspective of their alienation, they longed to go back, not to a Biblical promised land, but to a Spain where, with Muslims and Christians, they had been at home. Salomon Atijas, a Jew who helped the Consul and whose integrity impressed the European, speaks almost the last words in the novel, thanking Daville for unostentatiously treating his people as human beings.

France in 1807, and the Austro-Hungarians soon after, established consulates in Travnik to observe and influence events: the Roman Catholic Serbians were rising against the Ottoman Turks, 'a visible sign of the new times and new methods of struggle', and the great rival European powers wanted a stake in the outcome. *Bosnian Chronicle* starts with the impending arrival of 'Bunaparta's' consul, Monsieur Jean Daville, his wife and family, and ends with their departure seven years and 430 pages later. By the end, his world, and ours, has been unsettled by the curious magic of the place, its culture and corruption, its squalor and charm.

The 1961 Nobel Prize for literature was awarded to Ivo Andrić primarily for *Bosnian Chronicle* and two other books completed in the same years, *The Bridge Over the Drina* and *The Woman from Sarajevo*, all published in Serbo-Croat in 1945. They constitute his celebrated Bosnian Trilogy.

Almost half a century later this English translation of *Bosnian Chronicle* appeared, a collaboration by two translators. Andrić is 'notoriously difficult to translate', they say. There is the challenge of his language, and the choices he made which are politically charged, since he used Serbian norms when writing of Bosnia. These elements are lost on the English reader, but we do hear how each community he evokes has a different mind-set, a different idiom and rhythm of speech, and each has a different way of seeing. Then the European envoys bring their own gradually maturing points of view to bear. How does Andrić keep *himself* out of it? This is his art, foregrounding the voices of his narrative, never interposing a modern presence or directing the reader. The translators have managed to suggest this with great skill.

Andrić's approach is unusual for English readers. The translators call it 'clear-sighted, unsentimental irony'. We might rather regard Andrić's self-withholding as a refusal to take sides, an invitation to readers to enter, not into judgement, but into the living tense of the narrative. Intersecting and colliding lives and wider histories emerge in their own terms. The French consul's perspective is sympathetic: he is a newcomer, engaged in seeing and then in trying to make sense of this strange world and report back to his superiors. Sometimes he errs, and we know Travnik well enough by the time he does so to identify his errors. Sometimes in his reports he chooses to simplify, knowing that the reality of Bosnia will be incomprehensible to Paris. He grapples with a culture more complex than his own. And than ours, also.

Then 'Bunaparta' begins his retreats. The confident voice of the consul begins to stutter. What is modern Europe, exposed in this alien and inscrutable place? What is the staying value of the new ideas set against the layered history of Travnik and what it represents? The pace of the book – slow, accreting – is terrific in its way, revealing a world caught between east and west, past and future, between conflicting religious visions and a secular ideology.

Though the book is a *Chronicle*, it has novel elements, especially in the relations between the French and Austrian envoys and their entourages. When Daville's 'long-awaited opponent, the Austrian Consul General', Josef von Mitterer arrives, he is accompanied by his wife, a propertyless Hungarian baroness, hot-headed, romantic and frigid, always repelled when a suitor seeks to cash in sexually on her possessive flirtations. Her relations with Daville's first secretary Des Fossés, ten years her junior, nearly cause an incident: diplomacy is tried and triumphs. Andrić displays something like the tact of Stendhal in unfolding this relationship: despite the exotic setting, one is put in mind of that other classic provincial romance which ends so differently, in *The Red and the Black*. Des Fossés, like Daville himself, has literary pretensions: the promise and deceit of literature are embedded neatly in what is a compelling historical chronicle.

As in his novel *The Bridge on the Drina*, Andrić enjoys weaving stories together. *Bosnian Chronicle* is more deliberately constructed than *The Bridge*, more limited in its time span and specific in its themes. There are memorable minor characters. The humpless hunchback Niccolo Rotta and his friendly rival Cesare Davena are precisely balanced, and the ill-starred physician from the monastery Brother Luka is a resigned spirit, wryly aware that he will be punished if his cures fail a powerful Turkish client, and punished too if they succeed. Most of the characters are minor in relation to Andrić's larger purpose. Even the Viziers are temporary: almost visitors like the European Consuls, sent from some other province for a purpose and then replaced as the fortunes of state turn.

In a novel with the range and sweep of *Bosnian Chronicle*, the main conflict is between the large forces of history, religion and ideology, of east and west. Their passing embodiment in lives vividly portrayed gives history a hundred telling faces and voices. This book makes real what the Balkans were and, as the Yeni Mosque near Lutvo's café shows, this is how it will continue.

Andrić was never comfortable with set forms and genres. Fiction disconnected from history was for him artificial, purposeless. A novel that is a chronicle has responsibilities to history, geography and to a kind of truth with which a conventional novel need not concern itself. It has an inbuilt seriousness, it asks the reader to engage not only with the story, but with something which can be explored, verified, argued with; something that refuses to be, merely, art. Late in life Andrić wrote an essay-story entitled 'Conversation with Goya'. Goya was deaf, so it is hardly a conversation, but the artist who declared that the sleep of reason brings forth monsters, and who sketched and painted unforgettable monstrosities, says, 'those for whom there are a thousand ways of painting do not paint'. *Bosnian Chronicle* does not aspire to the condition of art, which is why there is so much oxygen in its lungs. It was the only kind of book Andrić could write, and perhaps for that reason it takes its place on a shelf with Stendhal's and Balzac's novels, but also with travel books like Rebecca West's *Black Lamb and Grey Falcon*, written at roughly the same time as *Bosnian Chronicle*, and Misha Glenny's classic histories of the place.

Michael Schmidt, 2016

Note on the Pronunciation of Serbo-Croatian Names

With the exception of some Turkish words and names Serbo-Croatian spellings have been retained. The language may be written in either the Cyrillic or the Latin alphabet. The Latin alphabet includes a number of unfamiliar letters listed below. Serbo-Croat is strictly phonetic, with one letter representing one sound. The stress normally falls on the first syllable.

C, c – ts, as in cats
Č, č – ch, as in church
Ć, ć – tj, close to č but softer i.e. t in future
Dž, dž – j, as in just
Đ, đ – dj, close to dž but softer i.e. d in verdure
J, j – y, as in yellow (Jugoslavija)
Š, š – sh, as in ship
Ž, ž – zh, as s in treasure

NB For a glossary of Turkish words used in the text, see page 518

Translator's Preface

The final version of this translation was completed in collaboration with Bogdan Rakić in his flat in Sarajevo, in April 1986. Andrić is notoriously difficult to translate: his distinctive rhythms cannot be reproduced easily in English. All consequent awkwardness in wording and structure is my responsibility. But I can at least feel confident that the translation is accurate in respect of its meaning, with all its nuances: Bogdan has an acute ear for both English and his native Serbo-Croat and he proved to be an exceptionally conscientious and demanding colleague. Those spring days in Sarajevo are for me the brightest in a series of happy associations with the land and people of Bosnia. I shall always cherish the memory of our working sessions round a table laden with dictionaries in which we frequently found that illustrations for rarely used words were taken from Andrić himself. Working painstakingly like that through what is at first sight a sombre text, we surprised ourselves by the frequency with which we laughed at the scenes and situations it evoked. The hall-mark of Andrić's style is just this clear-sighted, unsentimental irony.

Andrić's novel was written amidst the misery and tragedy of the Second World War. This translation is being prepared for publication as Sarajevo is racked once again by senseless violence. Nothing can reduce the pain of the knowledge of that grief, suffering and destruction, but Andrić's timeless wisdom can offer a counterweight of sustaining strength.

C.H.
July 1992

Prologue

For as long as anyone can remember, the little café known as "Lutvo's" has stood at the far end of the Travnik bazaar, below the shady, clamorous source of the "Rushing Brook". Not even the oldest people can remember Lutvo, its first proprietor. He has lain for at least a hundred years in one of the cemeteries scattered throughout Travnik, but everyone goes to Lutvo's for coffee and his name is still recalled and mentioned while so many sultans, viziers and beys have been long forgotten. In the garden of this little café, at the foot of a hill, a gentle secluded slope rises up against a cliff, in the shade of an old lime tree. Low benches of irregular shapes have been fitted together around the tree, among boulders and tufts of grass, making a place where it is pleasant to sit for a while and always hard to leave. The benches are weather-worn and warped by the years and long use – they have merged completely with the tree, earth and rock around them.

During the summer months, from the beginning of May to the end of October, this was by ancient tradition the place where the Travnik beys and other notables admitted to their company gathered, about the time of the afternoon prayer. At that time of day, none of the other townspeople would presume to sit and drink coffee here. The spot was known as "The Sofa". For generations this word had a clear social and political meaning in the popular speech of Travnik, because whatever was said, discussed and decided "on the Sofa" had almost the weight of a resolution of the counsellors at the Vizier's Divan.

On the last Friday of October 1806, some dozen beys were

sitting there, although the sky was already overcast and a wind was getting up, which always meant rain at this time of year. Each in his own set place, the beys were talking in low voices. Most of them were pensively watching the play of sun and clouds, smoking chibouks and coughing tetchily. They were discussing an important piece of news.

One of them, a certain Suleiman Bey Ajvaz, had recently travelled to Livno on business. While there he had met a man from Split, a reliable person, he said, who had told him the news he was now recounting to the others. They could not make it out and kept asking for details and making him repeat what he had already said.

"It was like this," Suleiman Bey explained. "The man simply asked me: 'Are you expecting visitors in Travnik?' 'Us?' I said. 'No, we don't want visitors.' 'That may be, but you'd better be ready for them,' he said, 'because you're getting a French consul. Bunaparta has asked at the Porte in Istanbul for permission to send a consul, to open a consulate in Travnik. And it's already been approved. You can expect the consul this coming winter.' I treated it as a joke: 'We've lived for hundreds of years without consuls, and that's how we'll go on. In any case, what would a consul do in Travnik?' But he persisted. 'Never mind how you lived in the past, now you're going to have to live with a consul. That's how things are. And the consul will find things to do. He'll sit beside the Vizier giving orders, watching how the beys and agas behave and what the Christians are up to, and keeping Bunaparta informed about it all.' 'There's never been anything of the kind; it couldn't happen,' I contradicted the foreigner. 'We've never had anyone meddling in our affairs and we won't let them start now.' 'Ah well, you see what you can do,' he said, 'but you'll have to accept the consul, because no one has ever refused what Bunaparta asked, and the Istanbul Government isn't going to. Far from it, as soon as Austria sees you've got a French consul, they'll ask you to take one of theirs as well, and then Russia will come along…' 'Now you're really going too far, my good fellow!' I stopped him, but he just smiled, the Latin bastard, tugged at his moustache, and said: 'You can cut this off, if things don't turn out just as I say, or very like it.' There, that's what I heard, my friends," said Ajvaz, concluding his story, "and I can't get it out of my head."

Given the circumstances – the French army had already been in Dalmatia for a year and Serbia was in a state of constant rebellion – a vague rumour like this was enough to upset and confuse the beys, who were already very worried. They brooded and fretted over what they had heard, although no one would have known it from their faces and their tranquil smoking. Speaking slowly and indecisively, in turn, they tried to guess what it could all mean, weighing up how much of it was a lie and what might be true, wondering what they should do to find out more about the matter and perhaps put a stop to it at the outset.

Some of them thought the whole thing had been made up or exaggerated to alarm them. Others commented, with some bitterness, that it was a sign of the times: there were such goings-on now in Istanbul, in Bosnia and the whole world, that nothing should surprise anyone and you had to be prepared for anything. Yet others consoled themselves by saying that this was Travnik – Travnik! – and not just any little provincial town, and that what happened to others need not, could not, happen here.

Everyone said something, just for the sake of speaking, but no one said anything very definite, because they were all waiting to hear what the oldest among them would have to say. This was Hamdi Bey Teskeredžić, a heavily built old man, whose movements were slow but whose gigantic body was still strong. He had fought in several wars, been wounded and captured. He had fathered eleven sons and eight daughters and had innumerable descendants. His beard and moustache were sparse and the whole of his sharp, regular face was sunburnt, covered with scars and blue marks from an old gunpowder explosion. He had heavy, drooping eyelids the colour of lead. His speech was slow but clear.

At last, Hamdi Bey put an end to the conjecture, foreboding and fear by saying, in his surprisingly youthful voice: "Come now, there's no sense trying to cross our bridges before we come to them, as the saying goes, or alarming people for no reason. You must listen and pay attention to everything, but you needn't believe every word straight away. Who knows what will happen with these consuls? Maybe they'll come and maybe they won't. And even if they do, the Lašva won't start flowing backwards: it'll keep on going the same old way. We're on our own ground here, and anyone else who comes is a stranger and won't be able to hold out for long. Many people have come here intending to stay, but so far we've seen the back of all of them. It'll be the same with the consuls if they do come. And there's not even any sign of them yet. That fellow may well have sent a request to Istanbul, but that doesn't mean it's decided. A lot of people ask for a lot of things, but you don't always get what you ask for…"

Hamdi Bey uttered these last words angrily then paused, and, in the complete silence, exhaled the smoke from his pipe before continuing: "And if it does happen! We shall have to see how it turns out and how long it lasts. No man's star shines forever, and it won't be any different with that… that…"

Here Hamdi Bey started to cough, choking with suppressed anger, and so he never did pronounce the name of "Bunaparta" which was in everyone's thoughts and on everyone's lips.

No one else said anything, and that was how the discussion of the latest news was concluded.

Soon the clouds completely covered the sun and there was a strong, cold gust of wind. The leaves on the poplars by the water's edge rustled with a metallic sound. The icy tremor passing through the whole valley of Travnik was a sign that for this year the meetings and conversations on the Sofa had come to an end. One by one the beys began to rise and disperse to their homes with a silent gesture of farewell.

1

Early in 1807 a number of unusual, previously unheard-of things began to happen in Travnik.

No one in Travnik had ever imagined that this was a town created for the commonplace. No one, not even the lowliest Muslim peasant from the slopes of Vilenica. This fundamental sense that they were in some way different from other people, destined for something better and finer, entered into every human creature with the cold wind from Vlasić mountain, with the biting water from the Roaring Brook, with the "sweet" wheat from the south-facing slopes round Travnik. It never left them, not even in their sleep, in poverty, or at the hour of their death.

This applied particularly to the Turks who lived in the town itself. But even the rayah of all three faiths, scattered over the steep outskirts or crowded together in their separate district, were filled with the same feeling, each in their own way and in accordance with their own condition. It applied to the very town, in whose position and layout there was something special, individual and proud.

Their town was in fact a deep, narrow ravine which generations had built up and cultivated, a fortified *pass* in which people had stayed to live permanently, adapting themselves to it over the centuries and adapting it to themselves. On both sides hills sloped steeply down to meet at a sharp angle in the valley where there was scarcely room for the narrow river and the road beside it. The whole place looked like a half-open book, with gardens, alleyways, houses, fields, graveyards and mosques drawn on each page.

No one has ever calculated how many hours of sunlight nature has denied this town, but it is certain that the sun rises later here and sets earlier than in any of the other numerous towns and villages of Bosnia. Even the people of Travnik do not deny this, although they insist that, when it does shine, it is nowhere so bright as over their town.

In this narrow, damp and draughty valley through which the Lašva flows and whose sides are studded with springs, dykes and brooks, there is virtually no straight road or any flat place where a man might step freely. Everything is steep and uneven, tortuous and intricate, connected or interrupted by private roads, fences, blind alleys, gardens and back-gates, graveyards and places of worship.

Here by the water, that mysterious, inconstant and powerful element, the generations are born and die. Here they grow, feeble and pale, but resilient and equal to anything. Here they live with the Vizier's Residence before their eyes – proud, slender, stylish, discriminating and shrewd. Here they work and prosper or sit idle and grow poor, all of them reserved and cautious, never laughing out loud, but inclined to sneer; not saying much, but enjoying whispered gossip. And here they are buried when their time comes, each according to his faith and customs, in water-logged graves, making way for a new generation of people just like themselves.

So the generations replace one another, handing down not only established characteristics, both physical and mental, but their land and their faith, not only an inherited sense of measure and proportion, not only a familiarity with all the roads, side-entrances and alleyways of their tortuous town, but an innate ability to understand the whole world and its people. The children of Travnik come into the world with all of this, but above all with a sense of pride. Pride is their second nature, a vital driving force which accompanies them throughout their lives, marking them out and distinguishing them readily from other people.

Their pride has nothing in common with the naïve brashness of well-to-do peasants or provincial townspeople who brag and bluster in ostentatious self-satisfaction. On the contrary, their pride is all inward; more a weighty heritage and a painful sense of responsibility to themselves, their family and town, or rather, to the grand, proud and unattainable image they have of themselves and their town.

Every human emotion has its limits, however, even the sense of one's own distinction. It was true that Travnik was the seat of the Vizier, and that its people were noble, smart, restrained and wise, fit to converse with kings. But even the people of Travnik had days when their pride stuck in their throats and they would secretly long to live, tranquil and carefree, in one of those ordinary, insignificant towns which do not enter into the calculations of emperors or conflicts between states, which do not bear the brunt of world events and do not lie in the path of celebrated and important figures.

The times were such that nothing agreeable could be expected and no good could come of anything. This was why the proud and cunning people of Travnik wanted nothing at all to happen but just to go on living, as far as possible without any changes or surprises. What good could be expected when the rulers of the world were at loggerheads, the peoples at each other's throats and their countries in flames? A new Vizier? He would be no better, probably worse, than the last, and his retinue would be unknown and numerous, hungry with God knows what new appetites. ("The best Vizier is the one who got as far as the border and then turned back to Istanbul without ever setting foot in Bosnia.") A foreigner? A distinguished traveller, perhaps? They knew all about such people. They would spend a bit of money and leave a few gifts in the town, but they would be followed by a search party or the very next day there would be questions. Who were they, what were they, where had they stayed, who had they talked to? By the time you had extricated yourself and shrugged it all off, you had spent that pittance ten times over. An informer? Or the agent of some unknown power with suspect intentions? After all there was never any way of telling what people might be carrying with them or who was working for whom.

In a word, there was no good anywhere these days. So, let's eat up the crust of bread we have and live out in peace what few days remain to each of us, in this noblest city on earth, and God preserve us from glory, important visitors and major events.

This was what the prominent people were secretly thinking in those first years of the nineteenth century, but it goes without saying that they kept it to themselves, for in every citizen of Travnik there is a long, tortuous path between a thought or desire and its visible or audible expression.

And there really had been a great many occurrences and changes of all kinds in recent years – at the end of the eighteenth and beginning of the nineteenth century. Events crowded in from all directions, colliding and rolling across Europe and the great Ottoman Empire and reaching even into this valley, to stop there like floodwater or its silt.

Ever since the Turks had withdrawn from Hungary, relations between Muslims and Christians had become increasingly difficult and complex and conditions in general had deteriorated. The soldiers of the great Empire, the agas and spahis, who had been obliged to abandon rich properties in the fertile plains of Hungary and return to their confined and wretched homeland, were bitter and resentful of everything Christian. Their presence increased the number of mouths to be filled, while the number of working hands remained the same. At the same time, those wars of the eighteenth century which had driven the Turks out of the neighbouring Christian lands and back into Bosnia, raised bold hopes among the Christian rayah, opening up previously unimagined prospects. And that inevitably also affected the attitude of the rayah towards their "Imperial masters, the Turks". Both sides, if it is possible to speak of two sides at this stage of the struggle, were now fighting, each in its own way and with the means appropriate to the circumstances. The Turks fought with pressure and force, the Christians with patience, cunning and conspiracy, or readiness for conspiracy. The Turks fought for the protection of their right to their way of life, and the Christians for the attainment of that same right. The rayah felt that the Turks were becoming even more of a burden, while the Turks observed with bitterness that the rayah were beginning to throw their weight around and were no longer what they had been. These clashes of such opposing interests, beliefs, ambitions and hopes, formed an intricate knot which the long Turkish wars with Venice, Austria and Russia complicated and tied ever tighter. Bosnia grew increasingly constrained and sombre, conflicts were more frequent and life more difficult, with less and less order and certainty.

Then, with the beginning of the nineteenth century, the uprising in Serbia came as a visible sign of the new times and new methods of struggle. The tangled knot in Bosnia tightened still further.

As time went on that uprising in Serbia was the cause of increasing anxiety, damage, expense and loss to the whole of Turkish Bosnia including Travnik. But far more so to the Vizier, the authorities and the other Bosnian towns than to the Travnik Muslims, who did not consider any war sufficiently large or important for them to contribute either money or men to it. The people of Travnik talked about "Karageorge's trouble-making" with forced scorn, just as they always found some disparaging word for the army which the Vizier had sent against Serbia and which the indecisive, quarrelsome local commanders were bringing slowly straggling into Travnik.

Napoleon's wars in Europe were a rather more worthy topic of conversation in Travnik. At first those wars were spoken of as distant events which are recounted and interpreted, but which do not and cannot have anything to do with real life. But the arrival of the French army in Dalmatia had brought that "Bunaparta" of the stories unexpectedly close to Bosnia and Travnik.

At the same time a new Vizier, Husref Mehmed Pasha, arrived in Travnik. He brought a personal respect for Napoleon and an interest in all things French, which appeared to the people of Travnik far greater than was appropriate for an Ottoman and a dignitary of the Empire.

All of this disturbed and irritated the Travnik Turks and they began to refer to Napoleon and his achievements in brief meaningless remarks or simply with a haughty and disdainful pursing of the lips. But none of that could distance them or altogether protect them from that "Bunaparta" or from the events which spread out from him with amazing speed across Europe, like a ripple of waves from their centre, and which, like a fire or a plague, overtook both those who fled and those who sat still. As in so many towns and cities of the world, that invisible, unknown conqueror had provoked anxiety, unrest and agitation even in Travnik. The brittle, resonant name of "Bunaparta" was going to fill the valley of Travnik for a number of years and, whether they liked it or not, the people would often have to break their jaws on its knotty, angular syllables. It was going to hum in their ears and flicker before their eyes for a long time. For *the days of the Consuls* had begun.

Without exception, all the people of Travnik liked to feign indifference and appear impassive. But the news of the consuls' coming – one moment French, the next Austrian, then Russian or all three at once – provoked either hope or unease, and aroused desires and expectations. None of this could be altogether disguised, as it made their hearts beat faster and brought a new liveliness to their conversation.

Few people knew what the reports circulating since the autumn actually meant. Nor could anyone have said either which consuls were supposed to be coming or what they would be doing in Travnik. In the present circumstances, a single piece of news or an unusual word was enough to stir the people's imagination, to give rise to conjecture, and even to suspicions and fears, secret desires and thoughts, which they kept to themselves and never expressed or articulated.

As we have seen, the local Turks were anxious and they alluded sullenly to the possibility of the consuls' coming. Mistrustful of everything that came from abroad and ill-disposed in advance to any innovation, the Turks still secretly hoped that these were only ominous rumours, a sign of the inauspicious circumstances, that the consuls might not come, or, if they did, they would soon depart along with the bad times that had brought them.

On the other hand, the Christians – both Catholic and Orthodox – welcomed the news and passed it on, whispering it to one another furtively, finding in it cause for obscure hopes and the prospect of change. And change could only be for the better.

Of course, each of them had his own way of looking at things, from different, often opposite points of view.

The Catholics, who were in the majority, dreamed of an influential Austrian consul who would bring them the help and protection of the powerful Catholic Emperor in Vienna. The Orthodox, who were few in number and had been continuously persecuted over the last few years because of the uprising in Serbia, did not expect much from either an Austrian or a French consul. But they took the news as a good sign, proof that Turkish power was waning and that favourable times of upheaval and salvation were on their way. And they added immediately, of course, that "there could be nothing without a Russian consul".

In the face of such rumours, even the Sephardic Jews, a small but lively community, could not maintain the proverbial reticence taught them by the centuries. They too were excited by the thought that a consul of the great French Emperor Napoleon – "as kindly to the Jews as a kind father" – might be coming to Bosnia.

Reports of the arrival of the foreign consuls, like all news in our lands, sprang up suddenly, grew to fantastic proportions, and then disappeared all at once, only to re-emerge some weeks later with new force and in a new form.

In the middle of the winter, which was mild and brief that year, these reports acquired their first semblance of reality. A Jew by the name of Pardo arrived in Travnik from Split and, with Juso Atijas, a Travnik merchant, began to look for a suitable house for the French Consulate. They looked everywhere, visited the Vizier's Deputy, and examined the state properties, accompanied by the caretaker. They decided on a large, somewhat dilapidated house belonging to the State, where Dubrovnik merchants had usually stayed and which was therefore known as the Dubrovnik Khan. The house was on a slope, above a Muslim school, in the middle of a large, steep garden, divided in two by a stream. As soon as terms had been agreed, builders, carpenters and craftsmen were found to repair the house and put it in order. And that house, which had stood until then on its own, unnoticed, its blank windows gaping at the world, now suddenly came to life, attracting people's attention and the curiosity of children and those with nothing better to do. For some reason people began to talk about the coat of arms and the flag which would be prominently and constantly displayed on the building of the foreign consulate. These were things no one had actually ever yet seen. But these two significant words, which the Turks muttered rarely, with a scowl, the Christians spoke often, in a malicious whisper.

The Travnik Turks were, of course, too wise and proud to show they were upset, but in private conversations they did not hide it.

They had long been troubled by the knowledge that the Imperial defences along the frontiers had collapsed and that Bosnia was becoming an unguarded country, trampled over not only by Ottomans but by infidels from the four corners of the earth, a country where even the rayah was beginning to raise its head more insolently than ever before. And now some faithless consuls and spies were supposed to be thrusting their way in, freely proclaiming their authority and the power of their emperors at every step. So, little by little, an end would come to the good order and "blessed silence" of Turkish Bosnia, which for some time now had in any case become increasingly difficult to protect and preserve. Divine Will had ordained that the Turks should rule as far as the Sava river and the Austrians from the Sava on. But everything Christian was working against that clear Divine Order, shaking the frontier fence and undermining it by day and night, both openly and in secret. And recently even Divine Will itself had become somehow less evident and distinct. "What else is going to happen and who else will be coming?" the old Turks wondered with real bitterness.

And, indeed, what the Christians were saying about the opening of the foreign consulates showed that the anxiety of the Turks was not unjustified.

"There'll be a flag flying!" people whispered and their eyes flashed defiantly as though it would be their very own flag. In fact no one really knew what kind of flag it was supposed to be, nor what could be expected to happen when it appeared. But the mere thought that different colours could unfurl and flutter freely beside the green Turkish flag brought a joyous gleam to people's eyes and raised hopes of a kind that only the rayah could ever know. Those mere words – "There'll be a flag flying!" – made many a poor man feel at least for a second that his hovel was brighter, his empty stomach more comfortable and his thin clothing warmer. Those few vague words made Christian hearts leap, their eyes blink with the dazzle of brilliant colours and golden crosses; and all the flags of all the Christian emperors and kings of the world seemed to unfurl, roaring triumphantly in their ears, like a whirlwind. For a man can live on one word, if he is resolute enough to fight and win through.

Apart from all of this, there was another consideration which made many a trader in the bazaar think of the changes with hope. There was a prospect of profit with the arrival of these unknown, but probably wealthy people, who would certainly have to buy and spend. For in the last few years activity in the bazaar had lessened and income had dwindled, particularly since the uprising in Serbia. The many army suppliers, compulsory labour demands and frequent requisitions kept the peasants away from the town, so that now they sold virtually nothing and bought only the barest essentials. State purchases were badly and erratically paid. Trade with Slavonia had ceased and, since the arrival of the French army, Dalmatia had become an irregular and uncertain market.

In these circumstances, the traders of the Travnik bazaar welcomed even the slightest chance of making money and sought everywhere the longed-for sign of a turn for the better.

At last, what had been talked about for months actually took place. The first of the consuls, the French Consul General, arrived in Travnik.

It was the end of February, the last day of Ramadan. An hour before the evening meal in the light of the cold, setting February sun, the people of the lower bazaar were able to witness the arrival of the Consul. The shopkeepers had begun to take in their goods and lower their shutters when the scampering feet of inquisitive Gypsy children announced the Consul's arrival.

The procession was short. At its head rode the Vizier's envoys, two of his closest attendants, with six horsemen. They had ridden out as far as the Lašva to meet the Consul. They were all mounted on good horses and well turned out. To the side and behind rode guards sent by the Governor of Livno. They had accompanied the Consul the whole way and looked rather nondescript: cold and weary as they were, on small, ungroomed ponies. In the middle of the procession, on a fat, ageing dapple-grey, rode the French

Consul General, Monsieur Jean Daville, a tall, fair-haired, red-faced man with blue eyes and a moustache. Beside him was a chance travelling companion, Monsieur Poucqueville, who was on his way to Yannina, where his brother was the French consul. Behind them, some paces distant, rode that same Pardo, the Jew from Split, and two burly men from Sinj, in the French service. All three of them were wrapped up to the eyes in black capes and red peasant scarves, and there was hay poking out of their boots.

The procession, as may be gathered, was not particularly brilliant or numerous, and the winter weather still further reduced its dignity, for the bitter cold necessitated thick clothes, a hunched bearing and rapid gait.

Apart from those few frozen gypsy children, the procession met with general indifference on the part of the townspeople. The Turks pretended not to see it, while the Christians did not dare watch it blatantly. Those who did see it, out of the corner of their eye or from some hidden place, were a little disappointed by so mean and prosaic an arrival of "Bunaparta's" consul, for the majority had imagined consuls as high dignitaries who wore splendid apparel, covered with braid and medals, and rode on fine horses or travelled in carriages.

2

The Consul's escort was lodged at the Khan, while the Consul himself and Monsieur Poucqueville were housed at the home of Josif Baruh, the wealthiest and most respected of the Travnik Jews, as the large house which was being repaired for the French Consulate could not be ready for another fortnight. So it was that on the first day of the Ramadan Bairam, an unusual guest awoke in Josif Baruh's small, pretty house. The whole ground floor of the house had been given over to him and Monsieur Poucqueville. Daville had a large room on the corner with two windows looking onto the river and two, with wooden lattices, onto the frozen, deserted garden, covered with hoar frost which did not thaw all day.

From the floor above the Consul came the constant thumping, running and shouting of Baruh's numerous children and the sharp voice of their mother trying vainly to calm them down with threats and curses. From the town came the boom of cannon, the banging of children's toy guns, and Gypsy music which grated on the ears. Two drums throbbed monotonously, and, against that dark background, a pipe wove and unfurled strange melodies with unexpected trills and pauses. These were the few days in the year when Travnik emerged from its silence.

As it would not have been appropriate for the Consul to go out before his formal audience with the Vizier, Daville spent the three days of Bairam in that large room, with the same little river and frozen garden constantly before his eyes, while his ears were filled with those strange sounds from the house and the town. A strong smell of oil, burnt sugar, onions and pungent spices wafted in from the rich, lavish Jewish dishes, with their mixture of Spanish and Oriental cooking.

Daville spent the time in conversation with his countryman Poucqueville, giving instructions and receiving information about the ceremonial associated with his first audience. This was to take place on the Friday immediately after the third day of Bairam. He had received a gift from the Vizier's Residence of two large candles and several pounds each of almonds and raisins.

The Vizier's doctor and interpreter César d'Avenat acted as a link between the Residence and the new Consul. To all the locals, Muslim and Christian alike, he was known as "Davna". That had been his name for the whole of the second half of his life. In fact his forebears came originally from Piedmont, but he had been born in Savoy and was naturalized French. As a young man he had been sent to medical school in Montpellier. In those days he was still called Cesare Davenato, but then he took his present name and opted for French nationality. From there he made his way in some unexplained manner to Istanbul and entered the service of the great Admiral Kuchuk Hussein, as surgeon and medical assistant. Mehmed Pasha had taken him over from the Admiral when he went to Egypt as Vizier, and had brought him to Travnik, as his doctor, interpreter and a man able for any task, capable and useful in any situation.

He was tall, strong, and long-legged, with dark skin and black hair, powdered and deftly gathered in a pigtail. There were a few deep smallpox scars on his broad, clean-shaven face with its large sensuous mouth and burning eyes. He dressed carefully in the old-fashioned French style. He approached his work with sincere goodwill, doing his best to be of genuine assistance to his eminent countryman.

Everything was new and strange and filled Daville's time. But it could not fill his thoughts, particularly in the slow night hours, when they raced swiftly and arbitrarily, from the present to the past, or tried to make out the shape of the future.

The nights seemed endless.

It was hard to get used to lying so unaccustomedly low down on the floor (it made him dizzy), or to the smell of wool in the full, recently "fluffed up" cushions. He would wake often, choking with heat from so many layers of woollen cushions and quilts, weighed down by the heavy Oriental foods, which were hard to eat and still harder to digest. Getting up in the dark he would drink the sharp, icy water, which seared his throat and felt painfully cold in his stomach.

During the day, talking with Poucqueville or d'Avenat, he was a calm, decisive man, with a definite name, profession and rank, a clear aim and set tasks which were the reason for his coming to this remote Turkish province, just as he might have come to any other part of the world. But at night, he was both all that he was now and all that he had ever been or should have been. And that man, lying in the darkness of the long February nights, seemed to Daville himself a stranger, complex, and at times quite unknown.

Even at first light, when he was woken by the sound of the Bairam drums and pipes or the children running on the floor above, it would take some time for Daville to come to and clear his head. He would hover for a long time between waking and sleep, for his dreams had more to do with the reality of the life he had led up to now, while his present waking life was more like a dream in which one is suddenly flung into a strange, distant land.

So the waking itself seemed like an extension of his night dreams. It took time and effort to cross over into the unusual reality of his consular work in this remote Turkish town.

And in the midst of this mixture of new and unusual impressions, memories would come to him irresistibly, merging with the tasks and anxieties of the present. Events from his life succeeded one another rapidly, at random, appearing in a new light and strange proportions.

His life had been full and turbulent.

Jean-Baptiste Etienne Daville was nearer forty than thirty, tall, fair, of resolute gait and steady gaze. He had been seventeen when he left his native town on the north coast of France and went to Paris, like so many before him, seeking a living and some way of making a name for himself. After his first attempts, he was swiftly caught up, along with millions of others, in the Revolution which became his personal destiny. He left a notebook of verses and the bold beginnings of two or three historical and social dramas in a trunk and abandoned his modest position as a junior civil servant. Jean Daville became a journalist. He continued to publish both verses and literary reviews, but his main job was at the Constituent Assembly. He poured all his youth and all the enthusiasm he was capable of into lengthy reports on the Assembly. But the millstone of the Revolution ground and altered everything, obliterating things rapidly and without trace. As happens in dreams, people passed swiftly, straight from one position to another, from honour to honour, from disgrace to death, from poverty to glory. Only, some went in one direction, and others in the opposite one.

During those extraordinary times and in circumstances to which we shall return, Daville was in turn a journalist, soldier, volunteer in the Spanish war, and a civil servant in the improvised Ministry of Foreign Affairs. He was sent on missions to Prussia, to Italy, to the Cisalpine Republic and the Knights of Malta. Then he became a journalist again, and the literary critic of the *Moniteur* in Paris. And now, finally, Consul General in Travnik, with the task of opening the Consulate, establishing and developing commercial links with this part of Turkey, assisting the French occupying forces in Dalmatia and following the actions of the rayah in Serbia and Bosnia.

This is how the life of this guest in Baruh's house would have appeared if he had had to summarize it in a few sentences for a short *curriculum vitae*.

But now, from this strange perspective and unexpected three-day imprisonment, Daville had frequently to make an effort to remember exactly who he was and where he had come from, all that he had been in his life, why he had come here and how it was that he was spending the whole day pacing out this red Bosnian carpet.

For, as long as a man is in his own society and normal circumstances, such facts from his *curriculum vitae* signify, even for him, the important stages and major turning points of his life. But as soon as chance, his work or sickness remove and isolate him, these facts begin to fade, to wither and disintegrate unbelievably fast, like a lifeless mask of paper and lacquer he had once used. And beneath them our other life begins to emerge, a life known only to us, the true history of our spirit and body, not recorded anywhere, and quite unsuspected. It has very little connection with our social successes, but for us and our ultimate good or ill, it is the only one that is important and "real".

Lost in this wilderness, Daville spent the long nights, when all sounds had died away, looking back over his life. What he saw was a long succession of undertakings and setbacks, battles, heroic acts, lucky breaks, successes, turning points, misfortunes, contradictions, unnecessary sacrifices and vain compromises, which only he knew about.

From the darkness and silence of this town, which he had not yet even seen properly, but where worries and difficulties no doubt awaited him, it seemed as though nothing in the world could be put into rational order. At times Daville felt that life required a great deal of effort and each effort a disproportionate amount of courage. And in this darkness one could see no end to the exertion. So as not to stop or despair, people cheat themselves, piling new tasks on top of unfinished ones, although they will not complete these either, searching in new undertakings and new efforts for new strength and greater courage. So they keep on robbing themselves and, as time passes, they become ever more hopelessly indebted to themselves and to everything around them.

But, as the day of the first audience approached, these memories and reflections gave way increasingly to new impressions and temporary but real anxieties and duties. Daville began to collect himself. His sensitivities and memories sank to the back of his consciousness, from where they would still frequently reappear, associated strangely and unexpectedly with day-to-day occurrences or the extraordinary experiences of his new life in Travnik.

At last, those three long days and their three strange nights were over. (With the kind of intuition that does not usually deceive the tormented, it had that morning occurred to Daville that these may have been the best and most peaceful days he was destined to live in this narrow valley.) Quite early then, horses were heard trotting and neighing under the windows. Solemn and formal, the Consul received the commander of the Vizier's Mamelukes, in the company of d'Avenat. Everything was as had been agreed and arranged beforehand. Here were the Vizier's twelve Mamelukes from the unit which Mehmed Pasha had brought from Egypt as his personal bodyguard. He was particularly proud of them. Their dexterously wound turbans of fine cloth, woven with threads of gold and silk, their curved sabres which hung in a picturesque manner by their horses' sides and their wide cherry-coloured uniforms attracted everyone's attention. The horses provided for Daville and his retinue were covered from head to tail with thick velvet cloth. The manner of command was brisk and the order perfect. Daville endeavoured to mount his quiet, ageing, broad-crouped horse as naturally as possible. The Consul was dressed in ceremonial uniform. His dark blue greatcoat was wide open on his chest, displaying his gilt buttons, silver trimming and medals. He looked well with his upright bearing and fine, manly head. All went well and the Consul had every reason to be pleased until they turned into the main street. Then as soon as they reached the first Turkish houses they began to hear curious sounds: people calling to one another, slamming their courtyard gates and the shutters of their windows. At the very first doorway, a small girl opened one of the double gates a crack and, muttering some incomprehensible words, began spitting rapidly into the street, as though she were laying a curse on them. One after the other, gates opened and shutters were raised to reveal for a moment faces possessed with fanatical hatred. The women, veiled, spat and cursed, and the boys shouted abuse, accompanied by obscene gestures and unambiguous threats, slapping their buttocks or drawing their hands across their throats.

As the street was narrow and the upper storeys of the houses jutted out on both sides, the procession was riding between two rows of insults and threats. At the beginning, taken by surprise, the Consul had slowed down his horse's trot, but d'Avenat urged his horse closer to him and, without moving or changing his expression, began to implore Daville in an excited whisper:

"I beg Your Excellency to ride calmly on and pay no attention to any of this. Wild people, uncouth rabble. They hate everything foreign and greet everyone like this. It is best to ignore it. That's what the Vizier does. They're just barbarians. I beg Your Excellency to continue."

The Consul was disconcerted and indignant, although he tried not to show it. When he saw that the Vizier's men really were not taking any notice, he rode on, but he could feel the blood pounding in his head. Thoughts raced through his mind, jostling and colliding with one another. His first reaction was to wonder whether, as the representative of the great Napoleon, he ought to tolerate all of this or whether he ought immediately to turn back and make a scandal.

He could not resolve the dilemma, because he was equally afraid of damaging the reputation of France and of acting too hastily and causing a conflict which would ruin his relations with the Vizier and the Turks from the very first day. Incapable of making a decision, he felt humiliated and angry with himself. And he was repelled by the Levantine d'Avenat, who kept repeating over and over again behind his back:

"I beg Your Excellency to ride on and pay no attention. These are simply uncouth Bosnian customs! Just keep going calmly!" As he vacillated, unable to find a solution, Daville felt that his face was burning and that, in spite of the bitter cold, he was sweating profusely under the arms. He found d'Avenat's insistent whispering loathsome. In it he began to glimpse what it must be like for a man from the West to transfer his life to the East, linking his destiny to it forever. But when they reached the last houses, unseen women spat from the windows right onto the horses and their riders. The Consul stopped again for an instant, but set off once more, submitting to d'Avenat's pleas and drawn on by the calm trotting of the escort. Then the houses came to an end and they entered the bazaar with its low shops. The Turkish shopkeepers and their customers were sitting in their raised shop-fronts, smoking or haggling. It was like passing from an overheated room into a completely cold one. The savage looks suddenly disappeared, together with the gestures showing the infidels' heads being cut off, and the women's superstitious spitting. Instead, on both sides of the street, there were blank impassive faces. Daville saw them dimly as though through an unpleasant veil trembling in front of his eyes. No one ceased working or smoking or raised his eyes to honour the unusual figure and his splendid retinue with so much as a glance. Here and there a shopkeeper turned his head away, as though searching for goods on the shelves. Only Easterners can hate and despise others to such an extent and display their hatred and contempt in such a way.

D'Avenat fell silent and reined his horse back to a proper distance, but for Daville this incredible mute contempt of the bazaar was no less painful or insulting than the outspoken loathing of the earlier curses. At last they turned to the right and there in front of them were the long high walls and white building of the Residence, a large, well-proportioned structure with a row of glazed windows. This sight offered him some relief.

This agonizing journey, which was now behind him, would remain in Daville's memory for a long time, tenacious as a bad dream filled with meaning. Over the years, he was to make the same journey countless times, in similar circumstances. For he would have to ride through the residential quarters and the bazaar on the occasion of every audience, and these were frequent, particularly in troubled times. He had to sit upright on his horse, looking neither to left nor right, not too high nor down between the horse's ears, neither vacantly nor anxiously, not smiling or frowning, but serious, attentive and calm, with roughly that slightly unnatural expression with which military commanders are shown in portraits gazing above a battle into the distance, somewhere between the road and the line of the horizon, from where planned reinforcements are certain to come. For a long time the Turkish children would continue to spit from their gateways briskly and rapidly at the horses' hooves, as though uttering imprecations, the way they had seen their elders do. The Turkish shopkeepers would turn their backs, pretending to look for something on the shelves. Only occasionally would he be greeted by one of the Jews who happened to be there and simply could not avoid the encounter. He would have to ride like that innumerable times, calm and dignified, inwardly fearful of the hatred and malicious indifference poured on him from all sides, of the unforeseen mishap which might occur at any moment, sickened by this work and this way of life, but making a strenuous effort to conceal both his fear and his disgust.

And even later when, with the years and the changes they brought, the people had grown accustomed to the presence of the foreigners, and when Daville had met many of them and was on good terms with some, this first ceremonial procession would remain in his consciousness like a black, but burning, painful line, only gradually erased and softened by forgetfulness.

The solemn procession clattered across a wooden bridge and found itself facing a great gateway. Suddenly, with the sound of clanging bolts and servants' running feet, both gates swung abruptly open.

And so the stage was revealed on which Jean Daville was to act out various scenes, in always the same difficult and thankless role, for the best part of eight years.

This disproportionately wide gate was to open in front of him many more times. It always seemed, as it opened, like a giant's ugly jaws, emitting the stench of everything which was living, growing, crumbling, reeking or lying sick in the vast Residence. He knew that the town and surrounding villages which were obliged to feed the Vizier and his household, flung into the Residence each day a couple of thousand pounds of provisions of various kinds, and that all of it was distributed, pilfered and consumed. He knew that, apart from the Vizier and those closest to him, there were eleven dignitaries, thirty-two guards and just as many, or more, Turkish loafers and boot-lickers, Christian employees and occasional labourers. In addition there was an unspecified number of horses, cows, dogs, cats, birds and monkeys. But above it all one could smell the heavy, obnoxious odour of butter fat and tallow which is nauseating to anyone unused to it. That insidious smell would stay with the Consul the whole day after every audience, and the mere thought of it would make him retch and want to vomit. It seemed to him that the whole Residence was permeated with this stench, like a church with incense, that it clung not only to the people and their clothes, but to the walls and everything within them.

Now, as this unfamiliar gate opened in front of him for the first time, the detachment of Mamelukes parted and dismounted and Daville rode into the courtyard with his personal escort. This first narrow courtyard was quite dark because the upper storey of the building jutted over its whole width. It was only after this that they entered the real, open courtyard, with a well and lawn and borders of flowers. At the end of the yard a high solid fence enclosed the Vizier's gardens.

Still upset by what he had experienced on his way through the town, Daville was now further confused by the agitated courtesy and formal attentiveness with which he was met by the whole population of attendants and dignitories of the Residence. They all bustled and jostled around him with a brisk urgency unknown in Western ceremonies.

The first to greet the Consul was the Chief Secretary for Finance. (The Vizier's local deputy, Suleiman Pasha Skopljak, was not in Travnik.) He was followed by the Keeper of the Weapons, the Master of the Wardrobe, the Treasurer and the Keeper of Seals, with a whole throng of men of unknown or indeterminate rank and occupation pushing and elbowing their way after them. Some, bowing their heads, muttered incomprehensible words of welcome, others spread their arms in greeting, and the whole crowd advanced towards the great hall where the Divan was to be held. The tall dark figure of d'Avenat moved to and fro among them, swiftly and roughly, shouting insolently at anyone blocking the way, organizing and commanding more ostentatiously and loudly than the occasion demanded. Daville, disconcerted, but outwardly dignified and calm, felt like one of those saints in Catholic paintings borne heavenwards by a seething flock of angels. And the throng did indeed lift him up the few broad steps which led out of the courtyard to the Divan.

The Divan was a spacious, dimly lit hall at ground level. There were several carpets on the floor. All round the walls stood low sofas, covered with soft cherry-coloured cloth. In the corner, by the window, there were cushions for the Vizier and his guest. The only picture on the walls was the Imperial emblem, the Emperor's monogram inscribed on green paper in letters of gold. Below this hung a sabre, two pistols and a red ceremonial mantle – gifts from Selim III to his favourite Husref Mehmed Pasha.

Above this hall, on the first floor, there was another, just as large, more sparsely furnished, but lighter. This was where the Vizier held his Divan during the summer. Two walls of this hall consisted entirely of windows, some looking over gardens and steep plots of land, the others at the Lašva and the bazaar across the bridge. These were those "glass casements" mentioned in stories and songs, the like of which were quite unknown in the whole of Bosnia. Mehmed Pasha had acquired them at his own expense from Austria and brought a special craftsman, a German, to fit them. Sitting on his cushion, a visitor would look through those windows at a roofed veranda under the eaves of which, on a spruce beam, there was a swallows' nest with stalks of straw sticking out and chirping coming from it, and he could watch the cautious swallows flying swiftly in and out.

It was always pleasant to sit by those windows. There were always light and green foliage or blossom, a breeze, and the sound of water, the chirruping of birds, peace for repose and quiet for reflection and reaching agreements. Many difficult and terrible decisions were taken or approved there, but somehow, everything discussed there seemed easier, clearer and more human than in the Divan on the ground floor.

These were the only two rooms in the Residence that Daville was to know during his stay in Travnik. They provided the stage for many torments and satisfactions, successes and failures. Here, over the years, he would come to know not only the Turks and their unique strengths and boundless weaknesses, but also himself and the extent and limits of his powers, people in general, life, the world and relations between people in it.

As always in winter, this first audience was held in the ground-floor Divan. From the musty air, one could tell that the present occasion was the first time it had been opened and heated this winter.

As soon as the Consul had set foot on the threshold, the door on the opposite side of the Divan opened and the Vizier appeared in splendid apparel, followed by attendants, who walked with their heads slightly bowed and their arms crossed humbly on their breasts. This was a great concession in protocol, which Daville had achieved in negotiations carried on for the previous three days through d'Avenat. He thought it just the thing to brighten up his first report to the Minister. For the Turks had wanted the Vizier to receive the Consul sitting on a cushion as he received all his other visitors. The Consul, on the other hand, had wanted the Vizier to rise when he came in and to greet him standing. The Consul had appealed to the might of France and the military glory of his sovereign, the Turks to their traditions and the greatness of the Empire. Eventually, they reached an agreement whereby the Consul and the Vizier should both step into the hall simultaneously, meet in the centre, and the Vizier should lead the Consul from there to the raised dais by the window where two cushions had been prepared, on which they were both to sit down at the same moment.

And that is what happened. The Vizier, who was lame in the right leg (which was why he was known among the people as "The Limping Pasha"), moved briskly and rapidly as lame people often do. He came up to the Consul and cordially invited him to sit down. The interpreter d'Avenat sat down between them but one step lower. Stooping, his hands folded in his lap and his eyes lowered, he endeavoured to make himself lower and smaller than he was and to have only as much wit and breath as were required for these two dignitaries to communicate their thoughts and messages to one another. All the rest of the crowd vanished silently. Only servants remained, stationed at short intervals, ready to pass what was to be served. Throughout the whole conversation, which lasted more than an hour, these boys, like soundless shadows, handed one another and presented to the Consul and the Vizier all that the ceremonial required. First came the lighted chibouks, then coffee, then sherbet. After this, one of the boys shuffled up to them on his knees, bringing strong perfume in a shallow dish which he passed under the Vizier's beard and the Consul's moustache as though it were incense. Then coffee again and new chibouks. All of this was served as they talked, with the greatest care, unobtrusively and swiftly.

For a man from the East, the Vizier was unusually lively, pleasant and open. Although he had been told in advance about these qualities, and although he knew that he should not take it all too much at face value, Daville found this courteous and amiable manner agreeable after the unexpected humiliations he had experienced on his way through the town. The blood which had rushed to his face subsided. The Vizier's words and the smell of the coffee and tobacco pleased and soothed him, although it could not erase his earlier painful impressions. In the course of the conversation, the Vizier made a point of stressing the savagery of this country, the crudity and backwardness of the people. The land was wild, the people impossible. What could be expected of women and children, creatures whom God had not endowed with reason, in a country where even the men were violent and uncouth? Nothing these people did or said had any significance, nor could it affect the affairs of serious, cultivated men. "Curs may bark, but the caravan moves on," concluded the Vizier, who had evidently been informed about everything that had happened during the Consul's ride through the town and was now trying to minimize the incident and alleviate its effects. And from these disagreeable trifles he passed immediately on to the unparalleled greatness of Napoleon's victories and to the importance of what their two Empires, the Turkish and the French, would be able to achieve, through cordial and well-conceived co-operation.

These words, spoken sincerely and calmly, pleased Daville, because they were an indirect apology for the recent insults, and he felt that they reduced the extent of the humiliation he had undergone. Already soothed and in better humour, he observed the Vizier carefully, recalling what he had learned about him from d'Avenat.

Husref Mehmed Pasha, known as The Limping Pasha, was Georgian. Brought as a slave to Istanbul while still a child, he had been in the service of the great Kuchuk Hussein Pasha. There he had been noticed by Selim III even before the Sultan came to the throne. Brave, astute, cunning, eloquent, sincerely loyal to his masters, this Georgian had become Vizier in Egypt at the age of thirty-one. In fact, that had all ended badly, for the great uprising of the Mamelukes had thrown Mehmed Pasha out of Egypt. But he had not fallen completely into disfavour. After a short stay in Salonika he was appointed Vizier to Bosnia. It was a relatively light punishment, and Mehmed Pasha made it lighter still by wisely behaving in public as though he did not see it as a punishment at all. From Egypt he had brought a unit of some thirty loyal Mamelukes, with whom he liked to carry out military exercises on the plain of Travnik. Splendidly dressed and well-fed, the Mamelukes aroused people's curiosity and increased the Pasha's standing. The Bosnian Turks watched them with loathing but also with fear and secret admiration.

More even than the Mamelukes, it was the Vizier's stud that provoked wonder: so many horses of such quality had never been seen in Bosnia before. The Vizier was young and looked even younger than he was. He was of less than average height, but his whole bearing, and particularly his smile, made him seem at least a hand's breadth taller than he was. He disguised his lameness as far as possible by the cut of his clothes and his deftly controlled, agile movements. When he had to stand, he always knew how to adopt a posture which would make his disability imperceptible, and when he had to move he would do it rapidly, nimbly and in stages. This gave him a special air of freshness and youth. There was nothing about him of the immobile Ottoman dignity of which Daville had heard and read so much. The colours and cut of his clothes were simple, but obviously chosen with care. There are people like this who give an extra brilliance and distinction to their clothing and jewellery simply by wearing them. His face, unusually red, like a sailor's, with a short black beard and slightly slanting black, bright eyes, was open and smiling. He was one of those people who conceal their disposition with a perpetual smile and hide their ideas, or absence of ideas, in lively eloquence. The way he talked about everything suggested that he knew a great deal more than he had said. All his civility and kindness, every favour, seemed to be only a prelude, the first stage of what might still be expected of him. No matter how well-informed and forewarned, no one could avoid the impression that here was a mild, reasonable man who would not only make well-meaning promises, but actually carry them out, wherever and whenever he could. But at the same time, there was no one shrewd enough to see through those promises and determine their limits or gauge the true measure of those good intentions.

Both the Vizier and the Consul turned the conversation to topics which they knew to be a secret weakness or favourite subject of the other's. The Vizier kept returning to the illustrious figure of Napoleon and his great victories, and the Consul, who had learned from d'Avenat of the Vizier's love of the sea and seafaring, to questions connected with sailing and naval warfare. The Vizier really did passionately love the sea and life on it. Apart from the hidden pain of his failure in Egypt, what grieved him most was being so far from the sea and shut in among these cold, wild mountains.

In the most secret depths of his soul, the Vizier cherished the desire that one day he might become the successor of his great master Kuchuk Hussein Pasha, and, in the capacity of Admiral, carry out his ideas for improving the Ottoman navy.

After an hour and a half's conversation, the Consul and the Vizier parted as close acquaintances, each equally convinced that he would be able to carry weight with the other and each well pleased with both his partner and himself.

There was a still greater flurry and clamour at the Consul's departure. Cloaks of great value were brought – marten for the Consul and woollen cloth and fox for his escort. A voice loudly intoned prayers and called for blessings on this Imperial guest, and others responded in chorus. High officials brought Daville to the mounting block in the centre of the inner courtyard. They all walked with their arms outspread, as though carrying him. Daville mounted. The Vizier's cloak was placed over his greatcoat. Outside, the Mamelukes were waiting, already on their horses. The procession set off in the same direction from which it had come.

Despite the heavy clothes he was wearing, Daville shivered at the thought that he would have once again to ride between the worn shutters and warped lattices, amid the insults and contempt of the mob. But it seemed as though his first steps in Travnik were always to bring surprises, even agreeable ones. It was true that the Turks in the shops were sullen and motionless, with deliberately downcast eyes, but this time there were no curses or threats from the houses. Uneasily tense, Daville had the feeling that many hostile and inquisitive eyes were observing him from behind wooden lattices, but without a sound or movement. For some reason he felt as though the Vizier's cloak were protecting him from the mob, and unwittingly he drew it a little more tightly around him, straightening himself in the saddle. So, with his head high, he rode up to Baruh's walled courtyard.

When he was at last left alone in his warm room, Daville sat down on the hard couch, unbuttoned his uniform and breathed a deep sigh of relief. He was over-wrought and weary. He felt empty, confused, as though he had been thrown from a considerable height onto this hard couch and had not yet come round, nor could he make out clearly how or where he was. At last his time was his own, but he did not know what to do with it. He contemplated rest and sleep, but his eyes fell on the hanging cloak he had just been given by the Vizier and it immediately occurred to him, like something unexpected and painful, that he would have to write a report about it all to the Ministry in Paris and the Ambassador in Istanbul. This meant that he would have to live through it all once again, presenting everything so as not to damage his reputation and yet not straying far from the truth. This task loomed before him like an impassable mountain which had nevertheless to be crossed. The Consul covered his eyes with his right hand. He drew in a few more deep breaths and, as he breathed out, said half aloud:

"Oh, dear God, dear God!"

And he stayed like that, leaning back on the sofa. That was all the sleep and rest he had.

3

L ike the heroes of Oriental tales, Daville had to confront the greatest difficulties at the beginning of his Consulship. It was as though everything was leaping up to frighten him and turn him back from the path he had embarked on.

Everything he found in Bosnia and all the information that reached him from the Ministry, the Embassy in Istanbul and the Commander in Split, was the opposite of what he had been told on his departure from Paris.

After a few weeks, Daville moved from Baruh's house into the building intended for the Consulate. He put two or three rooms in order and furnished them as best he could. And he lived alone, with his servants, in that huge empty house.

When he set out for Travnik, he had been obliged to leave his wife in Split with a French family. Madame Daville was expecting the birth of her third child and he did not dare bring her with him into this unknown Turkish town in that condition. She was making a slow and difficult recovery from the birth and her departure from Split had repeatedly to be postponed.

Daville was used to family life, and had never been parted from his wife before. In the present circumstances, the separation was particularly hard to bear. With every day he was increasingly oppressed by his loneliness, the disorder in the house and anxiety for his wife and children. Monsieur Poucqueville had left Travnik after only a few days, continuing his journey to the East. In every way, Daville felt forgotten and abandoned to his own devices. All the resources needed for his work, which he had been promised before leaving for Bosnia or which he asked for subsequently, were either inadequate or simply did not materialize.

Having no clerk or assistant, he had to write, copy and carry out all the office business himself. As he did not know the language, or understand the country and its circumstances, he had no alternative but to take d'Avenat into his service, as interpreter to the Consulate. The Vizier magnanimously assigned his doctor to him and d'Avenat was delighted at this opportunity to enter French service. Daville employed him with great misgivings and concealed disgust, determined to entrust him only with matters that even the Vizier might know about. But he soon began to recognize how truly useful, indeed indispensable this man could be. D'Avenat succeeded immediately in finding two reliable men, an Albanian and a Hercegovinian, as khavazes to take charge of the servants and relieve the Consul of many unpleasant, trivial chores. Working with him every day, Daville observed him and came to know him increasingly well.

D'Avenat had been in the East from his early youth and had acquired many of the characteristics and habits of the Levantines. A Levantine is a man without illusions or scruples, who wears a number of different masks, obliged one moment to act humility, the next courage, now despondency, now enthusiasm. These are all simply essential devices in life's struggle – harder and more complex in the Levant than in any other part of the world. A foreigner thrown into that unequal and difficult struggle founders in it completely, losing his true personality. He lives out his whole life in the East, but knows it only imperfectly and from one perspective, thinking only of gain and loss in the struggle to which he is condemned. Foreigners like d'Avenat who stay in the East generally take from the Turks only the worst aspects of their character, incapable of recognizing and adopting any of their better, finer qualities and customs. D'Avenat, of whom we shall speak again, was in many ways such a man. He had led a dissolute youth, and contact with the Ottomans had not helped. And when the turbulent life of the senses burns out, people like him become sullen and bitter, a burden to themselves and others. Infinitely deferential and self-effacing to the point of iniquity in the face of power, authority and wealth, he was insolent and merciless towards anything weak, poor or inadequate.

Nevertheless, there was something that redeemed this man. He had a son, a fine-looking, intelligent boy. D'Avenat lavished devoted care on his health and upbringing. He would do anything for him. This strong emotion of fatherly love gradually freed him from his vices, making him a better and more charitable man. As the boy grew, so d'Avenat's life became more virtuous. Whenever he did people good or refrained from doing some wrong, he did it in the superstitious belief that "the boy would be repaid". As often happens in life, this inept, misguided parent lived in the hope that his son should be a man who would live honourably and righteously. And there was nothing he would not do or sacrifice to this end.

Every care and attention was lavished on this motherless child and he grew up beside his father like a young tree, bound to a dry but sturdy stake. The boy was handsome, he had his father's features in a softened and noble form, and he was healthy in body and mind, showing neither base tendencies nor any troublesome obsessions.

D'Avenat nursed a secret desire: his highest objective was that his child should not stay in the Levant to be everyone's servant as he was, but should be first accepted for schooling somewhere in France and then taken into French service. This was the main reason for his zeal and dedicated service to the Consulate and the basis for trust in his real and enduring loyalty.

The new Consul had financial troubles as well. Money reached him slowly and irregularly. There were unforeseen and considerable losses in exchange transactions. Approved credits arrived late, and those he asked for to cover new expenses were refused.

Instead, he received incomprehensible, clumsily written directives from the Accounts Department, circular letters with no meaning whatever, that seemed to Daville, in his isolation, deeply ironic. In one, for example, the Consul was strictly ordered to limit himself to contacts with other foreign consuls and to attend receptions for foreign ambassadors and envoys only at the express request of his own ambassador or envoy. Another decreed how Napoleon's birthday, on 15 August, was to be celebrated. "The Consul General himself is to cover the expenses of the orchestra and decorations for the ball that is to be held on that occasion." Daville smiled bitterly as he read that circular. He immediately saw before his eyes the Travnik musicians, three ragged gypsies, two drummers and the third with a pipe whose "music" grated on the ears of the Europeans condemned to live here during Ramadan and Bairam. He remembered also the first celebration of the Emperor's birthday, or rather his pathetic attempt to organize a celebration. For some time before he had tried in vain, through d'Avenat, to get any of the more prominent Turks to visit him on that day. But even some people from the Residence who had promised failed to come. The friars and their congregation had refused politely but firmly. The Orthodox Abbot Pahomije had neither accepted nor refused, but he did not come. Only the Jews responded. There were fourteen of them, and, contrary to the customs of Travnik, some even brought their wives.

Madame Daville had not yet arrived in Travnik. With the help of d'Avenat and the khavazes, Daville had played the part of courteous host and, in all his finery, served refreshments and sparkling wine he had brought from Split. He even delivered a short speech in honour of his sovereign. In this speech he had flattered the Turks and praised Travnik as an important town. He assumed that at least two of these Jews were in the Vizier's service and would report everything to him, and that they would all relate what the

Consul had said throughout Travnik. The Jewish womenfolk, who sat on low sofas, their hands folded in their laps, had only blinked during the speech, their heads now on one side now on the other. The men had looked straight ahead, which was supposed to mean: this is how things are and they cannot be different, but we have said nothing. The sparkling wine livened them all up. D'Avenat, who did not care for the Travnik Jews and translated their pronouncements irritably, was barely able to satisfy them, for now each of them wanted to say something to the Consul. Some spoke in Spanish, at which the women's tongues were suddenly loosened, and Daville struggled to revive in his memory those hundred or so words he had once learned as a soldier in Spain. After a while, the younger ones began to hum. It was awkward that no one knew any French songs, and they did not want to sing Turkish ones. Finally Mazalta, Bencion's daughter-in-law, sang a Spanish romance, breathing heavily with emotion and premature corpulence. Her mother-in-law, a warm, lively woman, became so jovial that she began to clap her hands and sway the upper part of her body, straightening her ornamented cap, which kept slipping to one side with the effects of the sparkling wine.

The innocent merriment of this simple, good-humoured gathering was all that could be mustered in Travnik to honour the greatest ruler in the world. This both touched and saddened the Consul.

Daville preferred not to remember this occasion. And when he wrote, as was his duty, to the Ministry to describe how the Emperor's first birthday celebrations had gone, he had written with some embarrassment and deliberate vagueness that this great day had been celebrated "as befits the particular circumstances and customs of this land". And now, as he read this belated and inappropriate circular about balls, orchestras and decorations he was painfully ashamed all over again, not knowing whether to weep or laugh.

One of his constant problems was anxiety over the officers and soldiers travelling through Bosnia from Dalmatia to Istanbul.

There was an agreement between the Turkish government and the French Ambassador in Istanbul whereby the French army was to make available to the Turks a certain number of officers, instructors and specialists, gunners and engineers. When the English fleet broke through the Dardanelles and threatened Istanbul, Sultan Selim had begun to prepare the capital's defences with the help of the French Ambassador, General Sebastiani, and a small number of French officers. At that time a certain number of officers and soldiers were urgently requested by the French government. General Marmont was ordered by Paris to send them immediately in small groups through Bosnia. Daville kept receiving instructions to ensure their safe passage and to secure horses and an escort for them. This meant that he was able to see in practice the exact nature of an agreement reached with the government in Istanbul. The passes required for the transit of foreign officers did not arrive in time. The officers had to wait in Travnik. The Consul tried to speed things up through the Vizier, the Vizier through Istanbul. But even if the permit had arrived in time this would not have been the end of the matter, for unexpected problems kept cropping up. Time and again the officers had to interrupt their journey and hang around the Bosnian villages.

The Bosnian Turks looked on the presence of the French army in Dalmatia with hostile distrust. Austrian agents spread among them the rumour that Marmont was building a wide highway from one end of Dalmatia to the other with the intention of annexing Bosnia as well. The appearance of French officers in Bosnia seemed to confirm this mistaken belief. And those French officers who came as allies, at the request of the Turkish government, were met as early as Livno with abuse from the rabble and their reception became more antagonistic with every step.

There were times when several dozen such officers and soldiers who could not go any further and dared not go back gathered in Travnik at Daville's house.

It did not help that the Vizier summoned the ayans and leading men of the town, threatening them and ordering them not to behave like this towards allies coming at the request of the High Porte. In the end everything was usually smoothed over and settled with words. The local officials promised the Vizier, the Vizier the Consul, and the Consul the officers, that the hostile attitude of the population would cease. But when the officers set off the following day, they would meet with such a reception at the very first village that they would return, resentfully, to Travnik.

It did not help that Daville kept reporting on the real mood of the local Turks and the Vizier's inability to restrain them or make them do anything he ordered. Istanbul kept on making requests, Paris sending orders and Split carrying them out. So individual officers would suddenly turn up in Travnik to wait, angrily, for new instructions. It was all a chaotic muddle and in the end it was the Consul who had to bear the brunt.

It did not help that the French authorities in Dalmatia kept printing friendly proclamations to the Turkish population. No one wanted to read them since they were written in a refined literary Turkish which no one who did read them could understand. Nothing could counteract the innate distrust of the entire Muslim population who did not want to read, to hear or to look, but were simply following their deep instinct of self-defence and hatred towards any foreigner and unbeliever who approached the frontiers and tried to cross into the land.

It was not until the May coup in Istanbul and the change of ruler that the orders to send officers to Turkey came to an end. There were no new orders, but the old ones continued to be carried out mechanically. And so for a long time afterwards, small groups of French officers would suddenly appear in Travnik, complying with one of these outdated orders, although their journey was now entirely without sense or purpose.

But, if the events in Istanbul freed the Consul from one misfortune, they threatened him with another, far worse.

Daville's only source of real support was the Vizier, Husref Mehmed Pasha. Actually, the Consul had been able on several occasions to glimpse the limits of the Vizier's power and his real standing with the Bosnian beys. Many a promise remained unrealized and many an order was never carried out, although the Vizier himself pretended not to notice. But his goodwill was indisputable. Following both his own inner impulse and self-interest he wished to be seen as a friend of France and to prove it by his actions. In addition, Mehmed Pasha's cheerful disposition, his irrepressible optimism, and the smiling ease with which he approached everything smoothed over every setback, acting on Daville like a tonic, giving him the strength to withstand the many difficulties of his new life, both great and small.

Now, events threatened to snatch from the Consul this one great fund of help and solace.

In May of that year, there was a coup d'état in Istanbul. Selim III, the enlightened reformer, was overthrown by his fanatical opponents, incarcerated in the Seraglio and replaced by Sultan Mustapha. French influence in Istanbul was weakened and, still worse for Daville personally, the position of Husref Mehmed Pasha was called into question. With Selim's fall Mehmed had lost his backing in Istanbul, while he was hated in Bosnia as a friend of France and supporter of the reforms.

It is true that in public the Vizier lost nothing of his broad sailor's smile or his Oriental optimism which had no foundation in anything but itself. However, this could not deceive anyone. The Travnik Turks, to a man opponents of Selim's reforms and enemies of Mehmed Pasha, announced that "the Vizier's days were numbered". There was a confused silence in the Residence. Everyone tried, unnoticed, to prepare for a departure that could take place at any moment. And each, preoccupied with his own personal worries, said nothing and looked straight ahead. Even the Vizier himself was absent-minded in conversation with Daville, although he endeavoured with courtesy and bravado to conceal his powerlessness to assist anyone in any way.

Special envoys arrived and the Vizier sent his couriers to Istanbul with mysterious messages and gifts for those friends he still had left. D'Avenat got to know some details and maintained that the Vizier was, in fact, fighting not only for his position with the new Sultan, but for his life. Knowing what the loss of the present Vizier would mean for himself and his work, Daville had from the outset been sending urgent messages to both General Marmont and the Embassy in Istanbul. He urged them to use all their influence at the Porte to ensure that, regardless of the political changes in Istanbul, Mehmed Pasha remained in Bosnia. This was what both the Russians and the Austrians did for their friends and this was how the influence and strength of a Christian power was judged.

The Bosnian Turks were triumphant. "The Giaour Sultan has been overthrown," the hodjas muttered around the bazaar shops, "and now the time has come to wash away all the filth that has clung to the pure faith and true Turks in recent years. The Limping Vizier will go and take his consul friend with him, just as he brought him." The rabble passed on these words and became increasingly aggressive. They taunted and bullied the Consul's servants. They met d'Avenat in the street with mocking insults, asking him whether the Consul was getting ready to go and, if not, what he was waiting for. But the interpreter, tall and dark on his dappled mare, looked at them disdainfully and answered with deliberate insolence that they did not know what they were talking about. Only a fool whose brain was addled with Bosnian brandy could have given them such ideas. The new Sultan and the French Emperor were great friends. It had already been decreed from Istanbul that the French Consul would continue to be a "Devlet Musahfir, a Guest of the State" in Travnik and that the whole of Bosnia would be put to the flame should anything happen to him. Even the children in their cradles would not be spared. D'Avenat kept insisting to the Consul that this was the time to act boldly and ruthlessly, for nothing else would work with these savages who attacked anyone on the retreat.

The Vizier did the same in his own way. The unit of Mamelukes went every day to exercise in the field near Turbe and these athletic horsemen, as elaborately dressed as wedding guests, with their heavy, gleaming weapons, were watched by the townspeople with hatred, but also with fear. The Vizier would ride out with them onto the field, watch the exercises, race with them himself and fire at the target, like a man without a care in the world, who had not given a thought to the possibility of departure or death, but was preparing for battle.

Both sides, the Travnik Turks and the Vizier, were waiting for the judgement of the new Sultan, and for news from Istanbul of the outcome of the struggle being waged there.

In the middle of the summer a special envoy from the Sultan, a Kapidji Bashi, arrived with his retinue. Mehmed Pasha organized an unusually splendid reception for him. The whole unit of his Mamelukes, all the dignitaries and the Residence staff came out to meet him. Cannon were fired from the fort. Mehmed Pasha waited in front of the Residence to receive the Kapidji Bashi. Word immediately spread through the town that this must mean that the Vizier had succeeded in attaining the favour of the new Sultan and would be staying on in Travnik. The Turks refused to believe this, maintaining that the Kapidji Bashi would be returning to Istanbul with Mehmed Pasha's head in his horse's nosebag. Nevertheless, the rumours turned out to be correct. The Kapidji Bashi had brought a decree which confirmed Mehmed Pasha in his position in Travnik. At the same time he made him a ceremonial gift of a valuable sabre, a present from the new Sultan, and gave him the order to despatch a strong army against Serbia the following spring.

This happy occasion was disturbed in a strange and unexpected way.

The day after the Kapidji Bashi's arrival – it was a Friday – Daville had a prearranged audience with the Vizier. Far from cancelling the visit, Mehmed Pasha received the Consul in the presence of the Kapidji Bashi whom he introduced as an old friend and the welcome bearer of the Sultan's grace. And he showed him the sabre he had received as a gift from the Sultan. The Kapidji Bashi, who assured the Consul that he was, like Mehmed Pasha, a sincere admirer of Napoleon, was a tall man, evidently of mixed blood with very pronounced African features. His sallow skin had a greyish tint, his lips and nails were dark blue and the whites of his eyes were clouded, as though dirty.

The Kapidji Bashi spoke vehemently of his goodwill towards the French and his hatred for the Russians. As he spoke white foam gathered in the deep corners on either side of his curving African lips. Watching him, Daville secretly wished that the man would pause and wipe his mouth. But the Kapidji Bashi went on, as though in a fever. D'Avenat, interpreting, was barely able to keep up with him. With renewed hatred, the Kapidji Bashi spoke of the wars he once fought against the Russians and of his feats somewhere near Ochakov, where he had been wounded. And suddenly, with a brisk movement, he pulled up the narrow sleeve of his overshirt to show a broad scar from a Russian sabre on his forearm. His thin, powerful black arm was trembling visibly.

Mehmed Pasha revelled in the cordial conversation of his friends and laughed even more than usual, like a man who could not disguise the extent of his satisfaction and happiness that he had been graced by his Sultan's favour.

The Divan dragged on at unusual length that day. As they rode home Daville asked d'Avenat:

"How does that Kapidji Bashi seem to you?"

He knew that d'Avenat would always readily divulge all the information he had managed to glean in response to such a question about anyone. But this time he was unexpectedly brief: "He's a very sick man, Monsieur le Consul General."

"He does seem a strange guest, certainly."

"A very, very sick man," whispered d'Avenat, looking straight ahead and refusing to be drawn into any further discussion.

Then two days later, earlier than usual, d'Avenat asked the Consul for an urgent meeting. Daville received him in the dining room, where he was finishing breakfast.

It was Sunday, one of those summer mornings whose freshness and beauty are like a reward after the cold, gloomy days of autumn and winter. Numerous unseen streams cooled the air, filling it with murmuring and a bluish glow. Daville was thoroughly rested and pleased with the good news of Mehmed Pasha's staying on in Travnik. The remains of his breakfast lay in front of him and he was wiping his mouth with the gesture of a healthy man who has just satisfied his hunger, when d'Avenat came in, sombre and pale as ever, his lips tightly closed and his jaw muscles tense.

In a subdued tone, d'Avenat informed him that the Kapidji Bashi had died during the night.

Daville stood up abruptly, pushing the little breakfast table away, while d'Avenat, standing quite still, not altering his voice or attitude, answered his troubled questions briefly and vaguely.

The previous afternoon, the Kapidji Bashi, who had been ailing for a while anyway, had felt unwell. He had taken a Turkish bath and gone to bed. During the night, he had suddenly died, quite unexpectedly, before anyone could help him. He was to be buried during the morning. D'Avenat would report later anything else he might find out, either about the death itself or about reaction to the news in the bazaar.

Nothing more could be wrung out of him. In reply to Daville's question whether he ought to take some action, to express his condolences or something like that, d'Avenat answered that nothing should be done, because it was not the accepted custom. Here, death was ignored and everything connected with it was carried out swiftly, with few words or ceremony.

Left alone, Daville felt that his day, which had begun cheerfully, had suddenly clouded over. He could not stop thinking of that tall disagreeable man he had been talking with only two days earlier. Now he was dead. He thought also of the Vizier and of the embarrassment that the death of this important official in his house must cause him. D'Avenat's pale, funereal figure was constantly before his eyes, with his taciturn insensitivity and the way he had bowed and left, just as sullen and cold as when he came in.

Acting on d'Avenat's advice, the Consul took no action, but he kept thinking of the death at the Residence.

It was not until the following morning that d'Avenat came again and on this occasion, in the recess of a window, he explained in a whisper to the astounded Consul the true meaning of the Kapidji Bashi's mission and the cause of his death.

The Kapidji Bashi had in fact brought with him the Vizier's death sentence. The Imperial decree confirming him in his present position and the ceremonial sabre were meant only to conceal it, to reassure the Vizier and mislead the people. Immediately before his departure from Travnik, once the Vizier's vigilance was dulled, the Kapidji Bashi had been supposed to produce the other decree – the Katil-Ferman – which condemned the Vizier to death, along with all who had supported the former Sultan, directly or indirectly. He was to have ordered one of the officers of his retinue to execute Mehmed Pasha before any of his men could come to his aid. But, the cunning Vizier, who had foreseen just such an eventuality, had showered the Kapidji Bashi with attentions and honours, pretending to believe his words and to be delighted with the Sultan's clemency, and had immediately set about bribing his retinue. Then he had shown him the town, and introduced him to the French Consul at a Divan. The following day there had been a splendid luncheon in a meadow by the road leading to Turbe. When they returned to the Residence, after an excellent feast of rich foods, the Kapidji Bashi had been overcome by a high fever caused by the "icy Bosnian water". The Vizier had offered his guest the use of his fine hamam. While the Kapidji Bashi steamed himself on the hot stone tiles, perspiring abundantly and waiting for the masseur whom Mehmed Pasha had particularly praised, the Vizier's adept servants unpicked the lining of his coat where, as the officer he had bribed had told him, the Katil-Ferman lay hidden. It was found and handed to the Vizier. And when the Kapidji Bashi emerged, tired and flushed from the bath, he had been seized by a sudden, burning thirst which no liquid could quench. The more he drank, the more the poison spread. Before dark he collapsed, gasping like a man whose mouth and innards were on fire, and then he stiffened and fell silent. When they saw that he had lost the power of speech and was completely paralysed, that he could make no sound or sign, men were despatched from the Residence in great haste to find doctors and summon the hodjas. It was too late for the doctors, but the hodja is always in time.

Blue as indigo and stiff as a dead fish, the Kapidji Bashi was lying on a thin mattress in the middle of the room. Only his eyelids still flickered and he would from time to time raise them with difficulty, roll his eyes and survey the room with a terrible look, presumably searching for his coat or one of his men. Those large, clouded eyes of a betrayed and murdered man who had himself come to murder by treachery were all that was left alive in him and they expressed all that he could no longer say or do. The Vizier's servants moved around him on tiptoe, showing him every possible attention, and in awed silence, they communicated with each other only by signs and brief whispers. No one noticed the precise moment when he breathed his last.

The Vizier was seen to be an inconsolable host. The sudden death of his old friend had ruined his joy at the good news and great honour he had brought. His gleaming white teeth were now permanently covered by his thick black moustache. Quite changed, without a smile, the Vizier spoke with everyone, but only briefly, in a shaken voice, full of restrained grief. He summoned the Town Governor, the Kaymakam Resim Bey, a weak and prematurely old Travnik nobleman, and asked him to be at hand for the next few days, although he knew quite well that this man was incapable of looking after even his own affairs. And he lamented bitterly in his presence:

"It must have been written that he should make such a journey and die before my eyes... That could not be avoided, but I believe I would have preferred to lose my own brother," the Vizier said, like a man who for all his self-control could not quite conceal his anguish.

"What can you do, Pasha? You know what they say: 'We are all dead, just taking it in turns to be buried,'" the Kaymakam consoled him.

The Katil-Ferman, intended to condemn Mehmed Pasha and destroy him, was carefully sewn back in the same place, in the lining of the Kapidji Bashi's coat. He was to be buried that morning in one of the finest Travnik graveyards. And his whole retinue, well paid and rewarded, was returning that day to Istanbul.

So d'Avenat concluded his report of the most recent events in the Residence.

Daville was appalled, speechless with astonishment. It was like some improbable yarn and he had wanted several times to interrupt his interpreter. The Vizier's action struck him as not only criminal, but also dangerous and illogical. Tense with horror, the Consul strode up and down the room, staring at d'Avenat, as if trying to make out whether he really meant what he had said and whether he was in his right mind.

"What? What? Is it possible? How could he? How did he dare? He will be found out! And, after all, how can this help him?"

"It can help him. It seems it can help him," said d'Avenat calmly. He explained to the Consul, who had stopped pacing up and down, that the Vizier's calculations were not as misguided as they might seem at first sight, although they were very bold.

Firstly, by cheating his opponents and forestalling the Kapidji Bashi the Vizier had avoided the immediate danger very skilfully. There would be rumours and suspicions, but no one would be able to say anything and still less prove it. Secondly, the Kapidji Bashi had publicly brought the Vizier joyous news and exceptional marks of honour. Consequently, the Vizier would be the last person to want him dead. And those who had sent the Kapidji Bashi on his hypocritical mission would not dare, at least at first, undertake anything against the Vizier, because that would mean confessing that they had secretly intended him harm and that their plans had gone wrong. Thirdly, this Kapidji Bashi was a man with a bad name, widely hated, a half-breed, with no real friends, who had betrayed and deceived as naturally as he breathed, and whom not even those who used him had ever valued. Consequently his death would not surprise anyone, and still less provoke indignation or a desire for revenge. His bribed retinue would see to this as well. Fourthly, and most importantly, there was complete chaos in Istanbul now and Mehmed Pasha's friends, to whom he had sent "all that was required" just a few days before the Kapidji Bashi's unexpected arrival, would gain time to complete the "counter-attack" they had already launched and salvage the Vizier's standing with the new Sultan. And, if possible, strengthen him in his present post.

Frozen with terror, Daville listened to d'Avenat's calm account. Unable to contradict him, he simply murmured: "But still…still…"

D'Avenat did not consider it necessary to say anything further to convince the Consul. He only added that the bazaar was quiet and that the news of the Kapidji Bashi's sudden death had not provoked any particular excitement, although there was a great deal of comment.

It was only when he was left alone, that Daville became aware of the full horror of all he had just heard. And his disquiet grew as the day wore on. He ate little and could not settle in one place. He was on the point of summoning d'Avenat several times, to ask him anything at all, just to make sure that this morning's story was really true. He began to think what kind of report he would write about it and whether he ought to report it at all. He would sit down at his desk and begin. "Last night in the Vizier's Residence, there occurred…" No, that was insipid. "The events of the last few days show increasingly that, even in these altered circumstances, Mehmed Pasha will succeed in maintaining his position, by means and methods which are customary here, and, therefore, we may be assured that this Vizier, well-disposed to us…" No, no. That was dry and obscure. Finally, he himself saw that it was best to report the events just as they appeared to everyone: that a special Kapidji Bashi had come from Istanbul and brought a decree confirming the Vizier in his post and making him a gift of a sabre, as a mark of the Sultan's grace and the impending campaign against Serbia. At the end he would stress that this was a good sign for the future development of French endeavours in this region, adding in passing that the Kapidji Bashi had chanced to die suddenly in Travnik while carrying out his mission.

It soothed Daville a little to chop and change his official report like this. The crime which had taken place only the day before, right here before his eyes, seemed all at once less appalling as soon as it became the subject of these reflections about the report. In vain the Consul sought in himself for the shock and moral indignation of that morning.

He sat down and wrote the report, presenting the affair as it had appeared to the outside world. After that, copying it out neatly, he felt a still greater sense of relief, even a kind of satisfaction with himself, knowing that his report rested on sinister, momentous secrets, wisely left unspoken.

Soothed then, the Consul stood by the open window as the summer twilight gathered, full of silence and indirect light among the dark shadows of the steep hills. Someone came into the room behind him with a lighted taper and began to light the candles on the table. It was at that moment that the thought flashed into his mind: who could have prepared the poison, calculated the dose and expertly predicted its effect, so that it should be both sufficiently swift (each phase at its appointed moment) but not too sudden to be natural? Who, if not d'Avenat? That was his profession. He had been in the Vizier's service until recently, and perhaps he still was.

All Daville's apparent calm left him instantly. He felt again the shock of that morning. A crime had been committed right here, beside him, connected with his work, and therefore with him, and his interpreter was, perhaps, a despicable, hired accomplice. This feeling engulfed him like fire. Could anyone's life here be safe and protected from crime? And what was the good of such a life if this was how things were? He stood, rooted to the spot, between the light of the flickering candles being lit in the room one after the other, and the last, already dimmed glow on the steep slopes outside.

Evening was drawing in, and Daville faced one of those terrible, sleepless nights he had not known before Travnik. A night when one could neither sleep nor think properly. And if he did succeed in dozing for a moment, he would see in random order: Mehmed Pasha's broad and joyous smile of two days before, the thin, sinewy arm of the Kapidji Bashi with its wide scar and the grim, incomprehensible d'Avenat saying softly: "A very, very sick man."

And there was no rhyme or reason in all of this. The images came separately, with no logical connection, as though nothing were yet decided, as though the crime might happen, but could equally well be prevented.

Daville agonized in that half-sleep, wishing with all his heart that the crime should not take place, but sensing, somewhere in the depths of his consciousness, that it had in fact already occurred.

Often an oppressive, sleepless night like this determines the nature of a whole experience, shutting it off forever like a mute iron gate.

Over the next few days d'Avenat came with his reports as usual. He showed no sign of any change. The Kapidji Bashi's sudden death had not provoked any indignation among the Travnik Turks either; and even the suspicions and accusations did not last long. The fate of this Ottoman did not interest them much. The only thing they saw was that the hated Vizier was staying on in Travnik and that he had even been rewarded. From this they concluded that the May coup had changed nothing in Istanbul. So they withdrew into disappointed silence, clenching their teeth and lowering their eyes. They assumed that the new Sultan was also under the influence of infidels, or vile, corrupt officials, and that the victory of the forces of good had been postponed yet again. But they were equally convinced that the true faith would prevail in the end. They had only to wait. And no one was as good at waiting as the real Bosnian "Turks", people of unshakeable faith and rock-firm pride, who could be both fervent as a flood-tide and patient as the earth.

Daville had one more occasion to feel the astonishment of that first day and a painful, cold fear in his stomach. That was at his first audience after the Kapidji Bashi's death. Twelve days had passed. The Vizier was unchanged and smiling. He talked of his preparations for the campaign against Serbia and approved all Daville's plans for Franco-Turkish co-operation on the border between Bosnia and Dalmatia.

Making a great effort to be calm and natural, Daville expressed at last, in passing, his sincere regret at the death of the Imperial dignitary, the Vizier's friend. Even before d'Avenat had translated these words, the Vizier's smile was extinguished. His black moustache hid his gleaming white teeth. His face with its slanting almond eyes became suddenly shorter and broader. It stayed like that until the interpreter had finished translating Daville's expressions of condolence. His smile returned for the rest of the conversation.

Human indifference and a general tendency to forget appeased Daville as well. Seeing that life went on unaltered, he told himself that such things must then be possible. He did not talk even to d'Avenat about the crime in the Residence. His time was filled with work. With each day Daville felt a little freer from that stunning moral outrage and his initial sense of bitter astonishment. He let the current of his day-to-day life bear him along. It was true that he felt he would never be able to look at Mehmed Pasha without thinking to himself that here was a man who, in d'Avenat's words, had been "quicker and cleverer and forestalled his opponents". But he would continue to work with him and discuss everything other than that.

At about that time, the Vizier's Deputy, Suleiman Pasha Skopljak, returned from the river Drina. In the Residence the story went that he had completely routed the Serbian rebels. However, Suleiman Pasha himself spoke with more restraint and less specifically.

This Deputy, a Bosnian, came from one of the leading bey families. He had large estates in Bosansko Skoplje in the Kupres district, and dozens of houses and shops in Bugojno. Tall, wiry and slender despite his advanced years, with piercing blue eyes, he was a man who had seen many wars, acquired great wealth, and become a Pasha without flattering anyone or much bribery. He was austere in peace and cruel in war, greedy for land and unscrupulously acquisitive, but he could not be bribed and did not have the usual Ottoman vices.

One could hardly say that this half-peasant of stiff bearing, with the sharp eyes of the "best marksman in the whole of Bosnia" was particularly agreeable. Like the Ottomans, he was slow, mistrustful, sly and unyielding with foreigners. And in addition his speech was abrupt and crude. Suleiman Pasha spent the greater part of the year either in campaigns against Serbia or on his estates, and he stayed in Travnik only during the winter months. His presence now meant that, for this year at least, the war was over.

Altogether, things were beginning to calm down and less was happening. Autumn was approaching. At first early autumn, with its weddings, harvests, livelier trade and better income, and then the later season with its rain, coughs and worries. The mountains became impassable and people less mobile and enterprising. They were preparing to spend the months of winter wherever they happened to be, just trying to get through it. It seemed to Daville that even the great machinery of the French Empire was beginning to work more slowly. The congress in Erfurt was over, Napoleon was turning his attention to Spain, which meant that for the time being at least the whirlwind was shifting to the west. There were few couriers or orders from Split. It seemed that the Vizier was to stay in his position, which was what concerned Daville most. He had even regained his brightest smile. His friends' "counter-attack" in Istanbul had evidently succeeded. There was still no sign of the Austrian consul, whose arrival had been talked about for a long time. Daville was informed from Paris that by the end of the year he would be sent a competent assistant who knew the Turkish language. And during the most difficult days d'Avenat had proved himself skilful, trustworthy and devoted.

The greatest joy awaited Daville before the onset of autumn. Quietly and virtually unnoticed, Madame Daville arrived with their three children. These were three sons, Pierre, Jules-François and Jean-Paul. The eldest was four years old, the second two and the third had been born a few months earlier, in Split.

Madame Daville was fair, slight and slim. Under her thin hair which she wore up in a style quite outside any fashion, she had a little, lively face, with a healthy complexion, delicate lines and blue eyes which shone like metal. Behind what seemed at first an unremarkable appearance, there was hidden a wise, sober and capable woman of strong will and tireless body. She was one of those women of whom our people say that "nothing is beyond them". Her life consisted of dogged but sensible and patient service to her house and family. Her thoughts and feelings were devoted to this service, while her slender hands, always red, apparently feeble, never rested, mastering every task as though they were made of steel. Born into a good bourgeois family, which had been ruined in an unlucky turn of events during the Revolution, she had grown up at the home of her uncle, the Bishop of Avranches, and was sincerely devout, with that special French piety which was both firm and human, unshakeable, but free of bigotry.

As soon as Madame Daville arrived, a new era began in the large and neglected building of the French Consulate. Not saying a great deal, never complaining and not asking for anyone's assistance or advice, she worked from early morning until late at night. The house was tidied and put in order. A whole series of changes was carried out, so as to adapt it as well as possible to the needs of its new inhabitants. Rooms were altered, old windows and doors were filled in and new ones made. In the absence of proper furniture and material, Bosnian cloth and Turkish chests and carpets were used.

The house, clean and carpeted, was completely transformed. Footsteps no longer echoed unpleasantly through it as before. The kitchen had been entirely rebuilt. Little by little, everything took on the mark of the French way of life, sober and sensible but rich in genuine contentment.

The following spring would find the building and everything in and around it utterly changed.

Two gardens had been designed on the flat ground just in front of the house. Their layout and flowerbeds would be modestly reminiscent of French gardens. A chicken coop was constructed and store-rooms and pantries made behind the house.

All this was done according to Madame Daville's plans and under her supervision. But the Consul's wife had to contend with difficulties of every kind, particularly with the question of servants. These were not the kind of trivial problems all housewives the world over complain of. They were real. At first no one wanted to work in the Consulate. There could be no question of Turkish servants. No one from any of the few Orthodox houses wanted to work for them. And the Catholic girls, who would otherwise serve even in Turkish houses, did not initially dare set foot in the French Consulate, for the friars had threatened them with damnation and the harshest penance. The wives of the Jewish merchants eventually succeeded somehow in persuading some gypsy girls to work in the new Consulate for a good wage. Finally, Madame Daville showed by her visits and gifts to the church in Dolac that, although she was the wife of the "Jacobin Consul", she was a true Catholic. Only then did the friars become a little more lenient and give silent approval for the women of their community to work for the Consul's wife.

Altogether, Madame Daville endeavoured to create and maintain the best possible connections with the parish priest of Dolac, the friars of Guča Gora monastery and their congregations. And despite all the difficulties, ignorance and mistrust he encountered, Daville hoped that, before the Austrian Consul arrived in Travnik, he would be able to ensure for himself some influence with the friars and the Catholic population – at least through his clever, devout wife.

In short, during the first days of autumn everything became more tranquil and agreeable in the house and in his work. Daville was the whole time under the vague but constant impression that everything was falling into place and beginning to take a turn for the better. Or at least, things seemed easier and more bearable.

A pale autumn sky glowed above Travnik, and under it the streets with their rain-washed cobbles looked bright and clean. The bushes and copses changed colour and became thinner and transparent. The Lašva looked swift and clear in the sun. Constrained in its straight, narrow bed, it hummed like a wire. The roads were dry and hard, with traces of the squashed fruit which fell from carts and wisps of hay on the bushes and fences on either side.

Daville went out each day for long rides. He rode over Kupilo, along the straight road, under tall elms, looking down at the houses with their black roofs and blue smoke, the mosques and the white, scattered graveyards. It seemed to him that all of it, the buildings and the streets and the gardens, were settling into a pattern which was little by little becoming closer and more comprehensible to him. A breath of calm and relief spread everywhere. The Consul breathed it in with the autumn air and felt a need to turn round and share it, at least in a smile, with the khavaz who was riding behind him. In fact this was merely a lull.

4

In the reports he wrote during those first few months, Daville never stopped complaining about everything a consul in such circumstances could complain about. He complained about the truculent hostility of the local Turks, the indolence and unreliability of the state authorities, his meagre salary and inadequate credits, the roof which leaked, the climate which made his children ill, the intrigues of Austrian agents, the lack of understanding he met with from his superiors in Istanbul and Split. In short, everything was difficult, inefficient and a cause for dissatisfaction.

Daville complained particularly that the Ministry had not sent him a reliable man, a career civil servant, with a knowledge of the Turkish language.

D'Avenat served as a stop-gap, but the Consul could not have complete confidence in him. The great zeal he showed still could not quite dispel the Consul's doubts. Besides, while his spoken French was adequate, he could not carry on an official correspondence.

For contacts with the local people, Daville had taken on Rafo Atijas, a young Travnik Jew, eager to avoid work in his uncle's ware-house, preferring to be an interpreter of the "Illyrian" language to rummaging through tanned hides. He was even less trustworthy than d'Avenat. Consequently, in each report, Daville begged to be sent a civil servant. At last, when he was beginning to give up hope, gradually becoming accustomed to d'Avenat and gaining some confidence in him, the new Secretary and interpreter, young Des Fossés arrived.

Amédée Chaumette Des Fossés belonged to the youngest generation of the Paris diplomatic corps. That is, he belonged to the first generation after the troubled years of the Revolution to receive a regular education and to be given special training for service in the East. He was from a banker's family which had not quite lost its old established wealth either during the Revolution or under the rule of the Directoire. In the course of his education he had had the reputation of a prodigy and amazed his teachers and fellow-pupils with the power of his memory, the swiftness of his judgement and the ease with which he acquired the most varied knowledge.

The young man was tall, athletically built, ruddy-faced, with large brown eyes, shining with restless curiosity.

Daville's immediate impression was that he had before him a true child of the times, a new kind of young Parisian, carefree, bold and confident in his speech and movements, in touch with reality, confident of his strength and knowledge and inclined to overrate both.

The young man handed over the mail and briefly relayed the most essential information, not concealing the fact that he was tired and cold. He ate well. Then, without much ceremony, he announced that he wanted to go to bed. He slept through that night and until noon the next day. He rose fresh and rested, showing his satisfaction at this just as naturally and easily as he had his weariness of the day before.

The young man's directness, his assured bearing and easy tone caused a stir in the little household. At all times, he knew just what he wanted or needed, and asked for it without inhibition or wasted words.

After the first few days it became clear that the Consul and his assistant could never have much in common or even any mutual understanding. Only, each of them recognized and accepted this in his own way.

Daville was living through that stage of his life in which everything is liable to be a problem of conscience and a torment to the
spirit. Instead of relief, the arrival of young Des Fossés brought
him only new difficulties by raising a series of fresh, insoluble but
unavoidable problems, in the end creating around him an even
greater sense of emptiness and isolation. For Des Fossés on the
other hand, nothing seemed to represent a problem or insuperable
difficulty. At least, his superior, Daville, certainly did not.

Daville was a man approaching his forties, while Des Fossés
was just twenty-four. This difference in their ages would not have
been significant in other circumstances. But troubled times, with
their great changes and social upheavals, gouge out and continue
to deepen an unbridgeable gulf between the generations, making
of them two different worlds.

Daville remembered the Ancien Régime, even if only as a child.
He had experienced the Revolution, in all its forms, as his personal
destiny. He had greeted the First Consul and accepted his régime
with a zeal containing both suppressed doubts and boundless faith.

He had been about twelve years old when, lined up with other
children from bourgeois families, he had seen Louis XVI on a visit
to their town. That was an unforgettable event for the mind and
imagination of a child who kept hearing at home that his whole
family lived on "the King's goodness". Now that very King was
passing before his own eyes, in the flesh, the personification of
everything fine and great that life could bring. Besides, unseen
fanfares blared, cannon boomed and all the town bells were ringing
at the same time. The people in their best clothes nearly broke
down the barriers in their enthusiasm. Through tears, the boy saw
tears in everyone's eyes, and he felt his throat tightening with that
lump that always comes at moments of great emotion. The King,
himself deeply moved, ordered the coach to slow down to a walk,
removed his large hat with a sweeping movement and in response

to the chorus of "Long live the King!" kept replying in a clear voice: "Long live my people!" For the child watching and hearing all this, it seemed like an incredible dream of paradise, until the enthusiastic crowd behind him shoved his hat, brand-new and somewhat too tall, over his eyes, so that he saw nothing but the darkness of his own tears, in which yellow sparks flew and blue streaks swam. When he managed to push his hat back, it had all gone, like a vision. There was only the crowd pushing and shoving around him, with glowing faces and shining eyes.

Ten years or so later, as a young reporter for a Paris newspaper, Daville had listened with the same tears in his eyes and that same hard, indissoluble lump in his throat to Mirabeau thundering against the Ancien Régime and its abuses.

The young man's emotion sprang now from the same source, but its object was utterly different. Daville had changed and found himself in a completely changed world, flung into it by the Revolution as it swept him along violently and irresistibly with hundreds of thousands of young men just like him. It seemed as though the whole world had grown young with him and that new perspectives and unimagined possibilities were being opened up all over the globe. Everything had suddenly become clear, carefree, and straightforward, every effort had taken on a sublime significance, every step and every thought was filled with superhuman grandeur and dignity. This was no longer the King's goodness lavished on a limited number of people and families, but a general explosion of divine justice over the whole of humanity. Like everyone else, Daville was drunk with an incomprehensible happiness, as the weak always are intoxicated when they succeed in finding a common and generally recognized formula which promises to satisfy their needs and instincts at the price of other people's ruin, and which at the same time frees them from pangs of conscience and responsibility.

Although he was only one of numerous journalists reporting meetings of the Constituent Assembly, the young Daville felt that his articles, in which he recounted the speeches of the great orators or described rousing scenes of patriotic and revolutionary fervour among their audience, had universal and everlasting significance. And at first the initials of his name, at the foot of these reports, seemed to him like two mountains which nothing could either surpass or shift. He felt as though he were not writing parliamentary reports but, with his very own hands and the strength of a giant, moulding the soul of mankind like obedient clay.

But those years passed and, sooner than he would have thought possible, he saw the other face of the Revolution that had captivated him. He remembered how it began.

One morning, woken by a crowd shouting, he got up and opened his window wide. Suddenly he found himself face to face with a severed head, swaying, pale and bloody, on the pike of a sans-culottes. In that instant, something appalling and agonizing, like a cold, bitter fluid, ran from his stomach, his Bohemian stomach, which had been empty since the previous day, through his breast and through his whole body. From that moment, for many years, life never ceased forcing him to swallow that same draught which no one can ever get used to. He went on moving about, living, writing articles and shouting with the crowd, but now he was tormented by an inner gulf which for a long time he refused to admit even to himself, and hid completely from others. And when the time came to decide about the King's life and the fate of the Monarchy, when he had to choose between the bitter draught of the Revolution that had swept him up so violently, and "the Royal goodness" that had nourished his youth, the young man suddenly found himself once again on the other side.

In June 1792, after the insurgents broke into the Palace for the first time, there was a fierce reaction among the more moderate who began organizing a petition expressing sympathy for the King and the Royal Family. Carried along by that wave of indignation against violence and disorder, the young man overcame his inner fears, stifled his objections, and placed his signature alongside those of the other 20,000 Parisians. The inner struggle that preceded this signature was so great that Daville felt that his name was not lost among the other 20,000 names, for the most part weightier and better-known than his, but written in letters of fire across the evening sky over Paris. It was then that he discovered how a man could bend and break inwardly, how far he could fall and rise in his own eyes. In short: how transient exultation could be, how obscure and intricate it was while it lasted and how dearly it was paid for and bitterly repented when it passed.

A month later the great persecution began. Suspect persons and "bad citizens" were arrested, starting with the signatories of the petition of 20,000. In order to avoid arrest, to resolve or escape his inner conflicts, the young journalist Daville signed up as a volunteer and was assigned to the Pyrenean army on the Spanish frontier.

There he saw that war was a harsh and terrible thing, but that it was also good and healing. He recognized the value of physical effort and the limits of his own strength. He proved himself in danger, learned to obey and to command, and experienced all forms of suffering, but he also learned the beauty of comradeship and the purpose of discipline.

Three years after his first great inner crisis, soothed and strengthened by military life, Daville found his feet again. Chance took him to the Ministry of Foreign Affairs where everything was in a state of turmoil and upheaval. No one, from the Minister to the most junior clerk, was a career diplomat: they all had to learn together from the beginning the skill that had hitherto been the privilege of men of the old order. But when Talleyrand became Minister, everything began to make rapid progress. Once again, chance made Talleyrand notice young Daville's articles in the *Moniteur* and he took him under his special protection.

As happens with so many tormented, disturbed and basically weak spirits, Daville then saw one bright, fixed point in all his inner troubles: the young General Bonaparte, the victor in Italy and the hope of everyone who, like Daville, was seeking a middle course between the Ancien Régime and emigration on the one hand and the Revolution and Terror on the other. And when Talleyrand appointed him Secretary of the new Cisalpine Republic, before he left for his post in Milan, Daville was received by the General, who wanted to give him personal instructions for his emissary, Citizen Trouvé.

Daville knew Napoleon's brother Lucien well and had been recommended by him. So he was received with courtesy, in Napoleon's private apartment, after dinner.

Face to face with this thin man, with his martyr's pale complexion, his burning eyes but cold gaze, listening to his words, at once wise and warm – great, bold, clear and compelling words, which opened up unimagined vistas worth both living and dying for, Daville felt all his hesitations and doubts vanish. Everything in the world had become reconciled, all aims attainable and all efforts worthwhile and blessed in advance. Conversation with this exceptional man healed like the touch of a miracle-worker. In a moment, all the silt of the last years was washed away from his soul, and all his dulled ardour, all his agonizing doubts acquired meaning and justification. This extraordinary man pointed out that sure path between extremes and contradictions which Daville, like so many others, had been seeking for years, passionately, but in vain. And when, around midnight, the new Secretary of the Cisalpine Republic emerged from the General's apartment into the Rue Chanteraine, he suddenly felt tears brimming in his eyes and that same hard, indissoluble lump in his throat he had experienced once as a child waving to Louis XVI, and again as a young man listening to revolutionary songs and the speeches of Mirabeau. He felt drunk and as though he had wings, and the blood in his throat and temples was throbbing with the same rhythm as the great pulse of the world which he sensed beating high above him somewhere beneath the stars of this night.

The years passed. The thin general rose. He was now before everyone's eyes, moving along the horizon, a sun which knew no setting. Daville changed places and jobs, dreaming up literary and political plans and turning like all the rest of the world towards that sun. But his exultation, like the enthusiasm of all weak people in great and troubled times, betrayed him by not fulfilling all it had promised. And Daville felt that he was himself secretly betraying his own enthusiasm and becoming gradually estranged from it. When had this started? When had this indifference begun and how far had it gone? He could not find an answer, but with each day he saw more clearly that it was so. Only this time everything was more difficult, more hopeless. The Revolution had swept the old régime away like a whirlwind, and then Napoleon had appeared as salvation from them both, as a gift of Providence and the longed-for "middle way" of dignity and reason. Now the thought began to form that this path too might be just a dead-end, one of many deceptions. This so-called right path might not even exist and a man's life might be lost in perpetual longing for it and constant endeavour to straighten out the tortuous one he was treading. So he would have to continue to search for the right path. After all the peaks and troughs, it was not as easy as before. Daville was no longer young, and the years and his many painful inner crises had wearied him. Like so many of his contemporaries, he longed for peaceful work and stability. Instead of that, life in France was moving at an increasingly rapid pace and taking increasingly unusual directions. And France was infecting ever more peoples and an ever larger circle of countries with this restlessness. One by one they were falling into that ring dance of exulted, whirling dervishes. This was the sixth year already, roughly since the time of the treaty of Amiens, that hope and doubt kept changing places in Daville, like the play of light and dark. After each of the First Consul's or, later, the Emperor Napoleon's victories, it seemed as though a firm, secure, redeeming middle way could be seen. But just a few months later it all looked like an impasse. People were beginning to be frightened. They all kept going forwards, but many started glancing around them. During the few months he spent in Paris before being appointed Consul in Travnik, Daville had been able to see in the eyes of innumerable friends, as in a mirror, the same fear that kept appearing, unacknowledged and suppressed, in himself.

Two years earlier, immediately after Napoleon's great victory in Prussia, Daville had written an ode on "The Battle of Jena", perhaps precisely to stifle his doubts and drive away his fear, by praising the conquering Emperor extravagantly. Just when he was on the point of having his poem published, an old friend of his from the same part of France, a high-ranking officer in the Ministry of the Navy, said in a low voice over a glass of calvados: "Do you know what you are celebrating and who it is you are glorifying? Do you know that the Emperor's mad – mad! – and that he maintains his position only through the bloodshed of his victories which lead nowhere and have no purpose? Do you know that we are all rushing headlong into a great calamity whose name and scale we don't know, but which definitely awaits us at the end of all our victories? You don't know? There you are, that's why you can write poems celebrating those victories!"

His companion had had a glass or two too many that evening, but Daville could not forget his dilated pupils, staring prophetically into the distance, and his whisper which smelt of alcohol but contained also the breath of conviction. Sober people would mutter the same thought in different words, or hide it in a troubled look.

Daville decided nevertheless to publish his ode, but he did it hesitantly and with some misgivings as to its worth and the enduring nature of the victory. These misgivings, which were just starting to spread through the world, began to grow in his soul as his own private anguish.

Concealing these complex feelings, he arrived in Travnik as Consul. Nothing he had experienced here could have encouraged or soothed him. On the contrary, it had just disturbed him all the more.

All this was revived and stirred up with new force by his first contacts with this young man with whom he had now to live and work. Watching him behave so naturally and hearing him express himself so boldly and easily about everything, Daville thought to himself: "What is terrible is not that we grow old and weak and die, but that new people, young and different, come thrusting their way up behind us. That is death in fact. No one drags us towards the grave, we are pushed from behind." The Consul himself wondered in some surprise where these ideas came from, as they did not at all correspond to his natural way of thinking. He immediately rejected such thoughts, putting them down to the "Oriental poison" which sooner or later must infect everyone here and was gradually seeping into his own brain.

This young man, the only Frenchman in this wilderness and the only man he really had to work with, was so different from him in so many ways (or at least that is how it seemed), that Daville felt at times that he was living alongside a foreigner and an enemy. But what bewildered and irritated him most about the young man was his attitude (or rather absence of an attitude) towards the "fundamental things" which were the substance of Daville's life: towards the Monarchy, the Revolution and Napoleon. For the Consul and his generation these three concepts represented an intense and complex knot of conflict, inspiration, exultation, brilliant achievements, but also of hesitations, inner disloyalties and unseen crises of conscience, with no obvious solution, with increasingly little hope of being lastingly assuaged. This caused them constant pain which they had borne since childhood, and which would presumably accompany them to the grave. But at the same time, and precisely because of that, this pain was as close and dear to them as their life itself. For this young man and people of his age, however, as far as Daville could see, there was neither pain nor bewilderment, no reason for complaint or reflection. For them all these questions were simple and natural things it was not worth wasting words or beating one's brains over. The Monarchy was a fairy tale, the Revolution a dim childhood memory. The Empire was life itself, life and career, the straightforward, natural scene of unlimited possibilities, actions, exploits and glory. In fact, for Des Fossés the order he lived in, that is the Empire, represented the one and only completely coherent reality, stretching in a spiritual and material sense from one end of the horizon to the other and including everything which life itself comprised. But for Daville it was only one random, flimsy order of things whose painful beginning he had watched with his own eyes, and whose temporary nature he never quite forgot. Unlike this young man, he remembered quite well what had gone before this and he often wondered what might follow.

The "world of ideas" which was for Daville's generation their only spiritual homeland and their real life, appeared not even to exist for the new men. Consequently, what existed for them was "living life", the world of reality, the world of tangible facts and visible, measurable successes and failures, a terrible new world which was opening up in front of Daville like an icy desert, more terrible than the blood, suffering and spiritual turmoil of the Revolution. This was a generation born out of blood, stripped of everything, ready for anything, tempered as though it had run through fire.

As always, under the pressure of his unusual, difficult circumstances, Daville was undoubtedly generalizing and exaggerating. He would often tell himself as much, for by his nature he did not like contradictions or the realization that they were enduring and unbridgeable. But there in front of him, as a constant reminder, stood this young man with his keen look, cool but sensual, serene and full of self-confidence, unencumbered by doubt or consideration for others, looking at all things around him directly, seeing them for what they were, and calling them without second thought by their proper names. For all his talents and personal decency, he was a man of the new generation, one of the "animalized generation" as Daville's contemporaries used to say. So this was the product of the Revolution, the free citizen, the new man, Daville would think after every conversation with him, when he was left alone. "Perhaps revolutions breed monsters?" he would then wonder in alarm. And he would often reply: "Yes, they are conceived in greatness and moral purity, but they breed monsters."

And then, at night, he would be assailed by increasingly ominous thoughts, beyond his control, which threatened to overwhelm him.

While Daville struggled with the thoughts and moods which the arrival of his young Secretary provoked in him, the young man noted only the following in the short diary intended for his friends in Paris: "The Consul is just as I had imagined him." The picture he had of him was based on Daville's first reports from Travnik and still more on the account of an older colleague from the Ministry, a certain Kérène, who was famous for knowing all the civil servants at the Ministry of Foreign Affairs and being able to give a more or less accurate "moral and physical profile" of each of them in a few words. Kérène was astute and witty, but otherwise an arid man, for whom the sketching of such verbal portraits had become a life-long habit and passion. He entered completely into this barren business, which seemed at times an exact science, but at others the merest gossip. He could always repeat his "portraits" word for word, as though he had a printed text in his head. This was Kérène's account of Daville:

"Jean Daville came into the world an upright, sound and – average man. His whole nature, origin and education equipped him for a quiet, simple life, with no great heights or serious falls, without any sudden changes at all. A plant for a moderate climate. He has an innate ability to become easily enthusiastic and elated about ideas and people, and a special taste for poetry and poetic states of mind. But none of this goes further than a happy mediocrity. Peaceful times and orderly circumstances make mediocre people still more so, while stormy times and great changes complicate their natures. This is the case with our Daville, who kept finding himself at the centre of important events. None of it could alter his true nature, but it added new and contradictory features to his innate qualities. Incapable of acting in an inconsiderate, cruel, irresponsible or underhand way, in order to protect himself and survive, he became timid, secretive and superstitiously cautious. Naturally sound, honest, enterprising and cheerful, with time he gradually became touchy, hesitant, slow, mistrustful and inclined to melancholy. And as none of this suited his true character, it created in him a curiously divided personality. In short, he is one of those people who are the special victims of major historical events, for they are not capable either of resisting those events, as exceptional and strong individuals do, or of completely coming to terms with them, as the vast majority of ordinary people do. As a human type he is a 'moaner' and he will go on moaning about everything, including life itself, as long as he lives. A very common phenomenon in our times." Kérène concluded.

So, it was with this fundamental difference that their life together began. Although it was a cold, damp autumn, Des Fossés explored the town and its surroundings and met quite a number of people. Daville presented him to the Vizier and the most important people at the Residence, but the young man did all the rest himself. He made the acquaintance of the Dolac parish priest, Brother Ivo Janković, a man of some sixteen stone in weight, but with a lively wit and sharp tongue. He met the Abbot Pahomije, a pale, reserved monk who was at that time serving the Orthodox church of St Michael the Archangel. He called at the houses of the Travnik Jews. He visited the monastery at Guča Gora and there made the acquaintance of some friars who told him many things about the country and the people. He prepared to explore the old settlements and graveyards in the neighbourhood, as soon as the snow melted. After only three weeks he informed Daville of his intention to write a book about Bosnia.

The Consul had grown up before the Revolution and been educated along classical lines. So, despite his participation in the Revolution, he continued to operate within the limits such an upbringing imposes on a man's thinking and speech. That was why he looked with suspicion and unease on this undoubtedly gifted young man, his vast intellectual curiosity and astonishing memory, the bold disorder of his speech and enviable abundance of his ideas. He was frightened by the young man's energy, which nothing could check or throw off course. He found it hard to bear, but felt there was nothing he could do to curb or halt it. The young man had studied Turkish for three years in Paris and spoke boldly and directly to everyone. ("He knows the kind of Turkish you learn at the Collège de Louis le Grand in Paris, and not that the Turks in Bosnia speak," wrote Daville.) If he did not always succeed in making himself understood, he certainly attracted people with his broad smile and bright eyes. The friars, who avoided Daville, and the sullen, mistrustful Abbot, would all talk to him. Only the Travnik beys remained inaccessible. But the bazaar people could not be indifferent to the "Young Consul".

Des Fossés did not let a single market day go by without exploring the whole market place. He would ask about the prices, examine the goods and make a note of their names. People would gather round this stranger, dressed "alafranga", and watch him trying out a sieve or carefully examining displays of drills and chisels. "The Young Consul" would spend a long time watching a peasant buying a scythe, feeling its blade carefully with his hardened left thumb, then striking it many times against a stone step and listening attentively to the sound it made, finally looking down its length, with one eye closed, as though taking aim, assessing its cutting edge and its cast. He would approach the village women, hard, aged women, and ask the price of the wool lying in front of them in a goatshair sack smelling of the sheepfold. Seeing a stranger in front of her, the peasant woman would at first hesitate, thinking the gentleman was joking. Finally, at the insistence of the khavaz accompanying him, she would tell him the price and swear that the wool was "soft as the soul", as soon as it was washed. He enquired as to the names of cereals and seeds, examined the firmness and size of the grains. He was interested in various handles and hafts for axes, hoes, pickaxes and other tools, what wood was used and how they were made.

"The Young Consul" met all the notable figures in the market: Ibrahim Aga, the "scalesman", Hamza the town-crier, and the bazaar fool "Mad Fritz".

Ibrahim Aga was a thin, tall, stooping old man with a grey beard, of stern and dignified bearing. He had once been wealthy and had himself collected the local weight tax. Under his supervision his sons and assistants weighed and re-weighed everything that was sold at the market. With time he had lost his wealth and his sons and assistants. Now the Travnik Jews were in charge of the weighing scales and saw that the weight tax was paid, and Ibrahim Aga only worked for them, but you would not have guessed this at the market. For the peasants and everyone who bought or sold, the one true "scalesman" was Ibrahim Aga and he would remain so until his death. Every market day he stood by the scales, from morning until dark. When he began to weigh a solemn silence would fall around him. He would hold his breath as he set up the scales and, grave and concentrated, he would seem to grow and subside with the slow swaying of the pan. Squinting with one eye, he arranged the weight painstakingly, and carefully moved it along the scale away from the load in the pan, a little further, just a little further, until the scale stopped swaying and showed the correct weight. Then Ibrahim Aga would remove his hand, raise his head, without taking his eyes off the figure, and shout the weight clearly, sternly and indisputably:

"Sixty-one okes, less twenty-two drams."

There was no disputing this pronouncement. In all the bustle of the market, around him reigned order, silence and the respect everyone showed for conscientious work. Given the strength of Ibrahim Aga's personality, it could not be otherwise. And if some mistrustful peasant whose goods he was weighing came too close to the scale, in order to see and check the number of okes behind the scalesman's back, Ibrahim Aga would immediately place his hand on the weight, stop weighing and drive the importunate fellow away.

"Get away from here! Don't you go shoving your nose into the scales and coughing all over them! 'Right measure is real treasure' and the merest breath could upset it. And I'll be the one who burns in Hell, not you. Get away!"

So Ibrahim Aga spent his life hovering over the weighing scales, living with them, for them and through them, a living example of what a man can make of his profession, whatever it might be.

But Des Fossés had occasion to observe that same Ibrahim Aga, who guarded his soul against the slightest sin while he weighed, mercilessly beating a Christian peasant in the middle of the market place, in full view of everyone. The peasant had brought a dozen axe handles to sell and had leant them against the dilapidated wall surrounding a neglected graveyard and the ruins of an ancient mosque. Ibrahim Aga, who was supervising the work of the whole market, rushed furiously up to him and kicked the handles over, cursing and threatening the frightened man as he gathered up his scattered wares:

"Do you think a mosque wall is for you to lean your filthy handles on, you scurvy pig! There are no bells ringing here and no Christian trumpet blaring yet, you son of a swine!"

People carried on buying and selling, bargaining, weighing goods and making calculations, without paying much attention to this quarrel. The peasant managed to collect everything that belonged to him and disappeared among the crowd. (When he reached home, Des Fossés jotted down: "Turkish authority has two faces. For us their actions are illogical and incomprehensible and they constantly confuse and surprise us.")

Hamza the town-crier was a quite different kind of man, with a different destiny.

Once famous for his voice and his fine manly looks, he had been a layabout and reveller from his early youth, one of the worst Travnik drunks. In his younger years, he had been renowned for his daring and quick wits. His sharp, cheeky rejoinders were still remembered. When he was asked exactly why he had chosen the career of town-crier, he would reply: "Because there's nothing easier." On one occasion, several years earlier, when Suleiman Pasha Skopljak marched his army against Montenegro and burned Drobnjak, Hamza was ordered to announce the Turkish victory and to shout that 180 Montenegrin heads had been cut off. One of the crowd that always gathers around the town-crier asked him out loud: "And how many of ours were killed?" "The town-crier in Cetinje will announce that," Hamza answered calmly and continued shouting as instructed.

Hamza had long since ruined his throat with unruly living, singing and his professional shouting. He no longer roused the bazaar with his former resonant voice. Now, in a hoarse squeak and with great effort, he announced official and bazaar news, which would be heard only by those near him. But it never occurred to anyone that Hamza should be replaced by someone younger, in better voice. And he himself hardly seemed to notice that he scarcely had any voice left. He continued to announce to the world, as best he could, all that he had to, standing in the same position and with the same gestures with which he had once sent his famous voice ringing through the little streets. The children gathered round him and laughed at those gestures which for a long time now had not suited his strained guttural cooing, and they would watch with curiosity and alarm as his stretched neck swelled like a bagpipe with the tension. Nevertheless, he needed those children for it was only they who could hear his feeble call and they would immediately spread the news through the town.

Des Fossés and Hamza made friends quickly, for the "Young Consul" would from time to time buy a piece of jewellery or a carpet which Hamza advertised and that earned him good money.

"Mad Fritz" had been a familiar figure in the Travnik bazaar for years. He was a feeble-minded man of unknown origin, from somewhere across the border. And, as the Turks never touch madmen, he lived there, sleeping under benches, fed by charity. He was as strong as an ox. If he drank a bit too much brandy, the bazaar people would always play the same practical joke on him. On market days they would give him a couple of glasses to drink and thrust a cudgel into his hands. The simpleton would then stop the Christian peasants as they passed and start drilling them, always with the same words:

"Halbrechts Links! Marsch!"[1]

---

1   "Half-right! Left! March!"

The peasants got out of the way or clumsily ran off, because they knew it was the Turks who had put him up to it. And the Austrian chased them away to the laughter of the young shopkeepers and idle agas.

One market day, after he had been round looking at everything, Des Fossés was on his way back to the Consulate. The Turkish khavaz was walking behind him. When they reached the place where the market square narrowed and turned into the bazaar, Mad Fritz blocked the way. The young man saw in front of him a massive figure with a large head and baleful green eyes. The drunken madman blinked at the foreigner, then ran off, grabbed a pole used for hanging scales from in front of a shop and made straight for him.

"Halbrechts! Marsch!"

The bazaar people began to crane their necks from their shop-fronts in the malicious expectation of seeing the "Young Consul" hopping about in front of Mad Fritz. But that is not what happened. Before the khavaz had run up, Des Fossés ducked under the pole brandished high over him, and, with a swift, deft movement, grabbed the madman by the wrist. Turning his whole body, he twisted the huge man round him like a puppet. While the lunatic spun round the tall young man, the pole flew out of his clenched fist in a high curve and fell onto the ground. At that moment the khavaz ran up with a small flintlock in his hand. But the madman was tamed, with his right hand helplessly and painfully pinned behind his back. Des Fossés handed him to the khavaz like that, then picked up the pole and leaned it calmly back against the wall of the shop. The madman, his face twisted, looked from his aching arm to the young foreigner who wagged his finger reproachfully at him, as at a child, and said in his clipped, bookish accent:

"You are naughty. You mustn't be naughty!"

Then he called the khavaz and calmly continued on his way past the astonished shopkeepers in their shops.

Daville reprimanded the young man severely for this incident, maintaining that it proved he had been right in advising him not to go through the bazaar on foot, for one never knew what these malicious, wild and idle people would dream up next. But d'Avenat, who did not otherwise like Des Fossés and could not understand his unconventional behaviour, had to admit to Daville that people in the bazaar were talking of the "Young Consul" with admiration.

And the "Young Consul" continued to visit places round Travnik, through the rain and mud. He would approach people and talk to them without the slightest hesitation. He succeeded in learning things Daville, so serious, upright and rigid, could never have seen or learned. Daville who, in his resentment, responded to everything Turkish or Bosnian with revulsion and distrust, could not see much sense or professional benefit in these outings or the things Des Fossés learned. He was irritated by the young man's optimism, his desire to penetrate deeper into the past, the customs and beliefs of these people; to find explanations for their shortcomings; and, finally, to discover the good in them, stifled and distorted by the unusual circumstances in which they were obliged to live. This activity seemed a thorough waste of time to Daville, and a harmful distraction from his real tasks. Consequently discussions of these matters with his Secretary usually ended in argument or faded out in irritated silence.

Des Fossés would return from his outings on icy autumn evenings, with glowing cheeks, soaked and chilled through, full of impressions and eager to talk about them. Daville, who had been pacing round the heated, brightly lit dining room for hours already, churning over oppressive thoughts, always greeted him with a look of surprise.

Breathless, the young man ate avidly and told him enthusiastically that he had been to Dolac, a crowded Catholic village with closely packed houses, and that he had found the short distance between there and Travnik hard to negotiate.

"I don't believe there's a country in the whole of present-day Europe so lacking in roads as Bosnia," said Daville, eating slowly and without appetite, because he was not hungry. "Unlike all the other nations of the world, this people has some kind of incomprehensible, perverse hatred of roads, which are actually a sign of progress and prosperity. In this wretched country roads aren't maintained and they don't last, it's as though they destroyed themselves somehow. You see, the fact that General Marmont is building a highway through Dalmatia does us more damage in the eyes of the local Turks and the Vizier, than those enterprising, boastful gentlemen in Split can begin to imagine. These people don't like roads anywhere near them. But who could explain that to our people in Split? They brag to all and sundry that they are building roads which will ease the flow of traffic between Bosnia and Dalmatia, but they have no idea how the Turks mistrust them."

"Why, no one should be surprised at that. It's perfectly clear. As long as Turkey is governed like this and conditions in Bosnia are as they are, there can be no question of roads and traffic. On the contrary, for various reasons, both the Turks and the Christians are equally opposed to the opening and maintenance of all communications. This is precisely what I realized clearly today in conversation with my friend Brother Ivo, the fat parish priest of Dolac. I was complaining to him about the road from Travnik to Dolac, how steep and full of holes it is, and saying how surprised I was that the people of Dolac, who are obliged to use this road every day, took no steps to put it at least into some sort of shape. The friar gave me a mocking look, as though I didn't know what I was talking about. Then, closing one eye, he said in a whisper: 'Sir, the worse the road, the rarer our Turkish visitors. What we would like most would be to put an impassable mountain between them and us. And as for ourselves, whenever we need to use any road, with a little effort we always get through. Because we're used to bad roads and all kinds of difficulties. In fact, we thrive on difficulties. Don't tell anyone what I'm telling you now, but you should understand that as long as the Turks are in power in Travnik we don't need a better road. Just between the two of us, when the Turks repair it our people go out with the first rain or snow to dig and break it up. That goes some way to deterring unwanted visitors.' It wasn't until he'd finished that the friar opened his other eye, proud of his cunning, and asked me again not to say a word to anyone about it. There, that's one reason why these roads are no good. The other reason lies in the Turks themselves. Every link with Christian countries amounts to opening the doors to hostile influence, enabling the infidel to affect the rayah and threatening absolute Turkish power. After all, Monsieur Daville, we French have swallowed half of Europe and we shouldn't be surprised that those countries we haven't yet occupied look with mistrust at the roads our armies construct on their borders."

"I know, I know," Daville interrupted him, "but roads have got to be built through Europe and obviously one can't take account of such backward peoples as the Turks and the Bosnians."

"Anyone who considers that they must be built, will build them. Which means he needs them. But I am trying to explain to you why, on the other hand, the people here have no desire for roads, why they don't think they need them and why they believe roads could do them more harm than good."

As always, Daville was annoyed by the young man's need to explain and justify everything he saw here.

"It is indefensible," said the Consul, "and you cannot explain it with any rational interpretation. The backwardness of these people comes in the first place from their ill-will, their 'innate ill-will' as the Vizier puts it. This ill-will explains everything."

"All right, but then how do you explain this ill-will itself? Where do they get it from?"

"Where from? Where from? It's innate, I tell you. You'll have a chance to be convinced of that yourself."

"All right, but until I am convinced, allow me to stand by my view that both the ill-will and the goodness of a people are the product of the circumstances in which they live and develop. It is not goodness that drives us to build roads, but the need and desire to extend profitable communications and our influence, and many people regard that as 'ill-will' on our part. So our ill-will drives us to make roads while theirs drives them to hate and destroy them whenever they can."

"You've gone too far, my young friend!"

"No, life goes too far, further than we can follow it, and I am only trying to explain individual phenomena, since I can't understand everything."

"It is not possible to explain or understand everything," said Daville wearily and in a somewhat superior tone.

"No, it's not, but one should still endeavour to do so." After his cold ride, Des Fossés had now warmed up with the food and wine. He was at an age when he liked to reflect aloud, so he continued to talk. "Now, how does one explain this? That same sharp-witted and discreet Dolac priest, who has a lot of common sense and understanding of reality, gave a sermon last Sunday in the Dolac church. According to our Catholic khavaz, the priest spoke in his sermon about some pious friar who had recently died in the monastery at Fojnica. He maintained that he was, if not a saint, then at least in direct contact with the saints and that it was known on good authority that every night a special angel brought him a letter from some saint or other or from the Virgin herself."

"You still don't realize how bigoted these people are."

"All right, let's call it bigotry, but that word doesn't explain anything."

Daville, a reasonable and moderate liberal, did not like even the most innocuous discussions about questions of faith.

"It explains everything," he asserted a little caustically. "Why don't our priests say things like that in their sermons?"

"Because we don't live in similar circumstances, Monsieur Daville. I wonder what sort of sermons we should preach if we lived the way the Christians have been living here for the last three hundred years. Neither the earth nor the sky would have sufficient miracles for our religious arsenal in the struggle against the Turkish occupier. Believe me, when I look at these people and listen to them talking, I become more and more convinced of how wrong we are, as we conquer Europe country by country, to seek to introduce everywhere our own attitudes, our exclusively rational way of life and government. It seems to me more and more a senseless waste of effort. For it's pointless to want to remove all abuses and preconceptions if you haven't the strength or ability to remove what caused them."

"That would take us a very long way," Daville interrupted his Secretary. "Don't worry, there are people who are thinking about these things."

And the Consul rose from the table and rang impatiently for it to be cleared.

Whenever the young man began to criticize the Emperor's régime with his natural sincerity and ease, attributes he was not aware of and which Daville secretly envied, the Consul would recoil, losing all patience. Precisely because he was himself uncertain, and harboured unacknowledged misgivings, he could not listen calmly to other people's criticism. It was as though this young, carefree and incautious man exposed his tenderest spot, which he wanted to hide from others, and also to forget, if possible, himself.

Daville could not discuss literature with Des Fossés either, particularly not his own literary work.

This was something Daville was especially sensitive about. Ever since he could remember, he had been dreaming up literary works of various genres. Some ten years earlier he had been for a time the editor of a literary column in the *Moniteur* and had attended meetings of literary societies and salons. He had abandoned all this when he entered the Ministry of Foreign Affairs again and was sent first to Malta as Chargé d'Affaires and then to Naples. But he had continued his own literary activity.

The verses Daville published from time to time in newspapers or sent in his fine calligraphy to important personages, his superiors and friends, were neither much better nor much worse than thousands of similar contemporary poetic products. Daville called himself "a convinced follower of the great Boileau". And in articles, which it did not occur to anyone to refute, he took a decisive stand in favour of strict classical rules, defending poetry from excessive influence of the imagination, daring poetic innovations and spiritual confusion. In these articles Daville asserted that inspiration was essential, but it must be controlled by moderation and sound good sense without which there could be no art of any kind. Daville laid so much emphasis on these principles that he gave his readers the impression of being more concerned with order and strict moderation than with the poetry itself, as though order and moderation were somehow under constant threat from poets and poetry, and must be protected by all available means. His model among contemporary poets was Jacques Delille, the author of "Les Jardins" and translator of Virgil. Daville had published a series of articles in the *Moniteur* defending Delille's poetry, but again, no one took any interest in either praising or disputing them.

Daville himself had been wrestling for years with plans for a vast epic about Alexander the Great. Conceived in 24 cantos, this epic had become a kind of disguised intellectual diary for Daville. He took all his experience of the world, his ideas about Napoleon, about war and politics, all his desires and dissatisfactions and placed them in the distant times and hazy circumstances of his central hero's life, and there allowed them free rein, endeavouring to forge them into regular lines and more or less strict rhymes. Daville lived the life of his work to such an extent that he had named his middle child, in addition to Jules François, Amyntas, after the Macedonian king, grandfather of Alexander the Great. Bosnia had a place in his "Alexandriad" as well: a barren land with a harsh climate and savage inhabitants, under the name of Tauris. Mehmed Pasha, the Travnik beys, the Bosnian friars, and everyone else Daville had to work or contend with were there, disguised as some dignitary of Alexander the Great or his opponents. And here too was all the revulsion Daville felt for the Asiatic spirit and the East as a whole, expressed in his hero's struggle against distant Asia.

As he rode above Travnik and looked down at the roofs and minarets of the town, Daville would often compose in his head the description of an imaginary city which Alexander was at that moment in the process of conquering. As he sat with the Vizier at the Divan and watched the silent, bustling pages and courtiers, he would often make mental additions to the description of a meeting of the Senate in the besieged city of Tyre, from the third canto of his epic.

Like all writers without talent or real vocation, Daville laboured under the ineradicable delusion that poetry is made out of certain conscious intellectual acts and that poetic creativity can bring comfort or recompense for the ills life heaps upon us.

While he was young, Daville had often wondered whether or not he was a poet. Did his work at this craft have any point or future, or not? Now, after so many years and so much effort which had brought neither success nor failure, it might have been clear that Daville was not a poet. However, as often happens, with the years Daville "worked at his poetry" increasingly persistently, mechanically and simply, no longer asking himself that question so often put by the young in their honest and courageous self-observation. When he was younger and while there was still someone or other to encourage him with some acknowledgement, he had written less, but now, with his advancing years, just when there was no longer anyone to take him seriously as a poet, he worked regularly and assiduously. An unconscious need for expression and the deceptive energy of his youth had been replaced by stale habit and diligence. For diligence, that virtue which so often crops up where it should not, or when it is no longer needed, has always been the comfort of writers without talent and the misfortune of art. The exceptional circumstances, the solitude and tedium to which he was condemned for years drove Daville increasingly along this futile and misguided path, into the innocent sin he called poetry.

In fact, Daville had been on the wrong path from the day he wrote his first line, because he had never had any real relationship with poetry. He was incapable of responding to even its most direct expression and still less of composing it.

Daville's experience of evil in the world left him bitterly dejected while his experience of good aroused his enthusiasm and a kind of moral elation. It was from these moral reactions, which were really strong, if not constant or always reliable, that he created verses lacking in everything that would have made them poetry. To be fair, he was also encouraged in this misguided activity by the fashion of the times.

So Daville continued, increasingly assiduously over the years, to turn his not inconsiderable virtues into minor faults and to seek in poetry precisely what it does not contain: cheap moral euphoria and innocuous intellectual exercise.

Naturally, someone like young Des Fossés was not a welcome listener or critic, not even an appropriate companion for discussions about literature.

It was here that a new, huge gulf, which the Consul was particularly sensitive about, opened up between him and the young man.

A boundless store of facts, speed of judgement and daring conclusions were the main features of the young man's intelligence. Knowledge and intuition worked together in him, complementing each other in a magical way. For all their incompatibility and his personal aversion, the Consul could not fail to see this. At times he felt that this twenty-four-year-old had read whole libraries but did not consider this particularly important. And the young man kept astounding his companion time and again with his wide-ranging knowledge and daring judgements. As though he were playing a game, he talked about the history of Egypt or the relationship of the South American Spanish colonies with their mother country, about oriental languages or the conflict of faiths and races anywhere in the world, about the aims and likely success of Napoleon's continental system or about communications and tariffs. He would quote unexpectedly from the classics, always the less well-known parts, always in some bold connection and a new light. And although the Consul saw more youthful posing and exuberance than order and genuine worth in many of these things, nevertheless he always listened to the young man's expositions with a kind of superstitious and grudging admiration, but also with a painful sense of his own inadequacy which he tried in vain to repress.

And here was this young man, deaf and blind to what Daville held most dear and what seemed to him the only thing worthy of respect apart from his duties as a citizen. Des Fossés admitted openly that he did not care for verse and that contemporary French poetry seemed incomprehensible to him: insincere, insipid and redundant. But the young man did not for a moment deny himself the right or the pleasure of discussing what, by his own admission, he could neither respond to nor love, and of speaking of it freely, without malice, but also without respect or much thought.

For example, about Delille, his adored Delille, the young man remarked immediately that he was an astute salon gentleman, that he was paid at the rate of six francs per line and that was why Madame Delille used to lock him up every day and not let him out of his room until he had produced his quota. This arrogance of "the new generation" at times angered the Consul and at others saddened him. In any case, it made him feel still more isolated.

It sometimes happened that Daville, driven by the need to express himself and communicate with someone, would forget all this and embark on an intimate, frank conversation about his literary views and plans. (A perfectly understandable weakness in the circumstances!) So it was that one evening he outlined the whole scheme of his epic about Alexander the Great and explained all the moral intentions underlying the epic action. The young man did not for an instant enter into an assessment of those ideas or the beliefs that made up the brighter side of the Consul's life. Smiling and relaxed, he began unexpectedly to recite Boileau:

> *Que crois-tu qu'Alexandre, en ravageant la terre,*
> *Cherche parmi l'horreur, le tumulte et la guerre?*
> *Possédé d'un ennui qu'il ne saurait dompter*
> *Il craint d'être lui même et songe s'éviter.*[2]

And he added immediately, by way of apology, that he had once read these lines in one of the satires and happened to remember them.

Daville suddenly felt insulted and infinitely more alone than he had been a few minutes earlier. He felt that here before him stood the very embodiment of the new generation, that he could touch

---

2 What do you think Alexander, laying waste to the earth/Seeks amidst the horror, the tumult and war?/Possessed of a tedium he cannot overcome/He dreams of avoiding the self that he fears.

him with his hand. This was a diabolically restless generation of destructive ideas and instant, perverse associations, a generation which "did not care for verse" but still paid it some attention. A great deal, indeed, whenever it served their own misguided need to drag everything down, belittling and destroying it, because they wanted to reduce everything to what was worst and basest in mankind.

Not showing his displeasure in any way (there was so much of it!), Daville brought the discussion to an abrupt end and retired to his rooms. It took him a long time to get to sleep, and even in his sleep he was aware of the bitterness a quite innocent remark can leave. For some days he could not bring himself to touch the manuscript which lay in its cardboard binding, tied with a green ribbon. His beloved work seemed sullied, boorishly mocked.

Des Fossés, meanwhile, was not remotely aware that he could have offended the Consul in any way. On the contrary, lines of poetry were the rarest fruit at the disposal of his exceptional memory, and he was pleased that he had recalled them so appositely. He did not for a moment imagine that they could have any real inner connection with Daville's work and that they could upset him or in any way affect their relations.

It has always been the case that successive generations have the least mutual tolerance, and, in fact, know each other least well. But many of these divergences and conflicts between the different generations rest, as most conflicts do, on misunderstandings.

What particularly disturbed Daville's sleep was the thought that the young man who had offended him this evening and whom he thought of with bitter displeasure, was now sleeping a sound, healthy sleep, just as natural and heedlessly contented as everything he did and said during the day. As it happened, the Consul could have spared himself at least that bitterness, because he was mistaken. A person who smiles brightly and moves freely among people by day does not necessarily sleep and is not necessarily happy or tranquil. The young Des Fossés was not simply a strong, carefree young man "of the new type", nothing but a fortunate precocious child of the fortunate Empire, overloaded with learning and nothing more, as it often seemed to Daville. On this night each of these two Frenchmen was tormented by his own troubles, each in his own way, and with no possibility of fully understanding the other. In his way, Des Fossés too was paying the toll exacted by his new surroundings. However much stronger and more numerous his resources for struggle were than Daville's, he too suffered from tedium and the "Bosnian silence" and felt that this country and life in it were gnawing at him, wearying him, endeavouring to bend and break him, and so reduce him to the level of everything else around him. For it was no simple matter to be flung out of Paris into Turkish Travnik at the age of twenty-four, to have wishes and plans which went far beyond and above all that surrounded him, and to be obliged to wait patiently, while all the constrained energies and unsatisfied demands of his youth rebelled against any delay.

It had begun at once, in Split. Like the tightening of an invisible hoop: everything required a greater effort and at the same time one was less capable of making it. Every step was more difficult, every decision more laborious, and its outcome uncertain, while behind everything, like an ever-present threat, lurked distrust, poverty and trouble. This was how the East made itself known.

The local commander who had put at his disposal an unprepossessing carriage (and only as far as Sinj), horses for his bags and a four-man escort, was preoccupied, bad-tempered, almost malevolent. Despite his youth, Des Fossés was familiar with this type of disposition, which long drawn-out wars had induced in people. For several years now, people had seemed weighed down, each one dragging some trouble with him, and no one in his right place. As a result, everyone sought to off-load something of his burden onto someone else, in order to make things at least a little easier for himself, if in no other way then at least by a strong oath or sharp word. And so their common misfortune rolled on and was passed on ceaselessly, from place to place and from person to person. And as it moved it became, if not lighter then at least more bearable.

Des Fossés had felt this as soon as he made the mistake of asking whether the carriage had strong springs and soft seats. The commander had stared at him fixedly, his eyes glinting as though he had been drinking: "It's the best you can find in this infernal country. After all, anyone going to work in Turkey must have a rump of steel."

Without blinking, looking straight at him and smiling, the young man had said: "There wasn't anything about that in the instructions I received in Paris."

The officer bit his lip a little when he saw that he had come up against someone who did not run away from an argument, but he seized on the bilious exchange by way of relief.

"Ah well, sir, there wasn't much about it in our instructions either. It's added later, you see. *In situ*…"

And the officer maliciously mimed someone writing.

With this caustic blessing, the young man had set off along the dusty road and then over the bare rocky ground that rose up behind Split, moving further and further away from the sea, from the last well-proportioned buildings and the last Mediterranean plants. And on the other side of that rocky crest he had descended, as into an unknown sea, into Bosnia, the first great test on his entry into life. As he went further into the wild rocky landscape, he saw dilapidated huts and women guarding flocks by the roadside, lost among the stones and briars, their spindles in their hands, with no visible sign of livestock near them. And, looking at it all, he wondered whether this was the worst he would see, like a man who has to undergo an operation wondering at every moment whether this is the highest degree of pain, or whether he should expect more.

These were the kind of anxieties and fears youth indulges in. In fact, the young man was ready for anything and he knew he would come through it all.

After travelling nine miles, he stopped at a rocky pass above Klis and looked at the wild barren land opening out before him and at the grey crags, dusted with sparse, drab vegetation. And, from the Bosnian side, he caught a whiff of the hitherto unknown silence of a new world. The young man shuddered, trembling more at that silence and the starkness of the landscape, than at the fresh breeze blowing through the gorge. He hoisted his cape up onto his shoulders, pressed more closely against his horse and stepped out into that new world of silence and uncertainty. Bosnia could be sensed, a taciturn land, and one could feel in the air an icy suffering without words or obvious reason.

They passed through Sinj and Livno with no hitch. Then on the plain of Kupres they were caught in an unexpected snowstorm. The Turkish guide, who had met them at the border, managed with great difficulty to lead them to the nearest khan. There they dropped down, frozen and exhausted, by the fire where several people were already sitting.

Although he was tired, chilled and hungry, the young man sat upright and cheerful, bearing in mind the impression he would make on these foreigners. He rubbed his face with cologne and did a few of his habitual exercises, while the others watched him out of the corner of their eyes, as though he were carrying out some ritual according to his own law. It was not until he sat down that one of the men by the fire uttered a few words in Italian and told him he was a monk from the Guča Gora monastery, that his name was Brother Julian Pasalić and that he was travelling on monastery business. The others were carriers.

Slowly putting together sentences in Italian, Des Fossés explained who and what he was. When he heard the words "Paris" and the "Imperial French General Consulate in Travnik" the friar, who had a large bristling moustache and bushy eyebrows, under which his youthful face smiled as under a mask, suddenly frowned and immediately fell silent...For a moment the young man and the friar looked at each other warily, in silence.

The friar was very young, but stout. He was wearing a thick black cape under which one could glimpse his dark blue smock and a leather belt with a weapon stuck in it. The young man looked at him in disbelief, wondering, as in a dream, whether it was possible that this was a man of the church, a monk. And the friar observed the foreigner, the tall ruddy-faced young man of attractive, serene and carefree appearance, keenly and silently. He did not hide his disapproval when he heard where he came from and which government had sent him.

In order to break the silence, Des Fossés asked the friar whether his work was difficult.

"Well, you see, we are endeavouring, in really adverse circumstances, to maintain the reputation of our Holy Church, while you, in France, living in complete liberty, destroy and persecute it. It's a shame and a sin, sir!"

Des Fossés knew from a conversation he had had in Split that the friars and the whole Catholic population in that area were opposed to the "godless" "Jacobin" French occupying powers. But still he was surprised by the turn of the conversation and he asked himself how an Imperial consular official ought to react in such unforeseen circumstances. Looking into the friar's strange, bright eyes, he bowed slightly...

"Your Reverence is perhaps not well informed about matters in my country..."

"God grant it may be so. But from what one hears and reads, much ill has been done and is still being done to the Church, her leaders and congregation. And that never did anyone any good."

The friar too was having difficulty in finding the right expressions in Italian, and his measured words did not match the angry, almost wild expression on his face. The brandy brought by servants and the cheese dish sizzling on the fire beside them interrupted this dialogue. As they offered one another food and drink, the friar and the foreigner glanced at one another from time to time. Gradually the two frozen, hungry men warmed up, with the fire and the food.

Heat and oppressive drowsiness were gradually overcoming the young man. The wind howled in the high black smoke-vent and icy snow beat against the roof like gravel. The young man's head was reeling. "So my job has already begun," he thought, "and these are the kind of difficulties and tussles you read about in the memoirs of old consuls in the East." He tried to grasp his situation: snowed in somewhere in the middle of Bosnia, forced into an unaccustomed argument in a foreign language with this strange friar. His eyes were closing of their own accord and it was an effort for his brain to work. It was like a confused dream where one is subjected to unreasonable and difficult trials. He knew only one thing, that although his head was becoming increasingly heavy, he must not let it drop, or lower his eyes, nor leave the last word to his companion. It was all disturbing, but he was proud of having to take on part of his duties so unexpectedly, in this strange company, and to test both his ability to convince his opponent and the meagre command of Italian he had acquired at college. But at the same time, with this very first step, he seemed to have an almost physical sense of how immense and relentless a person's responsibilities were, meted out to every single individual, and scattered over the world like traps.

His frozen hands were burning. The smoke made him cough and pricked his eyelids. He was tormented by drowsiness and struggled against sleep as though he were trying to keep watch, but he kept looking into the friar's eyes, like a target. Through his drowsiness, as through a warm milky liquid which clouded his vision and hummed in his ears, the young man watched the unusual friar and listened, as though from a distance, to his disjointed sentences and Latin quotations. With his natural gift of observation, he thought: this monk has a great deal of accumulated energy and quotations which he cannot otherwise share with anyone. The friar went on, about how no one could have lasting success against the Church, not even France. And how it had been said long ago: "Quod custodiet Christus non tollit Gothus."[3] Again the young man explained, mixing French and Italian words, that Napoleon's France had proved its desire for religious peace and granted the Church its rightful place, correcting the mistakes and violence of the Revolution.

But, under the influence of the food, drink and warmth, everything began to thaw and relax. The friar's expression became less hard, it remained stern, but now it had a youthful smile. As he looked at him, Des Fossés felt that this could be a sign of truce and proof that the big, eternal questions could wait, and that they could not possibly be resolved in some Turkish khan, in the chance encounter of a French consular official and an "Illyrian" friar. And, consequently, there was a place for courteous withdrawal, without damage to the honour or reputation of his official position. Satisfied with himself and lulled by this thought, he gave in to his weariness and sank into a deep sleep.

When they woke him, it took him a few moments to come to and realize where he was.

The fire had burnt out. The majority of the travellers were outside. They could be heard shouting directions about their horses and cargo. Stiffly, the young man got up and began to make himself ready. He felt his money belt and called his men, more sharply and loudly than necessary. He was disturbed by the vague idea that he had forgotten or neglected something. It was only when he found everything in its place and his men ready beside the harnessed horses, that he calmed

3 "What Christ protects, the Goth does not take away."

down. His companion of the night before, the friar, came out of the stable, leading a good black stallion. His clothes and bearing were just like the pictures of Morlach frontiersmen and brigands. They both smiled as though they were old acquaintances and as though everything that needed resolving between them had been resolved. And the young man asked, naturally and without diffidence, whether they would be travelling together. The friar explained that he had to go a different way. He wanted to say "short-cut" but he could not think of the right word and simply pointed at a wooded slope. Not quite understanding, the young man waved his hat in farewell.

"Vale, reverendissime domine!"[4]

The snowstorm had passed like a crude joke. Only on the hillsides were there thin patches of white. The ground was soft as in spring, the vista clear and deep, the mountains blue. Above the line of the horizon, two or three fiery strips of bright cloud were stretched against the clear pale-blue sky, covering the sun which illuminated the whole landscape with a strange indirect light. It was somehow reminiscent of northern regions. And the young man remembered that in his reports the Travnik Consul had often referred to the Turks and Bosnians as wild Scythians and Hyperboreans, which had caused some amusement at the Ministry.

That was how young Monsieur Des Fossés had entered Bosnia. It had kept its promise and realized the threats of his first encounter with it, enveloping him increasingly in its sharp, cold atmosphere of poverty, and particularly in its silence and tedium with which the young man would wrestle for many a sleepless night, when there was no help to be had anywhere.

But we shall return to this in one of the subsequent chapters. Now another, more important event was looming, bringing great changes for the whole French Consulate: the arrival of the long-awaited opponent, the Austrian Consul General.

4 "Farewell, most respected sir!"

5

The months were passing and the year was nearing its end, but the Austrian Consul, who was supposed to follow on the heels of the French one, had still not arrived. People were even beginning to forget about the possibility. Then, at the end of summer, there was a rumour that the Austrian Consul was on his way. The word spread through the bazaar. Then the smiles, frowns and whispers began again and the weeks passed without any sign of the Consul. But with the last days of autumn he arrived.

While still in Split, before he had even set foot on Bosnian soil, Daville had heard the news that the Austrian government was also preparing to open a general consulate in Travnik. Later, when he was in Travnik, the prospect had hung over him like a threat throughout the year. But, after so many months of anticipation, now that the threat was actually to be realized it worried him less than might have been expected. With time, he had become reconciled to this eventuality. Besides, following the strange logic of human weakness, it flattered him that another Great Power attached importance to this benighted place. He grew in his own eyes and was conscious of a new energy and greater readiness to fight.

Ever since mid-summer, d'Avenat had begun to gather facts, to spread word of Austria's sinister designs and to prepare a net for the new Consul's welcome. Above all, he assembled all available information about how people viewed the innovation. The Catholics were triumphant and the friars ready to put themselves in the service of the new Consul with just as much whole-hearted dedication as they had met the French Consul with cold distrust.

The Orthodox, persecuted because of the Serbian uprising, for the most part avoided all discussion of it, but in confidence they still insisted steadfastly that "there couldn't be any consuls without a Russian one". The Ottomans at the Residence maintained a lazy, disdainful and dignified silence, preoccupied for the most part each with his own affairs and mutual intrigue. The Bosnian Muslims were even more upset than at the news of the French Consul's arrival. If Bonaparte was a distant, shifting and somewhat fantastic force which they had for the time being to reckon with, Austria was, on the contrary, a close, real and well-known danger. With the infallible instinct of a race which has ruled over a land for centuries exclusively on the basis of an established order, they were conscious of the slightest danger which threatened that order and their authority. They knew quite well that every foreigner who came to Bosnia would go some way towards treading out a path between them and the hostile outside world. But this Consul, with his special powers and resources, would throw that road wide open. Nothing good could come along that road for them, their interests or what they held sacred. But all sorts of bad things could. They were angry with Istanbul and the Ottomans who had permitted this. They were more anxious than they wished d'Avenat to see. They would not give clear answers to his insistent questions, concealing their resentment at this foreign invasion, but not their contempt at his insistence. And when he pressed one man in the bazaar to tell him which of the consuls would be the more welcome, the French or the Austrian, the man calmly replied that they were both the same: "One pug-nosed, the other lop-eared. One's a dog and the other's his brother."

D'Avenat swallowed this answer. Now at least he was clear about what the people thought and felt, only he did not know how to translate it to his Consul, without offending him.

In addition, the French were doing everything they could to impede their opponent's work and make his stay more difficult.

Daville had been trying for a long time, but in vain, to convince the Vizier of the danger to Turkey the new Consul would represent and that it would be best not to give him a permit and not approve his stay. The Vizier had looked straight ahead, not betraying what he thought. He knew that the permit for the Austrian Consul had already been issued, but he let the Frenchman talk, thinking only what damage might be done and what advantage he would have from the clash between the two Consuls which was evidently about to begin.

Nevertheless, d'Avenat did succeed in delaying the despatch of the permit, with new bribes and old connections. And the Austrian Consul General, Herr Oberst von Mitterer, met with an unpleasant surprise in Brod, because the Imperial decree and Consular permit had not reached the Austrian commander there, as promised. Von Mitterer had to spend a whole month in Brod, sending couriers to Vienna and Travnik to no avail. Finally he was informed that the permit had been sent to the Derventa military Commander Nail Bey for him to hand over to the Consul, so that he could bring it with him to Travnik. At that von Mitterer left Brod, with his interpreter Niccolo Rotta and two attendants. A new surprise awaited him. The Commander maintained that he had nothing for the Consul: neither the permit nor any kind of instructions. He invited him to stay with his escort in the Derventa fortress – in fact this was a damp prison – for the khan had recently burnt down. Although he had had plenty of experience, after long years of working and struggling with the Turkish authorities, the Colonel was simply beside himself with fury. The Commander, a sullen, obdurate Bosnian, spoke brusquely with him, over coffee.

"Hold on, sir. If what you say is true, that they've sent you a decree and a permit, then they'll get here. They can't fail. Because anything sent from the Imperial Porte must arrive. You just wait here. You're not in my way."

And as he spoke, both the decree and the permit for Josef von Mitterer, as Imperial and Royal Consul General in Travnik, were lying, wrapped in a waxed linen cloth and carefully folded, under the cushions where he was sitting.

The Colonel, perplexed and in despair, wrote urgent letters to Vienna once again, imploring them to ask for the permit from Istanbul. He begged them not to leave him in this position which was detrimental to the reputation of the country he represented and was undermining his work in Travnik in advance. He ended his letters: "Written in the Derventa fortress, in a small dark room, on the floor." At the same time he paid special couriers to take messages to the Vizier, urging him to send the permit or allow him to proceed to Travnik without it. Nail Bey held back the Colonel's couriers and took their letters, as suspect, putting them calmly under the cushions with the decree and the permit.

So the Colonel spent another fortnight in Derventa. During that time he was visited by a Travnik Jew who offered him his services, maintaining that he was in a position to spy on the French Consul. Accustomed to working with spies and on his guard, the Colonel was unwilling to accept the man's dubious services, but did use him as a messenger to take a letter for the Vizier. The Jew took his payment and carried the letter to Travnik where he gave it to d'Avenat, who had engaged him to go to Derventa and pretend to put himself at the disposal of the Austrian Consul. From this letter Daville saw what a difficult and comic situation his opponent was in and read with satisfaction his entreaties and helpless complaints directed to the Vizier. The letter was sealed again and delivered to the Residence. Surprised, the Vizier ordered that an enquiry be carried out to discover what had become of the decree and permit, sent a good fortnight earlier to the Derventa Commander, Nail Bey, to await the new Consul on his arrival there. The Vizier's Archivist turned his whole dusty archive upside down two or three times, striving in vain to discover where the package could have been held up. The messenger who had taken the letter to Derventa and returned, had proof that he had duly handed over the Vizier's mail to the Commander. Everything had been in order, but the Austrian Consul was still hanging around in Derventa, waiting impatiently and in vain for his permit.

The matter was quite simple, however. Through d'Avenat and the Jew, Daville had bribed the Derventa Commander to delay handing over the permit as long as possible. The Commander readily agreed to spend twelve days sitting on cushions with the decree and permit under him, to tell the Colonel every day with insolent serenity that nothing had come for him, and to receive a gold ducat for each day of this work. And there was nothing anyone could do about the Commander, because for a long time now he had not answered any complaints or letters which did not suit him, and he flatly refused to go to Travnik.

At last it was sorted out. The Colonel received a letter from the Vizier informing him that his documents were being looked for, and inviting him to set out for Travnik immediately, without the permit. The Colonel left Derventa joyfully that same day. And the very next day the Derventa Commander sent the Consul's documents to the Vizier, apologizing that they had been mislaid.

So the Austrian Consul General experienced what virtually always happened to foreigners coming to Turkey on business with the Turks. Such a man would be from the very first annoyed, wearied and humiliated by the Turks, partly wilfully and consciously, and partly unintentionally, by sheer force of circumstance. As a result he approached the work he had come to do with already diminished strength and weakened self-confidence.

It is true that even while he was waiting for his permit in Brod von Mitterer too had begun secretly opening the French Consul's mail on its way from Ljubljana.

The arrival of the Imperial and Royal Consul General in Travnik was quite similar to Daville's. The only difference was that von Mitterer did not have to spend any time waiting in a Jewish house, because the Catholic community was humming like a beehive and all the best merchants' houses were eager to receive him. According to d'Avenat's information, his reception at the Vizier's was somewhat briefer and cooler than that of the French Consul. But his reception by the local Muslim community was neither better nor worse. ("One's a dog and the other's his brother!"). The new Consul was accompanied through the street by the curses and threats of women and children, he was spat on from windows, and the men in the shops did not grant him so much as a single glance.

The new Austrian Consul first visited two of the most prominent Beys and the Apostolic Visitor who happened to be at the Guča Gora monastery at the time. And only then did he call on his French colleague. D'Avenat's agents dogged his steps during those visits and reported all that they found out, inventing and adding what they had been unable to discover. It emerged clearly that the Austrian Consul wanted to bring together all those who were opposed to the French Consul, unobtrusively, without saying a single word against him or his work, but accepting everything others had to say. He even expressed sympathy for his colleague, obliged to represent a government which had sprung out of revolution and was fundamentally godless. That is what he told the Catholics. To the Turks, he pitied Daville for having been allotted the thankless task of preparing the gradual penetration of French troops from Dalmatia into Turkey and so having to bring into this quiet and beautiful land of Bosnia all the pain and misfortune entailed by an army and war.

One Tuesday, precisely at noon, von Mitterer finally called on Daville.

Outside the late autumn sun was blazing, but in the large room on the ground floor of Daville's house it was cool, almost cold. The two Consuls looked each other straight in the eye, endeavouring not to be stilted in their conversation, but to say as naturally as they could what each of them had long since prepared for this occasion. Daville talked about his stay in Rome, adding in passing that his sovereign had successfully brought the revolution to an end and restored not only social order but also the standing of religion in France. As if by chance he found on his desk a decree about the creation of a new, imperial nobility in France and explained it in detail to his visitor. Von Mitterer, for his part, in an established formula, emphasized the wise policies of the Vienna court, which wanted nothing but peace and peaceful co-operation but had to have a powerful army, for this was demanded by its position as a Great Power in the east of Europe.

Both Consuls were entirely filled with the dignity of their calling and the initial zeal of a beginner. This prevented them from recognizing how comic much of the formal tone and ceremonial bearing of this meeting was, but it did not stop them observing and assessing one another.

To Daville, von Mitterer looked far older than he had imagined from what he had heard. And everything about him – his dark green military uniform, his old-fashioned hair-style and the waxed moustache on his sallow face – all looked outdated and lifeless.

Von Mitterer thought Daville looked too young and frivolous. His whole way of speaking, his drooping ginger moustache and the sweep of blond hair above his high brow, the lack of powder or pigtail, all of this seemed to the Colonel a sign of revolutionary sloppiness and an unpleasant excess of imagination and licence.

Who knows how long the Consuls would have gone on expounding on the high intentions of their respective courts, had they not been interrupted by shouts, squeals and a wild commotion in the courtyard.

Despite the strictest ban, numerous Christian and Jewish children had gathered in the street and clambered onto the fence, waiting to see the Consul in his splendid uniform. As they were incapable of waiting quietly, someone had given the youngest child a shove. He had slipped and thumped down from the fence into the yard where Daville's servants and von Mitterer's escort were waiting. The other children scattered like sparrows. After his first astonishment, the Jewish child who had fallen into the yard began to shriek as though he were being skinned alive, while his two brothers hopped about outside the closed gate howling and calling at the tops of their voices. The woeful cries and commotion this had occasioned turned the conversation of the two Consuls to children and family matters. Then they both seemed like soldiers ordered to stand "at ease" after some taxing exercise.

Now and then, as they remembered their calling and their duty, they both adopted an affected, formal posture. But it was no use. Their common misfortune and the similarity of their destinies were stronger than anything. Their common bitterness at the hard, degraded life they were both condemned to poured like a torrent over all their attitudes, their uniforms, medals and the phrases they had learned by heart. In vain did Daville stress the exceptional cordiality with which he had always been received at the Residence. In vain did von Mitterer emphasize the great, secret and significant appreciation which he enjoyed with the Catholics. The tone of their voices, the expression of their eyes reflected only the hidden sorrow and deep human understanding of two fellow-sufferers. And it was only ultimate considerations of duty and tact that prevented them from placing a hand on one another's shoulders, like two composed, reasonable men supporting one another in misfortune.

So their first meeting ended in discussing children's diseases and nutrition, and generally the difficult conditions in which they had to live in Travnik.

But that same day both Consuls were to be found, simultaneously, sitting for a long time over wads of rough draft paper, writing line after line of official report about their first encounter with their partner. Here, this first meeting looked completely different. Here, on paper, it emerged as a bloodless duel of sharp wits, subtlety and zeal between two giants. Each attributed to his opponent strengths and qualities entirely in keeping with the high opinion he had of himself and his task. Except that in the Frenchman's report the Austrian had in the end lain, morally speaking, flat on his back on the ground, and in the Austrian's report the Frenchman was left speechless at the dignified exposition of the Imperial and Royal Consul General.

It goes without saying that each of them laid great stress on the fact that his opponent was despondent because of the unusually difficult circumstances under which a cultured European had to live, with his family, in these wild, mountainous lands. And, of course, neither mentioned his own despondency.

So that day brought each Consul both solace and satisfaction. First, they had been able to converse and complain like human beings, as far as was possible at a first meeting. Then, each had been able to depict the other in the least favourable light, which meant giving the most flattering possible picture of himself. In this way each satisfied two personal needs. Both were vain and contradictory, but both were equally human and equally understandable. And that was at least something in this strange life where for each of them pleasures, real or imaginary, were rare and were to become ever more so.

And so from now on, the two Consuls were to live with their families and associates in houses facing each other on the two opposite sides of Travnik. These were two men expressly appointed as adversaries, and sent to wrangle and outdo each other. And they were to promote the interests of their own court and country with the authorities and the people, while damaging and undermining as far as possible the interests of the other. They did this, as we have seen and shall see again, each in the way he knew best, according to his temperament, upbringing and capabilities. Often they fought fiercely and ruthlessly, forgetting everything and giving themselves up wholly to their own instincts for survival, like two frenzied cockerels, loosed by unseen hands into this narrow, shady arena. Each of their successes meant failure for the other and each failure a small triumph. They minimized or concealed even from themselves the blows they received, and magnified those they inflicted on their opponent, stressing them in their reports to Vienna or Paris. Altogether in these reports the opposing Consul and his work were always depicted in black colours. Both these anxious fathers and tranquil middle-aged citizens appeared here, at times, as terrible and implacable as incensed lions or grim Machiavellian schemers. At least that is how they portrayed each other, each misled by his own difficult fate and deceived by the unusual surroundings he had been cast into, both of them rapidly losing all sense of proportion and all feeling for reality.

It would be a lengthy and superfluous process to recount all those consular storms in a teacup and all their battles and schemes, many of which were comic, some pitiful and the majority trivial and pointless. We shall not be able to avoid many of them in the course of our story in any case. The Consuls struggled for influence with the Vizier and his chief assistants, and bribed the ayans in the border towns, inciting them to plunder and raid their opponent's territory. The Frenchman directed his hirelings to the north across the Austrian border, and the Austrian sent his south, towards Dalmatia, which was governed by the French. Each used his agents to spread false information among the people and refute that spread by his opponent. They ended up slandering and maligning each other like two quarrelling women. They intercepted each other's couriers, opened their letters, lured away or bribed their servants. If one were to believe their words, it would seem that they really were poisoning each other or at least trying to.

At the same time there was a great deal that united the two Consuls and brought them together, in spite of everything. These two men, middle-aged, "burdened with families", each with his own complicated life and plans, anxieties and troubles, were obliged, in this unpleasant foreign land, to fight, reluctantly but persistently. And they imitated in their little actions the large-scale actions of their distant, unseen and often incomprehensible superiors. But their hard life and wretched fate drove them towards one another. And if there were in the world two men who could have understood, sympathized with and even helped one another, it was these two consuls who spent their energy, their days and often their nights putting obstacles in each other's way and making their lives difficult in every way they could.

In fact, it was only the aims of their official work which were different, all the rest was identical or similar. They fought each other under the same conditions, using similar methods, and succeeding by turn. In addition to their mutual struggle, they both had daily to contend with the slow and untrustworthy Turkish authorities and the unbelievably recalcitrant and malevolent local Muslims. Each of them had his own anxieties in his family, equal difficulties with his own government which never sent instructions on time and his Ministry which did not approve credits, with the frontier authorities who were forever making mistakes or overlooking things. Above all, they both had to live in this same little oriental town, without company or pleasure, without any comforts, often without the most essential things, among these wild mountains and uncouth people, struggling with distrust, inaccuracy, dirt, sickness and misfortunes of all kinds. In short they had to live in an environment which first exhausts a Westerner, then makes him chronically irritable, a burden to himself and others, and finally, with the years, completely alters and breaks him, burying him in dull indifference long before his death.

This was why the Consuls approached one another joyfully as soon as altered circumstances and better political relations between their countries permitted. At those moments of truce they would look at each other in shame and confusion, as though they had woken from a dream, seeking in themselves their other, personal feelings towards their opponent and wondering to what extent they dared give them rein. Then they would meet and console one another, exchange gifts, write each other letters, with a warmth and friendship known only to people who have done one another harm but who are at the same time thrown together and firmly linked by the same wretched fate.

But as soon as the brief truce drew to an end and relations between Napoleon and the Vienna court began to deteriorate, the Consuls too began cutting down their visits and measuring out their kindliness in doses, until the suspension of diplomatic relations or war completely separated them or made them enemies once more. Then both weary men would begin their battle all over again, imitating, like two obedient puppets on long strings, the movements of the great distant battle whose ultimate aims were unknown to them and whose scale and violence filled their souls with similar feelings of fear and uncertainty. But even then, the strong, invisible thread between the two Consuls, the "two exiles" as they called one another in their letters, was not broken. They and their families did not meet or see one another. On the contrary, they would work against one another by all possible means. During the nights, when Travnik would already have sunk deep into darkness, the only lighted windows one could see would be one or two in each of the Consulates. Those were the two Consuls sitting up over their papers, reading their spies' reports, writing memoranda. And then it often happened that Monsieur Daville or Herr von Mitterer, leaving his work for a moment, would go up to the window and gaze out at the solitary light on the hill opposite, by which his neighbour and adversary was forging unknown traps and plots, endeavouring to undermine his colleague from across the Lašva and thwart his intentions.

The crowded little town between them had disappeared. They were separated only by emptiness, silence and darkness. Their windows glinted at each other, like the pupils of men engaged in a duel. But hidden behind the curtain, one or other Consul, or both at the same time, would be staring into the darkness at the feeble ray of his opponent's light and thinking of the other with sympathy, deep understanding and sincere compassion. Then they would rouse themselves and go back to their work by the light of their low burning candles. They continued to write reports in which there was no trace of their feelings of a moment before and in which they slandered or disparaged one another, from that false official height from which civil servants believe they are looking on the whole world when they address their Minister in a confidential report they know will never be read by the people concerned.

6

It seemed that only unhappy, troubled destinies were to come together in the valley of Travnik during these painful years of widespread war. The life of the Austrian Consul General, Josef von Mitterer, consisted entirely of troubles. And not the least of them was his coming to Travnik.

He was a swarthy man, with a sallow face, a black waxed moustache, fixed gaze, slow speech and moderate manner. Everything about him was stiff, angular, clean and orderly, but unassuming and "regulation". It was as though everything, the man and the uniform, had been recently acquired from some Imperial and Royal military supplier for the urgent production of an average colonel. Only his round brown eyes, with their constantly inflamed lids, betrayed a goodness and sensitivity that were never expressed. These were the clouded eyes of a man with a liver complaint, the tired eyes of an officer who had served for years on the frontier imprisoned in his office, eyes which had worn themselves out watching over a border of the Empire under constant threat. They were sad, mute eyes which had seen much evil in the course of that work, and observed the limits of human power, freedom and decency.

Born fifty years earlier in Osijek, where his father was an officer in a Slavonian Hussar regiment, he had been sent to a military college and emerged as an infantry *Fähnrich*. When he became a lieutenant, he was transferred to Zemun as intelligence officer. There, with a few interruptions, he spent nearly twenty years, difficult years of war with Turkey and Serbian rebellion. During that time he received agents, gathered information, maintained contacts and submitted reports. And he also crossed into Serbia several times himself, under the most difficult circumstances, often disguised as a peasant or a monk, in order to assess the Turkish forces, record the fortified places and more important positions or sound out the mood of the people. Von Mitterer did well in this work, which wears a man out before his time. And, as often in life, it was his success that brought his downfall. After several years, the Ministry was so pleased with the information he gave them that he was summoned in person to Vienna where he was promoted to Captain and given a reward of 100 ducats. This success aroused in the young officer's heart the bold hope that he might be able to get out of the monotonous rut he was in, a rut where all his forebears had dragged out their hard lives before him.

The frontier officer in his early thirties, with the reward and certificate of promotion in his pocket, craved everything and above all a more peaceful, agreeable and socially more prestigious life. He saw the embodiment of such a life in a young Viennese lady. She was the daughter of an officer in the Military Court, a Germanized Pole, and a Hungarian baroness without property. They gave the beautiful, somewhat over-vivacious and romantic Fraulein Anna Maria in marriage without hesitation, a little too easily, to the nondescript, diligent frontier officer from the periphery of the Empire. It was as though his destiny had needed only to hang this woman round his neck for him to be definitively stuck in precisely that rut of a subaltern's life he had wanted to escape at all costs. That marriage, intended to open the door to a higher, pleasanter life, imprisoned and shackled him forever, depriving him of the tranquillity which is the only good and the greatest dignity of modest destinies and unremarkable people.

The "successful" intelligence officer soon discovered that there was something no one could assess or foresee, namely the moods of his wayward, restless wife. This "unfortunate Polish-Hungarian-

Viennese mixture", as the Commandant of the Zemun garrison called Frau von Mitterer, suffered from an over-active imagination and a morbid, irresistible, insatiable need of rapture. Frau von Mitterer was enraptured by music, nature, an unwholesome philanthropy, old paintings, new ideas, Napoleon or anything at all outside herself and her circle that was the opposite of her family life, its good name and her husband's reputation. The necessity for rapture in the life of Frau von Mitterer was very frequently linked with transient and capricious love affairs. A fatal need drove this hot-headed but frigid woman periodically to become infatuated with young men, usually younger than herself. She would always believe she had found in that particular man, in whom she sensed a strong spirit and courageous heart full of pure emotion, the knight she had dreamed of and a kindred soul. And by the same fatality, these were invariably inconsiderate, gifted men, who did in fact desire her, briefly and unambiguously, as they would have desired any other woman who came their way and offered no resistance. After the initial enthusiasm, at the first touch, when all the discrepancy between her exalted, spiritual rapture and the man's true intentions became quite clear, Anna Maria would fall into despair. "Love" was transformed into hate and revulsion towards the former idol and towards herself, love and life altogether. She would get over her pain, seeking sustenance in other kinds of enthusiasm and anger, thereby satisfying her innate need for crises and dramatic scenes. And so it would go on, until the first new opportunity, when everything would start all over again.

Von Mitterer had tried so often to explain his wife's delusion to her, to bring her to her senses and protect her, but nothing helped. With the regularity of an epileptic, his "sick child" who was already getting on in years, would fall every now and then into new crises in her search for pure love. The Colonel knew by heart the first symptoms and the progress of his wife's "aberrations" and could foresee well in advance the moment when she would fling her arms round his neck, disheartened and in tears, sobbing that everyone desired her but no one loved her.

How could such a marriage survive? How that conscientious, sober man bore it and why he forgave everything in advance, no one would ever be able to discover. It would remain one of those incomprehensible secrets which so often irrevocably divide two people, yet bind them indissolubly.

In the very first year of her marriage, Anna Maria had returned to her parents in Vienna, asserting that she had a mortal revulsion towards physical love and that she could not acknowledge her husband any rights in that respect. Agreeing to everything, the Captain succeeded in persuading her to return. After that, a little girl was born to them. That was a brief lull. Two years later, it all started again. The Captain bowed his head and buried himself in the demanding tasks of the Zemun quarantine and his security work, reconciled to the fact that he had to live with a fiery dragon to which everything must be sacrificed and which repaid all it received with nothing but new discontent and new restlessness.

Like all obsessive women, the beautiful, eccentric and extra-vagant Frau von Mitterer did whatever she wanted, never really knowing just what she wanted. She would plunge headlong into her temporary "enthusiasms" and return from them disillusioned. It was impossible to know what was harder for von Mitterer to bear and more painful to watch: her transports or her disappointments. The Captain endured them both with a martyr's serenity. In fact, he loved this woman whom fate had sent him as an unmerited punishment. He loved her boundlessly and constantly, as one loves a sick child. Everything to do with her was dear to him, noble and sublime. Everything in her, on her and around her, including the lifeless objects belonging to her, all seemed to him somehow higher and finer, worthy of adoration and deserving every sacrifice. He was hurt by her abrupt changes and embarrassing scenes, he was ashamed in the presence of others and inwardly tormented, but at the same time he trembled at the very thought that this enchanting woman might leave him or do herself some harm and disappear from his house or from this world. He was promoted to higher ranks. The little girl grew, frail, serious and silent. And Frau von Mitterer blundered on with undiminished energy, demanding from life what it could not give, transforming everything into either enthusiasm or bitterness, both of which were a torment to herself and all around her. With the years, the indomitable, baffling rage seething in this woman altered its direction and form but showed no sign of abating.

When von Mitterer was rather unexpectedly appointed Consul General in Travnik, Anna Maria happened to be going through one of her great disappointments. She began first to rant and weep, declaring that she would not go from one half-Turkish provincial town, where she had been languishing until then, into a "real Turkish graveyard" and that she would not allow her daughter "into Asia". The Colonel soothed his wife, pointing out that the new position meant an important change and a big step up in his career, that things would be a bit hard for a while, but their new income would enable them to ensure their child's future. In the end, he proposed that if she really did not want to go, she should stay in Vienna with the child. Anna Maria first agreed to this solution, but she soon changed her mind and decided on sacrifice. Evidently the Colonel was not destined on this earth to live even a few peaceful months in the heaven that was his wife's absence.

As soon as von Mitterer had found a house and rearranged it as far as possible, his wife and daughter arrived.

At the very first glance it was apparent that this was a woman who needed a lot of space in the world. She was still beautiful and youthful-looking, although a little overweight. Her whole appearance, the glow of her faultlessly white skin, the unusual brilliance of her eyes, now greenish, now dark gold, or grey as the waters of the Lašva, the colour and style of her hair, her walk, the way she moved and her commanding way of speaking, all of this brought into Travnik for the first time something of the power and nobility which in their imagination the townspeople associated with foreign consuls.

With Frau von Mitterer came her daughter Agatha, a child of about thirteen, who bore no resemblance whatever to her mother. Withdrawn and silent, too old for her years and over-sensitive, with thin, tightly drawn lips, and her father's fixed gaze, she accompanied her mother as a constant, silent reproach, never showing her feelings in any way and apparently indifferent to everything around her. In fact, from the outset the child had been frightened and perplexed by her mother's temperament and everything she sensed going on between her parents. She loved only her father, with a powerless, passive love. She was a short, fragile-boned girl, one of those girls who develop very quickly and become mature women in miniature, so that the combination of their childish bearing and unexpectedly mature forms constantly surprise and mislead. The absolute opposite of her mother in every way, the girl was unmusical and liked solitude and books.

Immediately after her arrival, Frau von Mitterer threw all her energy into putting the house and garden in order. Furniture was acquired from Vienna, workers were brought from Slavonski Brod. Everything was changed, moved round and turned upside down. (In the French Consulate, in the course of the inevitable gossip about "the people across the Lašva" they said that "Frau von Mitterer was building a new Schönbrunn". Actually, Frau von Mitterer, who loved the French language and nurtured what she considered to be French wit, was not to be outdone. Speaking scathingly of Madame Daville's furniture, which included, as we have seen, many skilfully disguised and covered chests, she maintained that Madame Daville had furnished her house in the style of "Louis Caisse".) The garden was separated from the busy, muddy courtyard of the bazaar khan and its stables by a high fence. The whole old-fashioned house was altered according to the Consul's wife's designs, whose end or sense no one could see, but which suited or were meant to suit her high conception, obscure even to herself, of perfection, brilliance and nobility.

As often happens with women of this kind, as the years passed she developed new eccentricities. Anna Maria now suffered from a mania for excessive cleanliness. But she tormented everyone around her more than she herself suffered. Nothing was sufficiently fresh or washed for her and no one sufficiently clean. With all the fervour she was capable of she entered into battle against disorder and dirt. She changed the servants, terrorized the household, ran about, flared up, wore herself out wrestling with mud, dust, vermin and the unusual customs of the new land. And then there would be days when, suddenly discouraged, Anna Maria would lose faith in the outcome of her struggle, withdraw and, her arms folded in despair, she would feel the disorder and dirt of this oriental land encroaching from all sides, bursting out of the earth and falling from the air, seeping in at the doors and windows, at every crack, slowly but irresistibly taking over the house and everything in it, objects, people and animals. Ever since she came to this desolate valley she had felt that even her personal belongings had been secreting mould and rust and becoming gradually shrouded in a thin layer of dirt which no amount of dusting or scrubbing could remove.

She would usually return from short outings shaken and still more discouraged. For at the very outset she would have come across some mangy or lame dog with a timid, pathetic look. Or she would have encountered a crowd of street curs fighting over a sheep's innards and stretching the guts across the street. She would ride outside the town, endeavouring from her big black horse not to see what was immediately around her. But that did not help either.

One day, after a brief spring shower, she was riding along the main road with her escort. As they left the town they met a beggar. A feeble-minded, sickly man, barefoot and in rags, he moved out of the way of the gentlefolk, climbing onto a little path that went up the slope above the road, parallel with it. Consequently, his feet were right in front of the face of the woman on horseback. For just one moment her field of vision was filled with trampled clay and the huge, filthy, bare feet of a disabled labourer, aged before his time. She glimpsed them for just one moment, but for a long time afterwards she could not rid herself of the sight of those inhuman feet, square, shapeless, gnarled, unspeakably deformed by long trudging and a hard life, cracked like the bark of a pine tree, yellow and black; enormous, crooked peasant's feet which could scarcely bear their own weight and shuffled, limping awkwardly, as they took perhaps their last steps.

Hundreds of suns and thousands of springs could not help those feet, thought Anna Maria in that instant. No care, food or medicine could put them right or alter them. Whatever was born and bloomed on the earth, those feet could only be yellower, more monstrous and more horrible.

That thought now haunted her constantly and the painful, monstrous vision did not leave her for days. Whatever she began to do or think, she would be brought up short, frozen at the outset by the idea that "that existed".

So Frau von Mitterer tormented herself and her torment was increased by the painful, offensive realization that no one understood her feeling of revulsion or shared her desire for perfection and cleanliness. But despite that or rather just because of it she had a constant need to talk about it and complain to everyone about the filthy town and slovenly servants, although she could see that there was no one who could sympathize with her and still less offer her any assistance.

The Dolac parish priest, the crude, fat Brother Ivo Janković, listened politely to her complaints, consoling her superficially and indifferently, as one consoles children, saying whatever came into his head and maintaining that one must endure everything calmly and humbly and that, after all, mud and dirt were also gifts of God.

"For you know the ancient words: 'Castis omnia casta'. All is pure to the pure in heart," the priest translated with the nonchalance characteristic of fat people and old friars.

After that, offended by everything around her, Frau von Mitterer would spend days in the house, avoiding contact with people and the gaze of the town. She would wear gloves all day long, sit in an armchair with a white cover which was changed frequently, not allowing anyone who spoke to her to come anywhere near or breathe in her face. But for all that, she had the constant sense that she was being submerged in mud, dust and foul stench. And when this nausea became insupportable, which happened often, she would get up, burst into her husband's office, interrupting his work, and reproach him bitterly for bringing them here, demanding through her tears that they leave this filthy, wretched country at once.

And it would all happen over and over again, until force of habit began to have an effect or one mania was succeeded by another.

In the Consulate itself, the main figure after the Consul General was the interpreter and office clerk, Niccolo Rotta. He had earlier served at the Zemun quarantine and von Mitterer had brought him with him to Travnik.

He was a small man, hunchbacked, but without a visible hump, with a broad chest and powerful head thrown back and sunk between his hunched shoulders. His striking features were his large mouth, lively eyes and naturally curly, greying hair. His legs were short and thin and he wore low boots, with their tops folded back, or silk stockings and shoes with large gilt buckles.

Unlike his superior, von Mitterer, who was a mild and approachable man, with a sad gentleness in his whole manner, his chief assistant was arrogant and irritable with Turks as well as Christians. His sullen silence was just as oppressive, unpleasant and insulting as his speech. Small and hunchbacked as he was, he somehow succeeded in looking down on even the tallest man, twice his height. His dark eyes with their heavy drooping lids looked out from his strong head thrown back against his hunched shoulders, with insulting boredom, contemptuously weary, as though seeing the person he was talking to somewhere in the distance and far beneath him. It was only when he was translating the conversation of important, influential people (and he well knew which of them were, and which were not or only appeared to be so) that these eyes would be lowered to the ground, becoming at once insolent, condescending and distant.

Rotta spoke many languages. (The people of Travnik had somehow counted ten.) But his greatest skill lay not so much in what he said, as in his ability to silence an opponent. He had the habit of throwing back his head, weighing up the person he was talking to through narrowed eyes, and saying drily and insolently:

"And then? So what? So what?"

Even the boldest people would often be disconcerted by these meaningless words, spoken in this way. The best reasons and evidence, the most justified demands would wilt and collapse.

It was only in Cesare Davenato that Rotta found a worthy rival and someone to talk to. Ever since d'Avenat had played that clever trick on them with the decree and permit, through the Derventa Commander, even before they reached Travnik, and obliged them to spend two weeks there like vagabonds, he had been in Rotta's eyes an opponent of class, who should be taken seriously. And d'Avenat did not underestimate Rotta either, having found out about him from a Belgrade merchant. They treated each other differently from others. With each other they almost always adopted an easy, joking tone which was supposed to convey indifference and scorn, but which hid a tense alertness and unacknowledged fear. They would sniff at each other like two wild animals and observe one another like two villains: both knowing quite well that they were villains, but not knowing exactly the other's methods and techniques.

Those conversations, which usually began in French, in a formal tone and diplomatic vocabulary, would sometimes turn into colourful squabbles in the crude, corrupted Venetian dialect spoken on all the shores of the Mediterranean. Then both interpreters would cast off their gentlemanly masks, wrestling and outdoing each other with words, in the Levantine manner, quite forgetting their dignity and using the most shameless expressions accompanied by indescribable gestures and grimaces.

"Give me your blessing, most reverend father, bless this humble servant of the Holy Mother Church," d'Avenat would then bow ironically before Rotta, mocking his good relations with the friars.

"All the Jacobin devils in Hell give you their blessing!" Rotta would reply, calmly as though reciting a part he had learned.

"You'd lick those friars' altar, you would!" said d'Avenat.

"You'd lick some other things, if only the priests would let you. But they won't! They won't have anything to do with you Frenchies. But I hear you're opening a synagogue in one wing of the Imperial French Consulate."

"Like Hell we are. What would we want with a synagogue? We'd far rather go to the Dolac church and see His Excellency the Imperial and Royal Consul General and his esteemed interpreter assisting Brother Ivo in the mass."

"Why not? Why shouldn't I do that?"

"I know, I know. You can do everything. There's only one thing you can't do. You can't grow!"

"Ah, you're right there. No I can't do that," said the hunchback, without so much as blinking, "but believe me I'm not sorry since I saw the size of you. And when I think how you'll stretch when you're dead. It'll be a job finding a coffin for such a massive corpse."

"Eh, if only I could see your end, I wouldn't spare any trouble or expense to find you a little box," and d'Avenat measured out an arm's length.

"Oh, no! I've no intention of dying. And why should I, if you're not my doctor?"

"Who'd be your doctor, cholera can doctor you!"

"A colleague of yours, I know. But at least it kills for free. Although to be fair, your hand is surer. Some people get cholera and survive, but with you – not a hope."

And so they would go on, until they both burst out laughing, still watching each other insolently and shrewdly.

These exchanges never had any witnesses, they were a kind of relaxation and exercise for both interpreters. And they would always end them in polite, ceremonious French again. Watching them take their leave of one another, removing their hats with a deep bow, the people of Travnik would draw all kinds of conclusions from such a long, friendly exchange between officials of the two Christian powers.

With everyone else in Travnik, Rotta was the same: insolent, morose, mistrustful, blunt and abrupt.

Born in Trieste, Rotta was the twelfth child of a poor shoemaker called Giovanni Scarparotta, who died of drink. This twelfth child was frail, deformed, hunchbacked and in his first months so weak that they kept lighting candles for him and once got as far as washing him and preparing him for burial. But when this little pale, hunchbacked boy went to school it emerged that he had the sharpest mind of all his brothers and was capable of becoming something higher and better than his grandfather or his father. And while all his other brothers, sturdy, healthy boys, became sailors, tradesmen, or took up those unspecified occupations from which people in Trieste live just as well as from real trades, the hunchbacked boy was taken on to work in the office of a shipping company.

Here, carrying the post and sharpening pens, the feeble, reticent child, with his pale face, large eyes and sensual mouth, saw for the first time what a gentleman's life in clean, spacious rooms was like, the life of civilized people in stable, favourable conditions, where people talked softly and behaved decently to one another, where food, clothing and all the other everyday needs were taken for granted, and all thoughts and efforts were directed above them, towards other, remote and higher goals. The boy compared that life into which he could only peer by day when he went round the offices, with the cramped, squalid poverty of his father's house, with its quarrels, spite and coarseness in the family and among their neighbours. And he suffered immeasurably from this comparison. Now that he knew such a life existed, he could no longer remain in that same shabby misery in which he had been born and in which he was supposed to live out his life. And one night, before dawn, after lying awake for a long time tormented by these thoughts, the boy got up out of the rags in which he slept and which filled him with unbearable revulsion, and, kneeling, his face bathed in tears, he swore, not himself knowing before whom or in whose name, that he would get out of the life his family was living or he would not live at all.

His numerous brothers, younger and older, were sleeping soundly here beside him under the same rags as himself – apprentices who were constantly beaten, or black and dirty idlers. He felt as though they were not his own brothers, but repulsive slaves among whom he could not survive and from whom he must escape as soon as possible, forever, at any price.

From that day, the hunchbacked boy turned completely towards that easier, brighter life "on the other side". He worked diligently and obediently, anticipating his employers' wishes, learning, watching, listening, and endeavouring with desperate efforts to discover the door into that pleasanter, finer life and the way to open it. An unconscious but deep desire to enter that world and stay there drew him forward, as he was pushed, with equal force, from behind, by his violent hatred of that other terrible life of his parents' house and an uncontrollable revulsion towards everything connected with it.

Such energy and such zeal could not remain unnoticed or fruitless. The boy gradually took on clerical work. He was entrusted with the more trivial jobs on the ships and with the authorities. He proved himself discreet and indefatigable, with a great gift for learning languages and perfect handwriting. He was noticed by his superiors. It was made possible for him to learn German. His salary was increased. He began to take French lessons from a Royalist émigré. This old man, paralysed and obliged to support himself by giving lessons, belonged to what had once been decent, cultivated Paris society. Young Niccolo Scarparotta learned a great deal from him, not only the language, but geography, history and what the old gentleman called generally "knowledge of the world".

When he had achieved all this, the young man abandoned his parental home in the poor quarter quite naturally and coolly. He rented himself a modest but clean furnished room in a widow's house. This was his first step onto the soil of that more agreeable world he had to conquer.

With time, he became indispensable in the company offices at the arrival of ships and in dealing with foreigners. He expressed himself easily and rapidly in five languages, knew in detail the names of all the government offices in the Empire and the functions of all the officials. He remembered everything that other people could not be bothered to remember but that they needed all the time. And at the same time he remained just as quiet and discreet, without personal needs or demands, always at people's disposal and never in the way.

As such he was noticed by the local commander, Major Kalcher, for whom the young hunchback had performed a few services and provided some quite useful information about the foreigners arriving or departing on the company's ships. And when the Major was transferred to Zemun, he invited the young man a few months later to enter the service of the Zemun Headquarters as interpreter and intelligence agent.

The shoemaker's son, who had run away from one world to gain a place for himself in another, saw in this invitation an omen and a welcome chance to distance himself physically from his family's poverty which was still here, just a few streets away from him.

So the young man came to Zemun. And he immediately made a mark with his zeal and efficiency. He crossed into Belgrade on confidential business, interrogating foreigners in the quarantine. (He had recently learned both Greek and Spanish.) Here the son of the Trieste cobbler, wishing to wipe out all trace of his origin, dropped the Scarpa and called himself Rotta. For a time he even wrote de Rotta. Here he married a Levantine girl, the daughter of an Istanbul export merchant who had come to visit relations in Zemun. Her father had been born in Istanbul, but was of Dalmatian origin and her mother was Greek.

The girl was beautiful, docile and plump, and she brought a dowry. It seemed to Rotta that the presence of such a wife was the final touch he needed to secure himself forever in the easier, brighter world and that the long years of working his way up, with all their effort and self-denial, had come to an end.

However, it was at just this stage of his life that Rotta began to realize that this was not the longed-for end of the road and the long awaited reward. In front of the already flagging man, life stretched ahead, an endless line, with nothing lasting or reliable, like the insidious play of innumerable mirrors in which ever new and ever more distant, probably equally deceptive, perspectives kept opening up.

His wife turned out to be unreliable, lazy, sickly, extravagant, and a nuisance in every way. (Had Rotta not broken off all connection with the life of his childhood so abruptly and completely, he would perhaps have remembered a Mediterranean proverb he had often heard mentioned at home as a child: "Chi vuol fare la sua rovina prende la moglie levantina.")[5] His work in Zemun was neither so well organized nor as innocuous as it had been in Trieste. He was entrusted with dangerous tasks that wore out his nerves and took up not only his days, but also his nights, disturbing his sleep. These colourful, sly, rough people who moved between Belgrade and Zemun, up and down the Danube on this great crossroads, were complex, untrustworthy and difficult to deal with. Enmities would spring up, unexpected conflicts and underhand revenge. Rotta had to make use of the same methods in order to survive. Bit by bit, he acquired that dry insolent tone which characterizes the khavazes and interpreters in the Near East and which is only the external expression of inner sterility, distrust of people and absence of all illusion.

After they had a second daughter die in the first months of her life, their marriage became filled with a sullen hatred. There were arguments which quickly turned into noisy quarrels and acquired a measure of ugliness and brutality, which were no less than the quarrels Rotta remembered from his childhood. Finally, his wife left him, without regret or scandal, and went back to Istanbul which they both agreed she should never have left.

Then it dawned on Rotta that the vow of a sensitive hunchbacked boy weeping in the night because of his poverty, was not enough. Twenty years of persistent, hard work and service were not enough

---

5   "Whoever seeks his own ruin takes a Levantine wife."

for a man to cross from the world he was born in into another which he had chanced to observe and for which his heart longed. And what was worse, this "new world" did not actually exist as something separate, specific and unmoving which could be reached and conquered once and for all, as it had seemed to him during the first years. And equally, that "old" world of poverty and degradation from which he had fled at the cost of the greatest effort, could not be so easily and simply cast off, as he had cast off his brothers and sisters and those rags in his parents' house – it pursued one unseen, fatefully, through all apparent changes and successes.

Still only in his forties, Rotta already felt cheated and exhausted, like a man who had strained himself beyond his strength and who had not been rewarded as he deserved. All abstract reflection was alien to him, but he could not avoid reflecting on his destiny and then he felt isolated and disillusioned. In order to escape these thoughts and himself, he threw himself completely into that murky life of the border and the quarantine, where people became crude beyond measure and old before their time. He became acquisitive, jealous of his position, touchy and irritable, easily aroused, obtrusive, rude, superstitious and inwardly afraid. His vanity appeared to others excessively exaggerated, for he was proud not only of what he had achieved, but of all his unseen efforts and the cost of that achievement.

But even this vanity was not true to him, for with the years we are abandoned even by the satisfactions afforded by our vices. Losing his faith in the purpose of further advancement along the road where he had so worn himself out and which had not brought him what he had expected, Rotta let himself go downstream, wanting nothing other than a life without illness and poverty, with the minimum exertion and anxiety, and as much trivial pleasure, stability and income as possible.

Like the interpreter of the French Consulate, d'Avenat, he too had grown close to the Turks, become used to their customs and ways and to that inhuman life which passed in constant association with the Turks, but at the same time in constant hatred, out-shouting and out-doing them, the rayah of all faiths and travellers of all kinds.

Worn out before his time, now he was a grey-haired, sullen, selfish hypochondriac, full of trivial manias and bureaucratic pedantry. He suffered from imaginary diseases, was afraid of spells and bad omens, hated the Church and everything connected with it. He felt isolated. He remembered his wife and their life together with loathing. He trembled at the very thought of those filthy, noisy, poverty-stricken people he had left behind him in Trieste and he did not want to hear so much as the name of his family. He found pleasure in saving and he saved passionately with the sense that in that way at least he was putting straight what was crooked and wrong in life and that money was still the only thing which could go some way towards raising up, saving and protecting a man.

He liked spicy food and good drink, but he had a horror of being poisoned, hated spending money and was afraid of saying the wrong thing when drunk and so giving himself away. (This unfounded fear of poison attacked him increasingly often, although he resisted it and defended himself against an obsession which alarmed him just as much or more than the possibility of actual poisoning.)

When he was younger, he had set great store by his clothing and found satisfaction in startling people with the stiff whiteness of his shirts and his lace ruffles and cuffs, the many colours and large quantities of his silk scarves, the faultless shine of his shoes. Now he had lapsed in these things. His passion for saving had suppressed everything else.

And his wealth itself, acquired with difficulty and jealously guarded, was becoming for him simply the fear of poverty. What was said about him was true: that once, as a young dandy, he had had 101 shirts and 30 pairs of shoes. His trunks were full even now. He did have some savings in gold. But what was the use of it all, when he could not for a moment free himself of the awareness that his shirts were slowly but constantly fraying at the edges, his shoes were wearing out and thinning at the tips and heels, that money could not be hidden in an entirely secure place. What was the use of it all? What was the point of twenty years of slaving and self-denial? When neither money, nor position, nor clothes could ward off fate ("that whore fate" as Rotta called it in his feverish monologues, at night). When all of it was torn, fraying, wearing out, and through the holes and tears on his clothes and shoes, despite all the abundance, he could always see what others could not – that same shameful poverty he thought he had left behind in Trieste, far behind him and forever. This anxiety about preserving his wealth was identical to his childhood anxiety about the constant lack of so much as a farthing, and these cares about saving and hoarding were the cares of poverty, want and denial. What was the use of it all? What was the use when after so much effort and empty successes, one was back where one started. What was the use when the same malice and coarseness came into his thoughts, the same brutality and crudeness into his words and actions, only from a different direction? When the same ugly torment that accompanied poverty was needed to maintain what he had acquired. In short, what was the use of having a lot and being something, when one could not free oneself from the fear of poverty, or base thoughts, or coarse speech, or uncertainty in one's behaviour, when bitter, relentless, but unseen, misery followed at one's heels, and that finer, brighter and more tranquil life kept slipping away, like a deceptive apparition?

And seeing that it was all useless, and that it was not easy to escape one's origin and childhood, Rotta threw his head still further back, stepped out with still more insolence, looked at people around him with still greater contempt, saved still more assiduously and maintained order in the office still more pedantically, ever stricter and more merciless towards his juniors and towards everyone who depended on him.

In addition to Niccolo Rotta, there were two other junior officials in the Austrian Consulate.

The office clerk, Franz Wagner, was the son of a German settler from Slavonski Brod, small, blond, obliging, gifted with perfect handwriting and tireless in his work. A small, grey man who melted with subservient servility under the glance of his superiors, but who concealed in himself, suppressed and crumpled, a large quantity of that soft and mute, but cruel, deadly bureaucratic spite which would later, as he advanced in his career, come pouring down on the head of some wretched subordinate, who was perhaps now still at school. This Wagner was Rotta's chief adversary. The two of them fought and quarrelled like two natural enemies.

The other, Petar Markovac, a junior clerk, was a Slavonian, a tall non-commissioned officer, smart, handsome, ruddy-faced, with a black waxed moustache, entirely taken up with his person, completely satisfied with himself and with no need whatever to think of anything else.

7

It was no longer autumn, but winter had not yet begun. That indeterminate freak season, neither autumn nor winter, but worse than both, had gone on for days, for weeks, for days which were as long as weeks, for weeks which seemed longer than months. Rain, mud and snow, which turned to rain while still in the air and to mud as soon as it fell to the ground. A pale, powerless sun coloured the east at dawn with a feeble pink glow behind the clouds, and did not appear in the west until towards the end of the grey day, as a bit of yellowish light, before the grey day passed into black night. All through the day, and during the night, dampness seeped from the earth and from the sky, drizzling, oozing, engulfing the town and permeating all things. Invisible but all-powerful, it changed the colour and form of things, the behaviour of animals, the bearing, thinking and mood of people. The wind, which swept twice a day through the valley, merely shifted the damp from place to place, bringing ever new masses of damp with sleet and the smell of wet forests. Damp simply replaced damp, the cold, sharp mountain dampness replacing the sated, stagnant dampness of the town. Bogs formed, springs overflowed and streams swelled on both sides of the valley. Thin streamlets, unnoticed till now, were turned into waterfalls, roaring and rushing down the slopes, falling into the bazaar like a drunken, blinded peasant. And through the middle of the town the Lašva rolled, humming, changed, clouded and swollen. There was nowhere one could hide from the sound of these rushing waters, nor protect oneself from the cold and damp spreading from them, for they penetrated into rooms and reached right into beds. And every living body had only its own warmth for defence, even the stone in the walls sweated a cold sweat, and the trees became slippery and flimsy. In the face of this deadly invasion of dampness, everything withdrew into itself, seeking the best form of resistance. Animals huddled against one another, seeds lay still in the earth, while the frozen, sodden trees concealed their stifled breath in their sap and warm roots.

The local people, accustomed to it all and hardened, put up with it, keeping themselves going, feeding and warming themselves by instinct and experience, each according to his own abilities, habits and the resources of his situation. The rich did not emerge from their houses without great need. They spent their days in the same stuffy rooms they slept in, warming their hands against the green tiles of their earthenware stoves and waiting, with a patience that was always one day longer than the longest winter or spell of bad weather. No one was afraid of missing anything, of being outdone or caught unawares, for they were all living under the same conditions, following the same rhythm and way of life. And they had everything they needed to hand and under lock and key, in the cellar, the attic, the barn or pantry, for they knew their winter and did not wait for it unprepared.

It was the other way round with the poor. Days like these drove them out of their houses, for they did not prepare winter stores, and even those who did not turn their heads to look at anyone during the summer, now had to come out and earn, borrow or beg, to "make money" out of nowhere and bring it home. Poor people with bowed heads, goose-pimpled, and stiff-limbed, gathered food and fuel, covered their backs and heads with old sacks turned inside out like hooded cloaks, wrapped scarves round their heads and waists, swathing themselves in rags until they lost all shape. They made themselves footwear of leather, rags and wood, crept by under the eaves and jutting-out upper storeys, stepping carefully round puddles, jumping over tiny rivulets from stone to stone, and shaking their feet like cats, humming, their teeth chattering, blowing on their hands or warming them against their thighs. They went to work, serve, or beg, finding the strength to bear everything in the thought of the food or fuel this outing would bring them.

So the people of Travnik would get through these difficult times, accustomed to them from birth.

It was different for the foreigners whom fate had cast into the narrow valley which, at this time of year, was as gloomy, damp and draughty as a prison corridor.

The damp had entered the Residence, where everything was usually as noisy and carefree as a cavalry barracks, bringing misery, like a disease. The Vizier's Mamelukes, for whom this was the first winter of their lives, shivered, pale and dismayed, they looked round with sorrowful, ailing eyes, like tropical animals transported to a northern land. Many of them spent the whole day lying down, their heads covered with a blanket, coughing, simply ill with longing for their warm, distant homeland.

And even the animals the Vizier had brought to Travnik, angora cats, parrots and monkeys, did not stir, shriek or entertain their master, instead they lay huddled in corners, dejected and silent, waiting for the sun to warm and cheer them.

The Secretary and other dignitaries did not emerge from their rooms, as though they thought there was a flood outside. All their rooms had large earthenware stoves which were stoked from the corridors. Servant boys stacked into them whole piles of heavy hornbeam logs, which gave out tremendous heat and kept burning throughout the night, so that in the morning a new fire could be lit from the remains of the still-glowing embers. In those rooms, which never grew cold, it was pleasant to listen, at dawn, to the stove being opened from the outside, the ash raked out and new pieces of wood being stacked in, log by log. But the misery penetrated here as well, long before the early dusk. People tried to ward it off, inventing games and amusements, visiting one another, conversing. Even the Vizier himself lost his natural gaiety and resourcefulness. He came several times a day into the gloomy ground-floor Divan, with its thick walls and few small windows, as the upper Divan, the airy, brighter one, had been abandoned in the battle with the cold and was not heated or opened during the winter. There he invited his older, closer officials to pass the time chatting with him. He talked for a long time about trivial things in order to stifle his memories of Egypt and drive away thoughts about the future and his craving for the sea, which tormented him even in his sleep. Ten times a day he would say ironically to each of his men:

"What a beautiful land, my friend! A blessed land! How have you and I sinned before God to be paying for it now like this?"

And each of them replied with a few crude and unkind words about the country and the climate. "A dog's land!" said the Secretary. "It's enough to make bears weep!" complained the Vizier's country-man and armourer Younuz Bey. "Now I see that we've been sent here to perish," maintained Ibrahim Hodja, a personal friend of the Vizier's, screwing his yellow face up into long creases as though he really were preparing to die.

They vied with each other in complaining, lessening their common boredom at least a little. And through all these conversations the roar of water and the drumming of rain could be heard, and the sea of dampness felt, laying siege to the Residence for days already, and penetrating through any opening and crack as soon as they appeared.

Regardless of the rain and cold, Suleiman Pasha Skopljak, the Vizier's Deputy, rode several times each day through the town. When he arrived at the Residence, they would break off their conversation and stare at him as at a marvel.

When he was talking to his Deputy, a tough, simple Bosnian,

the Vizier tried to speak moderately and to be considerate, but he would ask him jokingly:

"For God's sake, man, are misfortunes like this common in this town?"

Suleiman Pasha answered seriously, in his bad Turkish:

"There's no misfortune, Pasha, Allah be praised. The winter's begun well and as it should. Whenever it's wet at the beginning and dry at the end, you know it'll be a good year. Just wait and see when the snow comes and there's a sharp frost, when the sun shines, and it creaks under your feet and sparkles in front of your eyes. Beauty and delight, just as Allah made it and as it should be."

But the Vizier shuddered at these new wonders promised by his Deputy with such enthusiasm, as he rubbed his dry, reddened hands and warmed his damp gaiters by the stove.

"Oh, don't say that, my dear friend, haven't you anything better to offer?" the Vizier joked.

"Ah, no, no! Let these gifts of Allah be, let them be. It's no good when winter is not winter." The Deputy stuck firmly to his position, impervious to the subtle remarks of these Ottomans and insensitive to their sensitivity. And he sat upright, cool and tough, among these frozen, mocking foreigners, who were watching him with fear and curiosity, as though he were the one who had arranged the weather and the seasons so mercilessly.

And when the Deputy rose, wrapped in his wide red cape, to ride off through the icy rain, along the muddy road to his rooms, they looked at each other, shivering and desperate. And as soon as the door closed behind him, they carried on complaining of the Bosnians, and Bosnia, and the sky above it, until their bitter words and insults gave them some illusion of relief.

In the French Consulate life too had become more private and quieter. Madame Daville was acquiring her first experience of winter in Travnik and immediately making use of everything, remembering it all for the future, and finding a remedy and solution for every problem. Wrapped in a grey cashmere shawl, brisk and indomitable, she spent the whole day going round the huge Turkish house, deciding what needed to be done and giving instructions. She found it difficult to communicate with the servants because of her ignorance of the language and the slovenly ways of the local people. But in the end she always managed to make her will felt and get more or less what she wanted. It was only in weather like this that the house showed all its drawbacks. The roof leaked, the floorboards were rotting, the windows did not shut properly, the plaster was flaking, the stoves smoked. But Madame Daville succeeded eventually in patching, organizing and putting everything in order. Her dry hands, usually red, were now blue with cold, but they did not rest for a moment in the struggle against damage, breakages and disorder.

Daville and his young Secretary were sitting on the ground floor, where it was a little damp, but well-heated and bright. They were talking about the war in Spain and the French authorities in Dalmatia, the couriers who did not arrive or came at the wrong time, about the Ministry which did not reply to pleas or requests, and most of all about the bad weather, about Bosnia and the Bosnians. They talked calmly, in the discursive way people do when they are waiting for a servant to bring in the candles or to call them in to dinner, until the conversation moved imperceptibly on to general questions and so turned into a debate or quarrel.

This was the hour between day and night, when the candles had not yet been lit and one could no longer see well enough to read. Des Fossés had just returned from a ride, for even in such weather he did not miss going out into the surrounding countryside at least once a day. His face was still glowing and damp from the rain and wind and his short hair was tangled and stuck down. Daville had difficulty in concealing his dissatisfaction with these outings which he considered to be a danger to health and damaging to the reputation of the Consulate. He was altogether irritated by this active and enterprising young man and by his alert intellectual curiosity. But the young man, insensitive to the Consul's rebukes and completely impervious to his views, talked with enthusiasm of his discoveries as he roamed through Travnik and its surroundings.

"Ah," Daville waved his hand, "Travnik and a hundred miles around it, it's nothing but a muddy desert, inhabited by two kinds of wretch: torturers and tortured, and we are condemned to live in between them."

Unshakeable, Des Fossés argued that this region, although numbed and far removed from the world, was not a desert, but, on the contrary, varied, interesting from every point of view and eloquent in its way. Certainly, the people were divided by faith, highly superstitious and subject to the worst administration in the world and consequently in many ways backward. But at the same time they were full of interesting features of character, strange customs and spiritual wealth. In any case, it was worth making an effort to investigate the causes of their misfortune and backwardness. And the fact that M. Daville, Herr von Mitterer and M. Des Fossés, as foreigners, found life in Bosnia difficult and unpleasant was neither here nor there. The value and importance of a country could not be measured by the way the Consuls of a foreign state felt there.

"On the contrary," said the young man, "I think there are few parts of the world which are less empty and monotonous. You have only to dig a foot deep to find the graves and remains of former times. Every field here has been a graveyard, several times over. One necropolis on top of another, just as the various inhabitants were born and died over the centuries, one epoch after another, generation after generation. But graves are proof of life and not of a wilderness..."

"Well—" The Consul could not get used to the young man's way of expressing himself, and he brushed it aside with his hand, like an invisible fly.

"Not only graveyards, not only graveyards! Today as I was riding towards Kalibunar, I saw a place where the rain had eroded the soil under the path. To a depth of some dozen feet you could see, like geological layers, one on top of the other, the traces of former roads that had passed through this same valley. At the bottom were heavy paving stones, the remains of a Roman road, six feet above them the remnants of a medieval cobbled way and, finally, the gravel surface of the Turkish road where we walk today. So, in a chance cross-section, I was shown two thousand years of human history, and in them three epochs, each of which buried the other. You see!"

"I see. If we begin to look at things from that angle…" said Daville, for the sake of saying something. He was not so much listening as looking into the young man's brown eyes with their cold glint, as though he would like to understand better what kind of eyes these were that observed the world around them in this way.

The young man continued to talk about the traces of neolithic settlements on the road to the village of Zabilje, where, before the rains began, he had found flint axes and saws which had lain in the clay for perhaps tens of thousands of years. He had found these in a field belonging to a certain Karahodžić, a surly but vigorous old man, who refused to hear a single word about digging up anything at all on his land. And for a long time he had watched the foreigner and his escort angrily, as they made their way back towards Travnik.

And, as they rode, the khavaz told Des Fossés about the destiny of the Karahodžić family.

More than two centuries earlier, during the great wars, they had left this region and settled in Slavonia, near Požega, where they were given large estates. A hundred and twenty years later, when the Turkish forces had to withdraw from Slavonia, they too had abandoned their fine properties near Požega and returned to their less extensive and productive lands in Zabilje. The family still preserved a vessel, a copper cauldron they had brought with them, as a symbol of their lost estates and nobility when they returned, humiliated and embittered, to Bosnia. In addition to this cauldron, the first Karahodža had left them a pledge: that they should never shirk any war that might be waged against the Austrians, and that each of them should do all he could to ensure that one day the noble status they had lost in Slavonia was returned to them. And if, by some misfortune, Allah should permit the Austrians to cross the Sava river as well, he made them swear to defend these miserable fields in Zabilje as long as they could. And, when they no longer could, to run, even if they had to keep running, from place to place, through the whole of Turkey, right up to the furthest limits of the Empire, to the very ends of the Earth.

And, as he spoke, the khavaz had shown the young man a little Turkish graveyard above the road, beside a plum orchard, where two tall white tombstones stood out. These were the graves of the old Karahodža and his son, the grandfather and father of the old man who was standing by his fence bristling with anger, his lips moving and his eyes flashing, as he muttered furiously.

"You see," the young man said, looking out into the dusk through the misted window, "I don't know which I found more interesting, those traces of the Stone Age, tens of thousands of years before Christ, or that old man keeping the oath of his forebears and not allowing anyone to lay a finger on his land."

"I see, I see," said Daville vacantly, simply surprised that the young man saw these things at all.

As they walked about the room talking like this, the two men stopped by the window.

Outside, darkness was beginning to gather. There were no lights anywhere yet. Only far below in the valley, right by the water, a feeble glimmer flickered from Abdullah Pasha's tomb. That was a candle which burned constantly over the grave of the Pasha. Its feeble flame could always just be made out from the windows of the Consulate, when the other lights of the town were not yet lit or when they had already been extinguished.

Standing by the window, waiting for total darkness, the young man and the Consul would often talk about this "eternal light" and about the Pasha whose candle they were accustomed to as something constant and familiar.

Des Fossés knew his story as well.

Abdullah Pasha was born in this region. He had made a name for himself and grown rich while still quite young. He had seen much of the world, as a soldier and a high official, and when he became Vizier in Travnik, in the prime of his life, he had suddenly died and was buried here. (They say he was poisoned.) He remained in the people's memory as a mild and just administrator. One of the Travnik chroniclers had noted that "during Abdullah Pasha's rule the poor people did not know what evil was". Before his death he had bequeathed his estate to the Travnik Tekke and other institutions. He had left a substantial sum so that this fine tomb of good stone could be built, and in his will ordained that some of the income from his houses and serfs should be used to keep an exceptionally thick wax candle burning day and night. His grave was covered with a heavy green cloth on which was embroidered the inscription: "May the Almighty illumine his tomb". This had been composed by learned men from the Tekke as an expression of gratitude to their benefactor.

Des Fossés had succeeded in discovering where the Vizier's will could be found and he thought it must be an interesting document, characteristic of the people and their circumstances. And this evening he was complaining that he would never be allowed to see and copy it.

The conversation faltered. In the ensuing silence they heard from the darkness rapidly shrouding everything outside, the long drawn-out sound of an incomprehensible song, like a lament from deep under water. It was the voice of a man singing as he walked, interrupting the song and taking it up again after a few steps. It grew increasingly distant and weak.

Daville rang the bell impatiently and ordered that candles be brought.

"Oh, that music! My God, that music!" sighed the Consul, whom Bosnian singing drove to despair.

That was Musa, known as The Singer, going up the steep road, as every evening. He lived in one of the few houses lost among the steep gardens above the Consulate.

Des Fossés, who asked questions and found out about everything, had got to know the story of this drunkard and reveller who made his way home the same way every evening, staggering and hoarsely singing snatches of his long drawn-out melody.

A certain old Krdžalija had once lived in Travnik, a man of lowly origin and without particular standing, but very rich. He traded in weapons – merchandise which pays better than anything since anyone who needs a weapon does not ask how much it costs, but pays any price, just to have it when and where he needs it. He had only two sons. The older brother worked with his father, while Musa was sent to Sarajevo to school. Then old Krdžalija died suddenly, quite unexpectedly. He had gone to bed healthy, but in the morning they found him dead. Musa broke off his studies and returned to Travnik. When they came to divide the estate, it turned out that the old man had left unbelievably little ready money. All sorts of rumours about the old man's death began to circulate. People did not want to believe that he had left no money, and indeed it was hard to do so. Many suspected the older brother and tried to persuade Musa to take the matter to court and claim his rights. Besides, the older brother had tried to cheat the younger one when the rest of the estate was being divided. That older brother was a tall handsome young man, but one of those cold people whose eyes are icy even when they smile. While they were still dividing the estate and while Musa was hesitating between his innate indifference to money and everything connected with it and the advice of the townsfolk, something far worse and more difficult happened. Both brothers took a fancy to the same girl, from Vilici. They both wanted to marry her. She was given to the older brother. Then Musa disappeared from Travnik. No one mentioned the dubious settlement between the brothers, nor Krdžalija's death. The older brother looked after his business and increased his wealth. Two years later, altered, pale, thin, unshaven, Musa returned, with the heavy, uneasy look of a man who does not sleep much and who likes to drink. Since then he lived on his part of the estate, which was not small, but badly managed and neglected. So it was that with the years this handsome rich man's son, who had a wonderful voice and perfect pitch was transformed into this wasted wretch who lived by his songs and only for drink, a reticent, harmless, pitiful fellow, whom the children stared after. Only his famous voice remained the same for a long time. But now his voice too was impaired, just as his health had burned up and his wealth melted away.

The servant brought the candles in. Shadows danced over the room and then subsided. The windows were suddenly curtained with darkness. The drunken singer's song faded out completely, and the barking of the dogs answering him stopped as well. Silence closed in on everything once more. The Consul and the young man said nothing. Each was thinking his own thoughts, but each one was secretly wishing that he was far from this place with someone else to talk to.

It was Des Fossés who broke the silence again. He talked about Musa the Singer and people like him. Daville interrupted him, maintaining that their loud-voiced, drunken neighbour was far from being an exception, he was the true expression of an environment of which brandy, idleness and every kind of coarseness were the main characteristics. Des Fossés contradicted him. There were always such people in a place like this, the young man argued, that was inevitable. People regarded them with fear and pity, but also a kind of religious respect, roughly as the ancient Greeks respected the "enlision", the place where lightning had struck. But they were not at all typical of the society. On the contrary, they were regarded as lost and exceptional. The existence of such outcast and isolated people, abandoned to their passions, their disgrace and rapid ruin, just showed how firm the links were and how remorselessly strict were the laws of society, religion and family in patriarchal life. And this applied to the Turks as well as to the rayah of all faiths. In these societies everything was connected, one thing locked firmly into another, one thing supporting another, and watched over by everyone. Each individual took care of the whole, and the whole of each individual. Each house observed the next house, each street oversaw the next, for everyone was responsible for everyone else, and all were responsible for everything. Each person was closely linked with the fate not only of his relations and those in his household, but also of his neighbours, fellow-believers and fellow-citizens. This was both the strength and the enslavement of these people. The life of each individual was possible only within that pattern and the life of the whole only in accordance with those conditions. If anyone stepped outside that pattern, following his own instincts and will, it was as though he had committed suicide and, sooner or later, he would inevitably be destroyed. Such was the law of these communities, mentioned even in the Old Testament. It was the law of the classical world as well. Marcus Aurelius wrote somewhere: "Whoever avoids the obligations of the social order is an outcast." This was the law Musa had sinned against, and a law that has been transgressed and a society that has been wronged will exact their revenge and punishment.

Again Daville was observing the young man rather than listening carefully to him. And he was thinking: he has decided to explain and justify all the horrors and all the ugliness of this land tonight. This is probably the point he has reached in his book about Bosnia and now he needs to lecture me, or anyone else, about it. Or perhaps it has all only just occurred to him. But this is youth that I see before me. Ease, self-confidence, fluent self-expression and strength of conviction. Yes, that is youth.

"I hope, my dear friend, that we shall read all of this in your book, but now let us see what has happened to our dinner." Daville put an end to the young man's lecture and his own reflections about it.

During the meal, the conversation ranged over everyday things and events. Madame Daville joined in with her brief and practical observations. They talked mostly about cooking, evoking memories of dishes and wines from various parts of France, making comparisons with Turkish food, regretting that there were no French vegetables, French wines or spices available. A few minutes after eight o'clock, Madame Daville muffled a brief yawn. This was the sign for them to rise from the table and soon afterwards she withdrew and went into the children's room. Half an hour later the Consul and Des Fossés parted. That marked the end of the day. The other, nocturnal side of Travnik life was beginning.

Madame Daville sat beside her youngest child's bed, knitting, in just the same way as she carried out all her other chores through the day, and as she ate, swiftly and conscientiously, in silence, tireless as an ant.

The Consul was once again in his study, sitting at his small desk. Before him lay the manuscript of his epic on Alexander the Great. Daville had begun this opus long ago and had been working at it for years. He worked slowly and irregularly, but he thought about it every day, several times, in connection with everything he saw, heard and experienced. As we have said, this epic had become for him a kind of alternative, easier and better reality which he governed according to his will, in which there were no difficulties or obstacles and in which he found easy solutions to everything that was unresolved and insoluble both in him and around him. In it he sought solace for everything he found difficult and compensation for everything that real life did not offer or allow him. Several times a day Daville escaped into his "paper reality", leaning inwardly on an idea from his epic, as a lame man leans on a stick. And conversely, as he listened to news of the war, observed something or carried out some task, he often transposed them into his epic. And the fact that he cast them several thousand years back in time meant that all these things lost some of their oppressiveness and sharpness and at least seemed easier and more bearable. Naturally this did not actually make things easier nor the poem any nearer to resembling a real work of art. But so many people prop themselves up, inwardly, on some illusion, even stranger and vaguer than a work of poetry with its arbitrary content, rigid metre and strict rhyme.

This evening again, Daville placed the thick manuscript in its green binding in front of him, as a person carries out a habitual action. But since he had arrived in Bosnia and become involved in official dealings with the Turks, these evening hours brought ever fewer results and ever less satisfaction. Images would not come to him, the lines went into the mould with difficulty and emerged from it incomplete, the rhymes would not kindle each other, as they once had, making sparks fly from them, but remained unfinished, like one-legged monsters. Very often the green ribbons on the cardboard covers were not undone at all, but the manuscript lay there as a base for the little pieces of paper on which the Consul made a note of all the things he had to do the following day or had omitted to do in the day that had just passed. At these moments, after dinner, he would go over once again everything that had been done and said in the course of the day. But, instead of bringing rest and relaxation, this revived cares he had already forgotten and made new demands. The letters which had that day left for Split, Istanbul or Paris would appear complete before his eyes and he would suddenly see clearly everything he had omitted to say, everything irrelevant or awkwardly expressed. Exasperation and dissatisfaction with himself made the blood rush to his head. The conversations he had had that day loomed out of his memory, right down to the last detail, and not only the serious and important conversations concerning his official work, but even quite insignificant and trivial ones. He saw the person he was talking to clearly, heard every nuance of his words, he saw himself and recognized all the shortcomings of what he was saying and all the importance of what, for incomprehensible reasons, he had left unsaid. And suddenly there came to him the perfect, forceful sentences he ought to have spoken, instead of the pale, impotent words and answers he had actually uttered. The Consul now whispered them to himself, aware at the same time that it was all useless and too late.

Poems do not grow in such a state of mind, and such thoughts stop you sleeping. Or, if you do succeed in getting to sleep, they give you bad dreams.

This evening the whole conversation he had had with Des Fossés a short while before rang again in the Consul's ears. He suddenly realized how much immature swaggering there was in the stories of the three-fold layers of roads from different centuries, of neolithic weapons, of Karahodža and Musa the Singer, of the family and social organization in Bosnia. And to all the young man's fantasies, which he now felt could not stand up to the slightest criticism, he had only replied feebly, as though paralysed or bewitched: "I see, I see, but…" What the Devil did I see? he wondered now. He felt ridiculous and humiliated, but at the same time he was furious with himself for paying these insignificant conversations attention they did not deserve. After all, what did that conversation matter? And who had he been talking to? Not the Vizier, nor von Mitterer, he had simply been droning on with this callow youth about matters of no importance. But his thoughts would not be stopped or suppressed. And just when he was beginning to hope he had managed to forget these trivialities, he suddenly jumped up from his desk and found himself in the middle of the room, one arm outstretched, saying to himself: I should have replied to that whole immature exposition – this is the way things are – and put the young man properly in his place. One should always state one's opinion fully even in the most trifling matters, straight to a person's face, and let them worry over it afterwards, not keep it to oneself to wrestle with it later as with a vampire. Yes, that's what he should have done but he had not, and he would not do it the next day nor the day after that, never, not chatting with this raw youth nor in conversations with serious men. He would never realize it until evening, just before going to bed, when it was too late, when ordinary, everyday words became enormous and indestructible as apparitions.

That is what Daville told himself, returning once again to the little desk by the curtained window. But his thoughts followed him. He tried in vain to dispel them, for he was incapable of concentrating on anything else.

"He even found that dreadful singing of theirs interesting. He can even defend that," the Consul sighed to himself. Driven by this morbid need to argue and settle things with the young man in retrospect, the Consul wrote swiftly and without pausing on the white paper where line after line about the achievements of Alexander the Great should have flowed:

"I have heard these people singing and I have seen that they put into their songs the same savagery and unhealthy frenzy they put into every other aspect of their material and mental existence.

I once read the travel notes of a Frenchman, who had journeyed through these parts more than a hundred years ago and heard these people, he wrote that their song was more like the whining of dogs than singing. However, maybe because these people have changed for the worse, or maybe because that good old Frenchman did not know these lands sufficiently well, I find far less spite and insensitivity in the whining of dogs than in the singing of these people when they are drunk or simply carried away with their frenzy. I have seen them rolling their eyes as they sang, grinding their teeth and beating their fists against the wall, either because they were drunk on brandy or simply driven by an inner need to wail, draw attention to themselves and destroy things. And I have come to the conclusion that none of this has anything to do with the music and singing one hears among other peoples. It is simply a way for them to express their hidden passions and base desires to which, for all their lack of restraint, they could not otherwise give rein – for nature itself would prevent it. I spoke about this with the Austrian Consul General as well. With all his military rigidity, he too had felt the full horror of this wailing and shrieking which you hear at night in the streets and gardens, and during the day from some inns. "Das ist ein Urjammer,"[6] he said. But I somehow think that von Mitterer is, as usual, mistaken, overestimating these people. It is, quite simply, the fury of savages who have lost their simplicity."

The narrow sheet of paper was covered in writing. The last word barely fitted into the corner at the very bottom of the page. The rapidity with which he had written and the ease with which he had found words and comparisons warmed him, and the Consul felt something like relief. Exhausted, poisoned by worries, over-burdened with duties which seemed to him this evening beyond his strength, with bad digestion and insomnia as his only companions,

---

6 "That is an ancient, primeval sorrow."

he was sitting motionless over his manuscript when Madame Daville knocked on the door.

She was already prepared for bed. Under her white cap her face looked even smaller and sharper. A little earlier she had made the sign of the cross over her sleeping children and tucked their covers tightly round them. Then on her knees she had uttered the ancient evening prayer, praying God to grant her quiet rest that night and let her rise the next morning alive and well from her bed ("as she firmly believed she would rise from the grave on the Day of Judgment"). Now, with a candle in her hand, she peered round the half-open door.

"That's enough for today, Jean. It's time for bed."

Daville reassured her with a wave of his hand and a smile and sent her to bed. He stayed alone over his closely written sheet of paper, until his head swam and the lines ran into one another and everything became blurred like the night image of a world which by day appeared clear and comprehensible.

Then he rose from the desk, walked over to the window and, moving the heavy curtain slightly aside, he looked out into the impenetrable darkness, to see whether there were still lights, the last traces of that daytime world, in the Residence and the Austrian Consulate. Instead of that he saw in the misted glass his lighted room and the indistinct contours of his own face.

No one who had glanced at that moment, through the foggy darkness and cold drizzle, towards the French Consulate and seen that streak of light, would ever have imagined all that was troubling the sober and serious Consul and keeping him awake – a man who did not waste a single minute during the day on anything that was not practical, useful and directly linked with his work.

But the Consul was not the only person in that large building who was awake. Immediately above his room, on the first floor, three windows were lit, curtained with Bosnian linen. Here Des Fossés was sitting over his papers. For different reasons, he was not sleeping either, spending his night in a way he had no wish to and which he did not enjoy at all. The young man was not mulling over in his memory the conversations he had had during the day. On the contrary, he had forgotten both the conversation and the Consul five minutes later. He was not oppressed by weariness, a need for peace, or anxiety about the following day. He was racked by restlessness, choked by the appetites of his frustrated youth.

At night, he would be beset by images of women, not memories but real women, the whiteness of whose skin and the brilliance of whose smiles would shatter the darkness and silence like a shriek as they burst into his spacious room. He remembered all the grand, bold youthful plans with which he had left Paris, plans which had been meant to take him far from this little provincial town where he was bogged down, and he saw himself in some embassy, or in Parisian society, in the kind of place he ought to have been, the kind of person he wished to become.

His imagination played like this with his senses and ambitions every night and then deserted him, abandoning him to this deathly Bosnian silence. And now the breath of that silence preyed on him. During the day he could cheat it and stifle it in work, in his outings and conversations. But at night he could not manage it without great effort, and this was becoming increasingly difficult, for the silence overcame and wiped out, extinguished and hushed even that illusory, quiet life of the town, covering, enveloping and penetrating everything, alive and dead. In fact, from the day he left Split, and above Klis turned to take one last look at the mild landscape below him and the sea in the distance, the young man had been in constant contact with that silence and in perpetual conflict with it.

He found it in everything around him. In the architecture of the houses, with their faces always turned towards the courtyard, and their dumb defiant backs to the street; in the clothing of the men and women; in their eyes which expressed a great deal for their tongues were tied. And in their speech itself, when they did summon the courage to speak, it was easier to distinguish the significant hesitations than any actual words. He could hear in both sound and the meaning the way the silence seeped into each of their sentences, between the words and into each word between the letters, like pernicious water seeping into a flimsy little boat. He could make out their vowels, colourless and without clear limits, so that the speech of the boys and girls sounded like mindless cooing which dissolved in the silence. Even their singing which sometimes reached him from the street or a courtyard, was nothing but a long drawn-out wail, smothered at its source and at its ending in a silence which became an integral, and the most eloquent, part of the song. And any bit of life that could be seen in the sun and daylight and could not possibly be hidden – a little luxuriance or a brief flash of sensual beauty – that too begged for a quiet hiding place and fled, with its finger on its lips, into the first gateway of namelessness and silence. Every living creature, even objects, everything shrank from sound, hid from sight and trembled with fear lest it should have to pronounce a word or be called by its true name.

Looking at these men and women, stooped, bundled in their clothes and always silent, unsmiling and unmoving, he was impelled to discover more about their fears and hopes than their daily life betrayed, silenced and numb to the point of being life only in name. In the end, as he thought about this constantly, he began to find in everything examples to confirm his idea. In the very brutality of these people, which was considerable, and in their violent outbursts, he saw fear of true expression, a crude and special form of silence. And all his own thoughts about these people (Where did they come from? How were they born? What did they strive for? What did they believe in? How did they love and hate? How did they grow old and die?), these thoughts undeveloped and not articulated, vanished in that unspoken and oppressive atmosphere of silence which surrounded him completely, filling everything around him and striving to overcome everything within him.

With some alarm, the young man was beginning to feel increasingly clearly, that this silence was eroding and infecting him too, penetrating his skin and imperceptibly numbing his mind and freezing his blood.

The nights were particularly difficult.

At times there would indeed be a sound, sharp and unexpected: a shot somewhere on the edge of town, a dog barking at a rare passer-by or at its own dream. It lasted only a moment, making the silence still greater, for a hush would close in over it at once, like deep, endless waters. It was as impossible to sleep in this silence, as it would be in an orgy of noise. One could do nothing but sit and sense it threatening to corrode, crush, wipe one out of the ranks of conscious, living beings. Every night, as he sat like this by candles which quickly burned out, he imagined he could hear the speechless silence addressing him:

"You won't be stepping out like this for long, slender, looking straight ahead, a smile on your lips, thinking and speaking freely and openly. You can't stay like that here. I shall bend your spine, lower your eyes, make the blood choke your heart. I shall make of you a bitter plant in a windy place, on stony soil. And you will no longer be recognizable, not only in your French mirror, but in your own mother's eyes."

And this was not spoken abruptly, provocatively, but softly and relentlessly. And with these words, the silence was already bending and adapting him, like a step-mother dressing her step-child. He realized that the silence was in fact another form of death, a death which left a man his life, like a shell, while depriving him of the possibility of living.

But still, no one gives up without resisting or perishes without defending himself, least of all a man of Des Fossés's age, upbringing and race. His youth and sound nature contended in him against this affliction as against an unhealthy climate. And if it did sometimes happen that his strength and common sense deserted him at night, the morning always rescued him, the sun buoyed him up, water invigorated him, and his work and intellectual curiosity sustained him.

Tonight again he had made an effort and succeeded in wresting his thoughts away from the tedium and silence, to settle and focus them on the living, audible, visible and tangible things of daily reality and so defend himself from the silence which annihilated and buried everything, and which threatened to penetrate into his consciousness as it did into his room. He leafed through his day's notes, organized and re-worked them. His book on Bosnia was growing slowly and painfully, composed entirely from "true reality". Everything in it was supported by proof, confirmed by numbers and illustrated with examples. Without any eloquence or elegance of style, without any general observations, the pages were gradually accumulating, hard, smooth, cold and straightforward, as a defence against this insidious, seductive eastern silence, which blurred, softened, tangled and obstructed all things, giving them double or multiple meanings, or depriving them of meaning altogether, until they were all dragged off somewhere beyond the reach of our eyes and our reason into a deaf nothingness, leaving us blind, dumb and helpless, buried alive and cut off from the world while still in it.

But once he had arranged and copied out what he had jotted down that day, he found himself again face to face with the silence of the slowly advancing night. So he too sat with his arms folded over his manuscript, transported now into "unreal" contemplation, until his head too began to swim with fatigue and the large letters of his sober prose danced in front of his eyes like tiny ghosts and apparitions.

"Travnik! Trav-nik!" He repeated this word to himself, half aloud, like the name of some mysterious disease, like a magic formula it is hard to remember and easy to forget. And the more he repeated it, the more curious it seemed to him: two dark vowels between dull consonants. And now this formula encompassed for him more than he had ever imagined the world could contain. It was not a word, the dull cold name of a remote provincial town, it was not Travnik, for him it was now Paris and Jerusalem, the capital of the world and the centre of life. From his childhood a man may dream like this about great cities and glorious battlefields, but the real, decisive battles for the preservation of his being and the realization of everything concealed instinctively within it, must be fought wherever destiny happens to cast him, in who knows what narrow, nameless space with no splendour or beauty, with no witness or judge.

The young man stood up without thinking and went over to the window. Lifting a corner of the curtain he stared out into the darkness, not knowing himself what he was looking for in that night without sound or light.

That night, through the darkness filled with a damp that could have been either rain or snow, he could not make out the feeble light from the curtained windows of the Austrian Consulate. But candles were burning in that large house as well and people were sitting beside them, bent over papers and their thoughts.

The Consul's study was a long, unpleasant room, dark and airless, for its windows looked onto a steep orchard. Herr von Mitterer spent hours sitting here, at a desk piled with diagrams and military manuals.

The fire in the stove was forgotten, his long pipe had gone out and lay on the desk. The room was rapidly growing cold. The Consul wrapped his government-issue cape around him and wrote, tirelessly filling page after page of yellowish memorandum paper. When he had finished one page he would warm his numb, frozen right hand by the flame of the blazing candles and reach for a new, clean sheet, smooth it with his palm, rule the first line and rapidly fill the page with the large, regular handwriting used by all officers and non-commissioned officers of the Imperial and Royal Army.

This evening, after dinner, as so many times before by day or night, Frau von Mitterer had implored the Colonel, with tears, threats and entreaties, to write to Vienna and ask to be transferred out of this terrible wilderness. As always, the Colonel had consoled his wife, pointing out to her that it was not as easy or simple as she imagined to ask for a transfer and run away from difficulties, it would mean the end of his career and not a very honourable end either. Anna Maria had showered him with reproaches, refusing to listen to any of his reasons, and through her tears threatened to "take her child" and leave Travnik, Bosnia and him. In the end, to soothe his wife, the Colonel had promised, as so many times before, that he would write an application that very evening. And, as always, he had not kept his promise, because it was not easy for him to take such a step. He had left his wife and daughter in the dining room, lit his pipe and withdrawn into his study, not to write the application he found it so difficult to decide on, but to continue the work that gave him satisfaction and occupied all his evenings.

It was already the tenth evening that von Mitterer had been working on a lengthy paper for the military authorities in Vienna: he was describing the surroundings of Travnik from a military point of view. Now he was outlining, with a lot of drawings and sketches, figures and useful data, the fourteenth position which might be considered for a hypothetical army advancing along the Lašva valley towards the defences of Travnik. In the introduction to this lengthy work, he wrote that he had undertaken the job because of the benefit it could bring to the Supreme Headquarters, but also in order "to make the long monotonous evenings to which a foreigner was condemned in Travnik pass more quickly".

And indeed, the night was passing, albeit slowly. Von Mitterer wrote continuously, without a pause. He described the fortress of Travnik in minutest detail, its origin, what was thought and said about it, and its real strength, the value of its position, the thickness of its walls, the number of guns, the amount of ammunition it held, its ability to acquire supplies of food and water. His pen scratched on the paper, the candles sputtered, the lines followed one another, with their regular letters, precise figures and clearly presented data, and the sheets were laid one on top of the other, in a steadily growing pile.

These were von Mitterer's best hours, and this was his favourite place. By the candles, surrounded by silence, bent over the sheets filled with writing, he felt that he was himself in a well-built fortress, sheltered and protected, far from all doubts and ambiguities, with clearly defined tasks before him. Everything, from the manuscript and his way of expressing himself to the ideas he was expressing and the feelings that drove him on, all of it linked him to the great Imperial and Royal Army, to something firm, enduring and sure on which a man could rely and in which he could lose himself with all his personal worries and uncertainties. He felt certain that he was not isolated or abandoned to chance. Above him was a whole series of superiors, and below him a succession of subordinates. That supported and sustained him. Everything was permeated and connected with innumerable regulations, traditions and customs, everything was communal and everything thought out, constant, unchangeable and enduring.

On such a night and in such a place, where each individual sought salvation in his own illusion, there was no greater happiness or lovelier form of oblivion. And von Mitterer was writing, line by line, sheet after sheet, his lengthy paper on the strategic position of Travnik and its surroundings, which no one would ever read and which would remain, under the archive dust, marked with some official's casual signature, crammed into a virgin folder, unseen and unread, as long as the world lasted, with all its manuscripts and papers.

Von Mitterer wrote. The night seemed to hum, it was passing so swiftly. The heavy cape of his uniform warmed his back. His mind was alert but preoccupied with something which did not hurt but soothed, which speeded up the night hours, leaving a man weary, but with both the pleasant sense of a duty fulfilled and the precious desire for sleep.

So Colonel von Mitterer wrote but he was not growing tired, and his head was not swimming nor were the letters dancing in front of him. On the contrary, it seemed to him that between the regularly written lines he could make out others: masses of humanity drawn up as far as the eye could see, well-equipped and wearing splendid Imperial uniforms. He wrote, solemn and tranquil, as though he were working in the presence of the entire armed forces, from the Supreme Commander to the least Slavonian recruit. And when he stopped, he looked at his manuscript for a long time, not reading it but looking at it and losing himself in it, forgetting the Travnik night, himself and his family.

The Colonel was roused from this agreeable half-sleep by small but determined footsteps in the long corridor, approaching like distant thunder. The door was suddenly flung open. Frau von Mitterer burst loudly in. The room was immediately filled with the gust of a storm, and the air with a multitude of disconnected, angry words, which the woman had begun pouring out at the doorway and which merged with the tapping of her heels as she walked across the bare floorboards. As she drew nearer, von Mitterer slowly stood up and by the time she reached the desk he was already standing to attention. His happy, festive moments had vanished without trace. Everything had grown pale and dim and lost all meaning, value and purpose. The manuscript in front of him had dwindled to an insignificant little heap of paper. The armed forces had all retreated in disarray and evaporated in a pink and silver cloud. The pain in his liver he had forgotten all about reappeared.

Anna Maria stood in front of him, looking at him with a furious, unseeing gaze that trembled slightly, just as her whole face had now begun to tremble, eyelids, lips and chin. Red blotches appeared on her cheeks and under her throat. She was wearing a fine white woollen dressing gown with a low neck, tied at the waist with a belt of cherry-red silk. She had a small, light shawl of white cashmere over her shoulders, crossed over her breast and pinned with a large amethyst brooch in a gold setting. Her hair was piled up and tied with a broad band of muslin, over which brown curls and locks of her hair escaped in abundant disarray.

"Josef, for God's sake!..."

This was how it always began. This was the introduction to a frenzied charge and angry tapping of her heels through the house, to hurtful, ugly words without logical connection, unfounded statements, tears without cause, a spiteful, endless quarrel.

The Colonel stood at attention like a cadet caught off guard, for he knew that any movement and any word would provoke and fuel new explosions.

"Josef, for God's sake!..." his wife repeated, half-choking with sobs.

It took just one small, well-intentioned movement of the Colonel's hand for the storm to break over him, over the things around him, the manuscript on the table, through the chill air smelling of the pipe that had gone out. His wife erupted. The wide sleeves of her white peignoir flashed through the room so that the flame on the candles bent first one way then the other. From time to time her lovely firm arm would shine white, bare to the shoulder. Her light shawl shifted about and the amethyst brooch slipped from one side of her breast to the other. Locks of hair escaped from their band and curled on her forehead as though electrified.

She poured forth a torrent of words, now stifled and unintelligible, now loud, distorted with tears and saliva. The Colonel did not listen to them, for he knew them by heart, he just waited for the moment when they would begin to calm down and weaken, showing that the scene was nearing its end, for no one could repeat those several thousand words, not even Frau von Mitterer, until her next attack.

For the time being, the thunderstorm raged with full force.

She knew, she said, that he was not writing his application for a transfer tonight either, although he had promised he would, over dinner, for the fifteenth time. But still she had come to see this monster, more cold-blooded than any hangman, more heartless than any Turk, sitting over his stinking pipe, scribbling his nonsense which nobody read (which was just as well!), just to satisfy his own crazy ambition, the ambition of an inadequate man, who didn't know how to support and protect his family, his wife and child, who were dying, who were being destroyed, who, who...

All that was to follow was smothered by loud sobs and the rapid, spiteful beating of her two small but strong fists on the desk and scattered papers.

The Colonel moved his hand to place it gently on her shoulder, but he saw at once that it was too soon, that the cloud had not yet shed its load.

"Leave me alone, you gaoler, you heartless torturer, you unfeeling, unscrupulous beast. Beast, beast!"

There was a new torrent of words, then tears, heavy and abundant, then a trembling in her voice. And gradually it subsided. His wife was still sobbing, but now she allowed the Colonel to put his arm round her shoulder and lead her to a leather armchair. She sank into it with a sigh.

"Josef... for God's sake!"

This was the sign that the attack was over and his wife was ready to accept any explanation without objection. The Colonel stroked her hair and assured her that he would sit down straight away to write the application, decisively and without hesitation, that the letter would be copied out and sent off in the morning. He coaxed her, made promises, soothed her, fearing new words and new tears. But Anna Maria was tired and sleepy, unhappy but quiet and helpless. She let the Colonel take her into the bedroom, wipe the last tears from her eyes and lay her in the bed, cover and tuck her in, coaxing her with soft, meaningless words.

When he returned to his study and put the candlestick down on the desk, he was shivering and uneasy and the pain in his right side under his ribs was worse. For the Colonel the worst thing about these attacks was the moment when it had all passed, when he had succeeded in calming his wife and when, finally, he was left alone, each time with the clear realization that life could not go on like this.

The Colonel had again wrapped himself in his cape, which was heavy but cold, as though it were unfamiliar and not his; he sat down at the desk, took a clean sheet of paper and really did begin to write an application for a transfer.

Once again the Colonel was writing by the light of the blazing candles he had not trimmed. He listed his earlier merits in the service, emphasized his readiness now as ever to give all he could of himself, but he begged to be transferred from this post. He found reasons, pointing out and explaining that, under the present circumstances, only an individual without family could live and work in Travnik. The letters of his regular hand followed one another, but cold and dark now, like the links of chains. There was nothing of the former glow nor the sense of vigour and of being part of a whole. Now he was writing out his own weakness and shame, under a crushing pressure which no one could know or see.

The application was ready. The Colonel was resolved that he really would send it the next day and now he read it through for a second time, like his own condemnation. He read it, but his thoughts kept departing from this plaintive text and going back to the past.

He saw himself, a dark-haired, pale lieutenant, sitting lathered in shaving cream in front of the officers' barber. He watched him cut off the thick hair and handsome regulation pigtail he had been so proud of, shaving his head right down to the skin and preparing him to roam, dressed as a "Serbian lad", through the Turkish provincial towns and Serbian villages and monasteries. He remembered his journeys, his difficulties and fears. He saw his return to the Zemun garrison, after a successful reconnoitre, and heard the greetings of his friends and the warm words of his superiors.

He saw a soundless rainy night when he had crossed the Sava in a rowing boat with two soldiers and come below Kalemegdan, to the gate, for his agent to give him wax impressions of the keys to all the doors of the Belgrade fortress. He saw himself handing those keys to his major, overcome with delight, although he was shaking with fever and weariness.

He saw himself travelling by mail-coach to Vienna, as a man "who had been successful" and was to receive his reward. He saw himself carrying the commander's letter in which he was spoken of with the highest praise as a young man who was as sober as he was fearless.

He saw himself...

There was a soft bang outside in the corridor. The Colonel started in alarm, shrinking at the thought that he might again hear his wife's tempestuous footsteps. He listened. All was quiet. The insignificant little sound had tricked him. But the pictures from his memories of a moment before had been scattered and would not return. Before him lay the lines of his manuscript but now lifeless under his weary gaze. Where had that young man travelling to Vienna vanished? Where were the freedom and daring of youth?

The Colonel got up from the table with a sudden movement, like someone gasping for breath and looking for an escape. He went to the window, parted the green curtains a little, but there, right in front of his eyes, loomed the night, like a wall of ice and darkness. Von Mitterer stood in front of it, like one condemned, not daring to turn round and go back to the black lines of the application on his desk.

As he stood like that thinking about his transfer, it was just as well that he could have no inkling of how many more nights, how many autumns and winters he was to spend pressed like this between that black wall and his desk, waiting in vain for a decision on his application. The document would lie in the Geheime Hof und Staatskanzlei, in the archive, like his lengthy paper about the strategic positions around Travnik, only in a different section. For the application was to reach Vienna quickly and be seen by the appropriate official, a greying, weary Sectionschef. He read it one winter morning, in his high, warm and light office with its view of the Minorite church. He simply ironically underlined in red pencil the sentence in which von Mitterer suggested that he should be replaced by "ein familienloses Individuum", and wrote on the back that the Consul should be patient.

For the Sectionschef was a placid, immaculately groomed bachelor, a spoiled music lover and aesthete, who, in his lofty, secure and carefree position, could not begin to imagine the Consul's torments, what Travnik and women like Anna Maria von Mitterer were like, or all the possible troubles and needs human beings could have. Even at the hour of his death, as he breathed his last, this man would never find himself facing such a wall as the one before which Colonel von Mitterer was standing that night.

8

The year 1808 did not fulfil any of the beautiful autumn's vague promises, which Daville had sensed as he rode above Kupilo. In fact, nothing can mislead us so much as our own sense of tranquillity and agreeable contentment with the flow of things. And that was what had misled Daville.

At the very beginning of that year Daville experienced the hardest blow that could have befallen him in his thankless work in Travnik. In view of all he knew, it was what he could least have expected. D'Avenat had learned that Mehmed Pasha was definitely going to be replaced. The decree announcing his replacement had not yet arrived, but the Vizier was already secretly preparing to leave, with his belongings and all his retinue.

Mehmed Pasha did not want to wait in Travnik for the decree to arrive, d'Avenat explained. He would find some convenient excuse to leave the town earlier and never return. For the Vizier knew very well what a Turkish town was like the day the courier arrived with the Imperial decree announcing the recall of the current Vizier and the appointment of a new one. He could just imagine the insolent hired messenger who lived off such news and the morbid curiosity of the bazaar and scum of the town, who thrived on it. He could just see and hear him charging into the town at full gallop, cracking his whip and shouting at the top of his voice the names of the Vizier who had been replaced and his newly appointed successor.

"Mahzul Mehmed Pasha, mahzul! Khazul Suleiman Pasha, khazul!"

The rabble would stare at him, inquisitive and amazed, discuss the Imperial decision, rejoice, gloat, protest. As a rule, they would curse the one who was leaving and praise the one who was to come.

This was the moment at which the name of the replaced Pasha was thrown to the idle, common folk, like carrion to hungry curs, for them to defile with impunity, a cheap and easy excuse for them to swagger and boast and make tasteless jokes. Insignificant people who never dared so much as raise their heads when the Pasha rode past, suddenly sprang up as loud-mouthed avengers, even though this Pasha had not done them any personal harm nor indeed known of their existence. And often in such circumstances, you would see some student, a softa who had never finished his studies or a failed merchant loudly pronouncing judgement on the fallen Vizier over glasses of brandy, as though he personally had brought the Pasha down. Beating his breast the tipsy man would crow: "Oh, I'd rather have lived to see this day than be given half of Bosnia!"

Mehmed Pasha knew it was always like this, everywhere. Insignificant, nameless people would clamber onto the corpses of those who had fallen in the mutual struggles of the great. And it was understandable that he wanted at least to avoid that.

Daville immediately sought an audience. At this Divan, the Vizier divulged to him, in strictest confidence, that he really was going to leave Travnik, on the excuse that it was already time for him to supervise the preparations for the spring campaign against Serbia, and that he would never return. From the Vizier's words, Daville concluded that he had received news from friends in Istanbul that there was complete chaos there and that an insidious inner struggle was being waged among the groups and individuals who had overthrown Sultan Selim the previous May. The only thing they all agreed about was the persecution of all those who showed in any way that they approved of the deposed Sultan's reforms and plans. In these circumstances, the Bosnian beys' complaints against Mehmed as a friend of the French and a Selim man fell on fertile ground. The Vizier knew he had already been replaced. He hoped his friends had at least succeeded in preventing him being sent into exile, and obtaining for him some other pashalik far from Istanbul. In any case, he wanted to leave Travnik immediately, before the decree arrived, with the greatest discretion, so as not to give his Bosnian opponents the chance of gloating over his defeat and taking their revenge. And he would wait for the decree about his new posting somewhere on the way, in Sjenica or Prijepolje.

Mehmed Pasha told Daville all this in that equivocal oriental manner of speaking which does not entirely preclude doubt or the possibility of change or surprise even in the most clear-cut matters. The Vizier's face never lost its smile, or rather that row of regular white teeth which kept flashing between his beard and his thick, black, trimmed moustache, for neither the Vizier nor the Consul felt inclined to real merriment.

Daville watched the Vizier, listened to the interpreter and nodded his head in meaningless courtesy. In fact, he was stunned by the Vizier's announcement. The cold, painful constriction in his stomach, which always marked his visits to the Residence and every conversation with Turks to a greater or lesser extent, now rent him violently in two, like a numb paralysis, impeding his thought and speech.

In the Vizier's withdrawal from Bosnia Daville saw both a personal misfortune and a considerable setback for the French government. As he listened to Mehmed Pasha talking with forced calm about his departure, he felt cheated, misunderstood and abandoned in this icy land, among deceitful, malicious and incomprehensible people of whom you never really knew what they were thinking or feeling, among whom to remain might also mean to leave, whose smile was not a smile, nor their "yes" a "yes", just as their "no" was not altogether "no". He managed to compose a few sentences, and to tell the Vizier how much he would regret his departure, to express the hope that it would all nevertheless turn out for the best and to assure him of his own unwavering friendship and the goodwill of his government. He left the Residence with the feeling that the whole future was black.

In this mood Daville suddenly recalled the Kapidji Bashi, whom he had succeeded in forgetting. The death of that unfortunate man, which had not troubled anyone's conscience, began to disturb him once again, now that it had turned out to be of so little use.

At the beginning of the new year, the Vizier unobtrusively despatched his more valuable belongings and then, with his Mamelukes, he left Travnik himself. The joyful, vindictive whisper which began to spread among the Travnik Turks could no longer reach him. The only person who knew the date of his departure and went to see him off was Daville.

The parting of the Vizier and the Consul was cordial. On a sunny January day, Daville rode with d'Avenat four miles outside Travnik. In front of an isolated wayside inn, under a bower weighed down by snow, the Vizier and the Consul exchanged their last warm words and messages.

The Vizier rubbed his chilled hands, striving not to let his smile fade.

"Send my greetings to General Marmont," he said in that distinctive cordial tone which resembles sincerity as one drop of water does another and which leaves a convincing and soothing impression on even the most sceptical listener. "Pray tell him too, as well as anyone else who ought to know, that I shall remain a friend of your noble country, and a sincere admirer of the great Napoleon, wherever fate and circumstances cast me."

"I shall not fail to do so, I shall not fail," said Daville, genuinely moved.

"And to you, dear friend, I wish good health, fortune and success, regretting that I shall not be able to be at your side in the difficulties which you will always have with the uncultured and barbaric people of Bosnia. I have commended your affairs to Suleiman Pasha who will be deputizing for me temporarily. You may rely on him. He is a simple, uncouth man, like all Bosnians, but honourable and trustworthy. Let me say once more that it is only because of you that I regret leaving. But so it must be. Had I wished to be a scourge and a tyrant, I could have remained in this post and subdued those empty-headed arrogant beys forever, but I am not like that, nor do I wish to be. That is why I am leaving."

Shivering with cold and ashen pale, in his black cape which reached to the ground, d'Avenat translated mechanically and rapidly, as though he knew it all already.

Daville knew very well that what the Vizier was saying was not and could not be entirely accurate and yet every word touched him. Every parting arouses in us a double illusion. The person we are parting from, more or less forever, seems to us far worthier and more deserving of our attention, and we ourselves feel far more capable of generous and selfless friendship than we actually are.

Then the Vizier mounted his big sorrel horse, disguising his lameness with quick, sharp movements. His large retinue set off after him. And when the two groups, the Vizier's large one and the Consul's small one, had moved a little more than half a mile from each other, one of the Vizier's horsemen detached himself, like an arrow from a bow, swiftly reaching Daville and his escort who had halted. There he reined in his galloping horse and proclaimed loudly: "My fortunate master, Husref Mehmed Pasha, sends once more his respectful greetings to the esteemed representative of the great French Empire, and may his good wishes accompany your every step."

Surprised and somewhat bewildered, Daville removed his hat ceremoniously, and the horseman galloped off at the same speed after the Vizier's retinue as they rode over the snowy plain. In one's dealings with Eastern peoples, there are always details like this which give us a pleasant surprise and a thrill, although we know they are not so much a mark of attention or personal respect as an integral part of their ancient, inexhaustible ceremonial.

From the back, swathed against the cold, the Mamelukes looked like women. A powder of snow rose from under their horses' hooves, turning gradually in the winter sun into a pink and white cloud. The further it moved away, the tinier the group of horsemen seemed and the higher the cloud of powdery snow. Then they vanished in that cloud.

Daville went back along the frozen road that was barely distinguishable from the rest of the snowy whiteness. The roofs of the sparse peasants' houses, the fences and copses beside them were covered in snow and only suggested by a thin dark line against the white. The pink and yellow shadows were becoming blue and grey. The sky was darkening too. The sunny afternoon was passing rapidly into a wintery twilight.

The horses trod with strong, sure steps. Ice clung to the frozen tufts of hair behind their hooves, swaying as they walked.

Daville rode with the feeling that he was returning from a funeral.

He thought of the Vizier from whom he had only just parted, as though he were something long since irretrievably lost. He recalled details from their many conversations. He imagined he could see his smile, the mask of light which played all day over his lips and eyes, extinguished presumably only when he was asleep.

He remembered the Vizier's assurances, right up to the last moment, of his love of France and regard for the French. And now, in the light of this parting, he analysed their sincerity. He seemed to understand the Vizier's impulse clearly, as quite distinct from routine professional flattery. Altogether he felt that he now understood why and how foreigners admired France, the French way of life and looking at things. They admired her according to the law of opposites. They admired in her everything they could not find in their own country and for which their spirit had an irresistible craving. They admired France rightly, as an image of universal beauty and harmonious, rational living, which no momentary obscurity could alter or disfigure, and which after every inundation or eclipse reappears as an indestructible force and eternal joy. They admired France even when they knew her only superficially, slightly or even without knowing her at all. And she would be admired by many, always, often for the most contradictory reasons and motives, because people would never stop seeking a better life and wanting more than fate had granted them. And here he was himself thinking about France, not as his native land which he knew well and had always known and where he saw both good and ill, but about France as the kind of wonderful, distant land of harmony and perfection one always dreamed about in rough, wild surroundings. As long as Europe existed there would be a France and it could not disappear, unless in a certain sense (that is, in the sense of bright harmony and perfection) the whole of Europe were to become a France. But that was not possible. People were just too different, alien and distant from one another.

Then for some reason Daville recalled an experience with the Vizier from that summer. The lively and inquisitive Pasha had always enquired about French life and one day he told Daville that he had heard a great deal about the French theatre and would like at least to hear something of what was performed in France, since he could not see the real theatre.

Delighted with this request, Daville had arrived the very next day with the second volume of Racine's works under his arm, resolved to read the Vizier a few scenes from *Bajazet*. After coffee and chibouks had been brought, all the servants withdrew, apart from d'Avenat who was to translate. The Consul explained to the

Vizier, as best he could, what a theatre was, what it looked like and what was the aim and meaning of acting. Then he began to read from the scene which showed Bajazet entrusting Amurat with the care of the Sultana Roxane. The Vizier frowned, but he went on listening to d'Avenat's colourless translation and the Consul's impassioned reading. But when he reached the discussion between the Sultana and the Grand Vizier, Mehmed Pasha interrupted the reading, laughing heartily and waving his hand.

"Why, the man doesn't know what he's talking about!" said the Vizier reprovingly, but at the same time mockingly. "Ever since the world began, it has never happened that the Grand Vizier burst into the Harem and conversed with the Sultanas! It just couldn't happen!"

The Vizier had gone on laughing loudly and sincerely for a long time, not hiding the fact that he was disappointed and did not understand the purpose or value of such intellectual entertainment. And he said so openly, almost rudely, with the inconsiderateness of someone from a different civilization.

Cut to the quick, Daville tried in vain to explain the meaning of tragedy and the aim of poetry.

The Vizier waved him away implacably with his hand: "Ah yes, we too have all sorts of dervishes and pious folk who recite sonorous verses. We give them alms, but we never dream of treating them like people with a position and reputation. No, no, I don't understand."

From then on, Daville had thought of that experience as something both insulting and unpleasant, one of his secret failures. Now, however, he looked on it all more calmly, the way we look on comical situations which hurt us inordinately in our childhood. He was simply surprised that he should have suddenly recalled that trivial incident, at this moment, out of all the serious business and important things he had experienced with Mehmed Pasha.

Now, returning along the snow-covered road into the shrouded town after saying goodbye to the Vizier, everything seemed altogether clear, justified and appropriate. Misunderstandings are natural and failures inevitable. And even this painful departure of Mehmed Pasha's now hurt him in a different way. The full weight of his loss still confronted him. And he was also afraid of new misfortunes, new failures. But for now it all seemed muffled and distant, an inevitable part of life in which, according to some incomprehensible calculation, one both lost and gained along the way.

With these thoughts, which seemed new and unusual even to him, but at least momentarily comforting, he reached Travnik rapidly, before dark.

The departure of Husref Mehmed Pasha was the signal for a riot of the Travnik Turks. No one doubted any longer that the Vizier had cunningly escaped the wrath of the bazaar. It was known also that the French Consul had seen him on his way. This still further increased their anger.

Here, then, was a chance to see what a riot in the Turkish bazaar of a small Bosnian town could be like.

For several years the bazaar would work quietly, bored, subsisting, doing business, making calculations, comparing one year with another, but all the time people kept an eye on events, gathered news, acquired information and gossip, passing it in a whisper from shop to shop, avoiding any conclusion or opinion of their own. This is how the unique spirit of the bazaar was shaped. At first it was just a vague general mood, manifested only in brief gestures and curses with everyone knowing whom they referred to. Then it gradually evolved into an attitude which was not concealed. And finally it became a firm conviction which there was no longer any need to talk about as it was expressed now in actions.

United by this all-pervasive conviction, the bazaar whispered, prepared, waited, as bees wait for the time to swarm. It is impossible to penetrate the logic of these bazaar riots, blind, furious and always fruitless, but they do have a logic of their own, just as they have an imperceptible technique, based on tradition and instinct. All one sees is that they erupt, rage and subside.

Quite simply, one day, which dawns like so many others, the prolonged sleepy silence of the town is broken. Shutters clatter and the latches and bolts of shop doors thud shut. All at once, the shopkeepers leap from the places where they have sat cross-legged and motionless for years, calm, orderly, clean, proudly obliging, in their felt trousers, braided waistcoats and brightly striped shirts. This ritual stirring and the deafening banging of doors and shutters is enough for the word to spread like lightning through the whole town and neighbourhood: "The bazaar is shut."

These are grave, ominous words. Their implications are clear to everyone. The women and children go down into the cellars. The more prominent people withdraw into their houses, ready to defend them and die on their threshold. But the humbler Turkish folk begin to swarm down from the small cafés and remote quarters, people who have nothing to lose and can never gain anything except through riot and change. (For here too, as in all disturbances throughout the world, there are those who set things in motion and lead them, and others who carry them out.) One or two leaders spring up from somewhere at the head of the mob. These are usually loud-mouthed, violent, discontented underdogs and misfits whom no one has known or noticed until then and who will disappear again, once the riot has subsided, into their anonymous poverty in the steep outskirts they came from, or stay to rot in some gaol.

And this may last a day or two, sometimes three or five days, until something or other is broken or burnt, until blood is spilled or the disturbance simply abates of its own accord.

Then the shops open one by one, the rabble retreats, and the bazaar people, pale and solemn, as though ashamed or hung-over, carry on with their business and their ordinary life.

This is the typical pattern of the beginning, progress and end of riots in our towns.

And that is how it went on this occasion as well. For years the Travnik bazaar people, like all the Bosnian beys, had followed the attempts of Selim III to reorganize the Turkish Empire on a new basis, according to the demands and requirements of contemporary European life. The bazaar people did not hide their suspicious hatred of the Sultan's endeavours, expressing it frequently in direct petitions which they sent to Istanbul, and in their attitude to the Sultan's representative, the Travnik Vizier. For them it was clear that the reforms would only assist foreigners to undermine the Empire and destroy it from within, and that their ultimate consequences would mean for the Muslim population and consequently for each of them personally loss of their faith, possessions, family, and their life in this world, and eternal damnation.

As soon as it was discovered that the Vizier had set off ostensibly for the Drina, to inspect the situation and positions there, there was a spell of the tense silence that precedes explosions of popular fury. In whispers and glances people began to make arrangements no one else could understand. The riot was ready and awaiting its moment.

As usual, the pretext for the explosion was incidental and trivial.

César d'Avenat had in his service, as his trusted errand-boy, a certain Mehmed, known as "Whiskers", a broad-shouldered, tall Hercegovinian. Everyone who was employed by the foreign consulates was hated by the local Turks, but this Mehmed especially so. That same winter he had married a beautiful young Turkish girl who had come from Belgrade to visit relatives in Travnik. The girl had been married in Belgrade to a certain Bekri-Mustapha who kept an inn in a large house in the Dorcol district. Four witnesses, all Travnik Turks, had sworn on oath that Bekri-Mustapha had died from an excess of alcohol and that his wife was free. Thereupon the Cadi had married the girl to Mehmed.

Just at the time of the Vizier's departure, this Bekri-Mustapha suddenly turned up in Travnik, blind drunk, but alive, and looking for his wife. At first the Cadi refused him, as he was so drunk and had no documents. The inn-keeper kept explaining that he had spent eleven days on the journey from Belgrade to Travnik, through snowdrifts and terrible cold, and that was why he had had to drink so much brandy that now he simply could not sober up. He was only asking for his rights: to get back the wife someone else had married by fraud.

The bazaar became involved. Everyone felt that this was the best opportunity to get their own back on the hated khavaz Mehmed, his master d'Avenat, the Consuls and Consulates in general. They considered it their duty to help an honest Muslim in defence of his rights, against these foreigners and their servants. And Bekri-Mustapha, who had come through the terrible cold with no coat or proper footwear, "without a bean", warming himself only with brandy and eating onions, was now suddenly bundled into warm clothes, fed, wined and tended by the whole bazaar. Someone gave him a fur-lined woman's cloak with moth-eaten fox fur round the neck, which he wore with great dignity. Hiccuping and blinking, he made his way from shop to shop, borne along by communal care and benevolence, like a flag, demanding his rights more loudly and insistently than ever. He did not actually sober up, but this was not necessary for the defence of his rights, for the bazaar had taken the affair into its own hands.

When the Cadi refused decisively to return the woman to the drunken man simply on his word, the bazaar erupted. The long-awaited riot finally found its pretext and was able to break out openly and run its course unhindered. And it began, even though winter days are not suitable for such things which usually occur in summer or autumn.

None of the foreigners could have imagined the nature and

extent of this attack of collective madness which from time to time overwhelms the population of these small towns, lost and cramped between the high mountains. Even for d'Avenat, who knew the East, but not yet Bosnia, this was new and it made him anxious at least at times. Daville shut himself up in the Consulate with his family, expecting the worst.

That winter's day, an hour before noon, the bazaar was closed, as though at an invisible, secret sign. There was a clatter of shutters, doors and bolts which rumbled like the cracking and rolling of summer thunderstorms with hail and lightning, as though avalanches of rocks were hurtling down the steep Travnik slopes on all sides, with a loud roar, threatening to bury the town and all living things in it.

In the silence which set in immediately after this, a few shots and wild cries rang out, and then, first with a murmur and then with a deafening clamour, a crowd of the humblest people, children and youths, began to gather. When the mob had grown to two or three hundred, it set off, at first hesitating but then quickly and decisively towards the French Consulate. They brandished sticks, waving their arms as they went. Most of their shouting was directed against the Cadi, who had married Bekri-Mustapha's wife and was in any case known as a supporter of Selim's reforms and a Vizier's man.

One utterly unknown man with a long moustache shouted at the top of his voice that it was because of people like this that now true believers no longer dared raise their heads and their children were starving. He hurled abuse at the detested Mehmed who served the faithless and ate pork, telling them that they should arrest him at once and clap him in irons along with the Cadi who stole the wives of true Turks and married them off to others for money, and who was not in fact a Cadi, but a turncoat, worse than any Christian priest. As he listened attentively to the speaker with the moustache, a small sallow man, otherwise a modest, timid tailor from the lower bazaar who no one even in his own household had ever heard utter a loud word, suddenly screwed up his eyes, raised his head and bellowed with unexpected power, wildly and hoarsely, as though in revenge for his long silence:

"To Vranduk gaol with the priest-Cadi!"

This encouraged the others too. They began shouting, cursing the Cadi, the Vizier, the Consulate and, especially Mehmed-Whiskers. Timid youths would spend a long time getting ready, whispering to themselves like actors rehearsing a part, and then start to run, raising their heads in excitement, as though they were going to burst into song, shouting the cry they had composed. And then, blushing with excitement and trepidation, they would listen to the echo, loud or weak, of their cry in the muttering and cheering of the mob. So they encouraged one another, becoming increasingly caught up in the intoxicating sense that each one of them was free, within the limits of the riot, to shout and do whatever he liked, giving vent to everything that oppressed and troubled him.

Suleiman Pasha Skopljak, the Deputy Vizier, knowing quite well what a Travnik riot meant and how it would go, but without losing sight of his responsibility to the Consulate, did what was most sensible in the circumstances. He ordered that the Consul's servant Mehmed be arrested and shut up in the fortress.

The crowd which had gathered in front of the Consulate was incensed, because there was a broad courtyard and large garden round the house which prevented them from reaching the building even with a stone. Just as the mob was hesitating, wondering what to do, someone shouted that Mehmed was being taken away through the back streets. The rabble set off up the hill and ran to the bridge in front of the fortress. The servant had already been taken in and the great iron gates were locked behind him. Now there was some confusion. The majority began to go back to the town, singing, but several continued to stand by the moat looking at the windows in the gate tower, expecting something. And they shouted loudly, proposing the cruellest punishments and torture for the prisoner.

The empty bazaar, as though swept by a strong wind, was filled with the mumbling and cries of the idle people, who were only half satisfied by Mehmed's arrest. All at once that stopped as well. People began glancing and calling to one another. Heads began to turn inquisitively in all directions. The mob had reached that moment of boredom and fatigue when it is ready to accept any change or distraction, cruel and bloody, or benign and joking. Finally, the glances focused on the steep street leading from the French Consulate to the bazaar.

Out of that street, through the thinning crowd, armed and solemn, came d'Avenat on his big dappled mare. Everyone stopped wherever he happened to be in surprise and watched the horseman ride calmly and nonchalantly as though there were a whole company of cavalry behind him. Had just one person called out anything, they would all have started shouting and there would have been uproar and turmoil in which stones would soon have been thrown. The people would have engulfed horse and rider like water. As it was, everyone wanted to see what the Consul's bold interpreter intended to do and where he was going, and then to join in any ensuing action. So it happened that no one shouted anything and the mob stood expectantly, without common will or specific aim. Instead, d'Avenat yelled loudly and brazenly, as only a Levantine can, bending now to the left and now to the right as though herding cattle. He was deathly pale. His eyes were burning, his mouth wide open.

"Just you dare lay a finger on the Imperial French Consulate!" he shouted, looking straight into the eyes of those closest to him, and continued: "Have you come here to attack us, your best friends? Only an idiot with his brains addled by Bosnian brandy could have talked you into that. You don't realize that the new Sultan and the

French Emperor are the best of friends! Word has already come from Istanbul that everyone must take care of the French Consul and respect him as a Guest of the State."

Someone in the crowd mumbled something indistinctly, but the mob did not take it up. D'Avenat exploited this and, turning to that isolated voice, faced the speaker, addressing only him, as though all the others were on d'Avenat's side and he was speaking in their name.

"What? What did you say? You want to ruin everything the Emperors have agreed and decided? Okay, let everyone see who it is who's pushing these peace-loving people into disaster. For let me tell you the Sultan won't stand for it. The whole of Bosnia will be put to flames if anything happens to our Consulate. No child in its cradle will be spared!"

More voices were heard, but muffled and isolated. The crowd moved aside in front of the horseman who looked as though it had not occurred to him that he could come to any harm. And he rode through the whole bazaar like that, shouting angrily that he was on his way to Suleiman Pasha to ask him who was in charge here, and that after that, they could be sure, many people would regret having followed a few hotheads against the highest authorities.

And d'Avenat disappeared across the bridge. The furrow left behind him in the throng closed up again, but the mob felt defeated, tamed, at least for a moment. Now everyone wondered why they had let this infidel ride freely and impudently past them, why they had not crushed him like a bug. But now it was too late. They had missed their chance. The people were thrown off course. They would have to start all over again.

Taking advantage of this confusion and the temporary faint-heartedness of the rabble, d'Avenat rode back to the Consulate, just as boldly and unhurriedly. He did not shout now. He just looked defiantly around him, nodding his head meaningfully and threateningly as though he had fixed things at the Residence and knew exactly what was in store for them.

In fact, d'Avenat's attempt to speak somewhat sharply and haughtily to Suleiman Pasha had not met with any success. The Deputy was not going to be upset or alarmed by d'Avenat's threats or by the Travnik riot. He spoke of the riot just as he had once defended the Travnik winter, maintaining to the Vizier that it was no misfortune, but God's gift and a necessity. It was nothing, he conveyed to Daville, a rising of the populace, an ignorant herd. It happened from time to time. They would shout and yell for a bit, then calm down, and shouting never hurt anyone. No one would dare touch the Consulate. And the fate of the lad Mehmed was a matter for Islamic law. They would interrogate him, and if he was guilty, he would be punished and would have to give his wife back. If he was innocent, nothing would happen to him. Everything else was unchanged and in its rightful place.

That was the message Suleiman Pasha sent Daville, speaking slowly in his halting Turkish, with his coarse accent and numerous unintelligible local expressions. He had not wished to enter into any discussion with d'Avenat himself, however hard the interpreter tried to force him to. He dismissed him like a Turkish servant with the words:

"There. That is what I tell you. Remember it well and translate it accurately for the good Consul."

But the riot continued to swell. Nothing helped, neither d'Avenat's boldness nor Suleiman Pasha's Turkish deliberate belittling of it and looking on the bright side.

Towards evening that day an even larger and more unruly mob came down from the outlying quarters and poured through the bazaar, with the youths all yelling. During the night some dubious characters approached the Consulate building, making the dogs bark. The Consul's servants were keeping guard.

The following day hemp and tar were found, intended for setting fire to the Consulate.

The next day, with the same courage, d'Avenat sought and gained permission to enter the fortress and visit the prisoner. He found him tied up in a dark cell, known as the Well, where they lowered people condemned to death. The man really was more dead than alive, for the Fortress Governor, not knowing the real reason for his arrest, had ordered him to be beaten a hundred times on the soles of his feet, to be on the safe side. D'Avenat did not succeed in getting the unfortunate man released, but he found a way of bribing the guard to alleviate conditions for him.

To make things still more awkward for Daville, it so happened that two of the French officers sent from Split to Istanbul turned up in Travnik at precisely that time. For although it had long since become not only unnecessary but actually damaging to send these officers, and although Daville had been imploring the authorities for months not to send anyone or at least not to send them through Bosnia, where it provoked the hatred and distrust of the people, nevertheless it still happened from time to time that two or three officers would set off on the journey on the basis of some old order.

The riot confined these officers, like everyone else, within the Consulate building. But, on the first day, the officers, inconsiderate, arrogant and impatient men, had tried to ride outside the town regardless of the riot.

As soon as they had moved some way from the Consulate and reached the outlying quarters, snowballs began to fly at them. The town children ran after the horsemen, pelting them harder and harder. Small boys ran out of all the gates, with flushed cheeks and wild eyes, shouting and yelling:

"Look, a Christian! Get him!"

"Get the infidel!"

"Pay up, Christian scum!"

The officers watched them running to the fountain and soaking their snowballs in water, to make them heavier. They were in an awkward dilemma, for they did not want to spur their horses on and run away, nor would they fight with the children, but they could not calmly put up with their savage pranks. They returned to the Consulate, furious and humiliated.

And, with the yells of the crowd reaching them from the bazaar, the Engineer Major, imprisoned in the Consulate, wrote his report to the Command in Split.

"We are fortunate that there was snow," wrote the Major, "otherwise these savages would have hit us with stones and mud. I was seething with shame and fury and when this ridiculous situation became unbearable, I hurled my crop among the children, who scattered for a moment, but gathered again immediately and began to chase us with an even louder din. We only just made it to the town. The Consulate interpreter went so far as to maintain that it was lucky my crop did not hit one of the children, as it could have cost us our lives at the hands of the adults, for they are no better and it was they who put those wretched children up to it."

Daville endeavoured to explain it all to the officers, but was secretly mortified that he had the Frenchmen as witnesses of his impotence and the humiliation in which he lived.

On the third day, the bazaar was opened. One by one, the shopkeepers arrived, raised their shutters, sat down in their places and started work. They all looked stiffer and still more solemn, a little ashamed and pale, as after a wild spree.

That was the signal for things to calm down. Idlers and children still came, roaming through the town, blowing on their frozen hands. Sometimes one would shout something against anyone he could think of, but his yells did not meet with any response. No one emerged from the Consulate yet, except d'Avenat and servants on the most essential errands, and they were accompanied by threats, snowballs and an occasional gunshot. But the riot was drawing to its natural end. The French Consul had been shown what people thought of him and his stay in Travnik. D'Avenat's hated servant was punished. His wife, who was taken from him, was not given back to Bekri-Mustapha, but sent to her family. And Bekri-Mustapha himself suddenly lost all importance for the bazaar. No one took any notice of him. As though now sober, people asked who this drunken tramp was and what he was doing there. They would not allow him to approach their shops or warm himself at their braziers. He staggered about for a few more days, selling piece by piece the clothing people had given him in their first enthusiasm, for brandy, and then he disappeared from Travnik forever.

So the riot itself came to an end. But the difficulties the Consul had to contend with did not become any less. On the contrary, they were increasingly great and numerous. Daville came upon them at every step.

Finally, Mehmed Whiskers was released from prison, battered, crushed, and bitter at the loss of his wife. In response to Daville's strong protests, Suleiman Pasha did actually order the Fortress Governor to go and apologize to the Consul for the arrest of his servant, the insulting abuse against the French and the attack on the Consulate building. But the Governor, a stubborn proud old man, announced resolutely that he would relinquish his post and, if necessary, give the head from his shoulders, rather than go to the faithless Consul to beg for forgiveness. And that was the end of it.

All the other servants at the Consulate were alarmed by the example of Mehmed Whiskers. In the streets they were met by glances full of hatred. The shopkeepers refused to sell them anything. The Albanian khavaz, Hussein, proud of his position, would walk through the bazaar, pale with anger, and stop in front of the shops. Whatever he asked for, the Turkish shopkeeper would reply with a scowl from where he was sitting in the raised shop-front, that there wasn't any. The goods he had asked for were often hanging just there, within his reach, and when the khavaz pointed that out, the shopkeeper would either reply calmly that they had been sold, or else would flare up:

"When I say there isn't any, there isn't any. For you – there isn't!"

They acquired things surreptitiously from the Catholics and Jews.

Daville felt the hatred against him and the Consulate grow with every day. He felt he could see how that hatred would simply wash him out of Travnik. It deprived him of his sleep, paralysed his will and nipped every decision in the bud. All the servants felt powerless as well, persecuted and inadequately protected from the general hostility. Only their innate sense of shame and loyalty to good masters prevented them from leaving their posts in the hated Consulate. It was only d'Avenat who remained imperturbable and dauntlessly insolent. The hatred which was becoming increasingly dense around the isolated Consulate in Travnik did not disturb or alarm him. He remained unshakeably true to his principle: that one should flatter, consistently and single-mindedly, the few powerful people at the top, while to everyone else one should show nothing but force and contempt. For the Turks feared only those who were not afraid and shrank only from those stronger than themselves. Such inhuman behaviour was perfectly suited to d'Avenat's outlook and habits.

9

Exhausted by the demands made on him by the events of the last months, dissatisfied with the lack of understanding and inadequate support offered him by Paris, General Marmont in Split and the Ambassador in Istanbul, disturbed by the malice and distrust with which the Travnik Turks followed his every step and anything whatever to do with the French, Daville was increasingly conscious of the sad loss of Mehmed Pasha. Isolated and irritated, he began to look at everything in a particular light and from an unusual angle. Things had somehow become big, important, difficult and beyond redemption, almost tragic. In the replacement of the former Vizier, a "friend of the French", he saw not only his personal misfortune, but also proof of the weakness of French influence in Istanbul and a serious failure of national policy.

Privately, Daville increasingly regretted ever having accepted this post, which was evidently so difficult that no one wanted it. He particularly regretted having brought his family. He realized that he had both deceived himself and been deceived, that in this place he would, most probably, forfeit both his own prestige and the health of his wife and children. At every step he felt persecuted and powerless and, as a result he did not expect anything good or reassuring from the future either.

Everything he had so far been able to find out about the new Vizier alarmed him. It was true that Ibrahim Halimi Pasha was one of Selim III's men, and had even been his Grand Vizier for a time, but he was not himself particularly enthusiastic about the reforms and still less was he a special friend of the French. His unconditional devotion to Selim was well-known and this was the only thing for which he was renowned. After Selim was dethroned, it was said that he had been close to death himself, and the new government of Sultan Mustapha had sent him as governor first to Salonika and then straight to Bosnia, just as a corpse is removed from view. People said he was a man of good breeding but mediocre abilities, still completely bewildered by his recent fall and bitter about the unenviable post he was being sent to. What could Daville expect for the French cause and what could he hope for himself from such a Vizier, when even the adroit and ambitious Mehmed Pasha had been unable to do anything? So, Daville awaited the new Vizier with trepidation, as yet another misfortune in the long series of misfortunes his posting to Bosnia had brought him.

Ibrahim Pasha arrived at the beginning of March, with a whole host of staff and caravan of belongings. His harem had been left in Istanbul. As soon as he had settled in and rested, the new Vizier received the Consuls at a formal audience.

Daville was received first.

His ceremonial progress through the town did not pass off without threats and abuse this time either. (Daville had prepared his young Secretary for this.) But there was less of it and it was all far milder than the first time. A few loud curses and a few threatening or mocking gestures were the only expression of the general hatred of the foreign Consulates. Daville saw with sour satisfaction that his Austrian opponent, who was received the following day, did not fare any better at the hands of the common Turkish people.

The ceremonial with which Daville was met at the Residence was the same as under the former Vizier. The gifts were more lavish and the refreshments more abundant. The new Secretary at the Consulate was given an ermine coat, while once again Daville was draped with marten. But what was of particular importance for Daville was the fact that the Vizier kept him in conversation a good half hour longer than the Austrian Consul the following day.

Otherwise, Daville was really surprised by the new Vizier's style and his whole appearance. It was as though fate had wished to play a joke on the Consul by sending him the absolute opposite of Mehmed Pasha, with whom it was at least easy to work even if not always productive. (Isolated consuls easily begin to see themselves not only as abandoned by their government and persecuted by their opponents, but also as people whom destiny has singled out and attacked with special malice.) Instead of a young, lively and agreeable Georgian, Daville found himself at the Divan confronting a heavy, immobile and cold Ottoman whose appearance frightened and repelled him. Even if discussions with Mehmed Pasha had not always brought what they promised, they had at least left the Consul with a certain cheerfulness, a readiness for work and further negotiations. With this Ibrahim Pasha it seemed that every discussion would be bound to infect one with ill-will, sadness and quiet desperation.

He was a walking ruin. A ruin devoid of beauty or grandeur, or with only the grandeur of horror. If the dead could walk, they would perhaps inspire the living with more fear and surprise, but with less of that cold horror which freezes the gaze, stifles speech and makes the outstretched hand draw back. The Vizier had a broad, bloodless face, folded into a few very deep wrinkles, with a thin beard which was also in its own way colourless, like long-dead grass, flattened and bleached in the crevices of a cliff. This face stood out strangely from the huge turban which was pushed down to his eyebrows and over his ears. This turban was artistically wound of the finest material, white with pinkish glints, with a decoration in the front, just hinted at, embroidered in gold thread and green silk. And it stuck up curiously on his head as though someone else's hand had placed it, in the dark, on a corpse which would never again adjust or remove it, for it was destined to be buried and rot with him. Everything else about this man, from his neck to the ground, looked like one single block in which it was hard to distinguish arms, legs and waist. It was not possible to assess what kind of body it was that lived under this heap of thick cloth, leather, silk, silver and braid. It might have been small and weak, but just as easily strong and large. And, strangest of all, in the rare moments when it did move, this heavy mass of clothing and jewellery sometimes made the unexpectedly quick and energetic movements of a younger, nervous man. But all the while the large, ancient face remained immobile and expressionless. It looked as though this death's-head and stiff pile of clothes were being moved from the inside by unseen springs and coils.

All this gave the Vizier a ghostly appearance and filled whoever he was talking to with confused feelings of fear and disgust, pity and discomfort.

This was the impression the new Vizier made on the Consul on the occasion of his first visit.

With time, living and working with Ibrahim Pasha, Daville would grow accustomed to him, make real friends with him and recognize that under his unusual appearance there was hidden a man who was without neither heart nor brains, a man who had been driven to absolute despair, but who was not inaccessible to all the finer feelings known and permitted by his race and caste. But now, judging by this first impression, Daville thought with grim apprehension of his future co-operation with the new Vizier, who resembled a scarecrow, a sumptuous one, however, not suited to the meagre fields of this country, but intended in some fantastic landscape to ward off birds of paradise of unusual form and colour.

Among the throng at the Residence, Daville noticed many more new and unusual faces. As d'Avenat had gone over completely to the service of the French Consul, he no longer had free access to the Residence as in the time of Mehmed Pasha. Nevertheless, with time, he found ways and means of informing himself about everything: the Vizier, the main personalities, the relations between them and the way in which the more important business was conducted.

Not having much to do and driven by his natural zeal and curiosity, and partly also out of an unconscious desire to imitate the old royal ambassadors whose reports he enjoyed reading, Daville endeavoured to gain an insight into the personal life of the Vizier and the private affairs of his household. He tried, on the model of the old diplomacy, to get to know "the mood, habits, passions and inclinations of the rulers to whom he was accredited", so as to exert influence and carry out his intentions more easily.

D'Avenat, who deplored having to live in this Bosnian wilderness rather than at an Embassy or in the service of a Vizier in Istanbul, as suited his abilities and the opinion he himself had of them, was the very person to find out and pass on all this information. With all the brazenness of a Levantine, the conscientiousness of a doctor and the cleverness of a Piedmontese, he knew how to discover everything and recount it drily, factually and thoroughly, with details which were sometimes of interest to the Consul, invariably useful, but often disagreeable and repellent.

Just as there was no similarity between the two Viziers, so were their associates also completely different. The people whom Mehmed Pasha had brought and taken away with him had been on the whole quite young, mostly soldiers by profession, and in any case all good riders and huntsmen. There had been no unusual personalities among them, who would stand out from the others and attract particular attention for their physical or intellectual qualities, good and bad. They had all been capable, average people, unconditionally loyal to Mehmed Pasha, but they had resembled one another, almost like those thirty-two Mamelukes of the Vizier's who were like toys with expressionless faces, and all of the same build and features.

Ibrahim Pasha's "household" was altogether different. There were both more of them numerically and they were more various in character and appearance. Even d'Avenat himself, who knew most of the Turks' secrets, sometimes wondered in surprise where the Vizier had found this extraordinary gang, why he was dragging them about with him all over the world and how he managed to keep them all in one place. Unlike the majority of the viziers, Ibrahim Pasha was not a parvenu of unknown origin. His father and grandfather had both been high dignitaries and wealthy men. So the family had accumulated numerous slaves, agents, protégés and servants, adopted children, dependants and relatives of uncertain and indeterminate degree of kinship, sycophants and hangers-on of every kind. In the course of his long, turbulent life and career, the Vizier had made use of all kinds of people for various needs, particularly during the time he was the Grand Vizier to Selim III. The majority of these people no longer parted from him even when the task for which they were taken on had long since been completed. Clinging to the Vizier, "like clams to an old ship", they remained linked to his fate, or rather to his kitchen and his treasury. Some of them were very old and incapacitated, never going out into the light of day and having to be cared for in their little rooms, somewhere in the depths of the Residence. They had once been in Ibrahim Pasha's service and done him some considerable favour, which the Vizier had long since forgotten and which they themselves only dimly remembered. Others were young and stout, without specific occupation or position. Some of them had even been born in Ibrahim Pasha's "house", for their fathers were in his service. There they had grown up and there they would live out their lives without obvious reason or justification. And there were also some brazen spongers and the usual few begging dervishes.

In short, d'Avenat was not greatly exaggerating when in his reports to Daville he referred, with his insolent smile, to the new Vizier's Residence as a "museum of freaks".

The Vizier accepted all these people without any resistance, put up with them, dragged them about with him, tolerating their faults and their mutual conflicts, feuds and quarrels, with superstitious patience.

Even those who occupied the higher positions and did real jobs were mostly eccentric and only rarely ordinary, everyday people.

Among them the first place, both in importance and in official influence, was undoubtedly that of the Vizier's Secretary, Tahir Bey, who had Ibrahim Pasha's complete confidence and was his chief adviser in all matters. He was a sick, idiosyncratic man, but benign and exceptionally intelligent. Opinion about him was sharply divided both in the town and the Residence, but it was indisputable, and here the townspeople and the Consuls were all in agreement, that Tahir Bey was the brains of the Residence, "the Vizier's right hand and the pen in that hand".

As happened with every higher Ottoman dignitary, he too was preceded by his reputation, distorted and magnified along the way. The Travnik ulema, as numerous as they were envious, bit their lips spitefully and consoled themselves with the thought that he was just a man, and that there was nothing, apart from the Heavens above, which could not be "embellished or diminished". And in fact, before Tahir Bey was half way there, they had succeeded in both enhancing and detracting from his reputation. Someone who had come from Istanbul and talked about Tahir Bey's learning and intelligence said that while he was still at school he had been called the "Fount of Knowledge". In Travnik he immediately became known as "Fount Effendi".

That was typical of the prominent and well-bred people of Travnik, particularly these educated ones. They were adept at finding a vicious word or disparaging name for anything they did not have, did not know or could not do. This was their way of participating in everything, even the most exalted affairs, in which they could otherwise never have had any part.

But, when Tahir Bey arrived in Travnik, the sardonic nickname could not get a hold among the people. It went back to the ulema who had been too hasty in inventing it. Confronted with the new Secretary, every insult and thought of derision evaporated of its own accord. After just a few weeks the people called him only The Effendi, pronouncing this everyday word with respect and a special emphasis. So there were in Travnik at the time many effendis, literate and semi-literate scribes, hafizes, mullahs and hodjas, but only one Effendi.

Scholarship, the knowledge of foreign languages and a talent for writing were a tradition in Tahir Bey's family. His grandfather was a compiler of dictionaries and commentaries, his father a First Secretary at the Porte who had ended his days as Chief Adviser Reis Effendi. Tahir Bey would have succeeded his father had there not been the coup which dethroned Sultan Selim and drove the Grand Vizier Ibrahim Pasha first to Salonica and then to Travnik.

Tahir Bey was only just thirty-six, but he looked far older. He had grown from a precocious boy into a sickly, heavy, elderly man, virtually without transition. And that was the way he lived and worked. After all he had been through at Ibrahim Pasha's side as Grand Vizier in the most difficult times, and as a consequence of a disease which was making increasing inroads into his otherwise strong and well-proportioned body, he was now seriously ill. He moved slowly and reluctantly, but visibly exuded a desire for life and an unusual strength of mind.

Had he known how to live a little more moderately or had he been prepared to give up his work, it could be that his Istanbul doctor might have been able to cure him at an early stage. As it was, the unusual illness had established itself irreversibly and Tahir Bey had reconciled himself to living as an invalid. He had a raw wound on his left thigh, which would open and close up several times in the course of a year. This had made him bent at the waist and slow in his step. In winter or when there was a strong south wind, he was troubled by pains and insomnia and then he had to increase his dose of alcohol and sleeping draughts.

Since he no longer had his Istanbul doctor, Tahir Bey dressed his wound himself, just as he suffered his whole illness, secretly, never complaining and without disturbing anyone.

It is true that the numerous professions in Ibrahim Pasha's household included also the post of doctor to the Vizier. But the doctor was the ancient, witty Eshref Effendi, who had forgotten even what he had once known, to say nothing of the doctor's craft of which he had never had much inkling. In his youth he had been something like an apothecary, but he had spent half his life in the army, in battlefields and camps, where he "treated" people more by the power of suggestion of his warm nature and irrepressible goodwill than by knowledge or medicines. Ibrahim Pasha had long since removed him from the army and taken him with him wherever he went, far more as an agreeable companion than a doctor. Once an ardent hunter, particularly of wild duck, now he was almost completely paralysed by rheumatism in his legs and spent most of the time sitting somewhere in the sun or a warm room, always in boots with high cloth tops. He was a lively man, witty and sharp-tongued, but loved and respected by all.

Needless to say, it did not occur to Tahir Bey to consult this Eshref Effendi with whom he otherwise enjoyed joking and chatting.

He always kept ready and carefully arranged in a special chest both narrow and wide bandages, cotton wool, lotions and ointments. It was a finely carved and skilfully made little chest of the kind of rare wood that becomes lovelier as it ages and the longer it is used. Tahir Bey's grandfather used to lock his manuscripts in this chest, his father had kept money in it and now he used it for his medicines and bandages.

On the days when he was ill, specially heated warm water would be prepared for the Secretary every morning at the same hour, and then the long, painful, almost pious process of washing, cleaning and dressing the wound would begin. Alone, behind his locked door, he would carefully rinse his wound and change the ointments and bandages, his jaws tightly clenched and his brows deeply furrowed. And this often went on for hours.

These were secret hours of torment in the Secretary's life. But they also contained all his troubles and all his bitterness, unspoken and buried. For when, finally, he had bound and belted himself, laced himself up and finished dressing, the Secretary would emerge tranquil and strong, completely changed, among his fellow-men. His piercing eyes shone out of his cold, motionless face, and his thin lips trembled barely perceptibly. Now there was nothing daunting for him in the world, no insoluble problems, no dangerous people or insurmountable difficulties. This chronically sick invalid was more robust than the healthiest man and more adroit than the toughest.

It was his eyes that betrayed the true life and real strength of this man. At one moment they were the large, shining eyes of great men raised above everything by the power of their mind. Then they became the sharp, narrow, light-golden eyes of some wild animals – martens or weasels – gleaming and cold, with no discrimination or mercy. And then they were the laughing eyes of a capricious but generous boy, with the carefree beauty that is the natural gift of youth. The whole man lived through his eyes. His voice was hoarse, his movements rare and slow.

Tahir Bey had far more influence on the Vizier than any of his other associates. His was the advice the Pasha most often sought and always heeded. He was entrusted with difficult, delicate questions, which the Deputy often did not even know existed. He always solved them swiftly, naturally and easily, with few words, with that golden gleam in his eyes, never returning to the matter again.

He gave of his knowledge and cleverness lavishly and unselfishly, like a man who has too much and is accustomed to giving, and who needs nothing himself. He was equally well acquainted with Islamic law, military and financial affairs. He knew Persian and Greek. He wrote a perfect hand and had his own collection of verses which Sultan Selim had known and loved.

Tahir Bey was one of the few Ottomans in the Residence who never complained about his exile to Bosnia, about the wild land and crude populace. Privately, he missed Istanbul, being more used than the others to the luxuries and pleasures of life in the capital. But he kept this regret hidden too, like his wounds, "nursing" it unseen and alone.

The absolute opposite of Tahir Bey and his irreconcilable and helpless adversary was the Treasurer Baki, known in the Residence by the name of "Kaki". He was a physical and mental freak, a monstrous calculating machine, a man hated by all and who expected nothing different. It was out of habit rather than need that he had long since become indispensable to the Vizier. Ibrahim Pasha, who otherwise liked only quiet, generous-natured people, tolerated this malicious eccentric at his side through some superstitious instinct, as a kind of amulet which attracted to itself all hatred and evil from near and far, although he never admitted this even to himself. Tahir Bey used to say he was the "Vizier's house snake".

A man with no wife or friends, Baki had been keeping the Vizier's accounts for years now, conscientiously and accurately in his way, saving every last grosch with the tenacity of an inveterate miser and defending it from everyone, including the Vizier himself. His life, which was quite devoid of personal happiness, was completely dedicated to a selfish adoration of himself and a struggle against expenditure of any kind, anywhere and on anyone's behalf. Limitlessly and cruelly spiteful, he did not actually gain anything from his spite, for he needed nothing from life, apart from that spite.

He was a short, fleshy man, without beard or moustache, with thin, sallow, transparent skin which looked as though it were filled not with bones and muscle, but with a colourless fluid or air. His puffy yellow cheeks drooped like bags. Above them swam two shifty eyes, blue and clear, like the eyes of small children, but always worried and mistrustful. Those eyes never smiled. His coat and shirt were cut low at his neck which was swollen and ringed with a triple, deep furrow, like the necks of fat, anaemic women. The whole man looked like a large wrinkled wineskin which would pop with a hissing sound if punctured with a needle. The whole of his body quivered with its own breath and trembled with fear at any contact with anything that was not itself.

He knew nothing of joking or enjoyment. He said little, only what he had prepared in advance and as much as he needed. He would listen attentively, observing rapturously himself and everything he regarded as his. Had he had two lives, they would not have been enough for that activity. He ate little and drank only water, for he had no teeth to chew with or stomach to digest, and every mouthful he saved was sweeter than any he ate. But since it was necessary to eat, he would mould and reshape every crumb, studying it tenderly, for it was to become part of his body.

This man was always cold, everywhere, at any time of year. His sensitive skin and slack body did not allow him to put on as many clothes as he needed. The touch of a hem or seam irritated him and could make him pity himself to the point of tears. His whole life he sought light and soft but warm materials, and wore clothes and shoes in a style of his own – wide, comfortable, simple and without regard for custom or people around him. One of his recurrent dreams was about warmth. He imagined a little room, small and without furniture, which would be warmed from all sides by invisible flames, always steady and constant, and which would at the same time stay light, clean and full of fresh air. A kind of shrine to himself, a heated grave, but from which one could influence the world constantly, giving oneself pleasure while doing others harm. For, Baki was not only an absurd miser and selfish eccentric, but also an intriguer, informer and slanderer who had made many people's lives misery and cost more than one his head. This had been the case particularly in the Treasurer's time of glory, when Ibrahim Pasha was Grand Vizier and he himself, Baki, in the proximity of great figures and at the centre of events. At that time they used to say about him: "The man whose dish is overturned by Baki will never dine again." But even now, cast out so far away, without connections or influence, ageing and more comical than dangerous, he had not stopped writing to various dignitaries in Istanbul more out of habit than anything else, passing on information he thought he had, compromising and maligning whoever he could. Even now he could spend a night sweetly at that, hunched and cramped over half a sheet of paper, as others spend their nights in jovial company or the raptures of love. And he did it all naturally, almost always without personal profit, according to an inner need, without shame, without a pang of conscience, even without fear.

Everything that lived in the Residence hated the Treasurer, and he hated all of them, together with the rest of Creation. A maniac in economizing and calculating, he did not want to keep an assistant or clerks. He would spend the whole day over his accounts, whispering as in prayer, counting and making notes with a short blunt reed pen, on small scraps of paper of varying sizes. (He stole this paper from the other officials.) He spied on everything in the Residence, beat and dismissed the junior employees, tried the Vizier's patience with his denunciations and slanders against the more senior staff, and his pleas to forbid and prevent wastage and loss. He fought against expenditure and extravagance, against every pleasure and every joy, against virtually any activity at all, considering not only the cheerful and carefree, but also communicative and enterprising people idlers and dangerous spendthrifts. There were some comic and pathetic moments in this battle of his against life itself. He paid spies to inform him in which rooms light burned longer than it should have done, he measured how much everyone ate and drank, counted the onion plants in the garden, as soon as they appeared above the earth. In fact, all these measures cost him more in effort than the waste they prevented was worth. (Tahir Bey used to say, as a joke, that Baki's zeal brought the Vizier more harm than all the faults and vices of all the other employees put together.) Fat and asthmatic as he was, he would keep going down to the cellars and clambering up to the attic. He wrote lists of everything, labelling and supervising, but still things kept slipping away from under his eyes. He fought desperately against the natural course of life, and he would have most liked to be able to switch off the very life of the whole world, just as he snuffed out unnecessary candles in the rooms, with a moistened forefinger and thumb. He would have liked to stay alone in the dark, beside that extinguished candle of life, enjoying the fact that everyone was plunged in gloom, that, at last, there was no life – that is no spending – and that he was still breathing and enduring, the victor and witness of his triumph.

He was furious with the rich because they had plenty and spent and squandered it, but he passionately hated those who had nothing, that black, eternal poverty, that dragon with a million insatiable mouths. When people in the Residence wanted to annoy him, one of them would come up to him and in conversation, with an exaggeratedly sad expression and pitiful tone of voice, mention that someone deserved attention, "because he was poor". With the predictability of a machine, Baki would then jump up from his place, forgetting himself and shrieking in his high-pitched voice:

"What're you doing clinging to the poor? Let 'em go to the dogs, where they're heading. Am I God to make poor folk rich? Why, even *He* doesn't do that any more! He's got sick of it too."

He would bow his head and lower his voice pathetically, caricaturing whoever had accosted him.

"'Because he's poor!' So what? Since when is it some kind of honour to be poor? Is it a title that gives a man rights? 'He's poor!', as though you had said 'he's a Hadji' or 'he's a Pasha'!"

Then he would raise his voice and, foaming with rage, thrust his face right up to the other: "Why does he keep on guzzling if he's poor? No one eats as much as the poor! Why doesn't he economize?"

He praised the Bosnians for being simple and restrained and because their poor were not importunate and did not beg or attack you like the poor of Istanbul or Salonika, but just lived out their misery silently and patiently. He did not care for the people of Travnik, for he had observed that they liked jewellery and were virtually all well-turned out. He looked at the men's broad sashes, their trousers covered in silk braid, and the women's feradjees of heavy woollen cloth, at the veils embroidered with real gold covering their faces. And it all angered him, for he struggled in vain to explain to himself how all these people came to have money, how they bought such expensive and unnecessary things, and how they replaced them when they wore out and fell to pieces so fast. These insoluble calculations made him dizzy. And when, in the course of conversation, someone would start to defend the people of Travnik arguing that it was good to see them in the bazaar, clean and always well-dressed, Baki would fly at him:

"Well and good if they're clean! But where do they get the money for clothes like that? Eh? I ask you, where do they get money in this dump of a town?"

And as the other man deliberately went on praising the people of Travnik and justifying their extravagant dress, the Treasurer would become increasingly incensed. His blue eyes, worried and at the same time irresistibly comic, became suddenly stormily violet, brilliant and evil. Like a whirling dervish he moved quickly on his small invisible feet, in their rolls of fat, waving his short arms. Eventually, he would find himself in the middle of the room, legs apart, his arms outstretched and stubby fingers spread, repeating in a scathing hiss, faster and faster, in an ever higher and sharper voice:

"Where do they get the money? Where do they get it? Where do they get it?"

At this the mischief-maker, who had only come to annoy him, would go away, leaving the desperate Treasurer in the middle of the room without an answer, like a drowning man without hope or help on the seething ocean of boundless expenditure and insoluble calculations of this mindless, wretched world.

The person who knew the Treasurer best and could tell the most stories about him was Eshref Effendi, the Vizier's sick doctor. It was from him that d'Avenat learned most about the Treasurer.

Sitting in the sun, with his legs in their cloth boots stretched out, with his long thin hands covered in veins and scars on his knees, Eshref Effendi spoke in his deep, hoarse, hunter's voice: "Yes, he's ridiculous and quite worn out now. A pig wouldn't bother to rub itself against him. But you should have known him once. And even today he shouldn't be underestimated. You may say his skin's yellow and his hands tremble. That's true. Only you'd be mistaken if you conclude that he won't go on living for long or that he won't go on being dangerous and harmful to all living things around him, as far as he is able. Yes, he's yellow as a withered quince, but he's never been any different, he was born yellow. For more than fifty years he has been crawling over this world, coughing, sneezing, groaning, puffing and blowing in all directions like a balloon with a hole in it. From the first day, when for the first time he dirtied the floor where his mother gave birth to him, he has been sick, fouling everything around him. He has spent half his life in long, persistent constipation and the other half in terrible diarrhoea, running across the courtyard with a pitcher in his hand. But none of this has prevented him, no more than his eternal toothache, insomnia, rashes and bleeding, from moving about like a little barrel and doing evil with the speed of a snake and strength of a bull, every kind of evil, to anyone and anything. I myself protest when people say he is a miser. No, that's an insult to misers. For a miser loves money, or at least his miserliness, and is ready to sacrifice a great deal for it, but this one doesn't like anything or anyone apart from himself, he hates everything in the world, living beings and lifeless things. No, he's no miser, he's a putrid mould, the kind that destroys all it touches."

Eshref Effendi ended his tale with a brittle laugh: "Ah, I know that better than anyone, although he has never been able to do anything to me. You know I've always been a huntsman, a free man, and it's child's play to get the better of the likes of him."

In addition to these striking figures, d'Avenat managed to get to know the other important officials and to report back to Daville in detail.

There was the dark, thin Chief Archivist, the Tefter Khefay, Ibrahim Effendi, of whom it was said that he was incorruptible, a taciturn and withdrawn man who was concerned only about his numerous children and the Vizier's archive. His life passed in a battle with inept and negligent scribes, couriers and messengers and with the Vizier's papers which, as though under a spell, could never be put in order. He spent his days in a half-darkened room, full of chests and shelves. It was all organized in a way only he understood. And when he was asked for the copy of some document or old letter he would always get flustered, as though something completely unexpected and unheard-of were happening. He would jump up, stop in the middle of the room, press his hands to both his temples and start trying to remember. Then his black eyes would all at once become crossed and "he would look at two shelves on two opposite sides of the room simultaneously" as Eshref Effendi used to say. At the same time he would pronounce softly and repeatedly the name of the document he had been asked for, increasingly rapidly, briefly and indistinctly, until it became a long drawn-out hum through his nose. At a certain moment the unintelligible mumbling would be abruptly interrupted, the Archivist would jump as though he were catching a bird and reach up to a shelf with both hands. The paper he was looking for was usually there. If by any chance it happened that it was not, the Archivist would go back to the middle of the room and his inner concentration and mumbling through his nose would begin again, ending in a new leap to a different place. And so on, until the thing was found.

The Commander of the Vizier's "guard" was the frivolous, happy-go-lucky Behdjet, a man of indestructible health, stout and red-faced, brave, but an incorrigible gambler and sluggard. Those two dozen infantry men and hussars who made up the Vizier's motley guard did not give Behdjet many cares or much work. They generally fixed things in such a way that Behdjet did not worry much about them or they about Behdjet. They played dice, ate, drank and slept. The Commander's main and hardest task was his struggle with the Treasurer, Baki, when he had to extract from him the monthly wages or some unpredicted expenditure for himself or the soldiers, without dragging it out interminably or being refused. Unbelievable scenes would occur on these occasions. The Treasurer's spiteful hair-splitting managed to upset the calm even of the good-natured Behdjet, driving him to pull out his knife and threaten to chop the tight-fisted Treasurer up into little pieces "like a kebab". And the otherwise timid and feeble Baki would fly onto Behdjet's naked blade in defence of his cash box, blinded by the hate and revulsion he felt towards this squanderer, swearing that before he died he would see Behdjet's head stuck on a pole on that steep slope, below the graveyard, where criminals' heads were displayed.

Eventually, it all ended with the Commander getting the money and leaving the Treasurer's office laughing out loud, while Baki was left standing over the cash box, stroking the new emptiness like a wound, preparing to go to the Vizier for the hundredth time, to complain of this traitor and robber who had been raiding his treasury and making his life a misery for years. And with his whole Treasurer's soul he longed to experience the triumph of justice and order and really to see that empty, impudent head of Behdjet's grinning from a stake.

The Deputy was Suleiman Pasha Skopljak, who had held the same post under the former Vizier, as we have seen. He was rarely in Travnik. And when he was there, he showed far more understanding and goodwill towards the Austrian Consul than the French. But nevertheless, this Bosnian was the only man in that motley crew at the Residence of whom one could feel with any certainty that he had the intention of keeping to what he promised and the ability to carry it out.

10

The days of the Consuls brought changes and unrest into this Viziers' town. Directly or indirectly they caused many to rise and many to stumble and fall, they left many with good memories and many with bad.

But why was the barber's apprentice Salko Maluhija, the son of a poor widow, beaten by the bey's servants? Why was that the thing he remembered from the days of the Consuls? After all, he was not among the Imperial employees, the beys or ayans, ulema or bazaar people?

What was at work here was one of those life forces around and within us, which can lift and drive us, stop us still or knock us down. That force, which we call "love" for short, drove Salko the barber to clamber over the bushes in Hafizadić's hedge, tearing his clothes, and to climb trees in order just to glimpse the Consul's daughter Agatha.

Like all true lovers, Salko did not confess his love or show it, but he did find a way of satisfying it at least to a certain extent.

During the free hour he had for his midday meal, he would creep unseen into the Khan stables and from there, through an opening used for throwing out the dung, he would cross over into the bushes where he could observe the Consul's garden. There he would almost always see the Consul's daughter to whom he was drawn by something bigger and stronger than all the strength at the disposal of his feeble apprentice's body.

Between this hedge and the Consulate garden was a narrow, neglected plum orchard belonging to the Hafizadić Beys, but you could see through it clearly to the Consulate garden, laid out in the

European manner. Paths had been cut across it and the molehills flattened. In the centre, circular and star-shaped flowerbeds had been dug, flowers planted, and poles stuck into the ground, with red or blue glass balls on the top.

This whole area was both marshy and sunny, so that everything planted there grew rapidly, tall and abundant in flowers and fruit.

It was here that Salko the barber caught sight of Herr von Mitterer's daughter. Actually he had seen her in the town, when she drove by with her father. But that would happen so rarely and so briefly that he did not know what to look at first: the Consul's uniform, the yellow lacquered carriage or the girl, who always had a grey carriage blanket with a red crown and monogram embroidered on it wrapped tightly round her legs. That same distant girl, the colour of whose eyes he had not even been able to see, was now close at hand, moving about the garden alone, without any inkling that anyone was watching her, in front of the veranda which had been repaired and enclosed in glass last spring.

Completely hidden, Salko peered through the fence, crouching, his mouth half-open, furtively holding his breath. And the girl, convinced that she was quite alone, walked round the flowerbeds, examined the bark on the trees, hopped from one side of the path to the other. Then she would stop and glance now at the sky, now at her hands. (That is the way young animals will come to a halt in the middle of a game, not knowing any longer what to do with their bodies.)

And then she would start walking from one side to the other again, waving her arms and clapping her hands, first in front of her, then behind. And her form in her light dress was comically fragmented in those brilliant garden balls of different colours, together with the sky and foliage.

Salko completely forgot the world and lost all sense of time, place and the proportions of his own body. And only later, when he got up to leave, would he feel how numb his bent legs had become and how his fingers and nails hurt, full of earth and bark. And a great deal later, in the shop, where he would often be thrashed for getting back late, his heart would still thump excitedly and uncomfortably. But the next day he could barely wait for his meagre lunch to be over to go off and squeeze through the Khan stables by Hafizadić's hedge, trembling in advance both from fear of being caught and from the joy awaiting him.

One day, it was a bright, quiet afternoon after a rainy morning, the girl was not in the garden. The flowerbeds were wet and the paths beaten down by the shower. Washed by the rain, the glass balls gleamed in the sun, cheerfully reflecting the few white clouds. Seeing that the girl was not there, driven by desire and impatience, Salko climbed first onto the fence and then up an old plum tree which was growing right beside the fence, completely overgrown by a flourishing elder bush. He peered through the dense elder leaves.

All the windows on the veranda were wide open and the sun and bright sky sparkled in their panes. This made the veranda appear all the cooler inside. Salko could make out everything clearly: the red carpet on the floor and incomprehensible pictures on the wall. In one small, very low chair sat the Consul's daughter. She was holding a large book on her lap, but she kept raising her eyes from it and her gaze roamed over the veranda and through the windows. This new posture, in which he had never yet seen her, excited him still more. The more shadows there were on her and the further away she was, the longer she had to be watched. He trembled for fear that his foot might slip or a small branch break. He was weak with the delight of seeing her so motionless, her face even longer and paler in the shadow, and he kept thinking that something else was going to happen, something still more exciting and extraordinary, as unusual as the whole of this rainy day. He kept telling himself nothing was going to happen. And after all what could happen? – But still, something would.

There, she had placed both her hands on the open book. His

breath and thoughts stopped still. – Something was, something really was going to happen. – And truly, the girl got up, slowly and indecisively, closing her hands and then parting them again, leaving only the tips of her fingers joined. She stood looking at her nails. – Something was going to happen! – Suddenly she separated her fingers, as though she were breaking something thin and invisible, glanced down her body, moved her arms a little away from it and began to dance slowly in the middle of the red carpet.

She put her head a little to one side, as though listening, and, with her eyes lowered, looked at the tips of her shoes. Her face was motionless, entranced. The shadows and light of the rainy day shifted over it as she moved.

And Salko, seeing that what he had guessed was actually happening, completely forgot who and where he was and crossed from the main trunk to some young branches, lifting himself high above the fence and stretching further and further whenever she extended her leg more briskly in her dance. He pressed his face firmly against the leaves and young bark. He felt faint, his whole inner being was in turmoil. It was hard to bear so much rapture in such a position. But the girl did not stop dancing. When she repeated the same figure for a second and third time, a sweetness coursed through his whole body, as though he had caught sight of something long familiar and dear to him.

Suddenly, the tree cracked. The branch under him split and broke. He felt himself falling through the elder leaves, the branches tearing and lashing him, and he was hit twice, once on the back and once on the head.

He somersaulted over the fence into the Hafizadić garden. He fell first onto the fence, and then to the ground, among some mossy, worm-eaten boards covering a sewer. The rotten boards gave way under his weight and he plunged up to his knees into the mud and slime.

When he raised his filthy, scratched face, and opened his eyes, he saw standing over him a servant from Hafizadić's kitchen, an old woman with a sallow lined face like his mother's.

"Have you hurt yourself, you miserable wretch? What on earth are you doing in the sewer?"

But he just kept glancing around him, searching for at least a fragment of that beauty which just a moment before had flooded him on the height from which he had fallen. He listened to the old woman, but he did not understand what she was saying to him, just as he watched with wide-open eyes Hafizadić's servants running from the other side of the garden with clubs in their hands, but he could not work out what had happened or what these people wanted with him.

The girl, frail, joyless and lonely, continued to walk and play innocent games in the garden and the veranda. She knew nothing about all that had happened – because of her – in the garden next door, just as she had earlier had no idea that anyone was watching her.

After the thrashing he received in Hafizadić's garden and the cuffing he then got at the barber's shop, for coming back late, Salko had no supper that day. This was the usual punishment meted out by his mother, a sallow and prematurely old woman, whom poverty had wasted away and made sour. After that, the boy no longer stole into other people's gardens or clambered onto fences and trees to look at what was not for him. Even paler and sadder, he stayed in the shop dreaming of the beautiful foreign girl. She danced in front of him now just as his desire dictated and was able to imagine, but there was no danger of his falling into anyone's sewer, to be caught and flogged.

Nevertheless, even dreams of beauty must be paid for. He would stand, holding the dish of shaving soap in his thin, blue hands, in front of the stout barber, while he was shaving the crown of some effendi's head. The barber would notice his vacant gaze and motion with his eyes and a familiar gesture of his hand that he should be watching the master's razor and learning, not gaping mindlessly into the distance beyond the shop door. The boy would give a start, glance fearfully at the barber and then obediently fix his gaze on the razor. But just a minute later, the boy's eyes would again be vacant, looking at that bluish bare patch left on the crown of the effendi's head after the master's razor and seeing the heavenly garden and in it the girl with her light step and unusual appearance. And when the barber noticed his absent-mindedness again, he would give him a first slap with his free left hand where the foam he had wiped off would collect on the forefinger. All Salko's skill then went into not dropping the dish and calmly enduring the blow, for that would be the end of it. If he did not succeed, the blows would fall like rain and the barber's chibouk would also be brought into action.

That was how the barber Hamid cured his apprentice of his naughtiness, drummed sense into his head, driving out foolish whims and endeavouring to rivet his eyes on his work.

But that force which we referred to at the beginning sprang up, like underground water, unpredictably and unexpectedly in other places and different circumstances, striving to gain as much ground as possible and overwhelm the greatest number of human beings of both sexes. It would crop up in inappropriate places, where it could not possibly retain its hold because of the resistance it was bound to encounter.

From the outset, Frau von Mitterer had regularly visited the Catholic churches and chapels around Travnik, making them gifts. She did not do this so much from her own inclination as at the Colonel's bidding, so as to strengthen his influence with the Catholic clergy and congregation.

Vases of fake porcelain were ordered from Vienna, as well as thin candlesticks and gilt candelabras, all cheap and tasteless goods, but unknown in these parts. Embroidered brocade was acquired from Zagreb, stoles and chasubles made by the nuns there and given by the Consul's wife to the monastery at Guča Gora or the priests in the poor village churches round Travnik.

Anna Maria was unable to retain a sense of proportion even in this task, which was supposed to be practical and pious. As always, she was carried away by her unbalanced nature which tended always to distort everything she undertook, driving her along misguided paths. In her zeal she aroused the suspicion of the Turks, alarmed and embarrassed the villagers and friars of Dolac who were in any case mistrustful. In the course of distributing her gifts she behaved capriciously, bursting into churches, wilfully rearranging objects on the altar according to her taste, ordering them to be aired, cleaned and whitewashed. The friars, who shrank from any innovation and did not like anyone interfering in their affairs, even when it was with the best possible intentions, first watched it all in bewilderment, then began to exchange glances, make plans and prepare to resist.

For the chaplain in the nearest village of Orašje, this extraordinary zeal of Frau von Mitterer's became a hazard and a source of real danger. The chaplain, who was called Brother Mijat Baković, was alone at that time, because his priest, who was also called Brother Mijat, known as "The Wheelwright", was away on some business of the Order. The chaplain was a feeble, myopic young man, given to fantasy. He found the isolation and rigorous village life hard to bear, and had not yet quite found his feet as a member of the Order.

Anna Maria pestered this young chaplain with all the protective ardour she was capable of, and with that half-maternal, half-amorous attentiveness that so easily leads even more composed and experienced men into awkward misunderstandings. At one time, at the beginning of the summer, she rode two or three times a day to Orašje, dismounted at the church with her escort, summoned the chaplain and gave him instructions as to how to arrange the church and his house. She interfered in his household affairs, in the way he organized his time and the running of the church. And the young friar looked on her as an apparition, unexpected and wonderful, too beautiful and great for him to be able to rejoice in without pain. The narrow band of white lace around her neck glowed against the black material of her riding habit as though it were made of light, dazzling his eyes which did not dare look straight at the woman's face. In her presence, the chaplain quivered as though in a fever. And Frau von Mitterer looked with gratification at those thin, trembling hands and the monk's face, while he was mortified to find himself trembling.

When she had ridden off down the hill towards Travnik, the chaplain would sit for a long time on the bench in front of the old parsonage, as though struck down. Everything then seemed hard and disagreeable: the village, the church and his work. But everything would sparkle and blossom once more, as soon as he caught sight of the riders from Travnik. Only, the embarrassed quivering would start again together with the painful desire to be free of this blinding, paralysing beauty as fast as possible and forever.

Fortunately for the chaplain, Brother Mijat the Wheelwright soon returned to his parish and the young man made a thorough and sincere confession to him. The Wheelwright was a strong, vigorous man of fifty, with a broad face, snub nose and slanting eyes, experienced and considerate, robust, full of humour and wit, well-read and eloquent. He easily understood the whole affair and the unfortunate chaplain's position.

He immediately sent him back to the monastery. And the next time Frau von Mitterer rode up with her escort, instead of the embarrassed chaplain, the Wheelwright came out, smiling and tranquil, sat down on a tree-stump and responded over his heavy cigarette holder to the astonished Consul's wife's proposals for organizing the church: "I'm surprised at you, ma'am, breaking your bones on these country roads, when God has granted that you may sit in your own home in every comfort and ease. Bless you, you can't knock these churches and chapels of ours into order, even if you spend all the Emperor's treasure on them. Our churches are just like us. It wouldn't do for them to be any better. No, whatever you have in the way of gifts for these country churches, just send someone with them. They will be welcome and God will repay you."

Offended, Frau von Mitterer kept trying to start up a conversation about the church and the people, but Brother Mijat made a joke of all her remarks. And when she mounted her black horse angrily, the priest took his little monk's cap from his tangled hair, bowed in a devilish way, both humbly and mockingly, and said:

"That's a good horse, ma'am, just right for a bishop."

And Anna Maria never went to the church in Orašje again.

It was at about the same time that the priest of Dolac also had occasion to speak to von Mitterer on the same matter. Since the friars valued the Consul as a friend and protector and did not wish to offend him on any account, they selected the corpulent and cumbersome, but wily Brother Ivo to find a way of conveying to him, without offending either him or his wife, that Frau von Mitterer's zeal embarrassed them. And Brother Ivo, whom the Turks called "muzzevir" or "crafty", not without reason, handled the affair admirably. First he explained to the Consul that the monks were having to tread very warily for fear of the Turks, and to be particularly careful about who they were seen with. Then he said that the gifts Frau von Mitterer brought were welcome and they prayed constantly for her and the man who sent them. Finally, the unspoken conclusion emerged from the whole story that they would continue to accept the gifts, but that it would be better if Frau von Mitterer did not deliver them in person and that she did not interfere in their distribution or the way they were used.

But Frau von Mitterer had already had enough of churches and was disillusioned with the people and the monks. She flared up at the Colonel one morning, hurling a shower of hurtful words and insults at him. She shrieked that the French Consul was right to associate with the Jews who had better manners than these Turkish Catholics. Thrusting her face right into his, she asked whether he was the Consul General or a sacristan. She swore that she would never set foot in either the church or the parsonage at Dolac again.

That was how the young chaplain from Orašje was saved from what was for Anna Maria an inconsequential game but for him a serious predicament. That was also the end of the devout phase in the Travnik life of Frau von Mitterer.

The force to which we have been referring all this time did not spare the French Consulate on the other side of the Lašva either, because it respects neither coats of arms nor flags.

While Madame Daville was tending her children on the ground floor of the "Dubrovnik Khan", while Daville slaved over his comprehensive consular reports and confused literary plans, on the floor above them, the "Young Consul" was struggling with tedium and the desires it engenders but cannot satisfy. He continued to assist Daville in his work and to ride through the countryside, studying the language and customs of the people and working on his book about Bosnia. He did all this to fill his days and nights. But the young and blithe always have plenty of energy and time to spare for yearnings, and the kind of rambling known only to their age.

That was how the "Young Consul" noticed Jelka, a girl from Dolac.

We have seen that when Madame Daville arrived in Travnik, it had taken time and patience for her to gain the confidence of the monks and be accepted by the people of Dolac. At first not even the poorest wanted to let their child serve in the French Consulate. But when they got to know Madame Daville better, and when they saw everything the first girls who worked for her had learned, they began to vie for employment with the French Consul's wife. At any one time there would be several Dolac girls helping in the house or doing the embroidery Madame Daville taught them.

During the summer months there would be three or four girls sewing or knitting together. They sat on the wide veranda, under the windows, bowed over their work, singing softly. On his way to see Daville Des Fossés often passed these girls. Then they would bow their heads still lower, and break off their song. As he went to and fro across the wide corridor with his long stride, the young man often looked more closely at the girls and called out a word of greeting which they could not answer for shyness. And it would have been hard to answer, for it was a different word each time, the one he had just learned that day, and it would perplex them just as much as his free manner, swift movements and bold voice. As he passed them more frequently, some logic governing relations of this kind drove Des Fossés to notice particularly the face of the girl who bowed her head most deeply before him.

She was called Jelka and was the daughter of a humble shopkeeper who had a modest house in Dolac, full of children. The thick heavy fringe of her brown hair fell right to her eyes. She stood out from the other girls in some indeterminate way, which had something to do with both her style of dressing and her beauty. The young man began to distinguish the brown knot of her hair and strong white neck among the bowed heads of the others. And when he gazed for a little longer than usual at that bent neck, the girl unexpectedly raised her head, as though his look were burning her and she wanted to avoid it. He saw for a moment her young, broad face with shining but docile brown eyes, strong, not completely straight nose and her large, perfect mouth with its lips exactly alike and barely touching each other. Taken by surprise, the young man gazed at this face and saw that strong mouth tremble slightly at the edges, as though holding back tears, while her brown eyes shone with a smile they were unable to hide. The young man smiled too and called out to her some word from his "Illyrian" vocabulary – any one, because at that age and in such circumstances, all words are good and meaningful. In order to hide her eyes, which were smiling, and her mouth, with its barely visible tearful trembling, the girl bowed her head once more, displaying again her white neck in her brown hair.

This exchange between them was repeated several times, like a kind of game, over the next few days. But every game aspires to be prolonged, and this urge is irresistible when it involves such a girl and a lonely, full-blooded young man. So it happens that insignificant words, long looks and unconscious smiles become woven into a firm bridge, built up of its own accord.

He began to think of her at night and when he woke, to look for her, first in his thoughts and then in reality, and, as though by a miracle, to find her more and more often and see her for ever longer spells. Since at that time of year everything was sprouting, bursting into leaf, she seemed to him a part – a humanized and separate part – of that luxuriant vegetal world. "She is vegetal," he would say to himself, as people sing certain words, without thinking about the meaning of what they are saying or the reason for it. Rosy-cheeked, smiling and shy as she was, constantly bowing her head as a flower its crown, she really was linked in his thoughts with flowers and fruit, in some deep, special sense which he himself could not make out, something like the soul and consciousness of fruit and flowers.

When the spring was well-advanced and the trees full of leaves, the girls moved into the garden. That was where they did their embroidery throughout the summer.

If someone were to talk with two travellers one of whom had been in Travnik in winter and the other in summer, he would hear two quite contrary opinions of the town. The first would say that he had been in Hell, while for the other it was at least near Paradise.

Places like this with an unfavourable climate and position regularly have several weeks in the year when their beauty and charm are like a reward for all the adversity of the rest of the year. In Travnik this period comes between the beginning of June and the end of August, usually including the whole of July.

When the snow melts even in the deepest hollows, when the spring rains and snowstorms cease, when the winds have blown themselves out, now cold, now tepid, now violently raging, now soft and light, when the clouds withdraw once and for all to the high crest of the steep amphitheatre of mountains surrounding the town, when day holds back the night with its length, brilliance and warmth, when on the steep slopes above the town the fields turn yellow and the bending pear trees begin to scatter their abundant fruit over the stubble fields – then this brief and beautiful Travnik summer begins.

Des Fossés reduced his outings into the countryside, dawdling for hours in the big steep garden of the Consulate, going round the familiar paths and shrubs as though they were strange things he had never seen before. Jelka would come earlier than the other girls or try to stay after they had gone. From the patch of level ground where they worked, she went ever more frequently down to the Consulate for some thread, water or a snack. Then she would meet the young man on the little narrow paths overgrown with greenery. Here she bowed her broad, white face and he would pronounce with a smile his "Illyrian" words in which the letter "r" was muffled and protracted and the stress was always on the end of the word.

One afternoon they were alone together for longer than usual on one of the side paths among dense foliage, where the shadows breathed with warmth. The girl was wearing wide dove-grey shalwars and a tight light-blue silk waistcoat with one fastening. Her gathered blouse was done up at the neck with a silver clasp. Her arms, with their sleeves to the elbow, were full and had a network of rosy blood beneath the skin. The young man took hold of her forearm. The blood immediately drained away, leaving the pale traces of his fingers.

Her lips, pale-rose, firm and unusually symmetrical, began slowly to stretch at the ends into that pleading, half-tearful smile, but immediately afterwards the girl lowered her head and pressed against him, silent and submissive as grass and branches. "She is vegetal...," he thought again, but what was winding itself around him was a human being, a woman grown tender to the point of pain, her spirit still struggling, but already giving in to its breaking and its fall. Her arms hung motionless, her mouth half-open and her eyes closing as though in a faint. Here she was, on him, all around him, faint with love, with the ecstasy love promises and the horror that follows it, like a shadow. Bending away, broken, felled, she was the image of complete surrender, helplessness, defeat and despair, but also of unimagined grandeur.

The young man was transported by his racing blood, his sense of absolute joy and unrestrained triumph. Boundless vistas were lit and extinguished in him, like sparks. Yes, this is it! He had always felt and so often maintained that this poor, barren, neglected land was actually rich and luxuriant. This was the revelation of one of its hidden beauties.

The steep green, flowering slopes burst once again into flower and the air was filled with an unfamiliar, intoxicating scent which, he now felt, had always lain hidden in this valley. The secret riches of this apparently dark and desolate land had disclosed themselves and it was suddenly clear that its persistent silence concealed this rapid, uneven breathing of love in which the last gasp of resistance and the rapture of submission were still contending. Its eternally blank, drab appearance was only a mask under which light streamed and shimmered, glowing red with sweet young blood.

There was an old, thick, forking pear tree at this spot. It was bent and lay right along the steep bank, like a kind of sofa. Dried up towards the trunk, it was still putting out fresh leaves. They leaned against it, and then sank, in one another's arms, first the girl and then he onto her, into the forking trunk of the tree, as into a waiting bed. Making no sound or movement, she did not yet offer any resistance. But when the young man's hands slid down and clasped her waist, resting on her sides, between her shalwars and waistcoat, where there was nothing but her shirt, the girl twisted away, like a branch that has been bent down for the fruit to be picked but which springs away. He did not even feel her lift him from her or notice how he came to be on the path once more. The girl was kneeling at his feet, her hands clasped and her face turned up towards him, exactly as in prayer. Her face had become suddenly pale, her eyes full of tears which did not fall. Kneeling, her hands clasped, she uttered words he did not know, but which were at that moment clearer to him than his own native tongue: she was imploring him to be kind, to spare her, not to ruin her, because she could not defend herself from what had overcome her as irresistibly as death, but was more difficult and more terrible than death. She begged him on her mother's life and whatever was dearest to him, and kept repeating in a voice suddenly hoarse with passion and emotion:

"Don't, don't…"

The young man felt the blood pulsing in the veins of his neck, he struggled to compose himself and to take in this unexpected, abrupt transformation of the whole situation. He wondered in amazement what it was that had suddenly removed this swooning woman from under him and was holding them both now in this ridiculous position: he upright and aroused, like some pagan emperor, and she at his feet, kneeling, her hands clasped together and her tearful gaze fixed up at his face, like a saint from a pious painting. He wanted to lift her from the ground, to draw her to him and lay her once more on the forked trunk of the bending pear tree, but he could not find the strength. Everything was suddenly and incomprehensibly changed.

He did not know how or when it had happened, but he saw clearly that this weak girl, pliable as a reed, had passed mysteriously out of the "vegetal world" in which she had been up till then, into some quite other world. She had slipped perfidiously away under the secure protection of some stronger will, where he could no longer reach her. He felt cheated, beaten, painfully disappointed. He was overcome with shame, then anger, at her, at himself, at the whole world. He bent down and raised her carefully from the ground, mumbling something. She was just as yielding and compliant, responding to every movement of his hand as a short while before, but she continued with words and looks to beg him to have mercy on her and to spare her. It no longer occurred to him to renew his embrace. Stern-faced and with forced courtesy, he helped her to adjust the folds in her shalwars and the silver clasp at her throat, which had come loose. And then the girl, just as abruptly and for him incomprehensibly, vanished down the slope towards the Consulate building.

The young man spent a few troubled days. He was obsessed by the confusion, impotent fury and shame of those first moments in the garden. The question kept coming back: what was it that had happened to him and the girl, how had it come about? And he kept pushing it aside defiantly, endeavouring not to think of that brief encounter on the isolated garden path. But nevertheless, he often told himself with a mocking and ironic smile: "Yes, yes, you really are a faultless psychologist and a perfect lover. You dreamed up the idea that she belonged to the vegetal world, that she was the pagan spirit of this land, the undiscovered treasure which you had simply to pick up. And you deigned to bend down. Whereupon, suddenly, everything changes. She kneels like Isaac, whose throat his father

Abraham is about to cut, but at the last moment an angel saves him from death. Yes, that's how she knelt. And you played Abraham in front of her. Congratulations! You have begun to act parts in tableaux vivants with Biblical themes and a profound moral and religious message. Congratulations!"

Only long walks through the steep groves round the town could soothe him and make him think of other things.

So he was tormented by thwarted desire and youthful vanity for a few days, and then it too passed. He began to calm down and forget. He still saw the girls sewing in the garden as he passed, and Jelka among them with her head bowed. He did not falter or stop, but would call out jauntily and gaily some word he had learned that day, and pass on, always smiling, fresh and in a hurry.

Only, on one of those nights, in the manuscript of his book about Bosnia where he was describing the types and racial characteristics of the Bosnian people, he added the following paragraph:

"The women are usually shapely; many of them catch the eye with the fine, regular features of their faces, the beauty of their bodies and the dazzling whiteness of their skin."

11

As time went on it seemed that everything in this country tended to take a surprising turn and everything could, at any moment, become the opposite of what it appeared. Daville had already begun to reconcile himself to the unpleasant fact that he had lost Husref Mehmed Pasha, a lively, open man from whom he could always expect a warm reception, understanding and at least some assistance. And in his place he had the hard, cold, unhappy Ibrahim Pasha: a man who was a burden to himself and others and out of whom it was as hard to beat a kind word or human feeling as it was from a stone. Daville was confirmed in this opinion by his first contact with the Vizier and still more so by all he learned from d'Avenat. But soon the Consul was obliged to recognize once again that d'Avenat's clever, convincing assessment of people was in fact biased. As long as it was a question of ordinary things and regular, everyday relations, his judgement was truly penetrating, mercilessly accurate and reliable. But as soon as he found himself confronting more complex and subtle questions, his mental laziness and moral indifference drove him to generalize and reach hasty, simplified conclusions.

After his second and third conversations, the Consul had already observed that the Vizier was not as inaccessible as he had seemed at first sight. For one thing, the new Vizier too had his "favourite topic of conversation". Only in his case it was not the sea, as with Husref Mehmed Pasha, or some other real and useful matter. For Ibrahim Pasha, the starting and finishing point of every conversation was the fall of his master Selim III and his, Ibrahim Pasha's, own personal tragedy, closely linked with that fall. It was from that point that his views spread out in all directions. He saw everything that happened around him in the world through this event, and as a result of course everything was bound to appear sombre, difficult and hopeless. The main thing for the Consul, however, was that the Vizier was not simply "a physical freak and spiritual mummy": there were subjects and words which could arouse and excite him. What is more, with time, the Consul was able to perceive that this hard, forbidding Vizier, with whom every conversation was a lecture about the futility of things, was in many matters more reliable than the easy-going, radiant and perpetually smiling Mehmed Pasha. The way Daville listened to his pessimistic judgements and general observations appealed to the Vizier and inspired his confidence. The Vizier had never spoken for so long or so confidentially either with von Mitterer or with any other person as he came increasingly often to do with Daville. And the Consul became gradually accustomed to these conversations, in which the two of them would plunge into the many different adversities of this imperfect world, at the end extracting some minor concession which had in fact been the purpose of his coming to talk with the Vizier.

As a rule, these conversations began with praise of one of Napoleon's most recent victories or successes in international politics, but the Vizier would immediately pass, according to his natural inclination, from positive and joyous things to problematic ones. To England, for example, her inflexibility, arrogance and greed, against which even the genius of Napoleon struggled in vain. From there it was just a step to general observations about how difficult it was to govern nations and rule people, how thankless was the task of rulers and commanders, how things in this world usually went wrong, against the laws of impotent morality and the desires of honourable men. By then he was already passing on to the fate of Selim III and his associates. Daville listened with silent attention and profound sympathy, while the Vizier spoke with a kind of bitter elation.

"People do not wish to be happy. Nations do not want rational government or honourable rulers. Goodness is a naked orphan in this world. May the Almighty help your Emperor, but I have seen with my own eyes what happened to my master, the Sultan Selim. He was a man whom God had endowed with all good physical and moral qualities. He burned himself up like a candle for the well-being and prosperity of the Empire. Intelligent, gentle and just, he never thought of evil or betrayal, he never imagined what chasms of malice, hypocrisy and treachery lay hidden in people. That is why he did not know how to protect himself. And no one else was able to protect him. Spending all his energy in carrying out his ruler's duties and living a pure life such as none could remember since the time of the first Caliphs, Selim did not take any measures to defend himself from the sudden assaults and treachery of perfidious men. That is how it was possible for one detachment of 'yamaks', the dregs of the army, led by a raving barbarian, to cast such a sultan from his throne and lock him in the Seraglio, thus completely frustrating his far-sighted plans for the salvation of the Empire, and to put on the throne a shallow wretch, a libertine, surrounded by drunkards, barbarians and professional traitors. That's the way of this world! But how few people there are who see that and even fewer who want to prevent it and are in a position to do so!"

From that subject it was not far to the question of Bosnia and the circumstances in which both the Vizier and the Consul had to live. As soon as he started to talk about Bosnia and the Bosnians Ibrahim Pasha could never find enough harsh words and black images, and Daville would listen to him now with sincere compassion and genuine understanding.

The Vizier could not get over the fact that Selim's downfall had caught him at the head of an army which was just preparing to throw the Russians out of Wallachia and Moldavia, at a moment when success was certain. His fall had simultaneously deprived the Empire of its best Sultan and him, Ibrahim Pasha, of a great victory which was already within his grasp, to cast him suddenly, humiliated and crushed, into this remote, destitute land.

"You can see for yourself, my noble friend, the place we live in and the people I have to contend with. It would be easier to manage a herd of wild buffalo than these Bosnian beys and ayans. They are all savage, savage, savage and mindless, coarse and vulgar but easily offended and arrogant, pig-headed and stupid. Believe me when I tell you: these Bosnians have neither honour in their hearts nor sense in their heads. They vie with each other in wrangling and deceiving, that is all they are capable of. And these are the people I am supposed to use now to quell the uprising in Serbia! That is how things are in our Empire since Sultan Selim was overthrown and imprisoned, and Allah alone knows where it will all end."

The Vizier paused and fell silent. In his motionless face his deeply sunken eyes, where only despair ever shone now, flashed with the dull gleam of black crystals.

Daville interrupted the silence to observe with tactful circumspection: "And should the situation in Istanbul change by some happy force of circumstance, and you were to return once more to the post of Grand Vizier..."

"Why, even then!" The Vizier waved his hand. This morning he was enjoying driving himself and the Consul into the blackest despondency. "Even then!" he continued in a dull voice. "I would send orders which would not be carried out, I would defend the country from the Russians, the English, the Serbians and whoever else was beleaguering it. But I would be trying to save what can scarcely be saved."

At the end of these conversations, the Consul would usually raise the question he had come about, a permit for the export of corn to

Dalmatia, a border dispute, or something similar, and the Vizier, carried away by his gloomy reflections, would give his consent without much deliberation.

On another occasion, the Vizier would talk about other things during the audience, but always with the same heavy, despairing composure and the same bitterness. He spoke about the new Grand Vizier who hated him, envying him because he had been more fortunate in earlier wars, and now he would not send him instructions, reports or resources for the campaign against Serbia. Or he would pass on information he had received about his predecessor in Travnik, Husref Mehmed Pasha, whom that same Grand Vizier had exiled to Kesser.

All of this accumulated, forming a hard knot in the Consul's mind, and, despite the fact that he generally concluded his task favourably, he would return home as though poisoned. He could not eat, and at night he would continue to dream of misfortune, exile and all kinds of adversity.

Nevertheless, Daville was pleased that in the Vizier's incurable pessimism he had found, at least temporarily, a point of contact with him. In that rough Turkish world, without a ray of understanding or a trace of humanity accessible to the unfortunate foreign Consul this was a small private place, where the two of them met man to man. On occasions he felt that it would have needed only a little more time and effort for real friendship and a warm human relationship to develop between him and the Vizier.

But it was just then that something occurred which suddenly revealed the unbridgeable gulf dividing them, displaying the Vizier in a quite new light, worse and darker even than d'Avenat had painted him. It cast Daville once again into hopeless confusion, depriving him of the hope that he would ever find in this place a "spark of humanity" that would last longer than a tear or be deeper than a smile or a glance. With surprise and despair, the Consul then told himself that the hard school of the East went on forever and there was no end to surprises in these lands, just as there was no real sense of measure, constant judgement or enduring value in human relations.

One could not even remotely foresee or suggest all that these people were capable of.

One day the Vizier unexpectedly summoned both Consuls together, which was not otherwise his custom. Their escorts met at the gate. It seemed that the Divan was to be an especially ceremonial one. Attendants milled about, whispering to one another. The Vizier was affable and dignified. After the first coffee and the first chibouks, the Governor and the Secretary arrived and took their modest places. The Vizier told the Consuls that the previous week his Deputy Suleiman Pasha had crossed the Drina with his Bosnian troops and destroyed the strongest and best organized Serbian unit, trained and led by Russian officers. He expressed the hope that there would be no more Russians in Serbia after this victory and that this was probably the beginning of the end of the whole rising. The victory was important, said the Vizier, and the time was probably near when order and calm would be established even in Serbia. Knowing that the Consuls, as his good friends and neighbours, would also rejoice at this, he had invited them to share his satisfaction at the good news.

The Vizier fell silent. As though this were a sign, numerous attendants came into the Divan almost at a run. A rush mat was spread over the part of the room that was unoccupied. Several baskets, goatshair sacks and greasy black sheepskin bags were brought in. All these receptacles were hastily untied and opened and their contents shaken out onto the mat. During this time the Consuls were served with lemonade and fresh chibouks.

Onto the mat poured a huge quantity of severed human ears and noses, an indescribable mass of pathetic human flesh, salted and blackened with congealed blood. A cold, repulsive smell of damp salt and rancid blood filled the Divan. Hats, belts and cartridge cases with metal eagles on them were taken from the baskets, and from the bags narrow red and yellowish banners, fringed with gold, with the images of saints in the centre. After them two or three icons fell out with a dull thud. And finally they brought a sheaf of bayonets tied with bast.

These were the trophies of the victory over the Serbian rebel army "organized and led by the Russians".

Someone they could not see, in a corner of the room, uttered in a deep voice, like a prayer: "Allah has blessed the arms of Islam!" All the Turks present responded with an unintelligible murmur.

Daville, who could not have anticipated such a sight even in a dream, felt his stomach heave and the lemonade turn sour in his mouth, threatening to rise up his nose. He forgot about his chibouk and just looked at von Mitterer, as though expecting salvation from him. The Austrian was himself pale and subdued, but as he had long been accustomed to similar surprises, he was the first to find words to congratulate the Vizier and the Bosnian army. Daville's anxiety not to be outdone by his rival overcame his revulsion too and he uttered a few sentences in honour of the victory, expressing his wishes for the further success of the Imperial arms and peace in the Empire. He said it all in a wooden voice. It seemed to him that he could hear each of his words clearly as though they were being spoken by someone else. It was all translated. Then the Vizier began to speak again. He thanked the Consuls for their good wishes and congratulations, considering himself fortunate to have them at his side at this moment when he was so deeply moved to see the arms which the perfidious Muscovites had so shamefully abandoned on the battlefield.

Daville stole a glance at the Vizier. His eyes really were brighter and shining at the edges like crystals.

That same deep voice again intoned some formal, unintelligible words.

A barely audible murmur ran through the Divan. The reception was at an end. Seeing that von Mitterer was looking at the objects on the mat, Daville too summoned all his strength and glanced at the trophies spread out there. The lifeless objects of leather and metal were doubly dead, lying there, pathetic and abandoned, as though they had been excavated after centuries and brought out into the sun. The indescribable mass of severed ears and noses lay calmly, with salt scattered around it, black as earth with the blood and mixed with chaff. The whole thing gave off a thin, cold, pungent stench.

Daville looked at von Mitterer several times, and then at the mat in front of him, in the secret hope that the sight before him would vanish like a hideous vision, but each time his eyes fell on the same objects, improbable, but real and merciless in their immobility. "Wake up!" Daville told himself urgently, "wake up, shake off this nightmare and swim up to the sun, rub your eyes and breathe in a little fresh air!" But there was no waking, for this abject horror was the depths of reality. This is what these people were like. This was their life. This was how the best of them behaved.

Daville felt his stomach heave again. Everything was turning black before his eyes. Nevertheless, he succeeded in bidding the Vizier a polite farewell and riding calmly home with his escort. Once there, instead of sitting down to lunch, he went to bed.

The following day, Daville and von Mitterer met. They did not ask themselves who owed whom a visit and forgot how much time had passed since their last meeting. They were simply propelled towards one another. They shook hands for a long time looking in to each other's eyes without speaking, like two ship-wrecked voyagers. Von Mitterer had already been informed about the significance of the Turkish victory and the origin of the trophies. The weapons had been seized from a Serbian company, while the banners and everything else were the trophies of an ordinary massacre which the embittered and idle soldiers had carried out against the Bosnian rayah, somewhere near Zvornik, during a religious festival.

Von Mitterer was not a man given to reflection and it was not worth talking any further to him. But Daville kept fretting over this audience, asking himself constantly: Why these lies? Where did this futile, almost childish cruelty come from? What did their laughter and their tears mean? What did their silence conceal? And how could these people, the Vizier, with his exalted views, the apparently honest Suleiman Pasha and the wise Tahir Bey even conceive such things and participate in scenes from some other, lower, terrible world? What was their true face? What was life and what calculated acting? When were they lying and when telling the truth?

And along with his physical suffering he felt tormented by the realization that he never would succeed in finding a rational way of assessing these people and their actions.

Even more difficult and painful were similar experiences when they concerned French interests, and therefore Daville's personal pride and professional zeal.

Through informers, Daville had maintained permanent links with the Turkish commanders of the towns along the Austrian frontier. Even the least significant plundering foray out of these towns, or simply the word that such a foray was being prepared obliged the Austrians to send their troops into those regions and keep them there. By means of these contacts, Daville did what he could to weaken Austrian military strength and maintain a state of constant tension on their borders with Bosnia.

Among these commanders Ahmed Bey Cerić of Novi stood out. Daville knew him personally. He was a very young man, who had just acquired the post of Commander, with his father's death. A splendidly built man, of noble bearing, proud, eloquent and intractable, Ahmed Bey burned with the desire to distinguish himself in battle on the frontier which had so often been crossed and plundered by his forebears. He was quite injudicious in stressing his contacts with the French and he used to send the Austrian commander on the other side of the border threats and insulting messages "from Ahmed Bey Cerićand the French Emperor Napoleon". In keeping with the traditions of commanders from the border towns he hated and despised the Vizier, rarely came to Travnik and refused to accept instructions or orders from anyone.

Indirectly, through their people at the Porte, the Austrians had succeeded in blackening Ahmed Bey's name and presenting him as a traitor in French pay. This was a shorter, cheaper and more certain method than spending years skirmishing with the turbulent young commander on the frontier. A trap was carefully set. A Katil-Ferman for Cerić's execution arrived in Travnik, with a reprimand to the Vizier for tolerating such commanders and obliging the Porte to learn of their treachery from other sources. The issue was clearly posed: either the importunate commander must be removed and done away with, or the Vizier in Travnik would be replaced.

It was not easy to lure Ahmed Bey to Travnik, but the Austrians helped in this too. The commander was tricked into thinking that the French Consul had summoned him for talks. Once in Travnik he was immediately seized, put in irons and thrown into prison in the fortress.

This situation showed Daville the nature of Turkish terror, what the combination of deceit and violence could do and what kind of forces he had to contend with in this accursed town.

The very day after Ahmed Bey's arrest, a gypsy was hanged below the graveyard and the town-crier announced loudly and clearly that he had been hanged because "he had greeted the Novi commander" as he was being led to the fortress. This amounted to the commander's death sentence. Immediately everyone was filled with that blind, icy fear which descended on Travnik and Bosnia from time to time, paralysing for a few hours or days all life and even thought, and so enabling the forces which spread it to carry out what they intended rapidly and unhampered.

All his life Daville had hated and avoided everything dramatic. It was difficult for him even to imagine that the only solution to a conflict might be tragic. That went against his whole nature. And now he was entrammelled, indirectly, in a real tragedy, insoluble and without hope. In his present edgy state, hemmed in by mountains, troubled and oppressed for the second year now by difficulties and misfortunes of all kinds, Daville felt that he was involved in this drama of the Novi commander more than he actually was. He was particularly pained by the fact that, according to d'Avenat, the commander had been lured to Travnik by the abuse of Daville's name, so that the unfortunate man might well think that the French Consul too had had a part in his downfall.

After a sleepless night he resolved to seek an audience with the Vizier and to intercede on behalf of the commander, but tactfully, so as not to do him more harm. The conversation with the Vizier revealed a new side to Ibrahim Pasha. This was not the Ibrahim Pasha with whom he had only a few days before talked as with his closest and dearest friend about the disorder of the world and the necessity for agreement among all honourable and intelligent people. As soon as Daville mentioned the commander, the Vizier became cold and distant. He listened impatiently, almost with surprise, to his "noble friend", who, it seemed, had not yet learned that in life conversations were conversations and business business, and that everyone had to bear his own real troubles himself and solve them as best he could.

Summoning all his strength, Daville endeavoured to be decisive, convincing, sharp, but he felt his mind and will weakening and softening as in a dream and an irresistible torrent sweeping the handsome, smiling commander away from him. He pronounced Napoleon's name several times, asking the Vizier what people would say when they saw that the harshest possible punishment had been meted out to such a distinguished man simply because he was considered a friend of the French and because he had been falsely accused by the Austrians. But each of Daville's words sank immediately, impotent, into the Vizier's silence. Eventually, the Vizier said:

"I thought it would be safer and better to keep him here until all the hue and cry against him died down, but if you want I shall send him back to his post, to wait there. And whatever is decided in Istanbul shall be done."

Daville felt that none of these vague words had any connection with what was tormenting him, or with the commander's fate, but nothing more could be extracted from the Vizier.

The Consul also called on Suleiman Pasha, who had just returned from Serbia, and Tahir Bey, and was astonished when he was confronted by the same silence and the same expression of surprise. They too looked at him as at a man wasting words on an irrevocably lost cause, but whom politeness did not permit them to interrupt and who must be patiently and sympathetically heard out.

On their way back to the Consulate, the Consul asked d'Avenat what he thought. The interpreter, who had translated all three of the morning's conversations, said calmly:

"After what the Vizier said, it's clear that nothing can be done for Ahmed Bey. It's a lost cause. Either exile to Asia, or worse."

The Consul flushed with anger. "What? But didn't he promise at least to send him back to Novi?"

The interpreter fixed his burned-out eyes on the Consul's face for a moment and said in a dry, matter-of-fact tone:

"How could he send him back to Novi, where the commander has a hundred and one ways of defending himself?"

The Consul thought that his interpreter's voice had also conveyed something of that impatient surprise that had so confused and offended him while he was talking to the Vizier and his associates.

Daville was faced once again with a sleepless night, with dragging hours and that humiliating sense of utter hopelessness and impotence to defend his cause. He opened the window, as though seeking help from outside. He breathed deeply as he gazed out into the darkness. Somewhere in it was the grave of that gypsy who had had the misfortune to meet the commander on the bridge in front of the fortress and bid him a humble and fearful "Merhaba". For, even if he was a gypsy, he did not have the heart or the face not to greet a man who had once done him a great favour. Lost in it too, without trial or reason, was the young commander. As though he were able to read in that darkness far more clearly than in the false light of day, Daville became clearly aware both of his own powerlessness and of the commander's fate.

During the Revolution in Paris and the war in Spain he had seen many deaths and misfortunes, tragedies and fateful misunderstandings befall innocent lives, but he had never yet seen, from so close to, an honourable man relentlessly destroyed by the pressure of events. In unstable times and this kind of environment, governed by blind chance, caprice and the basest impulses, it happened that events would suddenly start spinning, like whirlpools or clouds of dust swirled up by the wind, around a man singled out quite fortuitously and he would sink in them irretrievably. And now this handsome, strong, rich commander had been suddenly caught in such a maelstrom. He had only been doing what all the frontier commanders had been doing all their lives, but a series of events had chanced to become meshed around him, linking into a firm chain.

It was by chance that the Austrian frontier captain had met with the understanding of his superiors in his proposal that the young

Novi commander should be destroyed. By chance at that moment the higher authorities attributed great importance to peace on that frontier. By chance Vienna had categorically demanded of its secret agent at the Porte that the commander should be removed. By chance that unknown high official, very interested in Austrian bribes at that particular moment, exerted severe pressure on the Vizier in Travnik. By chance the discouraged and irrevocably frightened Ibrahim Pasha put the whole affair into the hands of the merciless Governor, the Kaymakam, for whom the execution of an innocent man was nothing and who, by chance again, happened at that moment to need a terrible example to demonstrate his power and scare the ayans and the border commanders.

Each of these individuals was working independently, exclusively for himself, without the least connection with the commander himself. But in doing so, all of them together tightened the noose around his neck ever more firmly. And all by chance and unwittingly.

Such was the fate of the Consul's unfortunate protégé. As he gazed into the damp darkness, Daville began to see clearly what he had been unable to make out that morning from the impatient silence and those surprised looks at the Residence.

And on the other side of Travnik, as though on the opposite shore of that gloom, Herr von Mitterer was also sitting, still awake, beside a steady light, writing his report about the case of Ahmed Bey Cerić to his superiors. He endeavoured to emphasize his own merit in the fall of the Novi commander, without exaggerating it, so as not to offend the captain in Croatia and the others who had contributed to it. "Now this meddlesome and ambitious commander, a notable adversary of ours, is in chains in the fortress here on a serious charge. As things stand, there is no chance of his getting out alive. From what I know, the Vizier is determined to be rid of him. I shall not work particularly or openly to this end, but you may be sure that I shall do nothing that could prevent his neck being wrung once and for all."

The following morning, at dawn, the Novi commander was shot with a musket, as he slept, and buried the same day in the graveyard between the road and the Lašva. The word was put about town that he had tried to escape as he was being taken on his way to Novi and that the guards had had to fire at him.

Daville burned with fever, dropping with fatigue and lack of sleep. But as soon as he shut his eyes, he felt that he was alone in the world, surrounded by a conspiracy of infernal forces and fighting with his last strength, in fog and on slippery ground, all his senses exhausted.

He was roused with a start by the thought that he must at once write reports, to three destinations, Paris, Istanbul and Split. He would have to sit down and write, describing the steps he had taken with the Vizier as a dramatic struggle for the reputation of France, attributing his whole failure to unfortunate circumstances beyond his control.

Daville came to terms with the death of the Novi commander. And when he stood up, he told himself: it was a black day when you came to this country and now there is no going back, but you must always keep in mind that you should not judge the actions of these people by your own standards nor react to them with your own sensitivity, otherwise you will come very rapidly to a wretched end. With this decision he went back to work. In any case, in times like these one problem quickly drives another into oblivion. New tasks and directives were reaching the Consul. Seeing that his superiors did not attribute to the downfall of the Novi commander the same significance as he himself did in his isolation and bewilderment, Daville too endeavoured to bury that defeat in himself and silence the painful questions it raised. It was not easy to forget Ahmed Bey's glowing, girlish face with the shining teeth and bright brown eyes of a highlander, with the smile of a man who is not afraid of anything. Nor the Vizier's silence, before which the Consul had felt humiliated and incapable of defending his rights and his country's cause. But nevertheless, with the demands new days were bringing, these things had all to be forgotten.

The Vizier at once became his old self again. He invited Daville to see him, behaved affably towards him, did him various favours and carried on their customary conversations. Daville nurtured this curious friendship. They spent increasingly lengthy periods in amicable discussions which were often nothing but the Vizier's pessimistic monologues, but Daville always succeeded in the end in pushing through the trivial consular care he had come about. There were days when the Vizier would invite the French Consul of his own accord on any excuse, just to talk. In this respect, Daville left his rival von Mitterer far behind. The Austrian Consul was received only when he requested an audience and discussions with him were short, politely cold and formal.

Napoleon's reconciliation with Russia had caused great disappointment and hostility towards France in Istanbul, but even this could not affect relations between the Vizier and the Consul for long. As always with the Turks, the transition was abrupt and the surprise complete. As soon as he received this news from Istanbul, the Vizier had immediately cooled. He did not invite Daville to talk. When the Consul himself requested an audience he would reply curtly and drily. But this all lasted a very short time and, as usual, soon became its opposite. Without apparent reason, the Vizier softened. And the friendly conversations and exchange of small kindnesses began again. Even the reproaches for French behaviour, which the Vizier addressed to the Consul from time to time, were now only an excuse for their melancholy common reflections on the inconstancy of human relations. Daville unloaded the blame for everything onto the English: Ibrahim Pasha loathed the English as much as the Russians, ever since he had experienced the English navy's attack on the Bosphorus when he was Grand Vizier.

In the end, Daville began to get used to surprises and to the ebb and flow of the Pasha's disposition towards him.

Von Mitterer's attempts to win the Vizier over through gifts and to oust Daville were fruitless. He acquired a fine light carriage from Slavonski Brod and presented it to the Vizier. This was the first real luxury carriage Travnik had ever seen. The Vizier accepted the gift with grace. People went to the Residence to see the black, gleamingly lacquered coach. But the Vizier himself was indifferent and this was most chastening for von Mitterer whose official reports did not disclose the fact that Ibrahim Pasha had never so much as sat in the gift carriage nor driven anywhere in it. The coach continued to stand in the central courtyard of the Residence, a shining, cold, and inappropriate offering.

At roughly the same time, Daville, who had far fewer resources and far less influence on his government, succeeded in acquiring from Paris, as gifts for the Vizier, a small telescope and an astrolabe for measuring the position and height of the stars on the horizon. The Consul was not actually able to explain exactly how to use the telescope, and even thought that some parts were missing or broken, but the Vizier accepted the gift gratefully. For him in any case all objects in the world were dead and meaningless and he valued them only according to the person and intentions of the giver. The telescope was just an excuse for new conversations about the stars and human destiny which may be read in the stars, about the changes and catastrophes they predict. It was during that first year as well that the Vizier was dealt a new, severe blow which should have finished him off, had there still been any need to crush him.

That summer the Vizier went to the Drina with a large escort. He had the intention of detaining the Bosnian troops as long as possible by his presence and preventing them from returning too early to Bosnia for the winter. He might have succeeded, but in

Zvornik he received word of a new coup d'état in Istanbul and the tragic death of the former Sultan Selim III.

The messenger, who brought details of all that had taken place in Istanbul at the end of July, did not know that the Vizier was on the battlefield. He arrived first in Travnik, from where he was sent straight to Zvornik. Through this messenger, Daville sent the Vizier a crate of lemons, with a few touching words in which recent events in Istanbul were not mentioned, but which were obviously an expression of solicitude and compassion towards the Vizier in the calamity that had befallen his master. When the same messenger returned to Travnik, he brought a letter from the Vizier, thanking Daville for the gift and saying simply that it was the greatest joy to receive a present from a true friend and that "an angel of light guides the steps of the giver". Daville, who knew well what a severe blow the terrible death of Selim was for the Vizier, stood surprised and thoughtful over this warm, serene letter. It was one of those strange surprises one experiences in the East. There was no connection whatever between a man's true inner life and the words he wrote.

The Consul's surprise would have been still greater had he been able to see the Vizier immediately after he received the news from Istanbul.

The tents for the Vizier and his escort stood on a piece of flat ground below an abandoned quarry. There was always some cool air here even on such sultry nights as these, for all night long a constant breeze carried the freshness of water and willow trees down the narrow valley. The Vizier immediately withdrew into his tent and did not let anyone other than his closest and most devoted aides near him. Tahir Bey had ordered everything to be prepared for the return to Travnik but because of the Vizier they could not contemplate such a difficult journey immediately.

After receiving the distressing news calmly, the Vizier had, without looking at anyone, pronounced with equally perfect calm the surah for the dead and the rahmet for the soul of the man he had loved more than anything and anyone in this world. Then, with his slow step of a belated nocturnal apparition, he had gone into his tent. As soon as the heavy flap had been lowered behind him, he collapsed like a felled tree onto the mattress and began to tear off his clothes and weapons as though he were suffocating. His old servant, dumb from birth, tried in vain to remove his clothes and cover him, for the Vizier would not let himself be touched, as though even the lightest contact caused him unspeakable pain. With convulsive movements he refused a glass of sherbet. He lay like a stone which had rolled down from a great height, his eyes closed and his lips pressed together. The colour of his skin kept changing abruptly: it was yellow, then green, then brown as earth, from the sudden rush of bile. He lay like that, silent and motionless, for several hours. It was only towards evening that he began to moan, softly at first, and then to utter long drawn-out monotonous groans, with rare, brief pauses. Had anyone dared pass by the tent, they would have thought it was some foolish, feeble lamb, born the previous day, lost and bleating for its mother. But apart from the Secretary and the old servant no one could come anywhere near, nor see or hear the Pasha even from a distance.

All day and all night, the Vizier lay like that, refusing all help, not opening his eyes and emitting, straight from his throat, that long drawn-out, unmodulated sound of a soft, animal lament: "Ah – ah – ah – ah!"

It was not until the following dawn that Tahir Bey succeeded in getting through to him and persuading him to talk. Once he had come to, the Vizier quickly pulled himself together, dressed and became himself again. It was as though he had put on his rigid posture and his old infrequent movements together with his clothes. Now there was nothing about him that even the greatest catastrophe could alter. Then he wanted to set out immediately, but they had to travel slowly, in short stages from one halt to the next.

When the Vizier reached Travnik, Daville sent another crate of lemons by way of welcome. But he did not seek an audience, considering it better to let the approach come from the grieving Vizier himself, although he was burning with eagerness to see and hear him and to inform his Ambassador in Istanbul about his impressions of Selim's former Grand Vizier and what he had to say. Daville was doubly satisfied with his apt decision when he learned that the Austrian Consul had immediately sought an audience and been received, but in a cold, unfriendly manner. The Vizier had not wanted to say a single word in reply to all his probing about events in Istanbul. It was only a few days later that Daville reaped the fruits of his shrewd restraint.

The Vizier summoned the French Consul on the eve of the Friday holy day, with the excuse that on his return from the battlefield he wanted to inform him about the progress of operations against the rebels in Serbia. He received him warmly and to start with really did talk only about what he had seen of the fighting.

In the Vizier's account, everything seemed trivial and insignificant. In his deep, rumbling voice he spoke with the same contempt of both the rebels and the Bosnians fighting them.

"I saw what I had to see and my presence in that God-forsaken region became superfluous. The Russians, who had been helping the rebels to carry out their operations, have left Serbia. All that is left are the rebellious, misled rayah and it is not worthy of the Ottoman Empire that a former Grand Vizier should tackle them directly. They are miserable wretches, quarrelling among themselves, who will wreak havoc with each other and then fall at our feet. There is no need to sully our hands."

Daville looked in admiration at this statue of pain, telling lies so tranquilly and with such dignity. What the Vizier was saying was the direct opposite of reality, but the calm dignity with which he spoke was in itself a powerful, defiant reality. ("You see," Daville recalled his old familiar thought while the interpreter was stringing the last words together, "you see! The course of life's events does not depend on us in the least, or very little. But the way we bear these events is to a large extent in our own hands. So that's where we should concentrate our attention. Clearly!")

Soon after the contemptuous words about the Serbian uprising and the Bosnian army which was meant to crush it, the conversation turned of its own accord to Selim's death. Even now the Vizier did not change his tone of voice or expression. His whole being was saturated with mortal grief without any possibility of gradation.

For a time there was no one in the large Divan on the first floor. Even the servants with the chibouks had disappeared at an imperceptible sign. Only the Vizier and the Consul, and between them, a hand's breadth lower, d'Avenat, hunched on crossed legs, his arms folded and eyes lowered. He had transformed himself entirely into the low, monotonous voice, almost a whisper, in which he spoke the translation for the Consul.

The Vizier asked Daville whether he knew any details about all that had happened in Istanbul. The Consul said he did not and was anxious to hear them as soon as possible, for the French were grief-stricken at the death of such a true friend and a ruler of such rare qualities as Selim had been.

"You're right," said the Vizier thoughtfully, "the late Sultan, who is now enjoying all the bliss of paradise, loved and sincerely admired your country and your Emperor. All high-minded and noble men, without exception, have lost a good friend in him."

The Vizier spoke in a soft, muffled voice, as though the dead man were lying in the next room, but he kept to hard facts, as though avoiding what was most important and most difficult.

"No one who did not know him closely can begin to imagine

how great a loss it is," said the Vizier. "He was a many-sided man, perfect from every point of view. He sought the company of learned men. He himself wrote, under the name of Ilhami, The Inspired, verse which was a delight to the initiated. I remember the poem he composed the morning he ascended the throne.

"'God's mercy has destined me to hold the throne of Suleiman the Magnificent.' That's how it began, I think. But his real passions were mathematics and building. He himself participated in the reform of the administration and the taxation system. He toured schools himself, examining pupils and distributing prizes. He climbed onto buildings with an ivory ruler in his hand, supervising the methods of work, the quality and price of the materials. He wanted to know and see everything. He loved work. And he was sound in body, strong and deft, so that he had no equal with the lance or sabre. With my own eyes I have seen him cut down three rams with a single sweep of his sabre. They must have surprised him, treacherously, unarmed, for he would not have feared anyone with his sabre in his hand. Ah, he was too noble and too trusting!"

It was only because he was speaking about his beloved master in the past tense that one could have known he was talking about a dead man. Otherwise he avoided referring clearly to the Sultan's death.

He spoke rapidly and absently, as though he wanted to stifle another, inner voice.

D'Avenat translated softly, endeavouring to make his voice and appearance as unobtrusive as possible. At one moment, as he spoke the last words, the Vizier gave a slight start, as though he had just noticed the interpreter. He turned his whole body towards him, slowly and stiffly, like a carving pushed by unseen hands, directing the dead, terrible gaze of a stone statue at the interpreter, whose voice faltered and whose spine bent still lower.

This was the end of the conversation for that day.

Both the Consul and his interpreter emerged as out of a grave. D'Avenat was as white as a corpse, with drops of cold sweat on his brow. Daville was silent until they reached home. But he noted among the worst horrors he had experienced during those years in Travnik that ghostly movement of a living statue.

The murder of the deposed Sultan Selim strengthened the bond between the unhappy Vizier and the Consul who knew how to listen and to take a restrained and intelligent part in the Vizier's joyless conversations.

Only a few days later, the Consul was again summoned to the Vizier. Ibrahim Pasha had fresh news from Istanbul, from a servant who had witnessed Selim's murder, and he evidently wanted to talk to the Consul.

No one could have told from his external appearance what the Vizier had been through in these last ten days. But it was clear from his words that he had begun to come to terms with his loss and to be accustomed to the pain it caused him. Now he was already talking of the death as of something definitive.

In the course of the next fortnight, Daville saw the Vizier three times; twice at the Divan and once they went together to watch cannon being cast in the Vizier's new foundry. The Consul came each time with a list of requests and current problems. Everything was resolved quickly and almost always favourably. Immediately afterwards, the Vizier would turn with bitter and passionate satisfaction to the subject of Selim's tragic death, to the reasons for it and details of the event. His need to talk about it was great, and the French Consul was the only man whom he considered worthy of such a conversation. With a few apt questions, which were an expression of his sympathy, Daville filled out the account and encouraged him. So the Vizier told him all the details of the last act of Selim's and, in fact, his own tragedy. And it was clear that he badly needed to talk at length, precisely about those details.

A movement in favour of the deposed Sultan Selim III had been initiated by Mustapha Baryaktar, one of the better military commanders, an honourable, but impulsive and uneducated man. He had marched on Istanbul from Wallachia with his Albanian troops with the intention of overthrowing the objectionable government and its Sultan Mustapha, freeing Selim from his incarceration in the Seraglio and putting him back on the throne. He was well received everywhere and he reached Istanbul, where he was welcomed as a victorious liberator. He succeeded in getting as far as the Seraglio and had entered the first courtyard, but here one of the officers of the guard managed to close the great inner gate in his face. Then the brave but crude and maladroit Baryaktar made a fatal mistake. He began to shout, demanding the immediate release of the deposed lawful Sultan Selim. Hearing this and seeing that Mustapha Baryaktar was master of the situation, the feeble-minded, perfidious and cruel Sultan Mustapha had ordered Selim's immediate execution. A slave girl betrayed the luckless Sultan, who was just saying his afternoon prayer, when the Chief Eunuch and his four assistants came into the room. They stood for a moment, confused, and then the Chief Eunuch hurled himself on the Sultan, who was just then kneeling with his brow touching the prayer-rug. The slaves went at once to the Eunuch's assistance, grabbing Selim by the arms and legs and driving his servants away with knives.

The Consul suddenly felt a shudder run down his spine and, only half-hearing, it occurred to him all at once that he was looking at a madman. The Vizier's inner being was even more monstrous and deranged than his extraordinary outer appearance. D'Avenat interpreted with difficulty, skipping passages and missing out words.

"He's mad, there can't be any doubt about it," said the Consul to himself, "he's mad!"

And the Vizier continued his narration as though uttering a prayer, unfaltering, as though this were not a conversation with someone in front of him but an inner monologue. He kept recounting even the least details, painstakingly and conscientiously, as though they were of exceptional importance, as though he were casting a spell and through his magic saving the Sultan whom he could not save. Driven on by this incomprehensible but irresistible need, he was determined to repeat aloud everything he had heard from the witness who had escaped, the whole burden that was now oppressing him. Evidently the Vizier was going through a phase of temporary insanity. It was a kind of obsession of which the cause and focus was the downfall of Selim III. And it seemed that he was able to find at least some relief from this torment by presenting the whole drama to a kindly stranger exactly as he saw it.

And the Consul could visualize that struggle clearly. Against his will he had to follow it in every detail, each of which made him shudder repeatedly.

In the struggle which followed, continued the Vizier, Selim had succeeded in tearing himself away and knocking the fat Chief Eunuch down with one powerful blow. He stood in the middle of the room, flailing out with his arms and legs. The black slaves kept leaping at him, defending themselves from his blows. One of them had a bow without an arrow and kept trying to loop the bowstring over his victim's head, so as to strangle him with it. ("The Sultan did not have a sabre, but if he had, the situation would have been quite different," the Vizier repeated sorrowfully.) As he concentrated on warding off that bowstring, Selim lost sight of the prostrate Chief Eunuch. The fat, powerful Negro had clambered unnoticed onto his knees and with a swift movement he grabbed Selim, who was standing with his legs apart, by the scrotum. The Sultan howled with pain and bent down so that his head came close to the Chief Eunuch's sweating, blood-stained face. From that distance, he could not swing his arm to strike the Eunuch, who was rolling over the carpet without letting go of his victim. The slave took advantage of this moment and succeeded in throwing the bowstring over Selim's head. He twisted the bow several times, tightening the noose around his neck. The Sultan struggled, but with only half his strength, for he was rapidly losing consciousness from the pain in his groin. His face was changing colour. His mouth opened, his eyes started. His hands fluttered a few more times at the height of his neck, but pitifully and powerlessly, and then the whole man folded in on himself, bending at the knees, the waist, and the neck. Finally he collapsed by the wall and stayed crumpled up like that, half sitting, without a spasm, as though he had never lived or defended himself.

The corpse was immediately laid out on a carpet and carried on it, as on a stretcher, to Sultan Mustapha.

Outside the locked gate, Mustapha Baryaktar was banging and shouting impatiently: "Open up, you curs and sons of bitches! Let the true Sultan Selim go! Or I'll strike the heads from your shoulders!"

Baryaktar's Albanians yelled and shrieked, as though they wanted to reinforce his cries, and got ready to force the heavy gate.

At that moment one of the narrow, deep-set windows, cut high into the wall on either side of the gate, opened. The shutters parted slowly, for they were rusty and overgrown with lichen. A folded mat appeared in the half-open window and out of it slid the half-dressed corpse, landing with a dull thud on the small white cobblestones.

Mustapha Baryaktar was the first to run up. Before him lay the dead Sultan Selim, bare-headed and battered, his face blue. It was too late. Baryaktar had won, but his victory had lost all meaning. Evil and madness had triumphed over good and reason. Vice had remained on the throne and disorder in the state.

"That, sir, is how the noblest ruler of the Ottoman Empire perished," the Vizier concluded, as though waking with relief from a sleep in which he had been talking all this time.

When he returned home after these conversations, Daville always reflected that no one would ever know just how dearly he paid for all the small successes and concessions he obtained from the Vizier. Even d'Avenat was silent, lost for words of explanation.

12

That year – 1808 – was evidently to be a year of losses and misfortunes of all kinds. Instead of the damp Travnik season, "neither autumn nor winter", there was a sharp, early frost at the very beginning of November. During that time one of Daville's children fell suddenly ill.

Daville's middle son was two years old and until then had been thriving – unlike his younger brother born in Split on their way to Travnik, who had always been delicate. When the child fell ill, his mother treated him with infusions and household medicines, but when he became really weak, even the courageous Madame Daville lost her composure. They began to summon the doctors, those who called themselves doctors and anyone popularly regarded as one. This gave the foreigners a chance to see what health and sickness meant to these people and what being ill in this country entailed. The doctors were: d'Avenat, who was attached to the Consulate, Brother Luka Dafinić from the Guča Gora monastery, Mordo Atijas, the Travnik apothecary and Giovanni Mario Cologna, the titular physician at the Austrian Consulate. His presence had an official character and he announced ceremoniously that he had come "on the instructions of His Excellency the Austrian Consul General, to place his skill at the disposal of His Excellency the French Consul General". There was immediate disagreement and conflict between him and d'Avenat concerning both the diagnosis and the treatment. Mordo Atijas said nothing and Brother Luka asked leave to go to Guča Gora to fetch some of his special herbs.

In fact, all these Travnik doctors were confused and dissatisfied, for they had never had to treat such a small child. The range of their skill did not stretch to either the highest or the lowest limits of human life. In these lands small children live or die according to the will of chance, just as very old people may either fade away or their time may be drawn out a little longer. It is a question of the resilience of these children or old people, the care offered by those around them and, ultimately, of the whim of destiny, against which there is no doctor or medicine. That is why tiny, weak or worn-out beings, who do not stand firmly with both feet on the ground, are not considered suitable for treatment or the attention of doctors. And if prominent personages in the highest positions had not been involved, none of these doctors would have concerned himself with such a small creature. As it was, their visits were more an expression of attentiveness towards the parents than real interest in the child. And in this there was no great difference between Brother Luka and Mordo Atijas on the one hand and d'Avenat and Cologna on the other, for these two foreigners had also grown completely into the ways of Eastern lands. In any case, their knowledge did not go any further or deeper.

In the circumstances, Daville decided to take the child himself all the way to Sinj where there was a good, well-known French military doctor. In keeping with their outlook, the Travnik doctors were decisively and unitedly opposed to this extraordinary decision, but the Consul was adamant.

The Consul set off, accompanied by a khavaz and three grooms, in increasingly intense cold, along icy roads. He himself carried the sick child, well wrapped-up, in his arms.

The unusual procession set off at dawn from the Consulate. They had only just crossed Karaula mountain when the little boy expired in his father's arms. They spent the night with the dead child at a khan and the following day returned to Travnik. They reached the Consulate at dusk.

Madame Daville was lulling her youngest son to sleep and just whispering a prayer "for the travellers", when she was startled by the sound of hoof-beats and knocking at the gate. Paralysed, she could not move from where she was and it was there Daville found her when he came in, bearing the well-wrapped child in his arms as tenderly and carefully as ever. He laid the dead child down, threw off his wide black cape which spread a sudden chill through the room, and clasped his wife to him. Ice cold and beside herself, she was still whispering the last words of the prayer in which a moment before she had been praying that her child should return to her, recovered.

The Consul, frozen, shattered by his two days' riding, could hardly stand on his feet. His arms which had been in the same position for hours, holding first the sick child and then its body, were painfully numb. But, forgetting all of that now, he pressed her frail body to him, with a silent tenderness that contained the infinity of his love for his wife and his child. He closed his eyes and let himself go. Like this, forgetting his weariness and overcoming his grief, he felt as though he were still carrying his child towards recovery and that it would not die as long as he could continue, in pain and anguish, to carry it through the world. And, in his arms, his wife wept meekly and softly, the way courageous and utterly unselfish women do.

Des Fossés stood a little way off, embarrassed and superfluous, observing in surprise the unsuspected stature of an ordinary man.

The following day, in sun and dry frost, little Jules-François Amyntas Daville was buried in the Catholic graveyard. The Austrian Consul attended the funeral with his wife and daughter and came to the Consulate to express his condolences. Frau von Mitterer offered her services, and talked emotionally and at length about children, illness and death. Daville and his wife listened to her calmly, watching her with dry eyes and the expression of people for whom every word of consolation is welcome, but whom no one can actually help and who do not expect it of anyone in any case. That conversation evolved into a lengthy dialogue between Frau von Mitterer and Des Fossés, and finally ended as a monologue about destiny from Anna Maria. She was pale and solemn. Emotional upsets were her true element. Her brown hair curled in unruly locks, and her large eyes shone unnaturally in her pale face. This glow lit up grey depths in them, so that it was hard to look into them for long without turning away. Her face was full and pale, her neck without a single wrinkle, her breast that of a mature young girl. In this circle of death and grief, between her sallow, preoccupied husband and frail, silent daughter, she seemed to shine, standing out in her strange and dangerous beauty. Des Fossés looked for a long time at her strong, slender hands. The skin of these hands was white, but when they moved the joints became suffused with a dark, pearly sheen like the barely perceptible reflection of an unseen, pure white flame. Something of that white sheen stayed in his eyes the whole day. And when he caught sight of Anna Maria again, in the Dolac church, where the Requiem Mass was said for the soul of the dead child, the first thing he looked at was her hands. But this time they were both in black gloves.

After several unsettled days, everything returned to its usual course. The winter closed all doors, driving people into their heated houses. There was no further contact between the two Consulates. Even Des Fossés curtailed his outings. The conversations with Daville before lunch and dinner were now milder and warmer and generally turned on subjects which did not offer scope for differences of opinion. As always happens in the days immediately following a funeral, they avoided mentioning the death of the child, but since these thoughts could not be driven away, they talked a good deal about his illness, about health and sickness altogether, and particularly about medicine and doctors in this difficult land.

There are innumerable and varied surprises in store for a Westerner suddenly cast into the East and obliged to live there. But one of the greatest and most painful surprises occurs in questions of health and sickness. For such a man the life of the body suddenly takes on a quite new light. In the West illness exists in various forms and with all kinds of horrors, but as something which is quelled and mitigated or at least hidden from the eyes of healthy, cheerful, busy people, by the special organization of the community, conventions or traditional forms of social life. Here, on the other hand, sickness is not regarded as in any way exceptional. It appears and develops alongside health, alternating with it. It is seen, heard and felt at every step. Here a person takes medicine as naturally as he takes food, and is ill just as naturally as he lives. Sickness is the other, more difficult half of life. Epileptics, syphilitics, lepers, hysterics, idiots, hunchbacks, cripples, the dumb, the blind, the lame, all these people swarm about in broad daylight – shuffling and crawling, begging for alms or defiantly silent and bearing their terrible disability almost with pride. It is fortunate that women, particularly Turkish women, hide and cover themselves, otherwise the number of sick people one meets would be twice as great. Daville and Des Fossés would both think of this whenever they saw some peasant coming down a steep country road into Travnik, leading a horse by the halter with a woman swaying on its back, entirely enveloped in her long veil, like a sack filled with unknown suffering and disease.

But it was not only the poor who fell ill. Illness here was the destiny of the poor, but also the punishment of the wealthy. On the shoots of plenty, as of poverty, the same flower of sickness blooms. The people in the Vizier's Residence, seen from close to and better known, were not much different in this respect from the poor, simple folk to be found on bazaar days in the alleyways. If the manner in which they were ill was different, the attitude to illness was the same.

In the course of the Consul's son's illness, Des Fossés had occasion to get to know all four of the Travnik doctors. These were, as we have seen, d'Avenat, Cologna, Mordo Atijas and Brother Luka Dafinić.

We met d'Avenat right at the beginning as the interpreter and temporary clerk at the French Consulate. D'Avenat had not practised much medicine even under Mehmed Pasha. The title of doctor served him, as it did so many foreigners, only as a shield for carrying out all sorts of other tasks in which he showed far more knowledge and skill. Now he was satisfied with his new position, for which he had both the inclination and the ability. It seemed that he had studied some medicine in Montpellier as a young man, but he lacked everything needed for the vocation of doctor. He had no love of people or faith in nature. Like most Westerners who remain in the East by force of circumstance and adapt themselves to the Turks, he was infected with a deep pessimism and mistrust of everything. Healthy and sick humanity were for him two worlds without any real connection. He regarded recovery as simply a temporary state and not a transition from sickness to health, for, as he saw it, there could be no such transition. A man became ill, and that was his lot for this lifetime, and the other miseries, like pain, expense, treatment, doctors and other pitiful things, were a natural consequence. That was why he far preferred dealing with the healthy than the sick. He was repelled by the seriously ill, taking long drawn-out illness to some extent as a personal insult. He considered that such patients ought to make up their minds: to go either left or right, to join either the healthy or the dead.

When he did treat the Turkish gentry he served, he did so not through his knowledge or his more or less innocuous medicines, so much as by his strong will and reckless daring. He would flatter his well-born patients ingeniously, praising their strength and endurance, arousing their vanity and will to resist their illness;

or by suggestion, belittling the disease and its significance. This was all the easier for him, since he continued just as steadily and consistently to flatter the healthy gentry as well, only in a different way and to a different end. Very early on, he had grasped the importance of flattery and the powerful effect of fear. He realized the weight a kind or a harsh word could have, spoken at the right moment and in the right place. Uncouth and inconsiderate with the vast majority of people, he saved all his attentiveness for the powerful. In this he was both unusually skilled and brazen.

Such were the medical skills of César d'Avenat.

His absolute opposite was Mordo Atijas, a frail, taciturn Jew, who had a shop in the lower bazaar in which he sold not only medicines and medical instructions but everything, from spectacles and writing materials to potions for barren women, dyes for wool and good advice of all kinds.

The Atijases were the oldest Jewish family in Travnik. They had lived here for more than a hundred and fifty years. Their first house was outside the town in a narrow, damp gorge where one of those nameless streams which flow into the Lašva ran. This was a ravine within the Travnik ravine, almost entirely without sun, damp and full of rubble, overgrown on all sides with alder and traveller's joy. Here the Atijases were born and died, generation after generation. Later they managed to leave this gloomy, unhealthy place and move up into the town, but all the Atijas family retained something of their earlier dwelling. They were all frail and wan, as though they had grown up in a cellar, taciturn and withdrawn. They lived modestly, somehow imperceptibly, but with time they came by property and wealth. And some member of the family was always involved in medicine.

Of all the Travnik doctors and those who were regarded as such and summoned to the Consulate, there is the least to say about Mordo Atijas. What is there to tell about a man who says nothing, goes nowhere, is friendly with no one, asks for nothing, but minds his own business and looks after his home? The whole of Travnik and all the neighbouring villages knew of Mordo and his shop with its remedies, but at the same time that was all that was known about him.

He was a small man, completely swathed in beard, moustache and eyebrows, dressed in a striped smock and wide blue shalwars. As far as their family knew, their forebears had been doctors and apothecaries too, while still in Spain. The Atijas family had maintained that skill as exiles, first in Salonica and then in Travnik. Mordo's grandfather, Isaac the Doctor, had died here, in Travnik, as one of the first victims of the great plague, in the middle of the last century, and his son had taken over the shop and given it to this same Mordo some twenty years before. The family kept the books and notes of the famous Arabic and Spanish doctors which their forebears had brought with them when they set out as fugitives from Andalusia and they had passed them down from generation to generation as a precious secret. For more than twenty years, Mordo had been sitting in the raised, open front of his shop, every single day, apart from the Sabbath, his legs crossed, back bent and head bowed, always busy with customers and his powders, herbs and fluids. His tiny shop, no bigger than a large wooden box, brim-full from top to bottom, was so cramped and low that Mordo was able to reach everything with his hand, without getting up. So he would sit in his shop, winter and summer, always the same, in always the same clothes and the same mood: a huddled knot of silence which neither drank coffee nor smoked, nor participated in the bantering chatter of the bazaar.

One at a time, his sick customers or someone from their family would come, sit down on the edge of the narrow dais and tell him what they wanted. Mordo would then mutter his opinion through lips invisible in his dense black beard and moustache, hand over the medicine and take his fee. There was no possibility of anyone drawing him into any conversation. He did not talk more than was absolutely necessary, even with his patients about their illness. He listened to them placidly, watching them with his dark eyes out of that forest where there was not yet a single grey hair, and to all their tales he replied with always the same stock sentences. The last of these was: "The medicine is in my hands, health is in God's." This marked the end of the whole discussion and informed the customer that he should take what he wanted and pay or "leave it where it was".

"Oh, I'll take it, of course I'll take it. I'd take poison," the peasant would grumble, needing as much to complain and talk as he did the medicine.

But Mordo was unrelenting. He would wrap the medicament in blue paper, place it in front of the patient, and at once take up some small task he had put down a moment before, when the customer appeared.

On market days a crowd of peasant men and women would gather in front of Mordo's shop. One would be sitting on the dais whispering to Mordo, while the others stood in the street, waiting. They would have come for medicines or brought herbs to sell, and would talk quietly, negotiate, argue, and go home. Only Mordo remained where he was, motionless, indifferent and taciturn.

The noisiest and fussiest were the older peasant women who came for spectacles. First they recounted at great length how they had been able to thread even the finest needle until just a short time before, but that since the last winter for some reason, a chill or such, their eyes had begun to mist over and they found it difficult even to make out their knitting. Mordo looked at the woman in her forties, whose sight was naturally beginning to go, estimating the breadth of her face and thickness of her nose, then he took some spectacles with a thin frame out of a round black box and put them over the woman's eyes. She looked first at her hands, turning them up one way and then the other, and then at the ball of wool Mordo handed her, asking: "Can you see? Or can't you?" through his teeth, saving his breath.

"I can see, I can see: it's wool, only it's somehow far away, like at the end of the bazaar," said the peasant woman hesitantly.

Mordo took out another pair and asked: "Better?", sparing any other words.

"Yes and no. Now there's a sort of fog, like smoke, like something…"

Mordo calmly took out a third kind of spectacles and those were the last. The woman would have to see through those and buy them or "leave them where they were". She would not get another word out of Mordo for love or money.

Another patient came, a bony, wasted, ashen-faced peasant from the mountains, from the village of Paklarevo. Mordo asked him in his inaudible voice and Spanish accent what was troubling him.

"There's something like a live coal in my chest, Lord save you, and it hurts, it hurts…" the peasant said, pointing to the centre of his chest and he would have liked to tell him a few more times that it hurt.

But Mordo interrupted him drily: "There's nothing there, there can't be anything hurting there," he said categorically.

The peasant assured him that was exactly where the pain was, but nevertheless shifted his finger a little to the right.

"But it hurts…How can I explain? It hurts like this: it begins here, then the pain walks, that's what…it walks…"

In the end, the patient gave way a little, Mordo a little, and they came to an agreement about the place where the pain was more or less permanently situated. Then Mordo asked him briefly and in a business-like manner whether he had any rue in his garden and instructed him to crush this herb in a bowl, add a little honey, sprinkle it all with the powder he was going to give him, roll it into three little balls with his hands and swallow it before sunrise.

"Do that every morning for a week, from Friday to Friday. And the pain and sickness will go. That's two groats. Good luck!"

The peasant, who up to that moment had been trying to remember the instructions, his eyes wide-open, moving his lips, suddenly forgot everything, including the pain he had come about and reached for the place where he kept his linen purse. The difficult process of extracting began, with much sighing, hesitation, untying and counting out.

Then finally came the agonizing payment.

And once again, Mordo would be sitting, slight and motionless, bent over a new customer, and the peasant slowly left the bazaar and made his way along the edge of the stream to his high village of Paklarevo. On one side of his breast, the pain which did not ease, on the other, in his pocket, Mordo's powder, wrapped up in blue paper. And running through his whole body like another, separate pain, the pain of regret for his money, which seemed to him thrown away, of mistrust and the fear that he might have been cheated. He made his way straight towards the setting sun, completely distracted and despondent, for there is no creature so pathetically bewildered as a peasant who is ill.

Nevertheless there was one visitor with whom Mordo would talk for longer and more warmly and with whom he did not grudge wasting an extra minute or a word. This was Brother Luka Dafinić, better known as "The Medic". Brother Luka had worked with Mordo's father, David, and been on good terms with him. And he had been an inseparable friend and colleague of Mordo's for a full twenty years. (When he was younger, serving in the parishes, he would come to Travnik whenever he could and the first thing he did was to call on Mordo in his shop, and only afterwards go on to the priest in Dolac.) The Travnik bazaar had long been accustomed to seeing Mordo and Brother Luka with their heads together, muttering something or examining herbs and medicines.

Brother Luka was born near Zenica, but he had come to the monastery of Guča Gora as a child, when his family had all died of the plague. Here, with some brief interruptions, he had lived out his life among medicines, medical books and equipment. His cell was full of pots, jars and boxes, and on the walls and ceiling hung little bags or bundles of dried herbs, twigs and roots. In the window was a large bowl of leeches in clear water, and another, smaller one of scorpions in oil. He slept on a bench which was covered with an old, burnt, stained and patched rug, and beside it stood an earthenware brazier where a small pan of herbs would always be simmering. In the corners of the room and on the shelves were pieces of rare wood, large and small stones, animal skins and horns.

But for all this, the cell was always clean, aired, and usually fragrant with the scent of juniper berries or mint tea.

There were three pictures on the walls. Hippocrates, St Aloysius Gonzaga, and the portrait of an unknown knight in armour, with a vizor and a great plume on his head. How Brother Luka had come by this picture and what he wanted it for, no one was ever able to discover. Once, when the Turks had been carrying out an inspection of the monastery and found nothing they could object to, they focused their attention on this picture and were told it was the portrait of some sultan. An argument ensued about whether it was possible or permissible to paint sultans, and, as the picture was already quite faded and the Turks uneducated, that is where the matter rested. These pictures had been hanging here for more than half a human lifetime. They had never been particularly clear and had faded completely over the years, so that now St Aloysius looked like Hippocrates and Hippocrates like the "Sultan", while the "Sultan" in his faint print, on flimsy, cheap paper, no longer looked like anything and it was only Brother Luka who could clearly make out his sabre and helmet and still see his martial air of fifty years before.

While he was still a very young novice, Brother Luka had shown an inclination and gift for the medical vocation. Seeing this and knowing how great the need of the people and the monks was for a good doctor, his superiors had sent the young man to the Medical School in Padua. But the very next year, at the first change of authority, the new opposing group of superiors concluded that this was not quite appropriate for Brother Luka and too costly for the Monastery so they brought him back to Bosnia. Three years later, when the previous superiors were re-elected, they sent the young friar to Padua for a second time, to complete his medical studies. But after a year, the opposition faction returned, annulled everything that had been done up to then and, among other things, brought Brother Luka back from Padua to Guča Gora again, just out of spite.

With the knowledge he had gathered and the books he had managed to acquire, Brother Luka then established himself in this cell, continuing to study and collect medicines with passion and to treat people with love. The passion never deserted him and his love never cooled.

All was peace and order in this cell, where the tall, short-sighted, thin "Medic" moved noiselessly. Brother Luka's thinness had become proverbial in the whole province. ("There are two things even the most learned ulema do not know: what the earth rests on and how Brother Luka's habit stays up!") On top of this tall, thin body stood, upright and lively, a handsome head with blue eyes of a rapt and slightly absent air, with a thin wreath of white hair on his regular skull, and branching veins under its fine, pink skin. He remained vigorous and nimble well into old age. "That man doesn't walk, he flashes like a sabre," one of the Monastery Guardians used to say of him. And really, this man with his smiling eyes and quick, silent movements was never still. His long, frequently washed and dried fingers rummaged the whole day through numerous small objects, grating, pounding, pasting, tying, making notes, and cramming things into his boxes and shelves. Because, for Brother Luka, nothing was insignificant or superfluous. Under these thin fingers and in front of his smiling, short-sighted eyes everything came to life, spoke and sought its place among the medicaments or at least among his useful or unusual things.

As he observed, day after day, year after year, the herbs, minerals and living creatures around him, the changes in them and their movements, Brother Luka came to see increasingly clearly that there are only two things in the world as we see it: growth and decay, and they are everywhere closely and inextricably linked, in a constant state of flux. All the phenomena around us are simply isolated phases of this endless, complex and eternal ebb and flow, just fictions, passing moments which we arbitrarily isolate, define and call by fixed names, such as health, sickness and death. And none of that exists, of course. There are only growth and decay in various stages and under different aspects. And all the doctor's skill consists in recognizing, seizing on and exploiting the forces moving in the direction of growth, "as a sailor the winds", and avoiding and diverting all those which serve decay. Whenever a person manages to grasp that positive force, he recovers and sails on. Where he does not succeed, he simply sinks inexorably. And in the great, invisible account book of growth and decay a force is transferred from one side of the ledger to the other.

These were the broad lines of Brother Luka's picture of the world. In detail it was, of course, far more complex. Each living being, each plant, each illness, each season of the year, each day and each minute had its own growth and decay. And it was all fitted one into the other, linked by numerous obscure connections, and it all functioned, seethed, quivered and flowed, by day and night, deep under the earth, everywhere on it and high in the air, as far as the planets. And it was all governed by a single, twofold law of growth and decay, which was very difficult to grasp.

All his life, Brother Luka had exulted in this vision of the world and the perfect harmony which could only be glimpsed, which one could at times succeed in using, but never control. What could a man like himself do, to whom all this had been revealed, whose lot it was to work at a hopeless, boundless task: studying remedies and curing illnesses, according to God's ordinances? What should he first seize on and remember from that picture which would at one moment flash before him, clear, comprehensible, within his reach, and the next grow dim and swirl like a frenzied snowstorm in an impenetrable night? How was he to find his way through this flickering light, through this apparent chaos of disordered and interwoven mutual influences, blind forces and elements? How could he grasp at least some of the thickest threads and bind the consequences to their causes?

This was Brother Luka's only care and his dominant thought, apart from his duties to the Order and the church. That was why he was so preoccupied and absent-minded, thin as a taut wire. And that was why he threw himself with such passion at any blade of grass or patient, wherever they were, whatever they looked like and by whatever name they were known.

Brother Luka firmly believed that there were in nature as many healing forces as there were diseases among people and animals. One corresponded to another in every smallest detail. These were calculations on a grand scale for which there was no solution or standard, but at the same time there could be no doubt that they were accurate and balanced, with nothing left over, somewhere out there at the end, beyond sight. And those healing forces could be found, as the ancients taught, "in herbis, in verbis et in lapidibus".[7]

---

7 "in plants, in words and in stones".

Secretly Brother Luka boldly believed, although he did not admit it even to himself, that every adverse change in the human body may be suppressed, at least in theory, for the disease and its cure appear and exist at the same time, even if they are far, often inaccessibly far from one another. If the doctor succeeds in bringing them together, the disease will yield. If he does not, it will overwhelm and destroy the organism in which it has appeared. No failures and no disappointments could shake him in this secret faith. And it was with this unspoken faith that Brother Luka would approach every remedy and every patient. It is true that he fostered this inexplicable faith of his in so far as he, like so many other doctors, would quickly forget every incurable or dead patient entirely, while he remembered all successful cures, even fifty years later.

That was what Brother Luka Dafinić, the "Medic", was like. He was an enthusiastic and incorrigible friend of the sick half of humanity. He had the whole of nature for his ally and only two enemies: the friars and mice.

The business with the friars was a long, old story. The generations changed, differing from each other in many ways, but in one thing they were all agreed: the way they underestimated and criticized Brother Luka's medical skill. Ever since they had sent him as a student to Padua and brought him back, sent him again and brought him back again, he had lost all hope of any understanding or assistance from his brethren. The Guardian, Brother Martin Dembić, *vulgo* Dembo, used to speak about the harmony reigning between Brother Luka and the other friars: "You see this Luka the Medic of ours? Even when he's in the choir, praying with the friars, he's not thinking the same thoughts as them. While they recite the same prayer, Brother Luka is thinking: 'Lord, soften the hearts of these wicked Brethren of mine and make them see sense, so that they don't hinder me at every step in my good and useful work. Or, if You cannot do that, for I know how hard a friar's head can be even for the hand of God, then at least arm me with divine patience so that I may, without hatred or hard words, put up with them as they are and help them in sickness with my skill which they despise and condemn.' Meanwhile, the friars are thinking as they pray: 'Lord, enlighten the mind of this Brother Luka of ours, cure him of his terrible illness: of medicine and remedies. Blessed be all the illnesses You send (for a man must die of something!), only rid us of this fellow who wants to cure us of them.'"

Dembo was witty, forceful and mercilessly sardonic, but a good Guardian of the monastery and a faultless monk. For years, Brother Luka provided him with the theme of endless stories and jokes. But nevertheless, like so many others, Dembo was destined to die in Brother Luka's arms. He did smile even then, frowning in pain and breathing with difficulty, as he told the friars gathered round him: "Brethren, all the monastery accounts, the loans and ready cash, are in order. The Vicar knows all the details. And now forgive me my sins and remember me in your prayers. And know that two things did me in: my asthma and my doctor."

So Dembo joked, exaggerating things, until he died.

Only, that was all a long time ago, "in Dembo's day", when Brother Luka was younger and more sprightly and when his contemporaries, virtually all now dead, were still alive. For he had entered his eighty-first year on St John's Day. Brother Luka had long since forgiven the Brethren for not continuing to maintain him in Padua, and for never having given him as much as he needed for books and experiments. And with time they too had stopped teasing him so much on account of his unusual way of life, his passion for medicine and his friendship with Mordo Atijas. Brother Luka would still go into Travnik, sit with Mordo in the shop, exchanging observations and experience, bartering herbs and roots for sulphur and lapis lazuli, for no one knew how to dry linden flowers or to preserve willow-herb, St John's wort or yarrow as Brother Luka did.

The friars had long since become accustomed to this "friendship between the Old and New Testament".

Brother Luka's visits and ministrations to sick people outside the monastery, formerly the most frequent cause of conflict with the friars, were now reduced in scale. This activity had once been the source of constant tribulations for the monastery and the only reason for serious discord between Brother Luka and the monastery superiors. Even then it was not that Brother Luka used to look for patients among the laity, particularly not among the Turks. But the Turks sought him out, sometimes inviting and begging him, but more frequently commanding him and sending constables to take him to the patient. These visits caused Brother Luka and his monastery many headaches, and troubles of all kinds. He would be summoned with entreaties to cure some ailing Turk or Turkish woman, and then he and the monastery would be blamed if the patient took a turn for the worse or died. And even when the treatment succeeded and the satisfied relatives offered Brother Luka gifts, there were always some spiteful, greedy Turks who would complain about his going into Turkish houses. Witnesses always testified that the friar had been invited and that he had gone on honest business, but by the time that was all verified and the accusation withdrawn, it would have caused the monastery trouble, alarm and expense. That was why the friars did not allow Brother Luka to go and treat anyone in a Turkish house until that household had taken out a permit from the authorities in which it was clearly stated that they were summoning him of their own free will and that the authorities had nothing against it.

But even then, it did not always go smoothly. There were cases, quite a few of them, when the treatment was successful, and then generous, grateful people would heap praises and gifts on Brother Luka and the monastery.

A certain bey, one of the humbler, country beys, but an influential man, whose leg Brother Luka had successfully treated for a neglected wound below the knee, would say to the friar whenever he saw him: "When I get to my feet in the morning, you are the first person I praise, after Allah."

And as long as he lived, this bey defended the monastery and the friars and acted as their guarantor, whenever the need arose.

A wealthy Turk from Turbe, whose wife Brother Luka had saved, never said anything (for one never talks about women), but each year, after the Assumption, he would send the monastery two jars of honey and a sheepskin, with the message: "For the priest who heals the sick."

But, by contrast, there were also instances of black ingratitude and devilish spite. For a long time the monastery remembered the case of the young bride of Mustay Bey Miralem. Something came over the young woman, and she could find no ease anywhere, but for days on end kept twisting and turning, shrieking and grinding her teeth. Or else she would lie, motionless and silent, refusing to see anyone or touch any food. The family did whatever anyone advised them, but nothing helped, not spells, hodjas or amulets. And the young woman's life was ebbing away from day to day. In the end her father-in-law, old Miralem himself, sent to the monastery for the "Medic Brother".

When Brother Luka arrived, the woman had been lying for two days doubled up in a state of complete insensibility, and no one could rouse her from her grim silence. At first she did not want to turn her head. But then at one moment she parted her eyelids a fraction and caught sight of the friar's clumsy sandals, the edge of his habit and the white cord which friars tie round their waist. Then she raised her eyes slowly and morosely to look up at Brother Luka, thin and lengthy as he was, and it took her a long time to reach his grey head and meet his blue, smiling gaze. The woman suddenly burst out laughing, an unexpected, mad laughter, without end. The friar tried in vain to calm her with words and gestures. As he left the Miralem house, he could still hear her frightful laughter echoing after him from the large ground-floor room.

And the very next day, janissaries took Brother Luka to prison in chains. The Guardian was informed that old Miralem was accusing Luka of casting a spell over his daughter-in-law. This was the second day the young woman had not stopped laughing and she was driving the household to distraction. The Guardian argued that this could not be, a doctor's duty was to cure if he could, but they were prohibited from using spells and sorcery. At the same time, he distributed money right and left, giving more to some, less to others, but to no avail. He was only told that things looked very bad for the doctor, because the daughter-in-law maintained that the friar had secretly given her "something black and thick like grease" to drink and tapped her twice on the forehead with his large cross. And from then on she had not been able to restrain this laughter which tormented her ceaselessly.

Just when everything looked so bleak and hopeless, Brother Luka was suddenly released as though nothing had happened. It seemed that on the fourth day the young woman had all at once calmed down and then burst into prolific, soundless tears. She called her father-in-law and husband and announced that she had slandered the monk in her fits of madness, confessing that he had not given her any medicines at all, that he had not had a cross with him, but had simply spread his hands over her and prayed to God according to his law, and that had now made her better.

That is how the matter rested. Only the friars went on grumbling at Brother Luka for a long time afterwards. Brother Mijo Kovačević, who was then the Guardian and had the most fuss and bother over this affair with Brother Luka, told him later in the refectory, in front of all the others: "Now listen to me, Brother Luka, either you stop plaguing me with your demented infidel shrews or I'll take to the woods and you can be both Medic and Guardian. Because we can't go on like this."

And he angrily offered him the keys, in all seriousness.

Nevertheless, everything settled down and was forgotten. All that remained was what the Guardian had written in the Monastery register of fines and expenses:

On 11 January, the Mubassir came with a writ that Brother Luka Dafinić, Physician (woe the day he was made physician!) did give Miralem's daughter-in-law noxious potions… Wheretofore we did disburse, to the Cadi and the Emin, a fine of 148 groats.

Brother Luka's doctoring caused problems in later years as well. The friars forgot it all, but the register of fines and outlay on compensation preserved many references to Brother Luka:

Because Brother Luka has treated with medicines

a Turk...48 groats

incurred on behalf of the Physician............20 groats

Somewhere here there was also noted the number and date of the decree according to which the monastery elders forbade, in any circumstances, "prayers over any Turkish man or woman, or the giving of remedies", even if they had a permit from the Turkish authorities for it. But immediately afterwards a new fine was noted:

Because Brother Luka did omit to treat a patient

we disbursed a fine of...........................70 groats

And so it went on, year in, year out.

In the course of Brother Luka's long lifetime, there were two occasions when the plague raged through Travnik. People fell ill, died, fled into the mountains. The bazaar was closed and whole families perished. Even the closest bonds between people were loosed, and all courtesies were abandoned. In both epidemics, Brother Luka emerged as strong and fearless, both as doctor and monk. He visited the plague-ridden quarters, treating the sick, confessing and absolving the dying, burying the dead, helping and advising those who survived. Even the friars acknowledged this and it confirmed his reputation and good name as a doctor among the Turks as well.

But, anyone who lives long outlives everything, including his own merits. After disease and calamity came good, peaceful years. Everything was altered and forgotten, eased and faded. And in all of it, the successes and defeats, the praise and blame, disasters and victories, only Brother Luka remained the same, unchangeable and unwavering, with his absent look, thin smile and lightning movements, with his faith in the mysterious relationship between remedies and sickness. Not knowing any life other than concocting remedies, he felt that everything in the world had its place and its justification: disease, fines, the Guardian's anger, misunderstandings and slander. Even prison itself, after all, might be good, if it were not for that unpleasant iron on his ankles and the constant anxiety that his medicaments might go bad up in the monastery and the leeches die, the monks start rummaging through his bundles and packages and throwing them away.

For his part, Brother Luka treated his "great adversaries", the friars, with whom he was sometimes secretly, but only momentarily annoyed, devotedly and generously whenever they were taken ill. And he would advise them and worry about them when they were well. As soon as one of them began to cough, Brother Luka would put a little pot of herbs on his brazier and himself take the hot fragrant infusion to his cell and persuade him to drink it. There were some irascible friars, eccentric, morose or indifferent, old "uncles" who did not want even to hear of medicaments or the Medic and who would drive him from their cells or ridicule him and his cures. But Brother Luka refused to be deterred. He would pass over the joke or insult, as though he had not heard them, and persistently urge the sick monks to take care and to let him treat them. He would beg them, persuade and bribe them to swallow the medicine he had taken some trouble to prepare and often acquired at considerable expense.

One of these old "uncles" liked brandy more than the elders permitted or than was good for his physical health and spiritual progress. The old man had a bad liver, but he would not stop drinking. Among his notes, Brother Luka even had a recipe with the title "To deter a man from drink", and he treated the old friar, but with difficulty and no success. Every day the same conversation was repeated between them.

"Be off with you, Brother Luka, and tend those who wish to be cured and whom you can cure," the "uncle" would grumble.

"Come now, old fellow, pull yourself together! Everyone can be helped. There's a cure for everyone hidden somewhere in the world."

Brother Luka would sit beside the sick and morose old man. He had never cared for books and learning, even when he was well, but Brother Luka brought him books and spent hours expounding at length and in depth on all the riches of the earth and its bounty towards mankind.

"Do you know that Pliny called the earth 'benigna, mitis, indulgens, ususque mortalium semper ancilla'[8] and wrote: 'Illa medicas fundit herbas, et semper homini parturit.'[9] There, that's what Pliny said! And you keep going on: 'There's no cure for me.' There is, and we must find it."

The old man would only scowl with boredom, dismissing medicine and Pliny with a wave of his hand, but Brother Luka would not be stopped.

And when he could not cure him with his medicaments or soothe him with his quotations, he would secretly bring him a little brandy, pretending it was medicine, for the Guardian had completely forbidden it. And this would ease his suffering at least a little.

But Brother Luka did not concern himself only with the Brethren who lived in the monastery. He would fill yellowing sheets of paper with his small handwriting and sew them into little notebooks for those who were scattered through the parishes. These little

---

8 "benign, mild, indulgent, and ever a hand-maid to mortals".
9 "It produces medicinal plants and constantly bears fruit for mankind."

booklets, (known as "remedy books") would be copied again and distributed through other villages and parishes. They contained, in alphabetical order, popular cures interspersed with instructions on hygiene, superstitions and useful household hints. For instance: how to clean a habit spattered with candle wax or how to restore wine that was going sour. Alongside a cure for jaundice or for "fever not caused by bile" there would be a note, from Italian sources, of "how miners extract ore in the Indies and other places" or "how to make wine, so-called vermouth, which is good for strengthening the intestines". All the knowledge and information Brother Luka had collected over the years, from ancient "Compositiones medi camentorum" to Mordo's and old wives' cures, was contained in these notebooks. And here too Brother Luka came up against the ingratitude of the Brethren and many disappointments. Some copied them carelessly, others spoilt them out of ignorance or negligence, leaving out single words or whole sentences, yet others accompanied individual recipes by disparaging comments about medicine or even about the Medic himself. But Brother Luka would laugh at these comments when he came across them, consoling himself that his work on these "cure books" nevertheless did the people and the friars more good than the Brethren's carelessness and lack of understanding caused him offence.

There was one other, more harmless, thing that hindered Brother Luka in his work. As we have mentioned before, this was – mice. There were really a great many mice in the huge old monastery building. The friars maintained that it was Brother Luka's cell, which resembled Mordo's apothecary in Travnik, with its ointments, all sorts of balms and medicines, that was the main reason why the mice gathered in the building. But Brother Luka, on the other hand, said it was the age of the building and the untidiness of the cells which had allowed the mice to breed, ruining his medicaments and making all struggle against them useless. With time his battle with the mice became an innocuous mania. He made far more fuss than they did actual damage. He locked his ingredients away from them and hung things from the ceiling. He dreamed up all sorts of devices to outwit his unseen adversaries. He longed for a large metal box in which he could keep all the more valuable items locked and completely protected from the mice, but he did not have the courage even to mention such an expensive purchase to the friars or the Guardian. He was inconsolable when the mice really did devour the rabbit lard he had painstakingly prepared and rinsed several times.

He always kept two mousetraps in his cell, one large and one small. He set them carefully each evening, hanging in them a scrap of smoked ham or the remains of the tallow from a candlestick. And usually when he got up the following morning at dawn to go to the choir for prayers, he found both traps set and empty, the tallow and the ham eaten. But if it did happen that a mouse was actually caught, the snapping of the shutter would wake him and he would get up and walk round the terrified creature, shaking his finger at it threateningly.

"Aha! So now what, you little scoundrel? Up to mischief, eh? There you are, then!"

Then, barefoot and with just his habit around him, he carefully picked up the mousetrap and took it out onto the long gallery, to the top of the stairs, opened the little door and whispered:

"Come on out, you rascal! Come on, come on!"

The confused mouse would dart down those few steps, straight across the cobbles and vanish in the pile of logs heaped there throughout the year.

The friars knew of this method of Brother Luka's for catching mice, they often teased him and used to say that the Medic "had been hunting and releasing the same mouse for years". Brother Luka denied this vehemently, demonstrating at great length that he caught several in the course of a year, large, small and middle sized.

"Why, I've heard," said one of the elders, "that when you let the mouse go, you open the shutter and say: 'Come out and run into the Guardian's room. Go on!'"

"Just listen to the rogue! What nonsense you dream up!" Brother Luka would laugh, defending himself.

"I'm not dreaming anything up, Medic Effendi, people overheard you roaming about the gallery at night."

"Get away with you, you rogue, let me be!"

But others would immediately join in.

"If I caught one, I'd plunge it, trap and all, into boiling water, and then see if it came again," said one of the younger friars with deliberate provocation.

This would always upset Brother Luka tremendously.

"Oh, come now, are you in your right mind? What do you mean 'boiling water'? Are you a Christian?" the Medic would flare up.

And even half-an-hour later, after other jokes and talk of other matters, he would still snap at the young man:

"Boiling water! Imagine! One of God's creatures in boiling water!"

That is how Brother Luka struggled with his adversaries, large and small, how he treated them, fed and protected them. That is how his long, happy life was spent.

The fourth doctor who came to the Consulate at the time of Daville's little son's illness was Giovanni Mario Cologna, the titular physician of the Austrian General Consulate.

Now it is clear that we were mistaken when we said that of the four Travnik doctors there was least to say about Mordo Atijas. In fact there is as little to be said about Cologna as about Mordo. With Mordo it was because he never said anything, and with Cologna because he said too much and what he said changed constantly.

He was a man of indeterminate age, indeterminate origins, nationality and race, indeterminate beliefs and attitudes and just as indeterminate learning and experience. Altogether, there was not much about the man that could be defined at all clearly.

According to him, he was born on the island of Cephalonia, where his father was a renowned doctor. His father was Venetian, but born in Epirus, and his mother was Dalmatian. He had spent his childhood with his grandfather in Greece and his youth in Italy, where he had studied medicine. He had lived the rest of his life in the Levant, in Turkish and Austrian service.

He was tall and extraordinarily thin. He walked with a stoop and all his joints bent, as though on springs, so that at any moment he could contract and fold up, or unfold and stretch out. And he would do so constantly in the course of conversation, sometimes more, sometimes less. On this lengthy body there was a well-proportioned head, always restless, almost entirely bald, with a few long locks of lank, stringy hair. His face was clean-shaven, his eyes large, brown and always unnaturally bright under exceptionally thick grey eyebrows. In his large mouth there were only a few big yellow teeth which wobbled when he talked. Not only the expression of his face, but his whole appearance altered ceaselessly, completely and incredibly. In the course of a conversation he could change his appearance fundamentally several times. From under the mask of a feeble old man there would momentarily break out – another mask? – the image of a vigorous, composed middle-aged man or – a third mask! – the face of a volatile, impudent, lanky youth who had outgrown his clothes, who did not know what to do with his hands and feet or where to look. His expressive face was never still and betrayed the feverishly rapid working of his brain. Dejection, thoughtfulness, indignation, sincere enthusiasm, naïve elation, pure unadulterated joy, succeeded one another swiftly and unexpectedly on this regular and unusually mobile face. At the same time, his large mouth with its few, loose teeth would pour out words, a torrent of words, abundant, harsh, angry, bold, kindly, sweet, elated words. And they might be in Italian, Turkish, Greek, French, Latin or "Illyrian". With the same ease with which he altered his gestures and the expression of his face, Cologna would slip from one language to another, mixing and borrowing words and whole sentences. In actual fact, Italian was the only language he knew properly.

He did not even always write his name the same way, but differently in different circumstances and at different phases of his life, according to who he was working for and what kind of work he was doing: scientific, political or literary – Giovanni Mario Cologna, Gian Colonia, Joanes Colonis Epirota, Bartolo cavagliere d'Epiro, dottore Illyrico. Still more frequent and profound changes would affect the substance of what he professed and did under these various names. According to his fundamental convictions, Cologna was a man of up-to-date views, a "philosopher", a free and critical spirit, devoid of all prejudice. But this did not prevent him studying the religious life not only of various Christian churches but also of Islamic and other Eastern sects and faiths. And for him to study meant to identify himself for a certain time with the subject of his studies, to be excited by it, to adopt it at least momentarily as his only, exclusive faith, and to reject all that he had previously believed and that had thrilled him up to then. His spirit was in every way exceptional, capable of extraordinary transports, but composed of elements which easily fused with their surroundings and strove constantly to be identified with whatever was around them.

This sceptic and philosopher had attacks of religious fervour and phases of practical piety. Then he would go to the monastery of Guča Gora and irritate the friars, wanting to carry out spiritual exercises with them and finding that they lacked adequate zeal, theological knowledge and religious ardour. Like all Bosnian friars, the Guča Gora monks, sincerely devout, but simple, hard men, had an innate aversion to religious fanatics, and all those "who hang on God's skirts and lick the paving slabs in front of the altar". The old "uncles" would bristle and grumble, and one of them even left a note of the extent to which they found this outlandish doctor suspect and tiresome: "he professes himself a loyal follower of the Holy Catholic faith, hearing Mass each morning, and performing a variety of devotions". Nevertheless, because of their connections with the Austrian Consulate and their respect for von Mitterer, the friars were not able to reject his Illyrian physician entirely.

But Cologna used also to go to the Orthodox abbot Pahomije and visit the Orthodox households in Travnik, to observe their religious customs, hear their services and singing and compare them with the services in Greece. And he carried on scholarly discussions about the history of Islamic beliefs with the learned Travnik Muderris, Abduselam Effendi, for Cologna knew well not only the Koran but also all the theological and philosophical trends from Abu Hanif to Al Gazali. Whenever he had the opportunity, he would shower all the other learned gentlemen of the Travnik ulema tirelessly and inconsiderately with quotations from Muslim theologians whom, for the most part, they did not know.

The same consistent instability dominated his character as well. At first glance he would strike everyone as impressionable, malleable, and pliant to an unsavoury degree. He would regularly adjust his opinions to those of whoever he was talking to and not only adopt that person's point of view, but even surpass it in the keenness of his expression. But, just as often, entirely unexpectedly and abruptly, he would take up audacious attitudes, contradicting everyone, defending them bravely and stubbornly, committing himself absolutely to them, regardless of the harm and danger he brought on himself.

Cologna had been in Austrian service since his youth. This was perhaps the one thing in which he had been steadfast. He had spent a certain time as personal physician to the Pashas of Scutari and Ioannina, but even then he had not broken off relations with the Austrian consuls. Now he was appointed to the Consulate in Travnik, not so much as a doctor but far more because of these old connections and merits and because of his knowledge of languages and understanding of local conditions. In fact, he was not included in the staff of the Consulate, but lived separately, and was simply registered with the authorities as a physician under the auspices of the Austrian Consulate.

Von Mitterer, who did not display any imagination or understanding of philosophy, but who knew the language of the people and conditions in the country better than Cologna, did not know what to do with this unsolicited colleague. Frau von Mitterer felt a physical revulsion towards the Levantine and said heatedly that she would rather die than accept medicine from the hands of that man. In conversation, she referred to him as "Chronos", for she thought he resembled the symbol of time, only a Chronos who had no beard and who carried in his hands neither a deadly sickle nor an hour-glass.

That was how this doctor with no patients lived in Travnik. He lived outside the Consulate in a dilapidated house, right up against a sunless rocky slope. He had no family. One servant, an Albanian, ran his whole household which was meagre and unusual in every way, in its furnishings, food, and organization of time. He spent his days in vain attempts to find people he could talk to without their growing tired and running away, or over his books and notes which embraced the whole of human knowledge from astronomy and chemistry to military skills and diplomacy.

This man without roots or balance, but with a pure heart and enquiring spirit, had one obsessive, but great and selfless passion: to penetrate into the destiny of human thought, wherever it appeared and whatever form it took. He devoted himself entirely to this passion, without measure, without specific direction and regardless of everything. All religious and philosophical movements and endeavours in the history of mankind, without exception, engaged his mind and lived in it, shifting, colliding and crossing over into one another like waves on the surface of the sea. And each of them was equally close to him and equally remote and with each of them he was able to agree and completely identify for a certain time, as long as it concerned him. These inner exploits of the mind were his real world and this was where he had moments of genuine inspiration and profound experiences. But at the same time this set him apart and alienated him from people, bringing him into conflict with the logic and common sense of others. What was best in him remained unseen and inaccessible, and what could be seen repelled everyone. A man like this would not have been able to find himself a place even in a different environment, one less difficult and harsh. Here, in this town, among these people, it was inevitable that he should be seen as confused and ridiculous, suspect and superfluous.

The friars regarded him as a maniac and a gabbling layabout, and the townspeople as a spy or a learned fool. Suleiman Pasha Skopljak once said of this physician: "The greatest fool is not the one who does not know how to read, but the one who thinks that all he reads is true."

Des Fossés was the only man in Travnik who did not run away from Cologna and who had the patience to talk with him from time to time, openly and at length. But as a result, through no fault of his own, Cologna was accused in the Austrian Consulate of being in the pay of the French.

It was hard to say what Cologna's medical knowledge and profession consisted of, but it was certain that this was one of his least important concerns. In the light of the philosophical truths and religious inspirations which altered and succeeded one another constantly in him, human needs, pain and even life itself represented nothing of any great significance. For him both diseases and changes in the human body were simply one more pretext for the exercise of his mind which was destined to perpetual restlessness. Being himself very loosely attached to life, he was not able even to guess what ties of blood, bodily health and a longer or shorter span of life could mean for a normal person. In questions of medicine too, everything began and ended for Cologna with words, abundant words, animated discussions, debates and often abrupt and absolute changes in his opinion about an illness, its causes and method of treatment. Naturally, no one would call on or ask for such a doctor without dire need. It could be said that the main medical activity of this eloquent physician lay in his constant quarrel and passionate enmity with César d'Avenat.

As a student of the Milan school, Cologna was an advocate of Italian medicine, while d'Avenat, despising and belittling Italian doctors, would point out that the university of Montpellier had surpassed the Salerno school as out-of-date many centuries before. In fact, Cologna had drawn all his wisdom and his numerous sayings from the great compilation *Regimen sanitatis Salernitarum*, which he hid and protected jealously and from which he extracted and generously distributed rhymed rules about diets for the body and spirit. D'Avenat, on the other hand, lived from a few notebooks, the written lectures of renowned professors from Montpellier and from the great ancient handbook *Lilium medicinae*. But the basis of their dispute lay not so much in books or the knowledge neither of them had, as in their Levantine need for dissension and competition, their jealousy as doctors, their boredom in Travnik, and their personal vanity and intolerance.

Cologna's attitude to human illness and health, if one can talk of his having one constant attitude, was as simple as it was futile and hopeless. Faithful to his teachers, Cologna considered that life was "a state of activity tending constantly towards death and gradually drawing near to it; while death was the solution of that long illness we call life". But these invalids we call "people" might live long and with the least trouble and pain, as long as they followed well-tried medical rules about measure and moderation in all things. Pain, malfunctions and premature death were only the natural consequences of transgression of these rules. A man needs three doctors, Cologna used to say: "mens hilaris, requies moderata, diaeta".[10]

It was with such views that Cologna treated his patients. It made them neither better nor worse, and they either died when they had moved too far away from the line of life and too close to the line of death, or they recovered. That is, they were freed from their disorders and pain and came back into the scope of the salutary rules of Salerno. And Cologna would facilitate this for them with one of thousands of useful Latin precepts which are easily remembered but difficult to observe.

That, briefly, was the "Illyrian physician", the last of the four doctors in this Travnik valley waging, each in his own way, the difficult, hopeless struggle against sickness and death.

---

10 "a serene mind, moderate rest, diet."

13

Christmas, every Christian's holiday, came to Travnik too, bringing worries and memories, festive and sorrowful thoughts. This year it provided an excuse for the revival of contacts between the Consuls and their families.

Things were particularly lively at the Austrian Consulate. Frau von Mitterer was going through a phase of goodness, piety and devotion to her family. She ran to and fro, obtaining gifts and surprises for everyone. She locked herself in the drawing room, decorating the Christmas tree, and practised old carols on the harp. She even considered a midnight mass in the Dolac church, recalling Christmas Eve services in the churches of Vienna. She had sent a clerk to Brother Ivo in this connection, but he had replied so rudely that the clerk was unable to repeat his words to Frau von Mitterer. But he did succeed in convincing her that you could not contemplate such things in these lands. Frau von Mitterer was disappointed, but she continued with her preparations in the house.

Christmas Eve passed festively. The whole of the little Austrian community assembled round the tree. The house was heated and well-lit. Pale with excitement, Anna Maria distributed her gifts wrapped in fine paper, tied with gold string and decorated with twigs of juniper.

The following day they gave a lunch to which Daville, his wife and Des Fossés were invited. In addition there were the Dolac priest, Brother Ivo Janković, and the young Vicar of Guča Gora monastery, Brother Julian Pasalić, standing in for his Guardian who was unwell. This was that same gruff giant of a monk whom Des Fossés had met in the khan at Kupres on his arrival in Bosnia and whom he had seen again on the occasion of his first visit to Guča Gora, when he had the opportunity of continuing the discussion begun under such unusual circumstances.

It was warm in the large dining room, which smelled of cakes and fir. Outside it was bright with dry, powdery snow. This brightness was reflected in the silver and crystal on the richly laden table. The Consuls were wearing their parade uniforms and Anna Maria and her daughter were in light, fashionable dresses of embroidered tulle, with high waists and full sleeves. Only Madame Daville stood out in her black, which made her look even thinner. The two monks, both tall, heavily built men, in their feast-day habits, completely covered the chairs they were sitting on and among the gay colours around them, looked like two brown heaps of hay.

The lunch was abundant and good. Polish brandy, Hungarian wines and Viennese cakes were served. All the dishes were heavily seasoned and spiced. Frau von Mitterer's imagination could be detected in everything, down to the smallest detail.

The friars ate plentifully and in silence, perplexed at times by the unfamiliar dishes and tiny spoons of Viennese silver, which vanished in their huge hands like children's toys. Anna Maria turned to them frequently, encouraging them and offering them things, fluttering her hands, tossing her hair and flashing her eyes, while they wiped their thick peasants' moustaches and looked on this vivacious, pale woman, as on those unfamiliar foods, with tranquil bewilderment. Des Fossés did not fail to notice the natural dignity of these two simple men, their politeness, their restraint, and the quiet decisiveness with which they declined to eat and drink what they were not accustomed to. Even their awkwardness in handling forks and knives and the caution with which they approached certain dishes were neither comical nor uncouth, but rather dignified and touching.

The conversation became livelier and was conducted in several languages. Towards the end the friars decisively refused both sweetmeats and southern fruit. Anna Maria was astounded. But the incident was easily smoothed over when the coffee and tobacco were brought. The friars welcomed these with undisguised pleasure as a reward for all they had had to endure until then.

The men withdrew to smoke. As it happened, neither Daville nor Des Fossés smoked, but von Mitterer and Brother Julian made up for it by puffing out thick clouds of smoke, while Brother Ivo took snuff, wiping his moustache and red neck with a large blue handkerchief.

This was the first time that von Mitterer had invited his adversary and his friends together, and that the Consuls had met in the presence of the friars. It seemed that Christmas had brought a temporary solemn truce and that the death of Daville's little boy had softened or at least postponed the enmity and rivalry between the two men. Von Mitterer was pleased to have provided the opportunity for such noble sentiments to be expressed.

But at the same time, it was a convenient occasion for each of those present to display by his behaviour both his "politics" and his personality in the most favourable possible light. In a pleasant and restrained manner, von Mitterer drew Daville's attention to his great influence with the friars and their congregation, and the monks confirmed this by their words and behaviour. Daville, both out of duty and personal defiance, adopted the stance of a representative of Napoleon, and this "imperial" attitude, which so little suited his true nature, gave him a stiff appearance, altering his whole personality in a negative sense. The only one of them who behaved and spoke quite naturally was Des Fossés, but since he was the youngest he was for the most part silent.

The friars, in so far as they said anything, complained about the Turks, about fines and persecution, about the course of history, about their destiny, and a bit about the whole world, with that typical, strange relish with which every Bosnian likes to talk about difficult circumstances.

In such company, where everyone was seeking to say what he wanted known and spread abroad and endeavouring to hear only what he needed and what others concealed, it was inevitable that the conversation could not develop and follow a natural or cordial course.

As a tactful host, von Mitterer did not let the talk pass on to subjects that might have provoked an argument. It was only the old acquaintances Brother Julian and Des Fossés who took themselves to one side and embarked on a somewhat livelier discussion.

Since that very first meeting at Kupres, the Bosnian friar and the young Frenchman clearly understood and respected one another. Their later meetings in Guča Gora had only brought them closer. Both of them young, serene, robust men, they engaged in conversation and then in a friendly argument, with pleasure, and no ulterior motives or personal vanity.

Sitting a little to one side and looking through the misted window at the bare trees sprinkled with fine snow they talked of Bosnia and the Bosnians. Des Fossés asked for information about the Catholic population and the work of the friars. And then he himself outlined his impressions and experience up to then honestly and calmly.

The friar saw immediately that the "Young Consul" had not wasted his time in Travnik, but had gathered a great deal of information about the country and the people, and even about the Catholic population and the work of the friars.

Both men agreed that life in Bosnia was exceptionally hard and the people of all faiths wretched and backward from every point of view. Seeking reasons for this, the friar attributed everything to Turkish rule, arguing that there could be no improvement until this land was freed from Turkish power and until Turkish authority was replaced by Christian rule. Des Fossés would not be satisfied with this interpretation, but sought reasons also in the Christians themselves. He maintained that Turkish rule had created in all its Christian subjects certain characteristic traits, such as hypocrisy, obstinacy, distrust, laziness of mind and fear of any innovation, any action or movement. These characteristics, the consequence of centuries of unequal struggle and constant self-defence, had passed into the nature of the local people and become permanent features of their character. They had sprung from necessity and under pressure. But they were now, and would continue in the future to be a great obstacle to progress, the negative heritage of a difficult past, which must be eradicated.

Des Fossés did not conceal the fact that he was surprised at the obstinacy with which in Bosnia not only the Turks but people of all the other faiths too, resisted every influence, even the best, opposed every innovation, every advance, even what was possible in the present circumstances and depended on no one but themselves. He pointed out all the harm done by this "Chinese" rigidity, the way they cut themselves off from life.

"How is it possible", asked Des Fossés, "for this country to become stable and orderly and adopt at least as great a degree of civilization as its closest neighbours, if its people are divided as nowhere else in Europe? Four faiths live in this narrow, mountainous and meagre strip of land. Each of them is exclusive and strictly separate from the others. You all live under one sky and from the same soil, but the centre of the spiritual life of each of these four groups is far away, in a foreign land, in Rome, Moscow, Istanbul, Mecca, Jerusalem, and God alone knows where, but at any rate not here where the people are born and die. And each group considers that its well-being is conditioned by the disadvantage of each of the other three faiths, and that they can make progress only at their cost. Each of them has made intolerance the greatest virtue. And each one of them is expecting salvation from somewhere outside, each from the opposite direction."

The friar listened to him with the smile of a man who believed that he knew how things were and had no need to have his knowledge confirmed or broadened. Evidently determined to contradict Des Fossés at all costs, he pointed out that in view of the circumstances, his people could survive only the way they were, if they did not want to degenerate, to be estranged and destroyed.

Des Fossés replied that just because a people begins to adopt a healthier and more rational way of life, it need not necessarily renounce its own faith and its own sacred objects. In his opinion it was precisely the friars who could and should be working in this direction.

"Ah, my dear young man," said Brother Julian, with the affectation characteristic of people defending conservative views, "it's easy for you to talk about the need for material progress, healthy influences and 'Chinese' rigidity, but if we had been less rigid and opened our doors to all sorts of 'healthy influences', my parishioners Petar and Anton would today be called Muhammed and Hussein."

"With respect, there's no need to exaggerate or to be so obstinate."

"What can you do? We Bosnians are pig-headed people. That's what we're famous for," said Brother Julian with the same pomposity.

"But, forgive me, why are you concerned about how you look to others and what people think of you? As if that were important! What is important is how much a man has of this life, what he makes of himself and his environment and leaves for his descendants."

"We maintain our standpoint, and no one can boast that he has forced us to alter it."

"But, Father Julian, standpoints do not matter, life does! A standpoint is in the service of life. And what does your life, here, amount to?"

Brother Julian was just on the point of pronouncing some quotation, as was his habit, when their host interrupted their conversation. Brother Ivo had stood up. Red from his good meal, he offered his heavy hand, plump as a small cushion, to all in turn like a bishop, and, breathing heavily and hissing as he spoke, he pointed out that it was snowing, that it was a long way to Dolac and they ought to set out, if they wanted to arrive by daylight.

The young man and the friar were sorry to part.

From time to time during the meal, Des Fossés had glanced at Frau von Mitterer's white, restless hands. And, whenever he caught sight of that pearly gleam of her skin which appeared in the same places whenever she moved, he would close his eyes for a moment, with the feeling that there was an unbroken connection between him and this woman which no one could know or see. His ears were constantly filled with her uneven, strident voice. Even the somewhat harsh accent with which she spoke French seemed to him not a shortcoming, but a source of unusual charm which was hers alone. He felt that such a voice could speak every language of this world and everyone would find it as close and familiar as his own.

Before they parted, the conversation turned to music and Anna Maria showed Des Fossés her Musikzimmer, a small, light room with very little furniture, a few silhouettes on the walls and a large gilded harp in the centre. Anna Maria complained that she had had to leave her clavichord in Vienna and had been able to bring only her harp which was now a great comfort to her in this wilderness. With that she stretched out her arm, the sleeve slipping from it to the elbow, and carelessly ran her fingers over the strings. Those few haphazard sounds seemed to the young man like the music of the spheres breaking the leaden silence of Travnik and promising days of joy and luxury in the midst of this wilderness.

He was standing on the other side of the harp and saying softly how much he would like to be able to hear her play and sing. With a silent glance, she reminded him of Madame Daville's mourning and suggested some later date.

"You must promise me that you will come out riding as soon as the weather is a little better. Are you afraid of the cold?"

"Why should I be afraid?" replied the woman on the other side of the harp slowly, and for the young man her voice passing along the strings was like music full of promises. He looked at her eyes, grey and deep, with a glow somewhere in their depths, and it seemed to him that here too there were incomprehensible promises.

During this time, in the other room, von Mitterer had succeeded in telling Daville in the greatest confidence, quite naturally and as though by chance, that relations between Austria and Turkey were becoming increasingly bad and that Vienna had been obliged to undertake serious military measures not only on the frontier but within the country itself, because they did not exclude the possibility that Turkey might launch an attack the very next summer.

Daville knew of the Austrian preparations and, like everyone else, believed that they were directed not against Turkey but against France, and that Turkey served simply as an excuse. He found in von Mitterer's disclosure new confirmation of this belief. Daville pretended to accept the Colonel's words and at the same time he was working out when he would next have a courier through whom he could pass on this intentional indiscretion as one more piece of evidence as to the hostile intentions of the Vienna government.

As they parted, Anna Maria and Des Fossés confirmed in front of all the others that they would not let the winter stop them riding and that they would go out as soon as the weather was dry and bright.

In the French Consulate no one sat up long after supper on the evening of that first day of Christmas. Without consultation, they had each wanted to withdraw into their own rooms as soon as possible.

Madame Daville was subdued and had barely restrained her tears during supper. This had been her first outing and encounter with people since the death of her child and now she was suffering. This first contact had quite shaken her, reviving the weight of her loss and the pain which, in silence, had begun to abate. In the most difficult moments she had pledged that she would control her tears, overcome the pain and offer her child, together with her pain at his loss, to God as a sacrifice. But now her tears ran uncontrollably and the pain was as acute as on the first day, before that pledge. The woman wept and at the same time prayed to God to forgive her for not being able to carry out what she had promised in a moment when she overestimated her strength. And she gave way to her tears, bent double with pain that tore her womb more sharply than during her labour.

In his study, Daville was writing a report on his conversation with the Austrian Consul, pleased that his premonitions in this modest section of international politics and from this difficult observation post had been shown to be exact.

Des Fossés did not even light his candle, but strode up and down his bedroom, stopping from time to time at the window, looking for lights in the Austrian Consulate on the other side of the river. The night was soundless and impenetrable and nothing could be seen or heard outside. But the young man was himself filled with noise and brilliance. In the silent darkness, as soon as he stopped and shut his eyes, Anna Maria would appear as dazzling sound. Her words spread light, and that glow in the depths of her eyes spoke, as she had today, the serene and in some way significant words: Why should I be afraid?

An enormous harp screened the young man's whole world, and he fell asleep, rocked by the mighty, intoxicating play of his quivering senses.

14

Dry, sunny days, when it was possible to ride despite the intense cold, came with the inevitability of natural phenomena. The same inevitability brought riders from both Consulates, following their Christmas arrangement, onto the frozen road that led over Kupilo.

This road might have been made for walking and riding. Level, straight and well-drained, more than a mile long, cut into the steep slopes under Karauldžik and Kajabaša, it follows the Lašva, but high above the river and the town in the valley below it. At the end, the road becomes somewhat broader and more uneven and branches off into the rough country lanes which lead further uphill into the villages of Janković and Orašje.

The sun reaches Travnik late. Des Fossés and a khavaz were riding along the road which was bathed in sunlight, while below them the town was still in shadow, under a shroud of mist and smoke. Vapour streamed from the riders' mouths and horses' nostrils, and rose in a haze from the horses' croups. Their hooves made a muffled thud on the frozen ground. The sun was still in the clouds, but the valley was slowly filling with a rosy light. Des Fossés rode at an uneven pace, now a slow walk, so that it seemed as though at any moment he were going to stop and dismount, now a brisk trot so that the khavaz on his sluggish dun horse was left the length of a rifle range behind him. This was how the young man wiled away the time as he waited for the moment when he would catch sight of Anna Maria and her escort somewhere along the road. For people carried along by youth and driven by desire, even long drawn-out anticipation and the pangs of uncertainty are only constituents of the rapture which love always promises. The young man waited with trepidation – could she be ill? had she been prevented from coming? had something happened to her on the way? – but at the same time he was confident that in the end all his fears would prove to be unfounded. Because, in love affairs of this kind, everything bodes well, apart from their end.

And truly, every morning, when the sun had passed the sharp mountain crest and when the doubts and questions had multiplied, becoming increasingly unlikely, Anna Maria would appear, "with the inevitability of natural phenomena", "l'amazone", in her black riding habit, with its long skirt, as though moulded onto her side saddle and her big black horse. Then they would both rein in their horses and draw near to one another, just as naturally as the sun was rising above them and the daylight growing stronger in the valley. It seemed to the young man that at a distance of a hundred paces he could clearly see her hat à la Valois making an inseparable whole, as no other woman's did, with the wave of her brown hair and her face, pale with the cool morning air, and her tired, sleepless eyes. ("Your eyes look sleepy," he said to her each time, as soon as they met, filling the word "sleepy" with a particular bold, secret meaning, at which the woman lowered her eyes, showing their glistening lids with a bluish tinge.)

After the greetings and first words, they would stand still for a time. Then they would part and, after riding a short distance, meet again as though by chance, ride part of the way side by side, talking rapidly and eagerly, then separate and once again come together and continue their conversation. These manoeuvrings were occasioned by their position and social considerations. But in themselves they did not part for a second and as soon as they came together again, they would continue their conversation of a short while before with the same delight. To their escorts and to anyone who might have happened to watch them it must have looked as though they were both devoting the greatest attention to their horses and riding, that their meetings were accidental and their talk inconsequential – about the road, the weather and their horses' paces. No one could have known what was being conveyed by that cloud of white mist fluttering like a restless banner at one moment from her lips, the next from his, breaking and dispersing to unfurl once more, more animated and lengthier than ever in the cold air.

And when the sun had penetrated even to the deepest hollows of the valley and all the air in it became for a moment pink, when the half-frozen Lašva began to steam, as though invisible fires were burning throughout the whole town, the young man and the woman would take leave of each other, warmly and at length (it is in parting that lovers most easily give themselves away!), and go their separate ways down into the snow and hoarfrost covered town.

The first person to notice that something was going on between the young Des Fossés and the beautiful Frau von Mitterer, some ten years his senior, was Herr von Mitterer himself. He knew his "sick child" of a wife very well. He knew the upsurges of her spirit, her "aberrations" as he called them, and he easily foresaw their evolution and their end. It was not hard, therefore, for the Colonel to make out what was happening to his wife and to see in advance the whole course of the affliction: rapture, entrancement with the spiritual relationship, disillusion with the coarse male desire for sensual contact, flight, despair – "They all desire me and no one loves me" – and finally, oblivion and the discovery of new objects of entrancement and disillusion. Nor did it require great perspicacity to grasp the intentions of this tall young man who had been flung from Paris into Travnik and placed in front of the beautiful Frau von Mitterer, the only civilized woman for hundreds of miles around. What was so difficult for the Colonel this time was the question of his relations with the French Consulate.

The Colonel had laid down for himself, his family and associates the extent of relations with his rival Consulate and its personnel. From time to time he would test, revise and adapt it, in accordance with instructions from the Ministry and the general situation, as a clock is wound and regulated. This was a serious matter for him, because his sense of military precision and professional conscientiousness was stronger and more developed than any other feeling. Now Anna Maria's behaviour might spoil those relations to the detriment of the Colonel's work and his professional reputation. This had never been the case with her earlier "aberrations" and it presented the Colonel with a new, previously unknown torment.

Although he was only a tiny cog in the machinery of the great Austrian Empire, through his position as Consul General in Travnik the Colonel knew that his government was making preparations for war, counting on a new coalition against Napoleon, and that these preparations, in so far as they could not be concealed, were being presented as directed against Turkey. But he had express instructions to pacify the Turkish authorities and reassure them that, on the contrary, these preparations could not in any eventuality be intended for a war with Turkey. At the same time, he was receiving increasingly frequent and increasingly strict orders to keep watch on the work of the French Consul and his agents and to report on every smallest detail.

It was not hard for the Colonel to deduce from all of this with reasonable probability that a new rupture of relations with France, a new coalition and war could soon be expected.

In such circumstances, it was understandable that he found his wife's infatuation awkward, as he did her mid-winter lovers' rides for the servants and all the world to see. But he knew that there was no point in talking to Anna Maria, for rational arguments had quite the opposite effect on her. He recognized that there was nothing to be done but to wait for the moment when the young man would reach out to her as a woman and, as in all the earlier cases, she would retreat, disillusioned and in despair. And the whole affair would thus be automatically and definitively broken off. The Colonel fervently hoped that this moment would come as soon as possible.

On the other hand, even Daville, who was constantly wincing at the behaviour of his "gifted but unbalanced" secretary, could not fail to notice his rides and meetings with Frau von Mitterer. And as he too had firmly laid down for himself and his whole establishment the extent of his dealings with the Austrian Consulate, he also found these meetings inconvenient. (In this, as often happened in other regards, Daville wanted the same thing as his adversary von Mitterer.) But he too was still at a loss as to how to prevent them.

As far as women were concerned, ever since his youth Daville had been a man of great discipline of mind and body. This discipline sprang just as much from a strict, wholesome upbringing as from frigidity and a poor imagination. And, like all such people, Daville experienced a superstitious fear in the face of irregular relations of this kind. As a young man in Paris and in the army, himself chaste and restrained, he had always fallen into a guilty silence at lascivious talk about women. And now, he would have found it easier to express his displeasure and reprimand Des Fossés on any other matter than one involving a woman.

Apart from that, Daville was afraid (that is the right word), afraid of his young colleague. He was afraid of his restless cleverness, his varied, disorderly but wide knowledge, his carefree manner and frivolity, his intellectual curiosity, his physical strength and especially his capacity to be afraid of nothing. Because of this, Daville too waited, searching for a convenient and roundabout way of rebuking the young man.

So January passed and in February the weather was again damp and foggy, with deep mud and slippery roads which prevented what neither Daville nor von Mitterer knew how to prevent. Riding was out of the question. Actually, Des Fossés did go out even in that weather, walking in his high boots and brown cape with its otter fur collar, getting cold and tired to the point of exhaustion. But, even Anna Maria, with her illogical nature, could not leave the house in such weather. Like a captive angel, somehow light, with a melancholy smile, she would look out at the world through her bright "sleepy" eyes, walking vacantly past the members of her household, as past lifeless shadows and harmless visions. She spent most of the day at her harp, relentlessly draining her rich repertoire of German and Italian songs or losing herself in interminable variations and fantasias. Her strong, warm, but unreliable voice, in which one was aware of the constant threat of imminent tears and sobs, filled the small room and penetrated into the other parts of the house. From his study, the Colonel overheard Anna Maria singing, accompanying herself on the harp:

Tutta laccolta ancor
Nel palpitante cor
Tremante ho l'alma[11]

As he listened to these words, with their inappropriate feelings of passion, he trembled with helpless hatred of that incomprehensible world which caused him all his immeasurable domestic misery and shame. He would lay down his pen and put his hands over his ears, but he continued to hear his wife's voice and the dripping, flowing notes of the harp carrying up from the floor below, as from some mysterious depths. They came from a world which was the reverse of all that the Colonel considered important, sacred and serious. It seemed to him that this music had always accompanied him and would never cease. Feeble and tearful as it was, it would outlive him

---

11 The whole story anew in the throbbing heart.

and every living thing: armies and empires, order and justice, duty and courtesy, and it would continue to whine and trickle over all these things in just the same way, like a thin but continuous stream of water over their ruins.

Then the Colonel would take up his pen again and continue the report he had begun, writing convulsively fast, accompanied by the music from below, with the feeling that everything was unendurable and yet it had to be endured.

At the same time their daughter Agatha was also listening to the singing. The little girl was sitting in a low chair on a red rug in the heated veranda. This was Frau von Mitterer's "winter garden". In her lap, closed, lay the latest *Musenalmanach*.[12] Its pages were full of what were for her new, wonderful and exalted pieces of verse and prose, but she had been driving herself to read them in vain: a painful but irresistible force compelled her to listen instead to her mother's voice from the music room.

This frail creature with her intelligent eyes and fixed gaze, reticent and mistrustful since childhood, had an intuition of many things that were unclear even to her, but ominous. For years she had been dimly aware of relationships in the family, silently watching her father and mother, the servants and her acquaintances, discerning things she found problematic, ugly and sorrowful. And she felt increasingly ashamed, withdrawing into herself, but still finding ever new reasons to be ashamed. In Zemun she had had some companions, officers' daughters. At that time her life had been filled with school, her fiery adoration for her teachers, the nuns, and countless little worries and joys. But now she was totally isolated, left to her own devices and the uneasiness of her age, between her good, powerless father and her incomprehensible, crazy, mother.

As she listened to her mother's singing, the little girl hid her face in the pages of her *Musenalmanach*, overwhelmed by unaccountable

12 Poetry Almanac.

shame and a strange alarm. Pretending to read, she was in fact listening, her eyes closed, to a song she had known well for years, which she hated and which frightened her as something only older people knew and did, something unendurable, which made a lie of even the loveliest books and the best thoughts.

The beginning of March, exceptionally warm and dry, resembled the end of April and suited the riders from the two Consulates unexpectedly well. Once again they began to meet and wait for one another on that high, level road, to gallop gaily over the soft earth and yellow, flattened grass, through the cool but mild air of early spring. Once again both Consuls began to be concerned and to ponder how to curtail the riders' idyll, while avoiding major upset.

According to information which was reaching both Consulates, a clash between the Viennese government and Napoleon was inevitable. "Relations between the two countries are developing in a direction contrary to the cordial relations being woven in public on the bridle-path above Travnik," as Daville told his wife, permitting himself one of those domestic witticisms which husbands display in front of their wives at little intellectual cost and effort. At the same time he was rehearsing how he might begin to talk about this disagreeable subject with young Des Fossés. It really could not go on much longer.

However, that demon called "the need for a knight" which drove Anna Maria to look for young strong men, and at the same time repelled her from them as soon as her knight, a man of flesh and blood, betrayed human inclinations and desires, that demon took a hand now and made things easier for both Daville and von Mitterer, if it were at all possible to speak of anything becoming easier for von Mitterer. What had to come came: the moment when Anna Maria, disillusioned, horrified and disgusted, abandoned it all and fled, confining herself in her house, with a feeling of revulsion towards herself and everything in the world, haunted by thoughts of suicide and the need to torment her husband and everybody else.

This exceptionally warm beginning of March hastened the course of things, bringing on the crisis.

One sunny morning their horses' hooves were once again drumming along the level road edged with leafless undergrowth. Both Anna Maria and Des Fossés were intoxicated with the fresh beauty of the morning. They would both let their horses go at full gallop and then meet again further along the road, breathless and exhilarated, exchanging warm words and fragmented sentences which made sense only to the two of them, and which made their blood course still more wildly, aroused by their riding and the freshness of the day. In the middle of their conversation, Anna Maria would whip her horse and fly off to the very end of the road, leaving the excited young man in mid-sentence, and then she would return at a walk and the conversation would continue. This game had tired them. They rode their horses off in figures, like experienced equestrians, coming together again and then parting, like two balls which are constantly drawn towards each other and then suddenly cannon off one another. This game had left their escorts behind. Des Fossés's and Anna Maria's servants and the khavazes were riding slowly on their small ponies, taking no part in this noble entertainment, but not mixing either, all waiting for their master and mistress to have had enough, so that they could go home.

Racing along like this, independently, at one moment the young man and the woman came together at the end of the level road, at the place where it suddenly turns off and becomes stony and rough. At this turn in the road there was a small pine wood. In the sunshine, the trees looked like a compact black mass and the ground beneath them was reddish and dry with fallen needles. All at once Des Fossés dismounted and suggested that Anna Maria do the same so that they could take a better look at this wood which he maintained reminded him of Italy. The word *Italy* beguiled the woman. Looping their arms through the reins and walking over the smooth carpet of rust-coloured pine needles, their legs stiff from riding, they went a few paces into the wood which was becoming denser and closing behind them. The woman walked with difficulty in her boots, holding up the long skirt of her black riding habit with one hand. She stopped, undecided. The young man was talking, as though he wanted to drown the silence of the wood and reassure both himself and the woman. He compared this wood to a temple or something similar. But between his words there were spaces and silences, filled with his rapid, warm breathing and the faster beating of his heart. Then the young man threw both his reins and hers over a branch. The horses stood quietly, their muscles quivering. He drew the woman, who was hesitant, a few steps further, to a hollow where they were completely hidden by the branches and trunks of the pines. She resisted, slipping awkwardly and fearfully over the thick layer of pine needles. But before she could break loose or say anything at all, she caught sight of the young man's flushed face right next to her own. There was no more talk of Italy or temples. Those great red lips were approaching hers, wordless now. The woman turned white, opened her eyes wide as though she had suddenly woken up, trying to push him away, to run, but her knees gave way. His arm was already holding her round the waist. She cried out like some defenceless being about to be treacherously murdered: "No! Not that!" She rolled her eyes upwards. And dropping the long skirt of her dress, which she had been clutching tightly until then, she sank to the ground.

Their familiar world, conversation and rides, Consuls and Consulates, all disappeared. The two of them disappeared too in a writhing, twisting knot on the thick layer of pine needles which crackled beneath them. Clasping the swooning woman, the young man embraced her as though he had a hundred invisible arms.

Their saliva mingled with tears, for she was crying, and with blood, for someone's lips were bleeding. But their lips did not part, as though they were no longer actually two mouths. This embrace of the young man crazed with passion and the swooning woman did not last even a minute. Anna Maria suddenly came to, her eyes even wider open, as though she had just glimpsed an appalling chasm. She regained consciousness, and with unexpected strength furiously thrust the delirious young man away and then started hitting him indignantly and repeatedly in the chest with both fists, like an angry child, shouting with every blow:

"No, no, no!"

The heady bewitchment that had swept everything away was shattered. Just as they had not known exactly when they had sunk to the ground, so now they found themselves on their feet, without knowing how. She was sobbing with rage and straightening her hair and hat, while he, embarrassed and awkward, brushed pine needles from her black dress, handed her her crop and helped her out of the hollow. The horses were standing quietly, tossing their heads.

They came out onto the road and mounted, before their escorts could have noticed that they had got off at all. As they parted they glanced at each other once more. The young man's face was more flushed than usual and he was blinking in the strong sun. Anna Maria was utterly transformed. Her lips had become so bloodless that they were lost in her pale face, and her eyes were different, suddenly "fully awake", with two black circles round the pupils which it was even harder to look into than that earlier gleam in their depths. Her whole face was swollen, with an expression of ugly rage and boundless revulsion towards herself and everything around her, as though it had long since grown old.

Des Fossés, who did not easily lose his presence of mind or his innate self-confidence, was genuinely perplexed. He sensed that this was neither coquettishness nor a society lady's ordinary fear of disgrace and scandal. All at once he seemed to himself baser, weaker than this sick woman whose abnormal temperament and indignation created a world of their own, where she was content to be.

Everything seemed to him to have changed. Everything around him and in him, even the proportions of his own body.

So the winter riders, the former tender lovers of Kupilo, parted forever.

Von Mitterer saw at once that the relationship between his wife and her new knight "manqué" had reached the critical turning point, as so many had before, and now the private tempests would begin. And truly, after two days of total seclusion, without eating or saying a word, the scenes began, with their senseless accusations and entreaties ("Josef, for God's sake...") which the Colonel had foreseen with calm determination to endure them to the end, just as he had everything that had gone before.

Daville too soon noticed that Des Fossés was no longer going out riding with Frau von Mitterer. He was glad because it freed him from the uncomfortable obligation of speaking to the young man about it and telling him that all cordial contacts with the Austrian Consulate must cease. For all the reports showed that relations between the Vienna court and Napoleon were again becoming strained. Daville read them, alarmed, listening to the wild March wind raging round the house.

Meanwhile, the "Young Consul" was sitting in his heated room, swallowing his fury at Anna Maria and particularly at himself. He tormented himself in vain, trying to explain the woman's behaviour. But whatever explanations he found all left a feeling of disappointment, shame and injured pride and, besides, the acute pain of aroused and frustrated desire.

He remembered – but only now, when it was too late – his uncle in Paris and the advice he had given him one day when he had seen him at the Palais Royal, having dinner with an actress, famous for her eccentricity. "I see you've grown up," the old gentleman had said, "and that you've begun to burn your fingers like everyone else. That's how it has to be and so be it. I only give you one piece of advice: keep away from unstable women."

His good, wise uncle haunted his sleep.

Now that the whole thing had come to such a ludicrous end, he also saw clearly, as though his eyes had been opened, the moral repugnance of his "fooling around" with the capricious, middle-aged Austrian Frau Consul he had been so pathetically driven to by his momentary lack of self-control and this Travnik tedium.

Now he recalled also last summer's "tableau vivant" in the garden with Jelka, the girl from Dolac, whom he had forgotten. And there were nights when he would suddenly jump up several times from his desk or bed, the blood pounding in his head, his eyes swimming, filled entirely with that feeling of shame and anger at himself which can still be as acute as this in the young. Standing in the middle of the room, he would blame himself for behaving so stupidly, and at the same time he never ceased looking for an explanation for his failure.

"What kind of country is this? What kind of air is this?" he would ask himself then. "And what kind of women are these? They look at you tenderly and meekly like flowers in the grass, or so passionately (through the strings of a harp) that your heart melts. And when you respond to this pleading look, they fall to their knees and turn the whole situation upside down, beseeching you with the look of a sacrificial victim, so that you are sickened, everything becomes loathsome and you lose all will to live and love. And then others behave as though they were warding off a bandit, flailing around themselves like English boxers."

So, on the floor above Daville and his sleeping family, the "Young Consul" wrestled with his secret torment, until he conquered it and until it began, like all the troubles of youth, to pass into oblivion.

15

The news and instructions from Paris, which Daville had recently been receiving with considerable delay, showed that once again the great military machine of the Empire had been set in motion, aimed against Austria. Daville felt directly threatened. He saw it as his personal misfortune that this avalanche should be moving precisely towards these territories where he had his own small area of heavy responsibility. Even in his sleep, Daville was haunted by the morbid sense that he ought to take some action and the unpleasant feeling that he might make a mistake or omit to do something. Des Fossés's calm nonchalance irritated him more than usual. The young man found it natural that the Imperial army had to be engaged in war somewhere or other, and he did not see why that should alter his thinking or way of life in the least. Daville shook with suppressed rage as he listened to the casual, witty expressions which were now the fashion among the youth of Paris, and which Des Fossés used as he talked about the new war, without awe or elation, but equally without doubt in its triumphant outcome. That filled Daville with unconscious envy and an acute sadness that he had no one to talk to ("to exchange anxieties and hopes") about this war and about everything else, no one with attitudes familiar to him and his generation. The world seemed to him now more than ever full of traps and dangers, those vague black trepidations which war spreads through the land and into people's hearts, particularly the hearts of the ageing, the weakened and the weary.

It seemed to Daville at times that he was running out of breath, that he was bent double with fatigue, that he had been marching like this for years already, part of some grim, merciless column, with which he could no longer keep step and which was threatening to trample and crush him if he were only to falter and stop marching. As soon as he was left alone, he would sigh, saying softly to himself:

"Dear God, dear God!"

He spoke these words rapidly, unconsciously, without any real connection with what was happening around him at that moment; they were part of his breathing and sighing.

How could he not stumble with weariness in this dizzy rush which had been going on for years, but then, how could he throw it up and abandon all further effort? How could he see clearly and comprehend anything in this universal urgency and confusion, but how could he continue to march through exhaustion, adversity and uncertainty, into new obscurity as far as the eye could see?

It seemed only yesterday that he had been listening excitedly to news of the victory at Austerlitz, with its accompanying hopes for peace and a definitive solution. It seemed only this morning that he had written his verses on the battle at Jena. It seemed only a moment ago that he had read bulletins about the victory in Spain, the entry into Madrid and the expulsion of English troops from the Iberian peninsula. The echo of one triumph had not yet died away and it was already mingling with the clamour of new events. Would these truly natural laws be transformed by force or would they destroy everything in their relentless inflexibility? One moment it was the first outcome that seemed to prevail, and the next the second, but there was no clear conclusion. His spirit went numb and his brain refused to obey. And it was in such a mood that he was continuing to trudge on, with millions of others, to work and talk, striving to keep step, to make his contribution, saying nothing and not letting anyone see his wretched burden of perplexity and inner turmoil.

And now it was all going to happen all over again, exactly the same in every detail. The *Moniteur* and the *Journal de l'Empire* arrived with articles in which the need for a new campaign was explained and justified and its inevitable success foreseen. While Daville read them it seemed indisputable that this was so and could not be any other way. Then there would come days and weeks of reflection, anticipation and doubt. (Why war again? And how long would it go on? Where would this all lead the world, Napoleon, France and him, Daville and his family? Might not their good fortune run out this time, bringing the first defeat as a premonition of their ultimate downfall?) Then the bulletin would appear with news of successes, with the names of cities captured and countries overrun. And finally, complete victory and a victorious peace, with territorial gains and new promises of general conciliation which somehow never came.

And then Daville would celebrate the victory with the rest and louder than the rest, speaking of it as something self-evident in which he too had played his part. And no one would ever know those distressing doubts and hesitations, which the victory had dispersed like a mist and which he would now himself endeavour to forget. For a time, but only a short time, he would deceive himself. Soon there would be a renewed movement of the Imperial war machine and, simultaneously, a new play of emotions within him, absolutely identical to all the earlier ones. And all of this drained him and wore him out, creating a life which was apparently tranquil and orderly, but in fact unbearably distressing and in painful contrast to his inner constitution and his true nature.

The Fifth Coalition against Napoleon was formed in the course of that winter and was announced, suddenly, in the spring. As four years previously, only even more swiftly and audaciously, Napoleon replied to this perfidious attack with a lightning blow against Vienna. Now even the uninitiated could see just why the Consulates had been opened in Bosnia.

All contact ceased between the French and the Austrians in Travnik. The servants did not greet one another, the Consuls avoided meeting in the street. On Sundays, during High Mass at the Dolac church Madame Daville and Frau von Mitterer with her daughter stood apart and at some distance from each other. Both Consuls redoubled their efforts with the Vizier and his associates, the friars, priests and prominent citizens. Von Mitterer publicized the proclamation of the Austrian Emperor and Daville the French bulletin about their first victory at Eckmöhl. Couriers passed each other and caught each other up on the road between Split and Travnik. General Marmont wanted at all costs to reach Napoleon's army with his troops from Dalmatia before the decisive battle. So he asked Daville for information about the regions through which he had to pass, sending him new orders constantly. This greatly increased Daville's work, making it ever more difficult, expensive and complex, particularly since von Mitterer watched his every step and, as an experienced soldier, accustomed to plots and undertakings along borders, put every conceivable obstacle in the way of Marmont's progress through Lika and Croatia. Daville's strength, ingenuity and will for battle grew with the quantity and difficulty of these tasks. With d'Avenat's help, he succeeded in finding and bringing together everyone opposed to Austria by temperament or interests and willing to undertake anything at all. He contacted the town commanders from the Military Frontier, particularly the commander in Novi, the brother of that unfortunate Ahmed Bey Cerić whom he had not succeeded in saving, urged them to stir things up in the Austrian territories and offered them resources for raids.

Through the Livno friars, von Mitterer sent newspapers and proclamations to Dalmatia, which was under French occupation, maintained links with the Catholic clergy in Northern Dalmatia and assisted the organization of resistance to the French.

All the paid agents and voluntary assistants of both Consuls ran to and fro in all directions. And their work began to be felt in a general unrest and frequent conflicts.

The friars ceased altogether to see anyone from the French Consulate. In monasteries prayers were said for the victory of Austrian arms over the Jacobin armies and their godless Emperor Napoleon.

The Consuls went to visit and received people they would never otherwise have received, giving them gifts and dispensing bribes. They worked day and night, without many scruples about their methods. The Colonel's position was far more favourable. It is true that he was a tired man, oppressed by his domestic troubles and poor health, but for him this way of life and style of warfare were nothing new, it suited his training and experience. Faced with orders from above, the Colonel immediately forgot about himself and his family and stepped onto the well-trodden path of Imperial service, following it steadily, without any joy or enthusiasm, but without second thoughts or objections. Apart from this, he knew the language, the country, the people and the circumstances, and he had no difficulty in finding sincere and disinterested helpers at every step. None of this was the case with Daville who had to work under far harder conditions. Nevertheless, his intellectual vitality, sense of duty and innate Gallic belligerence sustained him, helping him not to fall behind in the contest. He too gave as good as he got.

Despite all of this, had it been up to the two Consuls themselves, relations between them would not have been so bad. Their worst affliction was petty officials, agents and servants. They knew no limits in their mutual denigration. Carried away by their professional fervour and personal vanity as hunters are by their zeal, they forgot themselves to such an extent that, in their desire to humiliate one another, they degraded themselves in the eyes of the rayah and the vindictive Turks.

Both Daville and von Mitterer clearly recognized that such reckless and ruthless methods of conducting the battle between them were damaging to both sides and to the reputation of Christians and Europeans altogether. How undignified it was for the two of them, the only representatives of the enlightened world in this wilderness, to be fighting in front of these people who hated and despised them both and did not understand them. And these were precisely the people they were calling on as witnesses and judges. Daville was particularly conscious of this, as his position was weaker. He decided to draw von Mitterer's attention to it, indirectly, through Doctor Cologna who was considered an unofficial figure, and to propose that they should both exert some restraint on their over-zealous associates. Des Fossés was to talk to Cologna, since d'Avenat was in permanent conflict with him. At the same time he wanted through his devout wife and in every other possible way to influence the friars and point out to them that as representatives of the Church they were wrong to give such one-sided and exclusive support to just one of the warring factions.

In order to demonstrate to the friars how mistaken they were in accusing the French régime of godlessness and to put them under as firm as possible an obligation, Daville hit on the idea of asking them for a permanent, paid chaplain for the French Consulate. And he sent a letter to the Bishop in Fojnica through the Dolac priest. As there was no answer, it fell to Madame Daville to talk the matter over with Brother Ivo in person and to assure him that it would be good and appropriate for the friars to appoint one of the Brethren chaplain and in general to change their attitude towards the French Consulate.

Madame Daville went to Dolac one Saturday afternoon, accompanied by the "Illyrian" interpreter and a khavaz. She had chosen a particular time for this conversation, that of the evening Benediction and not Sunday when there were a lot of people in the church and the priest was busy.

Brother Ivo received Madame Daville as graciously as ever. He told her that the Bishop's written answer had arrived "this morning" and that he was just about to pass it on to Monsieur le

Consul Général. The answer was negative, because unfortunately, in these hard times, persecuted, impoverished and few in number, the monks did not have even the bare minimum of clergy necessary for their parishioners. Besides, the Turks would immediately regard such a chaplain as an informer and the whole Order would be made to pay. In short, the Bishop regretted that he could not grant the French Consul's request, and begged him to understand his position, etc., etc.

That was what the Bishop had written, but Brother Ivo did not conceal the fact that, even if he had been permitted, he would never have agreed to allow a chaplain of theirs to serve at Napoleon's Consulate. Madame Daville endeavoured gently to correct his opinion, but the friar, in his armour of flesh, remained adamant. He respected Madame Daville, personally, for her sincere and unquestioned piety (in general the friars had far more respect for Madame Daville than for Frau von Mitterer), but he stuck resolutely to his point of view. He accompanied his words with a brisk, irritable gesture of his huge white hand which made Madame Daville flinch involuntarily. It was evident that the instructions he had were clear, that his position was firm and that he had no desire to discuss it with anyone, least of all a woman.

After he had told Madame Daville again that he was always at her disposal for any spiritual needs, but that in all other matters he would stand by his point of view, Brother Ivo went into the church where the Benediction was beginning. For some reason there were quite a few friars visiting Dolac that day, and the Benediction turned out to be particularly splendid.

Had it been up to her, Madame Daville would have returned home immediately, but considerations of duty required that she should stay for the Benediction, so that it did not look as though she had come in order to talk to Brother Ivo. This otherwise sober woman, with no trace of exaggerated sensibility, was upset by the priest's behaviour. The unpleasant interview had been all the more difficult for her as her nature and upbringing were such that all general issues and public affairs were remote from her.

Now she stood in the church by a wooden column and listened to the subdued and not yet harmonious singing of the friars, who knelt on either side of the main altar. Brother Ivo was taking the service. Large and heavy as he was, he succeeded, whenever necessary, in dropping easily and nimbly onto one knee and rising again at once. The woman kept seeing before her eyes his huge hand with its negative gesture and the look, bright with obstinate self-assurance with which he had watched her interpreter when he spoke with her a short while before. She had never observed such a look in France, in either laymen or a member of the clergy.

In their peasants' voices, the friars were quietly singing in chorus the Litany of the Virgin. A ponderous voice began:

"Sancta Maria…"

All responded in a muffled chorus:

"Ora pro nobis."

The voice continued:

"Sancta virgo virginum…"

"Ora pro nobis…" responded the other voices in unison.

The voice of the prayer-leader continued to drone the list of the virgin's attributes:

"Imperatrix Reginarum…"

"Laus sanctarum animarum…"

"Vera salutrix earum…"

And after each of them the choir would respond monotonously:

"Ora pro nobis."

The woman wanted to pray as well, to the familiar litany she used to hear in the shady choir of the cathedral of her native Avranches. But she could not forget her recent conversation or suppress the thoughts which kept mingling with her prayers.

We all say the same prayers, we are all Christians of the same faith, but the gulfs between people are great, she thought, and before her eyes she saw constantly the hostile, obdurate look and curt gesture of this same Brother Ivo who was now singing the liturgy.

The singing continued its catalogue:

"Sancta Mater Domini…"

"Sancta Dei genitrix…"

Yes, you know there are these gulfs and all these contradictions between people, but it is only when you go into the world and feel their effect on yourself, that you see just how great they really are, how difficult and impassable. What kind of prayers would there have to be to fill them in and smooth them over? Her despondent mood answered that there could never be any such prayers. But here her thoughts would stop, fearful and powerless. And the woman whispered softly, adding her inaudible voice to the friars' monotonous drone which kept returning like a wave, repeating:

"Ora pro nobis!"

When vespers were over, the woman meekly received a blessing from that same hand of Brother Ivo's.

Outside, in front of the church, in addition to her own escort she found Des Fossés with a servant. He had been riding through Dolac and when he heard that Madame Daville was in the church, he decided to wait for her and accompany her to Travnik. The woman was glad to see the familiar face of the cheerful young man and to hear her own language.

They returned to the town along the broad, dry road. The sun had gone down, but a strong yellow glow was falling indirectly over the whole region. The clay road looked red and warm, while the young leaves and flower buds on the bushes stood out from their black bark, as though they were made of light itself.

Flushed from his ride, the young man walked beside her, talking animatedly. Behind them they could hear the footsteps of the servants and the thud of Des Fossés's horses' hooves as they were led by the bridle. The litany was still echoing in her ears. Now the road began to slope downwards. The roofs of Travnik could be seen with thin blue smoke rising over them. And with them appeared real life with its needs and demands, dispelling all brooding, doubts and prayers.

It was at about this time that Des Fossés had his conversation with Cologna.

One evening, it could have been around eight o'clock, accompanied by a khavaz and a servant carrying a lantern, Des Fossés went to see the doctor.

The house stood on its own, on a steep rise, shrouded in dense night and damp fog. A murmur of invisible water came from a spring. This sound of water was dulled and altered by the darkness, and intensified by the silence. The road was wet and slippery, and under the feeble, flickering light of the Turkish lantern, it looked unfamiliar, like a forest clearing never before crossed by men. The gateway looked just as unexpected and mysterious. The doorstep and the knocker were illuminated, everything else was in darkness. It was impossible to make out the shape or dimensions of anything or to guess their true function. The wooden gate resounded dully when they knocked. Des Fossés felt that the knocks sounded boorish and out of place, almost painful, and the khavaz's excessive zeal struck him as particularly uncouth and obtrusive.

"Who's there?"

The voice came from above, more like an echo of the constable's knocking than a separate question.

"The 'Young Consul'. Open up!" shouted the khavaz in that unpleasant strident tone which subordinates always use to one another in the presence of a superior.

The men's voices and the noise of water in the distance all sounded like haphazard calling in a forest, without known cause or obvious consequence. Finally the clink of a chain was heard, the squeak of a lock and click of a latch. The gate opened slowly. Behind it stood a man with a lantern, pale and drowsy, wrapped in a shepherd's cloak. The two unequal lights illuminated a steep courtyard and low dark windows on the ground floor. Both lanterns vied with one another to light up the ground in front of the "Young Consul's" feet. Confused by these voices and the shifting beams of light, Des Fossés found himself all at once in front of the wide open door of a large ground-floor room. The stale air was full of smoke and the acrid smell of tobacco.

Cologna was standing, tall and stooped, in the middle of the room, beside a large candle holder. He was wearing a mixture of numerous bits of Turkish and Western clothing. On his head he had a small black cap with long thin locks of grey hair protruding out of it. Two tufts of completely white hair protruded from his ears. These tufts gleamed when he moved his head, first one, then the other, like two small white flames.

The old man bowed deeply, uttering sonorous greetings and compliments in his curious tongue, which could have been corrupt Italian or imperfect French. But they all struck the young man as superficial and half-hearted, empty formulas not only without warmth or genuine respect, but without the real presence of the man pronouncing them. And then suddenly everything he had found in the low, smoky room – the smell and look of the room itself, the appearance and speech of the man – was all condensed into one word, and so vividly that he almost spoke it aloud: age. Pathetic, toothless, forgetful, solitary and wearisome old age, which alters, disintegrates and embitters all things: thoughts, sights, movements, sounds; everything, everything down to light and smell themselves.

The old doctor ceremoniously offered the young man a chair, but remained standing himself, apologizing that this was required by the good old Salernitan rule: "Post prandium sta."[13]

---

13 "After dinner, one should stand."

The young man was sitting on a hard stool with no back, but with a feeling of physical and mental superiority which made his mission seem simple, almost agreeable. And he began to talk with the blind confidence with which the young often approach conversations with old people who seem to them out-of-date and decrepit, forgetting that slowness of mind and physical incapacity are often accompanied by great experience and accumulated skill in human affairs. He gave him Daville's message for von Mitterer, trying to make it seem what it really was: a well-intentioned suggestion in the general interest, and not a sign of weakness or fear. He gave the message, and was satisfied with himself.

While the young man was still speaking, Cologna hastened to assure him that he was honoured to be chosen as messenger, that he would pass on the message exactly, that he entirely understood the intentions of Monsieur Daville and shared his opinion, that his own origins, vocation and convictions made him the most suitable person for such a role.

It was evidently now Cologna's turn to be satisfied with himself.

The young man listened to him as one listens to the sound of water, looking absently at his long, regular face, with its lively, round eyes, bloodless lips, and teeth which moved as he spoke. Old age! thought the young man. The worst thing is not that you suffer and die, but that you age, for ageing means suffering without cure or hope, it is a lingering death. Only, the young man was not thinking about this process of ageing as the common lot, including his own, but as some personal affliction of the doctor's.

Cologna was saying:

"You need not explain things to me at length. I understand the position of Monsieur le Consul as I do that of any cultured man from the West, whose destiny drives him to these parts. For such a person to live in Turkey means to walk along a knife edge and to burn on a low fire. I know this, for we are born on that knife edge, we live and die on it, and we grow up and are burned out on that fire…"

Through his thoughts on age and ageing, the young man began to listen more attentively and to grasp the doctor's words.

"No one knows what it means to be born and to live on the brink, between two worlds, knowing and understanding both of them, and to be unable to do anything to help explain them to each other and bring them closer. To love and hate both, to hesitate and waver all one's life. To have two homelands, and yet have none. To be everywhere at home and to remain forever a stranger. In short, to live torn on a rack, but as both victim and torturer at once."

The young man listened, surprised. It was as though he were hearing some third person who had joined in their conversation. There was no longer any trace of empty words or compliments. Before him stood a man with shining eyes and long thin arms outstretched, demonstrating how one lived torn apart between two opposing worlds.

As often happens with young people, it seemed to Des Fossés that this conversation was not entirely fortuitous but that it had some close and special connection with his own thoughts and the book he was working on. There were not many opportunities for conversations of this kind in Travnik. It was pleasantly exciting, and in his excitement he began to ask questions and then himself to make observations and mention his own impressions.

The young man was speaking as much from an inner need as from a desire to prolong the conversation. But there was no need to goad the old man to talk. His thoughts flowed uninterruptedly. As though inspired, sometimes searching for French expressions and substituting Italian ones for them he spoke as though he were reading:

"Yes, these are the torments suffered by Christians from the Levant and which you who belong to the Christian West can never fully understand, while the Turks can understand them even less. That is the fate of a man from the Levant, for he is 'poussière humaine', human dust, drifting painfully between East and West, belonging to neither and beaten by both. These are people who know many languages, but none is their own, who know two faiths, but are steadfast in neither. These are the victims of the fatal division of humanity into Christians and non-Christians, eternal interpreters and go-betweens, but who carry in themselves much that is hidden and inexpressible; people who know well East and West, their customs and beliefs, but are equally despised and mistrusted by either side. One can apply to them the words written by the great Jelaleddin, Jelaleddin Roumi, six centuries ago: 'For I cannot know myself. I am neither Christian, nor Jew, nor Parsee, nor Muslim. I am neither from the East, nor the West, neither from the land, nor the sea.' That is how they are. They are a small, separate humanity, choking under a double burden of Original Sin, needing to be saved and redeemed anew, but no one can see how or by whom. They are people from the frontier, spiritual and physical, from the black and bloody line which was drawn, after some absurd misunderstanding, between people, God's creatures, between whom there should not and must not be any boundaries. They form the narrow edge between the sea and the land, condemned to perpetual movement and unrest. They are the 'third world', where all malediction settled as a result of the division of the earth into two worlds. They are…"

Elated, his eyes burning, Des Fossés watched the altered old man, still standing with his arms spread out in a cross, as he searched in vain for words and suddenly, in a broken voice, came to an abrupt end:

"It is heroism without glory, martyrdom without reward. And you at least, our fellow-believers and our kin, people from the West, Christians of the same sacrament as our own, should understand us, accept us and ease the burden of our fate."

The doctor lowered his arms with an expression of utter hopelessness, almost angrily. There was no longer any trace of that repellent "Illyrian doctor". Here stood a man with his own ideas, forcefully expressed. And Des Fossés was burning with the desire to hear and learn more, completely forgetting not only his feeling of superiority of a short time before, but even where he was and the business he had come about. And he felt that he had been sitting here far longer than he should have done or had meant to, but he did not get up.

The old man was looking at him now with an expression full of silent emotion, as one looks at someone moving out of sight, whose departure we regret.

"Yes, sir, you can comprehend this life of ours, but it is just a disagreeable dream to you. You may live here, but you know it is temporary and that sooner or later you will return to your own country, to better conditions and a worthier life. You will wake from this nightmare and be freed from it, but we never shall be, for it is the only life we have."

Towards the end of the conversation, the doctor became increasingly subdued and strange. He sat down, right next to the young man, bending towards him, in an attitude of the greatest confidence, and signalling to him with both hands to be still and not to let his words or gestures frighten and drive away something tiny, precious and fearful, like a bird which might have been there, on the floor in front of them. Staring at that spot on the carpet, he spoke almost in a whisper, but in a voice whose warmth betrayed inner joy:

"At the end, at the real, final end, all will nevertheless be well and everything will be resolved harmoniously. Despite the fact that here it all looks utterly discordant and hopelessly embroiled. 'Un jour tout sera bien, voilà notre espérance,'[14] as your philosopher put it. And one could not even imagine it any other way. For why should

14 "One day all will be well, that is our hope."

my thought, if it is good and true, be worth less than the same thought conceived in Rome or Paris? Because it was born in this pit called Travnik? And is it possible that this thought should not be noted in any way, not recorded anywhere? No, it is not. Despite the apparent fragmentation and chaos, everything is connected and harmonious. No single human thought or effort of the spirit is lost. We are all on the right road and we shall be surprised when we meet. But we shall meet and understand each other, all of us, wherever we are going now and however much we go astray. That will be a joyous meeting, a glorious, redeeming surprise."

The young man had difficulty in following the old man's thought, but he wanted fervently to hear more. With no apparent connection, but in the same confidential and excitedly joyful tone, Cologna continued to talk. And the young man nodded in approval, exhilarated, from time to time saying something himself, driven by an irresistible need. So he related his observations from the road by Turbe about the different historical epochs that could be seen in the various layers of that road. This was the same thing he had once spoken of to Daville, without much success.

"I know, you look around you. You are interested in the past and the present. You know how to look," said the doctor approvingly.

And as though he were telling him the secret of some hidden treasure and wanted to suggest with his smiling eyes more than he could say in words, the old man whispered:

"When you make your way through the bazaar, stop by the Yeni Mosque. There is a high wall round the whole grounds. Inside, under huge trees, there are some graves. No one knows any longer whose they are. The people know that once, before the arrival of the Turks, this mosque was the Church of St Catherine. And they believe that even now there is a sacristy in one corner which no one can open, however much force they use. And if you look a little more closely at the stone of that ancient wall, you will see that it comes from

Roman ruins and tombstones. And on one stone built into the wall of that mosque you can clearly read the steady, regular Roman letters of a fragmented inscription: 'Marco Flavio … optimo …' And deep beneath that, in the invisible foundations, lie large blocks of red granite, the remains of a far older cult, a former temple of the god Mithras. On one of these stones you can just make out an indistinct relief showing the young god of light slaying a powerful boar on the run. And who knows what else is hidden in those depths, under those foundations. Who knows whose efforts are buried there and what kind of traces have been erased forever. And that is on just one small piece of ground, in this remote little town. And where are all the other countless large settlements throughout the world?"

The young man looked at the old doctor, in the expectation of further explanations, but here he suddenly changed his tone and began to speak much more loudly, as though others were now allowed to hear him:

"You understand, it is all connected, one thing with another, and it is only apparently lost and forgotten, scattered, haphazard. It is all moving, even without realizing it, towards the same goal, like converging rays towards a distant, unknown focus. You should not forget that it is expressly written in the Koran: 'Perhaps one day God will reconcile you and your opponents and establish friendship between you. He is powerful, mild and merciful.' So there is hope, and where there is hope … You understand?"

His eyes smiled significantly, triumphantly, as though he were encouraging and consoling the young man, and with his hands he outlined in the air, in front of his face, something round, as though he wanted to suggest the closed circle of the universe.

"You understand!" the old man repeated meaningfully and impatiently, as though he considered it superfluous to find expression in words for what was so obvious and certain, so close and familiar to him.

But towards the end the conversation changed. Cologna was standing again, thin and straight, bowing and twisting, speaking sonorous, empty words, assuring the young man that he was honoured by both the visit and the message entrusted to him.

At this they parted.

Making his way back to the Consulate, Des Fossés strode mechanically in the circle of light which the khavaz's lantern spread before him. He did not notice anything around him now. He was thinking of the crazy old doctor and his unfathomable ideas, trying to get his bearings and make out his own thoughts which kept springing up unexpectedly and criss-crossing in his mind.

16

The news reaching Travnik from Istanbul was increasingly bad. Even after Baryaktar's successful undertaking and Selim III's tragic death things did not settle down. Before the end of that year there was a new coup in which Mustapha Baryaktar was killed.

The changes in the distant capital were reflected in this remote province, although much later, and altered and caricatured as in a distorting mirror. The Muslim population in the towns was racked by fear, discontent, shortages and anger which could find no outlet. In an accurate presentiment of the upheavals and damaging changes to come, these people felt betrayed from within and threatened from outside. Their instinct for survival and self-defence was driving them to action, but circumstances deprived them of the means and closed all roads to them. And so their energies spun about and were spent on the wind. And in the congested towns, among the high hills, where different faiths and opposing interests lived in their adjoining quarters, a tense and explosive atmosphere built up, in which nothing was impossible, in which blind forces clashed and frenzied brawls kept breaking out.

At that time battles of unprecedented scale and horror and as yet unpredictable historical consequences were being waged in Europe. In Istanbul one coup d'état followed another, Sultans were replaced and Grand Viziers perished.

Travnik was bustling. As every spring, on orders from Istanbul, the army was preparing to attack Serbia. The preparations were noisy, but the results meagre. Suleiman Pasha had already left with his small but orderly unit. In a day or two the Vizier was supposed to set off as well. In fact, Ibrahim Pasha did not himself know exactly what the plan of campaign should be or how large an army he should take. He was going, because there was nothing else he could do, because he had received orders and because he hoped that his presence would induce others also to do their duty. But no one could get the janissaries into rank and on the move, because they kept ducking out at every possible excuse. While some were being registered, others were already running away. Or they would simply provoke a fight or disturbance and take advantage of it to disappear and return to their homes, while their names stayed on the list as though they had gone to Serbia.

Both Consuls invested all their energy in informing themselves as fully as possible about the Vizier's intentions, about the size and competence of the troops he was leading and about the real situation on the battlefield in Serbia. Both they and their associates wasted days in these activities which looked at one moment exceptionally important and difficult and the next irrelevant.

As soon as the Vizier had followed Suleiman Pasha off to the Drina, leaving all authority and responsibility for order to the weak, frightened Governor, the Kaymakam – the Travnik bazaar was suddenly closed again, for the second time.

In fact, this was a continuation of last year's disturbance which had never altogether ceased but smouldered on in muffled silence, waiting for a convenient excuse to erupt again. This time the fury of the rabble was directed against the Serbs who had been captured in various parts of Bosnia and brought to Travnik, on suspicion that they had links with the rebels in Serbia and were preparing a similar uprising in Bosnia. But it was just as much against the Ottoman authorities, whom they accused of weakness, corruption and treachery.

Feeling clearly that this rising in Serbia threatened what was closest and dearest to them, that this Vizier, like all the Ottomans, was not protecting them as he should, and that they personally no longer had the strength or the will to protect themselves, the more prosperous Bosnian Turks fell into a state of morbid irritability typical of a group of people under threat. And they retaliated with quite arbitrary cruelty. Their example was often followed by the town's poor as well, the very lowliest who had nothing to lose.

Every day Serbs were brought, exhausted and in chains, from the Drina or the Austrian frontier, on serious but vague charges, in ones and twos, or in crowds, dozens at a time. There were people from the towns and priests among them, but they were mostly peasants.

There was no one to investigate their crimes or to judge them. They were cast into the seething Travnik bazaar, as into the crater of an erupting volcano, and it acted as their executioner, without inquiry or trial.

Despite Daville's pleas and warnings, Des Fossés went out to watch gypsies torturing and executing two men, in the middle of the cattle-market. On a rise, behind the crowd which was completely absorbed in the scene before it, he was able to watch unobserved and to see clearly victims, executioners and spectators.

There was chaos and commotion in the square. Soldiers brought in the two accused, who were barefoot and bare-headed, wearing thick trousers and unbuttoned torn shirts.

They were both tall, dark men, as alike as brothers. As far as one could make out from the remains of their clothes, ruined by their journey and ill-treatment, they looked as though they came from a small town. People said they had been caught just as they were about to smuggle some letters from the Bishop of Sarajevo into Serbia in hollow sticks.

The soldiers struggled to make enough space for the hanging. The executioners, gypsies, had no room to untwist their ropes. The seething crowd shouted abuse at the two unfortunates, the soldiers and the gypsies, surging in all directions and threatening to trample or carry off both victims and executioners.

The two bound men, with their long necks bared, stood upright and motionless, with the same expression of strange, confused uneasiness on their faces. They conveyed neither fear nor courage, neither enthusiasm nor indifference. The expression on their faces suggested only that they were worried, preoccupied with thoughts about some distant anxiety, and wanting only to be left to think about it, single-mindedly. It was as though all the activity and noise around them had nothing to do with them. They simply blinked and from time to time bent their heads slightly, as though that could protect them from the throng and din which was preventing them from devoting themselves entirely to the burden of their cares. Branching veins stood out on their brows and temples and they were bathed in sweat. They could not wipe it away, so the sweat poured down their sinewy, unshaven necks in glistening streams.

At last the gypsies managed to disentangle their ropes and they approached the first of the two condemned men. He backed slightly away, but very slightly, and immediately stopped, letting them do what they wanted to him. At the same time the other one also took an involuntary step back as though he were invisibly tied to the first.

Here Des Fossés, who had watched everything calmly up to then, suddenly turned away and went into another street. So he did not see the most harrowing part.

Two of the gypsies looped a rope around their victim's neck but they did not hang him. They stepped back and each one started pulling and tightening his end of the rope. The man began to choke and roll his eyes, to kick, twist his hips and jerk like a puppet on a taut string.

The throng started jostling and shoving. They all pressed towards the scene of the ordeal. The people responded enthusiastically and joyfully to the first movements of the tortured man, accompanying his movements with their cries, laughter and gestures. But when the spasms of the strangled man became deathly and his movements appalling and fantastic, those who were closest began to turn to move away. Undoubtedly, they had wanted to see something unusual, not themselves knowing exactly what, and through that to find some relief for their vague but profound general sense of discontent. For a long time they had wanted to get their fill of watching a defeated enemy being punished. But what had taken place in front of them had suddenly become agony and torture for them as well. Taken by surprise and frightened, they began all at once to turn their heads and get out of the way. But the throng of people who had not been able to see surged forward and pushed those who were in front ever closer. Then these people, horrified by the proximity of the unexpected agony, turned their backs to the site of the execution and made desperate efforts to force their way through, flailing around them with their fists in frenzy, as though escaping from a fire. Not knowing what was driving them and unable to understand their panic-stricken behaviour, other people responded to their blows with blows, forcing them back the way they had come. So it happened that, alongside the slow strangling and horrific twitching of the dying man, there were scuffles all around him, a whole series of individual clashes, quarrels and real fights. In the crush, people could not raise their arms to hit back, so they tore and scratched, spat and cursed, staring at each other's distorted faces with total incomprehension and the hatred they had stored up for the victim. They fled, appalled, from the sight of the strangled man, shoving and hitting out at each other in desperation but silently, while those who were thrusting forwards from all directions towards the site of the execution, in far greater numbers, were shouting loudly. Many of those who were furthest off and could not see anything of either the torture or the fighting going on all around the execution site, were laughing, borne along by the surging crowd. And, not knowing of the horrors going on so close to them, they were calling out the kind of wisecracks and banter that are always heard from any congested crowd. Completely different voices and exclamations mingled and collided with each other, angry, astonished, disgusted, furious, mocking, jovial, all mixed with the general inarticulate cries and clamour of a crowd of people, their stomachs pressed against one another and their lungs constricted.

"Heave ho!" shouted some unruly lads in chorus, as they tried to stir the crowd into movement.

"Sho-ve!" answered others, pushing in the opposite direction.

"Hey, stop hitting me! Are you crazy?"

"He's mad, mad! He's mad!" someone shouted, in a madman's voice himself.

"Hit him! Don't be soft! He's not your mother's son!" someone called from some way off, cheerfully, thinking it was all a joke.

There was a sound of scraping feet, stamping and thudding blows. And then more voices.

"There you are! You want more? Ha! You want a real thrashing?"

"Hey, you there with the cap!"

"Who's pushing? Come closer, let me talk to you."

"You're stroking him! Sock him in the gob!"

"Stop, sto-o-o-p!"

Meanwhile only those closest or those who were watching from high vantage points round about were able to see what was going on at the execution site. Both the strangled men had lost consciousness. First one, then the other. Now they were lying on the ground. The gypsies ran up to them, picked them up, poured water over them, hit them with their fists and scratched them with their nails. And as soon as the men came to and were standing on their feet, the torture was continued. Once again the rope was twisted and tightened, once again the two men twitched, their throats rasping, but for a shorter time now and with less resistance. Once again the closest of the spectators began to turn and run away, but the dense crowd would not let them through, turning them back with curses and blows to the scene they had wished to escape.

A little student with a face like a faun had a seizure, but he could not fall. Held in a vice and borne along by the surging mesh of bodies, he remained standing upright, although unconscious, his head thrown back, his face white as chalk, with foam on his lips.

The torture was repeated three times. And each time both men got up calmly and carefully bent their necks under the rope once more, like people who wanted very much to do all they could to make things go properly. Both of them were composed and calm, calmer than either the gypsies or any of the spectators, only thoughtful and worried, so worried that even their spasms could not quite wipe from their faces that expression of distant, leaden anxiety.

When they were unable to bring them round for a fourth suffocation, the gypsies went up to the fallen men, who were lying on their backs, and kicked each of them several times in the groin, to finish them off.

The gypsies coiled their ropes, winding them round their elbows and waiting for the crowd to disperse a little so as to continue their work. With shifting eyes, they interrupted their activities to draw greedily on cigarettes that someone had given them. They appeared to be equally furious with this mindless rabble milling round them and the two dead men, lying there, motionless and lost among the countless, rushing feet of the inquisitive people.

A little later the corpses of the two unknown martyrs were hung on special gallows, on the wall above the graveyard so that they could be clearly seen from all directions. Their bodies had lengthened again, and they had regained their former appearance, becoming once more straight and slender and as alike as brothers. They seemed light, as though made of paper. Their heads had become small, for the rope had cut deep under their chins. Their faces were calm and bloodless, not blue and disfigured like those of people who are hanged alive, and their legs hung together, their feet thrust a little forward, as though about to leap.

That was how Des Fossés saw them when he returned about midday. One of them had the sleeve of his filthy shirt torn off at the shoulder, and this piece of linen was fluttering in the light breeze.

His teeth clenched, consciously determined to see this too with his own eyes, shaken, but in a solemnly tranquil state of mind, the young man looked up at the two figures above him.

This heavy, solemn mood stayed with him for a long time. It was in this mood that he returned to the Consulate. Daville seemed to him small, confused and scared by trifles, while d'Avenat was coarse and ignorant. All Daville's fears appeared childishly unreal, and his remarks either insipid, bookish, or petty and demeaningly bureaucratic. Des Fossés realized that he would not be able even to talk to them about what he had just seen and experienced profoundly, at a level beyond words. And after dinner, in the same mood, he included in his book about Bosnia, faithfully and factually, a special paragraph about the way "sentences of death are carried out in Bosnia on the rayah and rebels".

People began to get used to hideous, bloody sights, immediately forgetting the old ones and seeking out ever new and more varied ones.

A new execution site was set up on a clear piece of level ground, between the khan and the Austrian General Consulate. Here the Vizier's executioner Ekrem cut off heads which were then stuck on stakes.

There was consternation in von Mitterer's house. Anna Maria flew at her husband, screaming: "Josef, for God's sake!" in all possible tones of voice, and, calling him Robespierre, she began to pack and get ready to run away. And then, exhausted and hysterical, she would fall into her husband's arms, sobbing like an unfortunate queen about to step onto the guillotine, with the executioner waiting outside the door.

Little Agatha, genuinely frightened, sat in the low chair on the veranda quietly weeping floods of tears, which von Mitterer found harder to bear than all his wife's scenes.

The pale, hunchbacked interpreter Rotta ran from the Residence to the official in charge, the Muteselim, threatening, bribing, demanding and imploring him not to have death sentences carried out in front of the Consulate building.

That very same evening a dozen Serbs, peasants from the borderlands, were brought into the square and executed by the light of lanterns and torches, to the sound of the hissing and shouting, running and jostling of the bloodthirsty Turks. The heads of the murdered men were stuck on stakes. All night long the growling of the hungry town dogs which had immediately gathered there permeated the Consulate. In the moonlight the dogs could be seen leaping up the stakes and tearing pieces of flesh off the severed heads.

It was not until the following day, after the Consul had visited the Kaymakam, that the stakes were removed and executions ceased to be carried out on that spot.

Daville did not emerge from his house and he could only hear, from time to time, the muffled, distant cheering of the crowd, but he received precise information from d'Avenat about the course of the riot and the series of executions in the town. When he learned what was going on in front of the Austrian Consulate, he suddenly lost all his fears and scruples and, without consulting anyone or asking himself for one moment whether it was in keeping with international customs and the interests of his position, he sat down and wrote von Mitterer a friendly letter.

This was one of those situations in which Daville knew, quite clearly, without his usual vacillation, exactly what to do and would have dared do anything.

In the letter he mentioned, of course, Bellona the goddess of war and the "rattle of arms" which was still going on and the dedicated service each of them owed his sovereign.

"But", wrote Daville, "I think that I shall not offend either your sensibility or my duty if, exceptionally, and in very special circumstances, I write you these few words. Disgusted and indignant, ourselves the victims of daily savagery, knowing what is taking place in front of your house, my wife and I ask you to believe that at all times our thoughts are with you and your family.

"As Christians and Europeans, despite everything that temporarily divides us, we would not like you to be without our expression of sympathy and some sign of condolence at this time."

It was only after he had sent the letter, by a roundabout way, to the Consulate on the other side of the Lašva, that Daville began to question whether he had done right or not.

That same summer's day when von Mitterer received Daville's letter – it was 5 July 1809 – the battle of Wagram began.

During the ten sunniest days of July there was total anarchy in Travnik. A general infectious madness drove people out of their houses, goading them to incredible and monstrous things they had never even dreamed of. Events developed of their own accord, by some warped logic. Situations grew up by chance, out of a cry or youthful prank, they followed an unforeseen course and came to an unexpected end or were simply broken off abruptly, in mid-stream. Crowds of young boys would set off in one direction with an aim in mind, but on the way, finding some other more exciting spectacle, they would abandon their initial purpose and throw themselves passionately into this new one as though they had been preparing it for weeks. The zeal of these people was amazing. Each one burned with the desire to contribute to the defence of his faith and good order and each wanted, with the greatest conviction and holy indignation, to participate, not only with their own eyes but with their hands, in the killing and torture of traitors and the wicked people who were to blame for all the great ills in the country and for all their personal misfortunes and the sufferings of each one of them. People went to the execution sites as one goes to a holy place which has miraculous healing powers and offers certain relief for every torment. Everyone wanted to bring in a rebel or a spy himself and to participate personally in his punishment and the selection of the place and means of his execution. And they quarrelled over it, transposing all their ardour and bitterness into this mutual dispute. You could often see a dozen destitute Turks round one of the bound prisoners, excitedly waving their hands, arguing and wrangling as over cattle up for sale. Quite small boys would yell to one another, running breathlessly, the long seats of their Turkish trousers swinging, to plunge their little knives into the blood of the victims so that they could later wave them about, frightening the younger children in their quarter.

And the days were sunny, the sky cloudless, the town full of greenery, water, early fruit and flowers. At night the moon shone, clear, glassy and chill. And the bloody carnival continued, day and night, with everyone bent on the same purpose and no one able to understand anyone else or recognize himself.

The general ferment spread like an epidemic. Long buried hatreds broke out and old vendettas were revived. Innocent people were caught or there were fatal misunderstandings and mistakes of identity.

The foreigners from both Consulates did not leave their houses. The khavazes brought them information about everything that was going on. Cologna was the only exception, unable to bear to stay in his damp, lonely home. The old doctor could neither sleep nor work. He went down to the Consulate, although it meant passing through the frenzied crowd or by places of execution which would spring up now in one place, now in another. Everyone noticed that he was in a state of constant agitation, that his eyes were burning with an unhealthy intensity, that he was trembling all over and stumbling in his speech. Like a straw in a whirlpool, the old man was drawn to the mindless maelstrom spinning through the town.

One day, at exactly noon, on his way back from the Consulate, Cologna came upon a mob of ragged Turks in the middle of the bazaar, dragging a bound man who had been beaten. He had time to turn off into one of the side streets, but the mob attracted him irresistibly. When he was just a few paces from them, a hoarse voice called from the middle of the crowd:

"Doctor, doctor, don't let them kill an innocent man!"

As though bewitched, Cologna went closer and with his short-sighted eyes recognized a man from Fojnica, a Catholic by the name of Kulier. The man was shouting, pouring out a torrent of words, not knowing what to mention first and begging them to let him go because he was innocent.

Looking for someone in the mob he could talk to, Cologna encountered many sullen glances. But before he was able to say or do anything, a tall man with pale, sunken cheeks stepped out of the group and barred the doctor's way.

"You get out of here."

His voice was trembling, brimming with fury that broke through his forced and ominous restraint.

Had it not been for this man and his voice, perhaps the old doctor would have continued on his way and left the man from Fojnica, whom no one could help, to his fate. But he was drawn to that voice, as into the depths of a whirlpool. He wanted to say that he knew this Kulier to be a law-abiding citizen, to ask what he had done wrong and where they were taking him, but the tall man would not let him speak.

"Get out of here, I said." The Turk raised his voice.

"Now wait a minute. Where are you taking this man?"

"If you must know, I'm taking the dog to hang him like the other dogs."

"How? Why? You can't hang innocent people. I'll call the Kaymakam."

Now Cologna was shouting as well, not noticing that he was becoming increasingly excited.

A murmur ran through the mob. From two minarets, one nearby and the other in the distance, the muezzins were summoning the faithful and their voices crossed, strained and wavering. People began to gather round the group.

"Well, since you've come to defend him," shouted the tall man, "I'll hang him right here, on this mulberry tree."

"You won't! You daren't. I'll call the police, I'll go to the Governor. Who are you?" the old man shouted shrilly and disjointedly.

"Someone who's not afraid of you. Now get out of my sight while your skin's still in one piece."

There was an abusive clamour from the mob. More and more people from the bazaar gathered around them. As he shouted, the tall man covertly caught their eye after every sentence, to see whether they approved. And they watched him, motionless, but with evident satisfaction.

The tall man moved towards the old mulberry beside the road and the whole crowd and Cologna followed him. Now they were all shouting and waving their arms. Cologna shouted ceaselessly as well, but no one wanted to listen to him, nor would they let him finish.

"Thieves, brigands, thugs! You are disgracing the Sultan's honour! Brigands! Renegades!" screamed the old doctor.

"Shut up, or you'll swing beside this one!"

"Who, me? You daren't lay a finger on me, you filthy renegade!"

All Cologna's joints had loosened and he lashed out with his hands and feet. He and the tall man were now the centre of the throng. The man from Fojnica was forgotten.

The tall man bent a little and shouted provocatively to his men:

"Did he curse the Faith and our Prophet? Did you hear him?"

They agreed.

"Hang them both, straight away!"

There was turmoil round Cologna.

"Who, who cursed the Faith? The Prophet? I know Islam better than you, you Bosnian bastard! I am…I am…," screamed Cologna, tearing himself away, foaming at the mouth and completely beside himself.

"Hang the infidel dog!"

Above the jostling and snatching, Cologna's indistinct words could be heard, like the gasp of a suffocating man:

"…A Muslim…I am, a better Muslim than you…"

Then the people from the bazaar joined in and pulled the doctor away from the rabble. Three of them had witnessed the fact that the old man had announced loudly and clearly three times that he accepted the pure faith as his own and as such he had become untouchable. Now they led him home, attentively and solemnly, like a bride. And this was necessary, for the old man was beside himself, his whole body was shaking and he was mumbling words without any connection or sense.

The disappointed people who had brought Kulier and were acting as his prosecutors, judges and executioners, now let him go, to rush headlong back to Fojnica.

The word soon spread that the Austrian Consulate physician had converted to Islam. Even for this completely crazed town where each day dawned madder than the last, and where things were happening which could not be told to the end or quite believed, the news of the doctor's conversion was a surprise.

As none of the Christians dared go outside, it was impossible to confirm or investigate the rumour. The Consul sent a servant to Dolac, to Brother Ivo Janković, but the priest was sceptical about the news and promised that he would come to the Consul as soon as the riot calmed down a little, perhaps even tomorrow.

Towards evening, on the Consul's orders, Rotta went out and made his way to Cologna's house by the steep rocky slope. But the interpreter returned barely half an hour later, pale and unusually quiet. He had been frightened by savage-looking strangers, covered in weapons, who had shouted into his face:

"Convert, Christian, while you've time!" and behaved as though they were drunk or deranged. But he had been far more shaken by what he had seen at Cologna's.

Once he had been reluctantly allowed into the house, which some quiet, unarmed Turks were just leaving, he came upon Cologna's confused Albanian servant. The floor of the outer room had been washed down and the room was in chaos, while the doctor's voice could be heard from inside.

The old man was striding about the room in great agitation. His normally grey and bloodless face was slightly flushed, his lower jaw was trembling. He looked keenly and sourly at the interpreter, for a long time, through lowered lids, as though he were staring into the distance, unable to see properly or make things out clearly. And as soon as Rotta mentioned that he had come on behalf of the Consul General to see what had happened, Cologna interrupted him irritably:

"Nothing has happened, and nothing will happen. No one need worry about me. I can defend my own position quite well. I'm standing here, defending it like a good soldier."

The old man stopped, suddenly threw his head back and thrust out his chest, then he whispered, in short breaths:

"Yes, here I stand. Here, here..."

"Just you stand...you stand there...sir," mumbled the terrified Rotta, all of whose usual brazen self-assurance had suddenly left him. At that he took a step backwards and, not taking his eyes off the doctor, felt behind him with a trembling hand for the door handle, repeating over and over again:

"Just you stand, you stand…"

Abandoning his stiff, strutting attitude, the old man suddenly leaned somehow confidingly and far more gently towards Rotta. On his old face, or rather only in his eyes, there appeared a significant, triumphant smile. And as though he were revealing some important secret, he said quietly, shaking his finger:

"Aleikhiselam says: 'The Devil runs through the human body like blood.' But Aleikhiselam also says: 'You will truly see your Lord as you see the moon when it is full.'"

Here he turned abruptly and suddenly took on a serious, offended air. But the interpreter, whom it would have taken far less to scare to death, took advantage of the moment to open the door without a sound and slip like a shadow through the outer room, with no word of farewell.

The moon was already up. Rotta hurried down the side streets shrinking from the shadows and feeling all the time a cold chill threatening him from behind. And when he reached home and went to see the Consul he still could not quite pull himself together or give a clear account of Cologna's condition and his conversion. He just kept stubbornly asserting that the doctor had gone mad, and replying to the Consul who wanted to know in a little more detail how one could tell he had gone mad:

"Mad, mad. As soon as a man starts talking about God and the Devil he must be mad. But you should have seen him, you should have seen him," the interpreter kept repeating.

By evening, the news had spread through the whole town that the doctor from the Austrian Consulate had publicly expressed his desire to convert to Islam and that he would be solemnly accepted the following day. However, no such ceremony was destined to take place and nor would the real truth about the doctor's "conversion" ever be discovered.

Next morning the news spread, more rapidly than that of the day before, that Cologna had been found dead on a path in the garden beside the stream, in that defile below the high rocky slope where his house was. His skull had been crushed. The Albanian servant had been unable to explain either when during the night the doctor had gone out or how he had fallen into the hollow.

When he heard of the doctor's death, the Dolac parish priest went down into Travnik to look into the whole affair because of the funeral. Risking attack by the rioting mobs, Brother Ivo managed to reach the doctor's house, but he did not stay there long. Despite his considerable weight, he flew lightly and swiftly down the steep road followed by the sticks and pickaxes of the frenzied Turks, who would not let him so much as peer into the house. The hodja had already prepared the body, because those three citizens had confirmed that the doctor had clearly stated three times, of his own free will, that he was prepared to receive the Islamic faith and that he was already a better Muslim than many who proclaimed themselves Turks around the Travnik bazaar.

And Rotta, who had come with the khavaz Ahmed at the news of the doctor's death, saw only a few bustling Turks in front of Cologna's house and returned to the Consulate. The khavaz stayed to attend the burial.

Had this occurred in calmer times, and had one of the senior officials been at the Residence, both the religious and the secular authorities would have become involved. The Austrian Consul would have acted more decisively. Brother Ivo would have visited government offices and influential Turks. And the matter of the unfortunate Cologna would have been clarified. But as it was, in the general anarchy which still prevailed, no one was prepared to hear anyone out. The riot, which was just subsiding, found new fuel, grabbing the corpse of the old man like a welcome trophy and refusing to let it go without bloodshed and sacrifice.

The doctor was buried, before noon, in a green bend of the steep Turkish cemetery. Although the bazaar was still closed, many Turks came out of their houses to attend the funeral of the doctor who had suddenly converted to Islam in such an unusual way. The majority, however, were armed riff-raff like those who had wanted to hang him the day before. With serious, sombre expressions now, they took it in turns to carry the body, rapidly and easily, so that the open coffin with the doctor's shrouded body went sliding over a constant succession of men's shoulders.

So this violent riot came to an end amid new, disturbing events. The capture and execution of Serbs ceased. The town fell once more into that shamefaced, befuddled mood, when everyone tried as soon as possible to forget what had happened, when the rowdiest throng of trouble-makers and bullies sank back into the outlying quarters, as water returns to its channel. And when order was restored, everyone felt, for a while, that things were better and more bearable than before. A heavy silence closed in over Travnik, as though it had never even been disturbed.

The process of appeasement was speeded up also by the return of Suleiman Pasha Skopljak. The presence of his authoritative word and skilled hand soon made itself felt.

As soon as he arrived, Suleiman Pasha summoned the most prominent men of the bazaar to ask them what had become of the peaceful town and its peaceful population. He stood in front of them, simply dressed and thinner, as he had returned from the battlefield, tall, with his slender, prominent rib-cage like that of a good greyhound, with his large blue eyes, questioning and reprimanding them like children. This man, who had spent six weeks on a real battlefield and now two on his estates at Kupres, looked at them sternly. They were pale and crushed, abruptly sober. And he asked them sharply since when the bazaar had taken it on itself to judge and carry out sentences, who had given them that right, and whether they had taken leave of their senses these last ten days.

"People say the rayah have become lawless, the rayah are disobedient and wicked. It's true. But you must know that the rayah do not breathe with their own lungs, they listen to the breathing of their masters. You know that quite well. It is always the masters who are corrupted first, and the rayah simply catch on. And once the rayah become disobedient and full of themselves, you had better go straight to find others somewhere else, because these people will be no good for anything any more."

Suleiman Pasha spoke like a man who had been looking at painful and serious things up until yesterday, things of which they, with their narrow Travnik outlook, could not have the slightest inkling and which had to be explained to them.

"God, praise and honour to Him, has given us two things: to hold land and to dispense justice. And you just sit with your legs crossed on your sofas, letting converts and riff-raff do the judging. Of course your serfs rebel. The serf's business is to do the work and the landlord's is to be vigilant, for even a blade of grass needs both dew and the scythe. You don't get one without the other. You see me," (he turned to the nearest man to him, not without pride,) "I am fifty-five years old, and I still visit all my estates by lunch-time. And let me tell you, there's not one rotten or disobedient serf on my land."

And truly, his long neck and sinewy hands were as sunburnt and hard as a labourer's.

No one knew what to say, each of them simply wanted to get out of his sight as quickly as possible, to forget what had happened and be forgotten himself.

As soon as the riot had subsided, von Mitterer began to investigate the matter of Cologna's inexplicable conversion and mysterious death. He did not do this for the sake of Cologna himself whom he had always considered unbalanced and a nuisance in his service. Knowing him well, von Mitterer believed that the doctor was quite capable of suddenly proclaiming himself a Muslim in a quarrel, just as it was perfectly possible and probable that he had committed suicide or lost consciousness and fallen into the ravine in a moment of agitation. Apart from that, now that the riot had died down and things and people had changed, it was not easy to investigate what had taken place in quite different circumstances, in that atmosphere of general madness, bloodshed and mayhem.

Von Mitterer had to take these steps because of the standing of the Emperor and in order to prevent similar attacks on any other Imperial subjects or Consulate personnel. And Brother Ivo urged him on as well, for the sake of the Catholic population, somehow to elucidate Cologna's change of faith and burial.

Suleiman Pasha from the very beginning was the only person in the Residence to have any sympathy for von Mitterer, and had always been on closer and friendlier terms with him than with Daville, with whom he had to converse through an interpreter and whose appearance he did not like. He endeavoured now to do what the Colonel asked. But at the same time, he advised him sincerely not to make things worse by pressing too far.

"I know that you have to intervene on behalf of an Imperial subject," he said to the Consul with that cold, reasonable and deliberate manner which everyone, including himself, considered infallible. "I know, and it cannot be otherwise. But it is not good to link the reputation of the Emperor with every Imperial subject. For there are subjects of all kinds and the Empire has only one reputation."

And Suleiman Pasha explained, drily and coldly, what the chances were of finding a solution that would satisfy everyone.

As far as the question of whether Cologna had converted or not was concerned, it was best not to discuss that any further, for the riot was such that there was no distinction between night and day, let alone between one faith and another. And to be honest, the man was such that his conversion did not represent much of a loss to Christianity nor much of a gain for Islam.

As for the matter of his obscure death, however, immediately after his mysterious conversion, that was even less worth investigating. For, dead lips do not speak and a man carried away by his thoughts and not looking where he was going, could always easily lose his footing. This was the most natural solution which could not offend anyone. And why go looking for other possibilities now, since they could never be fully elucidated and the Consulate would never be able to obtain the kind of satisfaction it wished.

"I can no longer find and arrest those fools and vagabonds who wanted to act like ardent Muslims and administer justice all over Travnik," Suleiman Pasha concluded, "nor can you raise up that dead man who has been laid in the Turkish cemetery and question him. Who can put that right? Rather, let us leave it and concern ourselves with more sensible matters. I understand your cares as though they were my own. That is why I shall order that the death of this doctor be investigated, so that it is seen that no one is being blamed for it, and have that recorded. And you will send that information to your superiors, so that there shall be no suspicion or argument on either side."

Von Mitterer saw for himself that this was, if not the best, then the only possible solution. Nevertheless, he asked for and received from the Deputy some decrees which could from a distance appear to provide some satisfaction and compensation for the Consulate.

All of that, with Rotta's report on his last visit to Cologna, could satisfy the people in Vienna, portray the affair of Cologna as the misfortune of an unbalanced man and save the Consul's reputation. But in himself, von Mitterer was dissatisfied both with the way things had gone and with himself.

Pale and alone, in his half-lit study, von Mitterer thought about it all and felt disarmed and powerless in the face of a whole combination of the most varied circumstances, in which he was now carrying out his duty conscientiously, exhausting himself beyond his strength, while clearly seeing that it was all futile.

The Colonel was shivering despite the oppressive July heat outside, feeling for a moment as though he too were losing consciousness and stumbling over an unknown ravine.

17

The second, more horrifying riot had nothing whatever to do with the French Consulate. On the contrary, towards the end its focal point had become the Austrian Consulate and Cologna. Nevertheless, it brought difficult days and sleepless nights to everyone in the French Consulate. As long as it lasted, apart from Des Fossés's two brief outings, no one dared even appear at the window. Daville himself found this riot more difficult than the first, for one does not get used to such disturbances – quite the reverse, they become increasingly hard to bear the more often they occur.

As during the first riot, Daville had considered fleeing from Travnik, to save his life and his family. Shut up in his room, he was tormented by the direst thoughts, foreseeing the grimmest possibilities. But in front of his servants and staff, and even with his wife, he let nothing betray his thoughts.

However, not even this shared misery could bring the Consul and his Secretary any closer. He would start a conversation with Des Fossés several times in the course of a day. (As they were shut up in the house, they would meet even more frequently than before.) But not one of these conversations did any good or brought reconciliation. On top of all his other worries, doubts and disappointments, Daville had to keep telling himself that he was living with a man who was alien to him, that there was an unbridgeable gulf between their ideas and attitudes. Even the young man's good sides, which were indisputable and particularly apparent in circumstances such as these – courage, altruism, composure – even these could not win Daville over. For even people's best qualities can only be fully valued when they are presented to us in a way which conforms with our own views and inclinations.

As had always been the case up to then, Daville watched what was going on around him with bitter disdain, attributing everything to the innate iniquity and barbaric way of life of these people, concerned only about safeguarding French interests. Des Fossés, on the other hand, with an objectivity that astonished Daville, analysed all the phenomena around him, endeavouring to find reasons for them both in themselves and in the conditions which had given rise to them, regardless of the damage or benefit, comfort or discomfort which they might momentarily afford the Consulate. Daville had always found the young man's cool, disinterested objectivity disturbing and disagreeable. All the more so, since at the same time he could not avoid seeing it as a clear sign of the young man's superiority. In the present circumstances, he found this even more difficult.

Every conversation, official, semi-official or unofficial, aroused in the young man a multitude of associations, independent reflections and icily objective conclusions, while in the Consul it provoked irritation and an offended silence which the young man did not even notice.

This child of a wealthy family, gifted in so many ways, behaved like a millionaire even in his thinking; and was daring, capricious and extravagant. He was not much use to Daville in the real work of the Consulate. Although it was the young man's duty to copy up the Consul's reports from rough draft, Daville avoided giving him this work. As he wrote, he would find himself inhibited by the thought that his report would be exposed to the critical examination of the young man, whose intellect seemed to have a hundred eyes. Daville was angry with himself, but he could not help wondering at every other sentence how it would look in his Secretary's eyes. Consequently, in the end he preferred to write and copy up his more important reports himself.

In short, in all business dealings, and, more importantly, in all the inner trepidations aroused in Daville by the events connected with Napoleon's new campaign against Vienna, Des Fossés was of no use at all, and often only a nuisance. The differences between them were so great that they could not even share joy. In the middle of July, at roughly the same time as the end of the riot, when the news reached them of Napoleon's victory at Wagram and shortly afterwards of the truce with Austria, Daville entered one of his periodic bouts of cheerfulness. Everything seemed to him to have ended well. The only thing that marred his good humour was the young man's indifference. He knew nothing of the excitement of success, just as he knew nothing of the doubts and fears that precede it.

Daville found it painfully incomprehensible to see the young man with always the same intelligent and indifferent smile on his face. "That man seems to have an advance subscription to victory," he told his wife, as he had no one else to complain to and was unable to stay silent any longer.

The warm, lush, late summer weather came again, the best and finest days in Travnik for those for whom all was always well and the least difficult for those whose life was hard, summer and winter alike.

In October 1809, peace was concluded in Vienna between Napoleon and the Viennese court. The Illyrian provinces were created, including Dalmatia and Lika, which were both in Daville's area of responsibility. A Governor General and an Intendant General arrived in Ljubljana, the capital of this new Illyria, with a whole staff of police, customs and tax officers, to start organizing the administration and, particularly, trade and communications with the Levant. Before this, General Marmont, the Commander of Dalmatia, who had reached the battle of Wagram on time, had been made a Marshal. Now Daville, seeing all this going on around him, had the melancholy but pleasant sensation of a man who has contributed to the victory and glory of others while he himself remained in the shadows, without glory or reward. This feeling appealed to him and made it easier to bear all the difficulties of Travnik which no kind of victory could alter.

What tormented Daville now, as always before, was the question he dared confide in no one: whether this was, at last, the final victory, and how permanent was this peace?

He could find no answer anywhere, either in himself or outside, to this question which would determine not only his inner calm but the fate of his children.

At a particularly solemn audience, Daville acquainted the Vizier with the details of Napoleon's victories and the provisions of the Peace of Vienna, particularly in so far as they referred to the territories immediately bordering on Bosnia. The Vizier congratulated him on the victories and expressed his satisfaction that their good neighbourly relations were going to continue and that, under French rule, peace and order would now reign in the lands around Bosnia.

But, on the Vizier's lips, all these words, "war" and "peace" and "victory", were dead, distant things, and he pronounced them in a cold voice, with a stony expression on his face, as though they were talking of events in the remote past.

The Vizier's Secretary, Tahir Bey, with whom Daville spoke on the same day, was far livelier and more talkative. He enquired about the position in Spain, the situation in Poland, and asked for details about the organization of the administration in the new Illyrian provinces. It was evident that he wanted to inform himself and make his own assessment. But all his affable readiness to talk and his intelligent curiosity communicated no more than the Vizier's dumb, lifeless indifference had done: from his words one could deduce that he saw no end to the warfare nor to Napoleon's conquests. And when Daville tried to drive him to express his thoughts more clearly, the Secretary avoided replying.

"Your Emperor is the victor, and everyone sees the victor in a shining light, or, as the Persian poet has it: 'The face of the victor is like a rose,'" the Secretary concluded shrewdly, with a smile.

Daville was always made unaccountably uncomfortable by this strange smile which never left the Secretary's face, giving his eyes a devilish slant and making them seem slightly crossed. And, after every conversation with him the Consul always felt disturbed, as though he had been robbed. Each conversation of this kind, instead of supplying an answer, would frighten him with new questions and new ambiguities. But he was the only man in the Residence who was prepared to talk business.

As soon as peace was concluded, contact between the two Consulates was re-established. The Consuls visited one another, expressing, in many words, their precarious joy at the attainment of peace, disguising under this exaggerated enthusiasm their embarrassment at all the measures each of them had undertaken against the other over the last few months. Daville strove not to offend von Mitterer by behaving like a victor, but at the same time not to lose anything of the advantage which victory afforded him. The Colonel expressed himself with great caution about everything, like a man who wishes to acknowledge the disagreeable present as little as possible, while expecting everything from the future. They both concealed their true thoughts and real fears under the veil of the kind of melancholy conversation which is often the recourse of older people who still expect something from life, but are conscious of their powerlessness.

Frau von Mitterer had not yet begun to exchange visits with Madame Daville, and she succeeded in avoiding meeting Des Fossés who had, of course, been "dead" to her since the spring and now rested in the large necropolis of her other disappointments. Throughout the whole campaign against Vienna she had been stubbornly and aggressively "with all her heart on the side of the incomparable Corsican". This had soured von Mitterer's life by day and night, for not even within the four walls of his bedroom could he bear indiscreet talk and every inappropriate word caused him physical pain.

That summer, Anna Maria suddenly returned to a long-standing passion: love of animals. At every step she found material for her exaggerated and unhealthy pity for draught animals, dogs, cats and cattle. A glance at small, mangy, and exhausted oxen wearily dragging their thin legs, while swarms of flies sank into the soft places round their meek eyes, would throw Anna Maria into a nervous attack. Prompted by her passionate nature, she intervened on behalf of these animals regardless of the place or circumstances, with no sense of proportion, thereby courting ever new disappointments. She would collect lame dogs and scabby cats and tend them. She would feed birds, which were in any case cheerful and well-fed. She would turn on peasant women carrying chickens over their shoulders, upside down and tied by the feet. She would go round the town stopping overloaded carts and overburdened horses, ask the peasant to unload them, to dress their wounds, fix the harness that was rubbing them or the girth that was too tight.

This was all impossible behaviour in this country. No one could understand it and it was bound to lead to absurd scenes and awkward conflict.

One day, Anna Maria noticed a long cart in a narrow, steep road, overloaded with sacks of grain. Two oxen were struggling in vain to drag the load up the slope. Then people brought up a thin horse, harnessed it in front of the oxen and began shouting and yelling to drive it up the hill. The peasant who was walking beside the oxen kept hitting them, now on their skinny flanks, now on their soft muzzles, while the horse was thrashed with a whip by a sturdy, bare-chested, sunburnt Turk from the town, a certain Ibro Zvalo, the most disreputable man in town, a carter and drunkard, who from time to time also acted as hangman, depriving the gypsies of their earnings.

The oxen and the horse in front of them could not pull together, in step. Every now and then the peasant ran to put stones under the back wheels. The animals were panting and trembling. The carter cursed hoarsely, shouting that the left-hand ox was shirking and not pulling at all. The animals braced themselves once more, but that same left-hand ox gave up and fell onto its front knees. The other ox and the horse continued to pull. Anna Maria screamed, ran up and began shouting at the carter and the peasant, her eyes full of tears. The peasant replaced the stone and stared at the foreign woman, perplexed. But Zvalo, perspiring and furious with the ox which was only pretending to pull, turned all his rage on the Consul's wife. Wiping the sweat from his brow with the bent forefinger of his right hand and shaking it off onto the ground, he cursed poverty and Him who had inflicted it on the world, and then, with the whip in his left hand, he made straight for Anna Maria.

"You get out of my sight, woman, don't make things worse, for I swear to God, if I…"

So saying, the carter brandished his whip. Anna Maria saw Zvalo's face bending right over her, twisted in a grimace, covered in wrinkles, scars, sweat and dust. It was an evil and angry face, but mostly tired, almost weeping with fatigue, like that of the winning runner in a race. At that moment the frightened khavaz ran up, shoved the demented man away and escorted the Consul's wife to their front gate as she wept aloud with impotent fury.

Anna Maria shivered at the memory of that scene for two whole days and through her tears she demanded that the Consul should see to it that all those people were severely punished for their cruelty and for the insult they had inflicted on his wife. At night she would wake with a start and jump out of bed, warding off Zvalo's face with a shriek.

The Consul calmed his wife with soothing words, although he knew he could do nothing. The load of oats was for the Vizier's granary. Zvalo was a man with no standing to whom nothing could be done and with whom no one should get involved in an argument. And, after all, the main blame lay with his wife, who, as so often in other circumstances, had interfered in an inappropriate way in things she should not have meddled with. And, as usual, she was now quite inaccessible to any kind of reasoning. Consequently, he soothed her as best he could, promising her everything, as with a child, patiently enduring her reproaches and the insults directed against him personally, and waiting for her to forget her obsession.

There was news at the French Consulate.

Madame Daville was in the fourth month of pregnancy. Virtually unchanged, tiny and light, she moved swiftly and silently about the large house and Consulate garden, preparing things, getting in supplies, planning ahead and giving instructions. This fourth pregnancy was a difficult one. But all these tasks, and even the physical discomforts of her pregnancy, helped her to endure more easily the pain for the little boy who had been so suddenly snatched from her the previous autumn and of whom she thought constantly but never spoke.

Young Des Fossés was spending his last days in Travnik. He was only waiting to travel with the first courier from Istanbul or Split on his way to Paris. He had been transferred to the Ministry, but he had already been informed that in the course of the year he would be sent to the Embassy in Istanbul. The material for his book on Bosnia was ready. He was pleased that he had got to know this country and glad that he was able to leave it. He had struggled with its silence, its many deprivations, and now unbeaten and cheerful, he was leaving.

Before he left, on the Feast of the Nativity of the Virgin Mary he went with Madame Daville to visit the monastery at Guča Gora. As relations between the Consulate and the friars had cooled completely,

Daville had not wanted to go with them. And their relations were really more than cold. The conflict between the Imperial French government and the Vatican was at its height just then. The Pope had been imprisoned, Napoleon excommunicated. The friars had not been to the Consulate for months. Nevertheless, thanks to Madame Daville, the Guča Gora friars received them kindly. Des Fossés had inwardly to admire the way the friars were able to separate what was due personally to these visitors from what their vocation and a serious sense of their duty required of them. In their behaviour there was just as much restraint and injured solemnity as their dignity demanded, and as much warmth as was required by the ancient laws of hospitality and the basic humanity which must prevail over all temporary disputes. A little of everything and in the right measure, and all together joined in a perfect, rounded whole and expressed in an easy bearing and free, natural gestures and expressions. He would never have expected so much poise and innate sense of propriety from these rough, heavy, quick-tempered men with their drooping moustaches and comically shaven round heads.

Here he had occasion to see again the piety of the Catholic villagers, to get to know more closely the life of the Franciscan friars in its "Bosnian form", and to talk and argue again with "Monsieur mon adversaire", Brother Julian.

The Feast fell on a fine warm day, at the best time of year, when the fruit was already ripe and the leaves still green. The bulky, white-washed monastery church quickly filled with villagers in their clean Sunday best, predominantly white in colour. Just before the beginning of High Mass, Madame Daville entered the church as well. Des Fossés stayed in the plum orchard with Brother Julian, who was free. They walked there, talking.

As always when they met, they were discussing relations between the Church and Napoleon, Bosnia, the vocation and role of the friars and the fate of the people of all faiths there.

All the church windows were open and from time to time they would catch the sound of the server's bell or the Guardian singing the Mass in his deep, old man's voice.

These two young men found as much pleasure in their discussion as healthy children in play. And their conversation, carried out in bad Italian, full of naïveté, bold assertions and barren insistence, moved constantly in the same circle, always returning to its starting point.

"You cannot understand us," the friar would reply to all the young man's remarks.

"I think that during this time I have got a clear grasp of conditions in your country. And, unlike many other foreigners, I have had some understanding of the good qualities hidden in this land, as well as the shortcomings and backwardness which a foreigner sees so quickly and so easily condemns. But allow me to say that I often find the attitude of you friars incomprehensible."

"Well, I keep saying that you can't understand."

"But I do understand, Brother Julian, only I cannot approve of what I see and understand. This country needs schools, roads, doctors, contact with the world, work and activity. I know that as long as Turkish rule lasts and until communications are established between Bosnia and Europe, you cannot achieve any of that. But, as the only educated men in this country, you should be preparing your people and pointing them in the right direction. Instead, you support the feudal, conservative policies of the reactionary European powers and you seek to link yourselves with that part of Europe which is doomed to destruction. And that is incomprehensible, for your people are not overburdened with traditions or class prejudices and everything points to their place in the world being on the side of the free, enlightened states and powers of Europe…"

"What good is enlightenment to us without belief in God?" the friar interrupted. "That enlightenment will last only a short time even in Europe and, as long as it lasts, it will bring nothing but unrest and unhappiness."

"You are wrong, dear Brother Julian, you are fundamentally wrong. A little more of that unrest would do you no harm. You can see that the people of Bosnia are divided into three or even four faiths, divided and in bloody conflict with each other, and all of them separated from Europe, that is, from the world and life, by an impassable wall. Take care that you friars are not answerable for the historical sin of not having grasped that and for having led your people in the wrong direction, without preparing them in good time for what is inevitably in store for them. Among the Christians of the Turkish Empire you often hear talk of liberty and liberation, and increasingly so. And, truly, one day liberty must come even to these parts. But it was said long ago that it is not enough to achieve freedom, it is far more important to become worthy of freedom. Without more up-to-date education and more liberal ideas, it will not help you at all to have freed yourselves from Ottoman power. In the course of the centuries your people have become in many ways so like their oppressors that it will not be much use to them if the Turks one day depart, leaving them, in addition to the faults they have as rayah, the Turks' own vices: idleness, intolerance, the spirit of violence and the cult of brute force. That would, in fact, be no kind of liberation, for you would not be worthy of liberty or know how to enjoy it, and, just like the Turks, you would know nothing other than being enslaved or enslaving others. There is no doubt that one day your country will join the European community, but it could happen that it joins it divided and burdened with inherited ideas, habits and instincts which you won't find anywhere else any more. And, like ghosts, they will hinder its normal development and create of it an outdated monster which would be prey to everyone, as it is to Turkey today. And these people do not deserve that. You see that not a single nation, not one country in Europe bases its progress on a religious foundation."

"That is what is so disastrous."

"It is disastrous to live like this."

"It is disastrous to live without God, betraying the faith of your fathers. And we, for all our mistakes and faults, have not betrayed it, and it can be said of us: 'Multum peccavit, sed fidem non negavit.'"[15] Brother Julian broke in, satisfying his passion for quotation.

The young men's discussion was returning to its starting point. Each, convinced of his argument, neither expressed himself clearly nor listened properly to what the other was saying.

Des Fossés stopped beside an ancient plum tree, bent and overgrown with thick greenish lichen.

"Have you honestly never thought that one day, when the Turkish Empire collapses and abandons these parts, these peoples who are now under Turkish rule, called by different names and confessing different faiths, must find a common basis for their existence, a broader, better, more rational and humane formula?"

"We Catholics have had that formula for a long time. That formula is the Credo of the Roman Catholic Church. We don't need a better one."

"But you know that not all your compatriots in Bosnia and the Balkans belong to that Church and not all of them ever will belong to it. You must see that no one in Europe unites on that basis any more. Consequently you have to find another common denominator."

The singing of the people resounded from the church and interrupted them. At first hesitantly and out of time, but then increasingly harmoniously, women and men sang together, in an unsophisticated, drawling monotone:

"*Hai-ai-ail, body of Christ!...*"

The singing was increasingly strong. The squat, heavy church

---

15 "He sinned greatly, but he did not deny his faith."

with no belfry, with its black wooden roof, slightly crooked from the apse to the façade, began to thunder and echo like a ship or the waves, its sails billowing in the wind, full of invisible singers.

They both stopped speaking for a moment. Des Fossés wanted to know the words of the song the people were singing with such pious exultation. The friar translated word for word. The meaning reminded him of the ancient hymn:

"*Ave verum corpus natum*
De Maria virgine…"[16]

While the friar was searching for the words of the second verse, the young man absently followed his efforts, but was in fact listening only to the heavy, simple, melancholy, raw melody which seemed to him now like the uniform bleating of an endless flock of sheep, now like the roar of the wind through black forests. And he kept wondering whether it was possible that this peasant wail echoing through the crooked church expressed the same idea and the same faith as the singing of the corpulent, learned canons and pale seminarians in French cathedrals. "Urjammer," he thought to himself, remembering Daville's and von Mitterer's opinion of Musa's song, and he started to walk, unwittingly, further into the plum orchard, fleeing from the tune, as a man turns his head away from an overwhelmingly mournful landscape.

Here Des Fossés and the friar took up their conversation once more, exchanging blows which left each of them in his former position.

"Ever since I came to Bosnia, I have been wondering how it is that you friars, who have seen the world and had some schooling, who are essentially good people, sincerely altruistic, do not have a broader, freer outlook, do not grasp the demands of the times and do not feel the need for men to draw closer as men, to seek together a worthier and healthier way of life…"

16 "Hail the true body, born of the Virgin Mary…"

"With Jacobin clubs!"

"But, Father Julian, there haven't been any Jacobin clubs for a long time, even in France."

"There haven't, because they've gone into the ministries and schools."

"But you've got *no* schools here, you've got nothing, and when one day civilization reaches you, you won't be able to accept it and you will remain a fragmented, confused, shapeless mass, without direction or aim, without organic links with humanity or your compatriots, or even with your immediate neighbours."

"But with faith in God, sir."

"Faith, faith! Why, you're not the only people who believe in God. Millions of people believe. Each in his own way. But that doesn't give anyone the right to cut himself off and shut himself up in morbid arrogance, turning his back on the rest of humanity, often even on those nearest to him."

The people were beginning to come out of the church, although the peasant song was still going on, reverberating like a swinging bell whose oscillations were slowing down. Madame Daville appeared, breaking off their interminable discussion.

They had lunch in the monastery and then turned back to Travnik. Brother Julian and Des Fossés continued to chivvy each other all through lunch. And then they parted, forever, as the best of friends.

Daville took Des Fossés to an audience with the Vizier to pay his respects and bid him farewell. So he saw Ibrahim Pasha once more. He was heavier and grimmer than ever. He spoke in a deep, gruff voice, rolling his words slowly, as though he were grinding them with his lower jaw. He made an effort to look at the young man, almost crossly, through his red, tired eyes. You could see that his thoughts were far away, that he found it difficult to comprehend this youthfulness that was moving on somewhere, taking its leave and travelling, that he had no desire to comprehend it, but wanted to be rid of it as soon as possible.

The formal visit to the Austrian Consul was also brief and turned out well. The Colonel received him with a sad dignity, but kindly, and expressed his regret that Frau von Mitterer was unable to receive him as well, because of a persistent migraine.

With Daville things were more difficult and tedious. In addition to written reports, the young man was supposed to take a large number of verbal messages, very complex and subtle. As the day of departure approached, these messages changed and were accompanied by more and more reservations and new suggestions. In the end, the young man could not make out clearly what he was supposed to say about life in Travnik and the work of the Consulate because the Consul had made innumerable complaints, pleas, remarks and observations. Some of these were personal messages for the Minister, some for the Minister and the Ministry, some only for Des Fossés himself, some for the world at large. The caution, subtlety and pedantry of these countless communications confused the young man, making him yawn and think of other things.

Des Fossés left on the last day of October, just as he had come – through frost and an early snow flurry.

Travnik is a town which is not gradually lost from the sight of people leaving it, but which vanishes all at once, in a hollow. So it sank also into the young man's memories. The last thing he saw was the fortress, low and compact, like a helmet, and beside it the mosque with its lovely slender minaret, like a plume. To the right of the fortress, on the steep rocky slope, he glimpsed the large dilapidated house where he had once visited Cologna.

As he made his way along the fine, level road towards Turbe, Des Fossés thought of this man, of his fate and that strange nocturnal conversation with him.

"... You may live here, but you know it is temporary and that sooner or later you will return to your own country, to better conditions and a worthier life. You will wake from this nightmare and be freed from it, but we never shall be, for it is the only life we have."

As on that night, when he had sat down beside him in the smoke-filled room, he felt again the breath that had hovered round the doctor – like some great excitement – and heard again his warm confidential whisper:

"At the end, at the real, final end, all will nevertheless be well, and everything will be resolved harmoniously."

So Des Fossés left Travnik, remembering nothing but the unfortunate "Illyrian doctor" and thinking for a moment of him.

But only for a moment, for youth does not dwell on memories nor remain long on the same thoughts.

18

From the very first days family life had been firmly established in the French Consulate. This was that real family life which depends so much on the wife, in which no changes or blows can disturb the strength of family feeling, a life with births, deaths, troubles, joy and beauty unseen by the outside world. This life radiated out of the Consulate, achieving what nothing else could have achieved, not force, nor bribes, nor persuasion: to an extent at least, it brought the inhabitants of the Consulate closer to the people of the town. And it did so despite all the hatred that was still directed, as we have seen, towards the Consulate itself.

Even two years earlier, when the Daville family had so suddenly lost their child, every single household had known all the details of that misfortune and every family had participated in it. And for a long time afterwards, people would turn compassionately after Madame Daville as she passed on her rare excursions into the town. In addition, the servants in the house, and the Dolac and Travnik women (especially the Jews) spread through the whole town tales of the Davilles' harmonious family life, of Madame Daville's "golden hands", her versatility, thrift, and cleanliness. Even in the Turkish houses, where the foreign Consulates were never mentioned without superstitious spitting, they knew, down to the last detail, how the French Consul's wife bathed her children and lulled them to sleep, what their little clothes were like, how their hair was done and what colour ribbons she used to tie it up.

It was therefore natural that all the women followed Madame Daville's pregnancy and the birth of her baby attentively and anxiously, as though she were a close neighbour. They tried to guess "how far gone" she might be, telling each other how she was carrying the child, discussing every change in her condition and the preparations she was making for her confinement. Then it was clear what great and important things birth and motherhood were in the life of these people, a life otherwise so monotonous and lacking in joys.

And when the time came, old Mother Matišić, the widow of a respected but ruined merchant, was up at the Consulate. This old woman was considered the best midwife in the whole of Dolac, and no birth could possibly take place in any of the more prosperous houses without her. She contributed still further to the tales about Madame Daville as a mother and housewife. She talked in detail of the order and comfort and all the pretty things in the house which was "as clean as paradise", fragrant, warm and well-lit even in the remotest corner; of the Consul's wife who, right up to the last minute, in the midst of her labour pains, had been giving instructions and organizing everything from her bed, making her wishes known "only with her eyes"; of her piety and incredible fortitude in enduring her pains; and, finally, of the behaviour of the Consul, dignified and full of love, quite different from that of our own men. For years afterwards, if any young mother became too upset, giving in to her fear and pain, old Mother Matišić would tell her of the example of the French Consul's wife, in order to shame and calm her.

The child, which came into the world at the end of February, was a girl.

Then gifts began to arrive from the households of Travnik and Dolac. (This again showed to what extent the people had become, if not reconciled to the existence of the Consulate, then at least close to the Daville family.) The ladies from the more prosperous Dolac houses arrived, ruddy-faced and rustling, in fur-lined satin cloaks, moving smoothly and solemnly like ducks on ice. Each of them was followed by a shivering apprentice, stepping carefully, his ears burning, with frozen drips under his nose, which he could not wipe, for he was carrying carefully wrapped gifts in front of him in his outstretched hands. Many of the beys' wives sent a gypsy woman with presents to enquire about the Lady Consul. The presents were set out in her room. Large pans of baklava; little date-shaped cakes, arranged crossways as logs are stacked; embroidery and rolls of fine rich baize; flasks and glass flagons of brandy or malmsey, corked with a few leaves from some house plant.

Just as before in her sorrow at the death of Daville's little son this time too Frau von Mitterer took a lively part in the joyous event. She brought the child a gift of a beautiful and costly Italian gold medallion, decorated with flowers of black enamel and diamonds. And she also told its complicated and touching story. Anna Maria called several times during those days and was a little disappointed to find that it was all going so simply, easily and smoothly, without unforeseen occurrences or cause for alarm. She would sit by Madame Daville's bedside, talking at length and disconnectedly about all that lay in store for the little creature, about the fate of women in society and about fate in general. From the whiteness of her bed, tiny and pale, Madame Daville listened to her without any sign of comprehension.

The largest and finest gift came from the Vizier. This was a huge copper pan full of baklava, covered first with a silk cloth and then with a broad piece of pale red Brusa brocade. The pan was carried by several servants, preceded by one of the clerks. They walked in procession through the whole bazaar, just before noon.

D'Avenat, who always got to know everything, learned of the difficulties with which this huge pan had left the Residence. The difficulties lay with the Treasurer. As always, Baki endeavoured to reduce every expenditure and take something back from any gift the Vizier made.

There had been a lot of discussion about the choice of pan and consultation over the material which was to be presented. The Vizier had ordered that the baklava must be in the largest copper pan to be found in the Residence. Baki first argued that there was no need to send anything, since it was not the French custom, and when that did not help, he hid the largest pan, substituting a somewhat smaller one, but Tahir Bey's servants found it. The Treasurer shrieked in his shrill voice, choking with rage:

"Why don't you take an even larger one! Give them the courtyard, that's the best idea. Hand everything over, we've got too much anyway."

When he saw that they were taking the best piece of material for the cover, he shrieked again, flung himself on the floor, lying on the cloth and wrapping the ends round him:

"No, you won't have it, I won't let you! You thieves, why don't you give something of your own?"

They tore him away from the precious material with great difficulty and covered the pan with it. Baki went on groaning as though wounded, cursing all the consuls and consulates in the world, all births and mothers, stupid customs and birth gifts, and even this wretched Vizier himself who was no longer able to protect the little he had, but listened to that deranged spendthrift, the Secretary, showering presents and money left and right, to Turk and Infidel alike.

The child in the French Consulate was not baptized until a month later, at the end of the cold spell which had set in that year right at the end of winter. The little girl was given the name Eugénie-Stéphanie Annonciade and was entered in the baptismal register of the Dolac parish on 25 March 1810, exactly on the Feast of the Annunciation.

That year, tranquil and full of promise, brought everyone a little of what they wanted and were hoping for.

At last, von Mitterer received clear instructions as to how to conduct himself towards the French Consul. ("In your personal relations, you may be amiable, even to the extent of cordiality, but in public no sign of friendship should be shown, in front of either the Turks, or the Christians. You should, rather, maintain a certain dignified coldness and restraint," etc.) Armed with these directions, von Mitterer moved more easily and at least to an extent more naturally. The only inconvenience was Anna Maria who never recognized anyone's instructions nor wished to know the meaning of measure and limits.

The engagement and marriage of the Austrian Princess Marie Louise to Napoleon were subjects of great excitement for Anna Maria. She followed all the details of the ceremony in the Viennese newspapers, she knew the names of all the personages who had participated and remembered every word that, according to the newspapers, had been spoken on that occasion. And when she read somewhere that Napoleon, unable to await the arrival of his Imperial fiancée in the agreed place, had rushed off in an ordinary carriage, incognito, to meet her and had burst into her coach somewhere in the middle of her journey, Anna Maria wept with enthusiasm and flew like a whirlwind into her husband's study, to tell him that she had always been right to see in the Corsican an exceptional man and a unique example of greatness and sensitivity.

Although it was Holy Week, Anna Maria went to visit Madame Daville, to tell her all she had learned and read, and to share her feelings of admiration and elation.

Madame Daville was making use of the unusually sunny April days and had given herself up completely to work in the garden.

Since the first year all the work in the garden and with the flowers had been done by the deaf and dumb gardener Munib, known as "Mumbler". Madame Daville had grown so used to him that she could easily make herself understood about everything concerned with the gardening through signs and gestures of the face and fingers. And not only that. They would talk, all by means of such signs, about other things as well, about events in the town, about the gardens of the Residence and the Austrian Consulate, but particularly about children.

Munib lived with his young wife in one of the tiny, poor houses under Osoj. Everything in the house was clean and orderly and his wife was healthy, pretty and hard-working, but they had no children. This was a great sorrow to them. That was why Munib gazed with emotion at Madame Daville's children when they came to watch him working. Always clean, quick and sprightly, he worked like a beaver and, without interrupting his task, he would smile at them with his sunburnt, furrowed face, as only those who do not speak can smile.

Wearing a large straw gardening hat, Madame Daville was standing in front of him while he dug. She was keeping an eye on the manuring, and herself crumbling lumps of earth with her fingers to prepare suitable beds for a particular kind of hyacinth she had managed to acquire that spring. When she was told that Frau von Mitterer was to pay her a visit, she received the news like a natural disturbance or change in the weather, and went off to dress.

In a warm, bright corner, where both the windows and the walls were draped with white linen, the two women sat down to exchange countless words and fine feelings. Anna Maria supplied both, for her loquacity and sensibility simply took Madame Daville's breath away. The only topic of conversation was the Emperor's marriage. There was nothing that Frau von Mitterer did not know. She knew the number and rank of the people present in the church during the wedding, the length of Marie Louise's Imperial train, which had been held by five real queens – it was nine feet long, made of heavy velvet, with golden bees embroidered on it, the same ones that could be seen on the coat of arms of the Barberini family, which, as everyone knew, had produced countless popes and statesmen, who, again, as everyone knew...

Frau von Mitterer's discourse came to an end somewhere in the distant past with an incomprehensible exclamation of pure elation.

"Ah, we should be glad to live in these great times, even if we ourselves are not, perhaps, aware of their true greatness and do not know how to value it," said Anna Maria, embracing Madame Daville who endured everything, unable to defend herself, and who had always been glad to be alive, even without Imperial weddings and historical facts, as long as her children were healthy and all was well in the house.

Then came the story of the great Emperor, rushing along the highway like an ordinary traveller, in a simple uniform, and bursting unexpectedly into his Imperial fiancée's coach, unable to wait for the ceremonial meeting.

"Isn't that wonderful? Isn't that wonderful?" exclaimed Anna Maria.

"Indeed, indeed," said Madame Daville, although she did not quite see where the greatness lay, for she herself would really have preferred the fiancé to wait for his betrothed as arranged and not to upset the plans.

"Ah, magnificent, simply magnificent," squealed Anna Maria, pushing back her light cashmere shawl.

Her intense enthusiasm had made her hot, although she was wearing a thin dress, a pink "belle assemblée" too light for this time of year.

Simply out of politeness, Madame Daville would have liked not to be left completely behind Frau von Mitterer, but to say something agreeable as well. For her all the actions of rulers and great personages were remote, foreign things, she had no real conception of them and was unable to say a single word about them, even if she had wanted to pretend. But, nevertheless, in order to say something, she told Anna Maria her plan for the new kind of especially lush hyacinths, explaining enthusiastically how the four beds of different coloured flowers would look, stretching down the middle of the whole large garden. She showed her the boxes in which the rough, brown, unremarkable bulbs of these future hyacinths lay, arranged by colour.

In a separate box lay the bulbs of a particularly rare variety of white hyacinth, which the courier had brought from France and of which Madame Daville was especially proud. A band of these was to run across all four beds, linking them all like a white ribbon. No one here had a variety so fine in scent, colour and size. She described the difficulties she had had in coming by this precious plant and added that, in fact, all of it together had not really even been very expensive.

"Oh, oh!" Anna Maria cried, still in the grip of her wedding mood, "oh, that is magnificent. Those will be Imperial hyacinths in this savage land. Oh, chère Madame, let us christen this variety of hyacinth and call it 'Wedding Joy' or 'The Imperial Bridegroom' or…"

Enchanted by her own words, Anna Maria kept searching for ever new names, while Madame Daville gave her approval to everything in advance, as when she was talking to the children whom it was not worth contradicting or the discussion would simply drag on.

After this the conversation was bound to falter, for when two people are really talking together, their words spark and set light to each other, but in this case they slipped past one another, each on its own account. And it could not have been otherwise. For Anna Maria was excited by all that was remote, foreign and outside herself, while Madame Daville was concerned only with what was close and intimately connected with her and her family.

In the end, and this was the end of every conversation with Madame Daville, the children came in to say "Good day" to the visitor. Both the boys came, while the little girl, who was only two months old, slept, well wrapped-up and fed, in her cradle draped with white tulle.

The fragile, pale-faced Pierre, now in his eighth year, wearing a dark-blue velvet suit with a white lace collar, was a fine-looking boy, as meek as an acolyte. He led in his younger brother Jean-Paul, a sturdy, healthy child with fair curls and rosy cheeks.

Anna Maria did not like children, while Madame Daville could not even imagine that anyone could be indifferent to them. Anna Maria regarded time spent in the company of children as time wasted. In the presence of children she was tormented by an infinite emptiness and tedium. Tender children's bodies, still growing, repelled her like something raw and unripe, arousing in her a feeling of physical discomfort and inexplicable fear. She was ashamed of this feeling (without even herself knowing why) and she concealed it under the sweet words and vivacious exclamations with which she always approached children. But in herself, deep in herself, she was disgusted by children and a little afraid of them, these little people who look at us with their large, new eyes, keenly and inquisitively, as coldly and sternly as judges (at least that is how it seemed to her). She always lowered her eyes before a child's steady gaze, while this never happened with an adult glance, probably because adults are so often either corruptible judges or willing accomplices in our weaknesses and vices.

And now Anna Maria had the same feeling of uneasy boredom in the presence of these children. But, in the absence of genuine delight in the little creatures, she kissed them ardently, drawing the necessary enthusiasm from her inexhaustible supplies of elation over the Imperial wedding in Paris.

When she finally took her leave, Anna Maria walked at the pace of a wedding march between the freshly dug flowerbeds, while Madame Daville and the bemused children watched her from the doorway. She turned once more from the garden gate, waving her hand, and calling that they must see each other often now, in order to discuss as fully as possible the wonderful, wonderful, great things that were happening.

This enthusiasm of Frau von Mitterer's did not seem to the Colonel in keeping with the instructions he had received, but still he and the whole household were glad that Anna Maria had found a distant and harmless but lasting object for her exultation. For, throughout the whole of that year, neither Travnik nor the trivial and dreary consular life in it existed for Anna Maria. She even forgot the question of the transfer and lived entirely in the glow of Imperial conjugal bliss, general conciliation and a mystical union of all the contradictions in the world. This coloured her conversations, her behaviour and her music. She knew the names of all the ladies-in-waiting of the new French Empress, the value, form and quality of all the wedding gifts, the way Marie Louise lived and organized her time. She followed the fate of the divorced former Empress Joséphine with much understanding. So her need for tears also found a distant and worthy object, which saved the Colonel many an unpleasant hour.

In the French Consulate too life passed that year without changes or excitement. Towards the end of the summer, Daville sent his eldest son to France, to the lycée. D'Avenat's son was also accepted as a state scholar, on Daville's recommendation, and sent to Paris.

D'Avenat was beside himself with happiness and pride. Dour and burnt-out, he was unable to rejoice out loud or visibly, like other people. Only his whole body trembled as he thanked Daville, assuring him that he was ready at all times to lay down his life for this Consulate. Such was his love for his son and his desire to ensure him a better, worthier and happier life than his own.

In other ways as well this year could be called happy, for it passed uneventfully, tranquilly and imperceptibly.

Peace reigned in Dalmatia, there were no border conflicts. Nothing happened in the Residence. The Consuls met on feast days, as hitherto, without warmth or closer contact. And they followed each other's activities attentively on working days, but without hatred or exaggerated zeal. The people of all faiths became slowly accustomed to the Consulates and when they saw that none of the difficulties and troubles they had experienced so far had driven the Consuls out of Travnik, they began to be reconciled, to work with them and to take them into account in all their affairs.

So the life of the town and the Consulates went on, from summer to autumn and from winter to spring, without incident or changes other than those brought by everyday life and the progress of the seasons in themselves.

But the chronicle of happy, peaceful years is brief.

19

In April 1811 a courier brought to Travnik a newspaper announcing the birth of Napoleon's son, who was to bear the title King of Rome. That same courier handed von Mitterer a decree stating that he was to be transferred from Travnik and placed at the disposal of the Ministry of Military Affairs. This then was the salvation the Colonel and his family had been awaiting for years. And now that it was here it seemed very simple, obvious and, like every salvation, it had arrived both too late and too soon. Too late, for it could not alter or assuage all that had been endured in anticipation of salvation; too soon, for like every change, it raised a whole series of new questions (moving, money, future career), which had not been thought of before.

Anna Maria, who had been surprisingly calm and withdrawn in recent months, burst into tears, because, like all people of her kind, she wept with both illness and its cure, with both desire and its fulfilment. And it was only a stormy scene with the Colonel (in which she accused him of everything that he could have accused her of had he wanted to), that gave her sufficient energy and the stimulus to start packing.

A few days later, the new Consul General, Lieutenant-Colonel von Paulich, who had until then been commanding a frontier regiment in Kostajnica, arrived to take over the duties of his new position personally from von Mitterer.

The arrival of the new Austrian Consul, on a sunny April day, was very splendid and dignified, although the Vizier had not sent a particularly large number of men to meet him. The youthful, well-proportioned von Paulich, on a fine horse, attracted everyone's attention, arousing curiosity and secret admiration even in those who would never have admitted it. Everything about him and his entourage was neat, polished and brushed, as though they were on parade. Those who had seen him told those who had not happened to be in the bazaar or at their windows, what a fine, handsome fellow the new Austrian Consul was ("Even if he *is* a Christian!").

And when the new Consul set out two days later in a ceremonial procession, accompanied by von Mitterer, to his first audience with the Vizier, there was a quite unexpected marvel. The people watched the procession, trying to pick out the new Consul and following him with their eyes in silence for a long time. The Turkish women watched from behind their lattices, the children clambered onto fences and walls, but there was not a sound from anywhere, not one offensive word. Although it is true that the Turks in the shops did all sit motionless and sullen as ever.

That is how the new Consul's procession rode to the Residence and that is how it returned.

Von Mitterer had described to von Paulich in advance the way he and his French colleague had been received on their first ride through Travnik a few years before. He was disappointed at this change, and, in a fit of pique, which closely resembled envy, he told the new Consul in detail of the insults that had been hurled at him in his time. He talked in a pained tone, slightly reproachful, as though it were he, von Mitterer, who had through his sufferings cleared this easy path for his successor.

However, the new Consul General was the kind of man for whom it always seemed that every path had been cleared for him.

Paulich came from a wealthy Germanized Zagreb family. His mother was an Austrian from Styria, one of the prominent von Niedermayer family. He was thirty-five years old, of exceptional masculine good looks. Well-proportioned, with fine skin, a small brown moustache which shaded his mouth, large dark eyes in which the dark blue pupils shone out of a deep shadow, and thick, naturally wavy hair, cut and brushed in a military style. The whole man radiated something monastically pure, cold and restrained, but without any of those traces of inner conflicts and scruples which so often give a troubled stamp to the appearance and bearing of monks. This unusually handsome man lived and moved as though in a kind of icy armour behind which every sign of personal life or human weakness and need quite disappeared. That was how his conversation was: factual, amiable and completely featureless, as was his deep voice and the smile which shone from his regular white teeth from time to time, illuminating his unmoving face, like chilly moonlight.

This tranquil man had once been a rich man's son, a prodigy of good memory and precocious intellectual development, and then one of those exceptional pupils who appear once in ten years, for whom school presents no problems and who complete two years' exams in one. The Jesuit fathers, with whom this unusual child studied, were already thinking that their Order was going to acquire in him one of those perfect figures who stand like cornerstones in the edifice of the Order. However, when he was fourteen, the boy suddenly turned his back on the Order, betraying all the hopes of the Jesuit fathers and showing an unexpected inclination to a military profession. His parents helped him in this, particularly his mother in whose family there was a strong military tradition. And so this boy, who had amazed his teachers of classical languages with the speed of his understanding and breadth of his knowledge, became a slender, capable cadet for whom all foresaw a great future, and then a young officer who neither drank nor smoked nor had affairs with women, nor conflicts with his superiors, nor duels nor debts. His company was the best maintained and equipped, he came first in examinations and exercises, and all without the zeal that tends to dog the ascent of ambitious people like an unpleasant shadow.

Von Paulich passed all his examinations and completed all his courses, coming first in everything. And then, surprising his superiors again, he devoted himself to service on the frontier, which was where officers with less knowledge and poorer qualifications would usually remain. He learned Turkish, got to know service in the field, methods of work, the people and conditions. And when von Mitterer's frequent requests finally caught his superiors' attention, von Paulich was fortunately discovered to be just that "familenlose Individuum"[17] for whom the Colonel had been appealing from Travnik.

And now, exhausted and frightened by the intricacy of life, von Mitterer was able to observe this young man and his unusual method of work. Before his eyes and under his hands all tasks became transparently clear and arranged themselves so easily and naturally in time and space, that there could be no pressure of work, no mistake, nothing hasty or too late. Everything was completed naturally and smoothly, like a sum with nothing left over. The man himself was somewhere high above and outside all that, inaccessible, and he participated in these tasks only as a consciousness and an energy which arranged, directed and resolved them. He was quite unfamiliar with all those doubts and compulsive weaknesses, sympathies and idiosyncrasies, all those emotional shadings which sometimes accompany the people and tasks placed before us, upsetting us, confusing and inhibiting us, and so often taking our work in a direction we had not wanted. He had none of these burdens. At least that is how it seemed to the exhausted von Mitterer, to whom it appeared that this man functioned like a higher spirit or like indifferent nature itself.

Moving house lays bare a person's life in the most intimate detail. Von Mitterer had the opportunity of observing and comparing

17 "a man without family".

his move (which, had Frau von Mitterer permitted it, he would have dearly liked not to think about at all) with the arrival of this unusual man. As in his work, everything had gone smoothly here as well. No disorder in his luggage or confusion among his staff. Things found their place of their own accord and all were useful, straightforward, clearly designated by number and purpose. The servants communicated with each other by glances, without any words, shouts or spoken instructions. There was no doubt about anything, no shadow of ill-will, uncertainty or disorder anywhere.

Always, in everything, a faultless calculation, with nothing left over.

The Lieutenant-Colonel was just the same when receiving the inventory and discussing the work and personnel of the General Consulate.

As he told him about Rotta, their main associate, von Mitterer unwittingly lowered his eyes and his voice became uncertain. Dragging out his words, he said of the interpreter that he was a little…well…unpredictable and that he was not exactly the most…the choicest flower, but that he was very useful and loyal. Von Paulich had been looking a little askance, throughout this discourse. His large eyes now narrowed and took on a cold, malign gleam in their outer corners. He received all these explanations of von Mitterer's silently, without a single sign of approval or dissatisfaction, evidently waiting to make up his own mind about their content, as about the whole inventory he was taking on, according to his own findings and calculations in which there must be no mistake. A man like this, appearing suddenly in Travnik, before the volatile Anna Maria, inevitably attracted her attention and aroused her feelings of amorous admiration and her vague desire for a harmony of souls, feelings which were always the same and never satisfied. She immediately called him "Antinous in uniform", which the Lieutenant-Colonel took without a word or any change in his expression, as something which did not and could not have any connection with him and the world around him. She introduced him to her musical studies. The Lieutenant-Colonel was totally unmusical and did not hide it, nor would he have been able to even if he had wished, but he lacked even that false affability with which unmusical people generally participate in conversations about music, as though that were a way of redeeming some of their fault. Their conversation about mythology and Roman poets went far better, but this time Anna Maria was weaker and this unusual Lieutenant-Colonel answered every couplet of hers with a whole series of lines. In the majority of cases, he was able to recite by heart the whole poem of which she knew one line, and he would in addition correct the mistake she usually made in that line. But von Paulich uttered it all coldly, factually, making no connection whatever with himself personally, with his surroundings or with living people at all. And each of her lyrical allusions rebounded off him like an unintelligible noise.

Anna Maria was astounded. Every one of her previous encounters, and there had been so many, had ended in disillusion and flight. But in her "aberrations" she had always succeeded in making the man take a step forwards or a step backwards, or first one and then the other, but there had never been a case when he had stayed in the same place, like this heartless Antinous, before whom she was now performing her futile dance. This was a new and particularly cruel form of torment. It was immediately felt in the life of the house. (On the very first day, Rotta had said in the office, expressing himself in that coarse language which petty officials use when they are speaking of those above them, that "Madam was dancing round him like a chorus girl.") While von Mitterer was introducing the new Consul to his duties, Anna Maria kept fretting hysterically about the house, altering her husband's instructions, sitting down on the full chests and weeping. One moment she would seek to delay their departure, the next to hasten it. At night she would wake her husband from his first sleep to tell him the reproaches and insults she had thought up as he slept.

As soon as the packing was finished, it became clear that nothing was in its proper place, that no one knew where anything had been put or how it was packed. When the things were due to be despatched, the horses which the Travnik Muteselim had promised the Consul did not arrive on time. Anna Maria went from furious scenes to sullen apathy. Rotta ran to and fro, shouting and threatening. When, on the third day, sufficient horses had finally been collected, it turned out that many of the trunks were too big and they would have to be repacked. And it would have been done somehow had Anna Maria not herself wanted to organize it. As it was, things were broken and spoiled before they even set out on their journey. And a whole caravan of horses and carriers waited, encamped around the Consulate.

Finally, everything was loaded and despatched. And the following day the von Mitterer family set off as well. With an insultingly cold expression on her tightly shut lips and dry, malicious eyes, Anna Maria took her leave of the Lieutenant-Colonel in front of the desolate Consulate, in the courtyard full of straw, broken boards and hoofmarks. She drove off ahead with her daughter. Von Mitterer and von Paulich followed on horseback.

Daville, attended by d'Avenat and a khavaz, accompanied von Mitterer from the French Consulate to the first crossroads. Here the two men parted and bade each other farewell. Their bearing was stiff and artificial rather than cold and insincere. And that was how they had greeted one another for the first time that autumn day a little more than three years earlier, and how they had lived and associated for the whole of that time.

At the crossroads, Daville was able to see Catholic women and children coming up to von Mitterer from both directions. He was clearly moved as they kissed his hand or took hold of his stirrup tenderly, with whole crowds waiting their turn by the roadside.

With this image of von Mitterer's last triumph in his eyes, Daville returned home, himself in some way moved, not because of von Mitterer's departure, but because of the memories this man aroused and his thoughts about his own fate. The departure of this man in itself seemed to him a kind of relief. Not because it freed him of a dangerous adversary – for, by all accounts, this new Consul was both stronger and cleverer than von Mitterer – but because the Colonel with his sallow face and sad, weary eyes had with time become a kind of embodiment of their common misery in these wild surroundings, a misery they had never confessed to anyone. Whatever was to come after him, it gave Daville greater satisfaction to part from this difficult man than he had felt on meeting him.

At the first halt, which was at about noon, beside the Lašva, von Paulich took his leave of his predecessor. Anna Maria was punishing him and did not give him the chance to say goodbye to her again. Leaving the carriage to go uphill empty, she walked along the grassy verge of the road and did not want to turn to look into the valley where the two men were taking their leave by the stream. Anna Maria was now choked by that tearful melancholy to which even healthier women are prone when they leave a place where they have spent a few years of their life, whether good or bad. The tears she was restraining with difficulty caught her throat and twisted her lips. But more than that she was tormented by the thought of the handsome, cold Lieutenant-Colonel whom she now no longer called Antinous, but *Glacier*, for she found him even colder than the marble statue of the beautiful classical youth. (That was what she had called him the previous night, so satisfying her need to give everyone a special name, which denoted her attitude to that person at the time.) Anna Maria stepped stiffly and solemnly up the mountain road, as though climbing to tragic heights.

Beside her, on the inner edge of the road, silent and fearful, walked her daughter Agatha. Unlike her exhilarated mother, the girl did not have the feeling that she was moving magnificently upwards, but slipping wretchedly downhill. She too was choked by stifled tears, but for quite other reasons. She was the only one of them who was sincerely sorry to be leaving Travnik with the silence and freedom of their garden and veranda, to be going back to huge, hateful Vienna where there was no peace, no sky and no view, where even from the gates the houses gave off a heavy odour which oppressed her, and where this mother of hers, of whom she felt ashamed even in her sleep, would be before her eyes, every minute.

But Anna Maria did not notice that her daughter's eyes were also full of tears. She had even forgotten her presence, and just kept whispering furious, disjointed words, angry with her husband for staying so long "flirting with that monstrous glacier", instead of coldly turning his back on him, as she was doing. And, as she whispered, she felt the wind lift her long, light, green veil, tied at the nape of her travelling hat, pulling at it and making it flutter. This seemed pretty and touching to her, so her mood changed abruptly for the better, raising her up in her own eyes so that all the details of her present life vanished and she saw herself as an exalted victim, marching, before the wondering gaze of the world, along the path of denial.

This would be all that insensitive Hyperborean would have of her and no more! Only her indistinct outline on the horizon and the last, proud message of her veil, irrevocably departing!

With these thoughts, she climbed up the edge of the hill, striding as though she were stepping across a large, deep stage.

And from below in the valley it was only her husband who caught sight of the green veil on the hill and sent anxious glances in its direction, while the 'Glacier', noticing nothing in the world, took his leave of him in the most courteous manner.

But the emotional and easily excited Anna Maria was not the only one whom the personality of the new Consul had charmed and disappointed.

On the occasion of the very first visit von Paulich made him, in the company of von Mitterer, Daville saw that he had now to deal with a quite different kind of man. Von Paulich expressed himself more clearly and freely about consular business. And it was possible to talk with him about all kinds of other subjects as well and notably about classical literature.

During the later visits which the two of them exchanged, Daville could see how comprehensive and profound was the Lieutenant-Colonel's knowledge of the texts and commentaries. Von Paulich looked over Delille's translations of Virgil into French which Daville sent him, and gave his opinion seriously, maintaining that only a translation in the original metre was a real translation and condemning Delille's use (and misuse) of rhyme. Daville defended his idol Delille, happy that he had someone to discuss him with.

But Daville's initial satisfaction at the arrival of this educated, literary man quickly waned. It did not take him long to see that his conversations with this learned Lieutenant-Colonel left none of the satisfaction which usually remained after an exchange of ideas with a noble collocutor about a loved subject. Conversation with the Lieutenant-Colonel was, in fact, an exchange of information, always precise, interesting and plentiful, on each and every topic, but not an exchange of ideas and impressions. Everything in those conversations was featureless, cold and generalized. After them, the Lieutenant-Colonel would leave with his rich and precious collection of facts, just as handsome, clean, cold and upright as he had come, and Daville would remain just as lonely and eager for good conversation as he had been before. Conversation with the Lieutenant-Colonel left nothing in either the senses or the heart; one could not even remember the tone of his voice.

The Lieutenant-Colonel carried on every conversation in such a way that his collocutor could not learn anything about him or say anything about himself. In general, everything that was close, intimate and personal rebounded off him as off a stone. So Daville was obliged to abandon all hope that he would be able to talk to this cold lover of literature about his poetic work.

On the occasion of the joyous occurrence at the French court, Daville wrote a special poem for the baptism of the King of Rome and sent it to his Ministry, with the request that it should be passed on to the highest level. The poem began with the words: "Salut, fils du printemps et du dieu de la Guerre!"[18] It expressed hopes of peace and prosperity for all the peoples of Europe and included mention also of those who were working humbly to this end in these "wild and sorrowful lands".

On one of his visits, Daville read his poem to von Paulich, but without any effect whatever. Not only did the Lieutenant-Colonel not wish to understand the allusion to their mutual co-operation in Bosnia, but he did not utter a single word about either the poem or its subject matter. And, worst of all, he remained throughout the same polite, pleasant man that he always was, in all things. So Daville was disappointed and inwardly aggrieved, but without the possibility of showing he was hurt.

---

18 "Greetings, son of the Spring and of the God of war!"

20

The years after the Peace of Vienna (1810 and 1811), which we have referred to as a peaceful spell, were in fact a time of great activity for Daville.

There were no more wars, no obvious crises and open conflicts but instead the whole Consulate was taken up with commercial activity, collecting information, writing reports, issuing certificates about the origin of goods and recommendations for the French authorities in Split or the customs office in Kostajnica. "Trade has taken over Bosnia," as the people put it, or, as Napoleon himself said somewhere: "The days of the diplomats are over and now the days of the consuls are beginning."

Three years earlier, Daville had made suggestions as to how to develop trade between Turkey and France and the countries under her rule. He warmly recommended that France organize a permanent postal service through the Turkish lands so as not to be dependent on the Austrian postal service and subject to arbitrary Turkish chaos. All these suggestions lay somewhere, in the overcrowded Paris archives. Now, after the Peace of Vienna, it was obvious that Napoleon himself was very keen that it should all be put into practice, and quickly, on a far wider and grander scale than the Travnik Consul would ever have ventured to suggest.

Napoleon's continental system demanded great changes in the network of communications and trade routes on the continent of Europe. According to his conception, the creation of the Illyrian provinces, with their centre in Ljubljana, was intended solely to serve that end. France had formerly been supplied with raw materials, particularly cotton, from the Levant by the old Mediterranean routes, but because of the English blockade, these had become difficult and dangerous. Now trade would have to be transferred to land routes and the newly created Illyria was to serve as a link between the Turkish lands and France. These routes had always existed – the route from Istanbul to Vienna by way of the Danube and the overland route from Salonica through Bosnia to Trieste. They had been used for a long time for trade between the Austrian lands and the Levant. Now they would all have to be expanded and adapted to the needs of Napoleon's France.

As soon as the direction of Napoleon's thinking became clear from the first circulars and newspaper articles, there was general competition between all French authorities and institutions to see who would serve the Emperor's wishes best and most zealously. There was copious correspondence and lively co-operation between Paris, the Governor General and Intendant General in Ljubljana, the Ambassador in Istanbul, Marshal Marmont in Dalmatia and the French consulates in the Levant. Daville worked with enthusiasm, referring proudly to his reports of three years before, which showed how close to the Emperor's views his way of thinking had been even then.

Now, in the summer of 1811, this activity was well under way. Over the last year, Daville had put a great deal of effort into finding trustworthy people in all the places French goods passed through, acquiring horses and at least some supervision of the carriers and cargos. It was all very problematic, slow and imperfect, like everything in this country, but there was still the possibility of improvement everywhere. And it was all done gladly and willingly, "with Napoleon's breath in the sails".

At last, Daville was able to see the day when one of the most important commercial firms in Marseilles, Les Frères Frayssinet, which had earlier been involved in the transport of goods from the Levant by sea, opened an agency in Sarajevo. The agency was approved by the French government and instructed to co-operate with the Consul. One of the Frayssinet brothers, a young man, had arrived in Sarajevo a month earlier, to manage the business in person. And now he had come to Travnik for a couple of days, to call on the Consul General and to discuss the next steps.

The lovely but brief Travnik summer was at its height.

A dazzling, translucent day, all brilliant sun and blue sky, was shimmering over the valley of Travnik.

A table had been laid on the large terrace, in the shadow of the Consulate building, and around it stood a set of white wicker-work chairs. The shade exuded coolness, although one was aware of the stifling heat weighing on the houses crammed together down in the bazaar. The dry heat evaporated from the steep green sides of the narrow ravine and it seemed that they were breathing, moving, like the sides of a green lizard lying in the sun.

On the terrace, Madame Daville's hyacinths were long since over, the white ones and the coloured ones, the double and the single ones, but now the edges of the beds were blooming with red pelargoniums and tiny violet Alpine flowers.

Daville and the young Frayssinet were sitting at the table, in the shade. Writing materials and copies of their reports were spread out in front of them, along with editions of the *Moniteur* containing the texts of regulations and decrees.

Jacques Frayssinet was a plump young man, with pink and white cheeks and that calm assurance in his voice and movements which characterizes the children of wealthy families. Commerce was evidently in his blood. No one in his family had ever done or wanted to do anything else or to belong to any other class. And he was no different from the rest of them in any way. He was, as all his family had always been, clean, polite, sober, considerate, decisive in the defence of his rights, concentrating on his own advantage, but not blindly or slavishly.

Frayssinet had made the journey from Sarajevo to Kostajnica in both directions, hired a whole khan in Sarajevo and already begun to enter into negotiations with merchants, carriers and local authorities. Now he had come to exchange information with Daville, communicate his observations and put forward some proposals. The Consul was pleased that he had acquired this vivacious but polite southerner to work with on business which often seemed unmanageable to him.

"So, once again," said Frayssinet with the certainty with which businessmen assert facts that are in their interest, "once again I repeat, one must reckon a week from Sarajevo to Kostajnica, with resting places for caravans at Kiseljak, Busovača, Karaula, Jajce, Zmijanje, Novi Han, Prijedor and, finally, Kostajnica. In winter one must reckon twice as much, that is fourteen stops. At least two more caravanserais will have to be built on that route if the goods are to be protected from the weather and theft. The costs of transport have soared and are still rising. They are being raised by Austrian competition and, I believe, by certain Sarajevo merchants, Serbs and Jews, who are working on English instructions. Nowadays you have to reckon with these prices: from Salonica to Sarajevo, 155 piastres a load, from Sarajevo to Kostajnica 55 piastres. Two years ago the prices were exactly half that. And everything must be done to prevent a further rise, because that could bring the whole route into question. And then there's the self-will and greed of the Turkish functionaries, the inclination of the populace to theft and plunder, the dangers of an expansion of the rebellion in Serbia and banditry in the Albanian districts and, finally, the danger of epidemic."

Daville was inclined to find the English intelligence service's fingerprints in everything, so he wanted to know why Frayssinet had come to the conclusion that the Sarajevo merchants were working for the English, but the young man would not be deflected from his theme.

Holding his notes in front of him, he continued: "To sum up then, and conclude. The dangers that threaten traffic are: the rebellion in Serbia, Albanian bandits, thieving in Bosnia, the rising costs of transport, unforeseen taxes and duties, competition and, finally, the plague and other infectious diseases. The measures that must be taken are: first, between Sarajevo and Kostajnica, two caravanserais; second, the prevention of immoderate fluctuations of Turkish currency and the establishment, by special decree, of an exchange rate of 5.50 piastres to the thaler of 6 francs and the Maria-Theresa thaler; 11.50 to the Venetian zecchino, etc.; third, the extension of the quarantine station at Kostajnica; a bridge must be built to replace the ferry, the warehouse altered to take at least 8,000 bales of cotton, there must be an inn for travellers, etc.; fourth, in connection with these demands special gifts must be presented to the Vizier, Suleiman Pasha and a few other prominent Turks. All this would come to roughly 10,000 to 13,000 francs. I believe that these measures would safeguard our route and remove the main obstacles."

Daville made notes of all these facts, so as to include them in his next report and at the same time he prepared, with satisfaction, to read the young man his 1807 paper, in which he had so clearly anticipated Napoleon's intentions and all that they were now working on.

"Ah, my dear sir, I could tell you a great deal about the difficulties that threaten every useful undertaking in these lands. I could tell you a great deal, but you will see for yourself what this country and its people are like, what sort of administration it has and what kind of endless problems there are at every step."

But the young man had nothing more to say, for he had defined precisely both the problems and the measures for overcoming them. He evidently had no inclination to complaints of a general nature, nor to "psychological phenomena". He agreed, politely, to listen to Daville's 1807 paper, which the Consul began to read.

The shadow they were sitting in was becoming increasingly long. In front of them stood tall crystal glasses of lemonade, growing steadily warmer, for both men had forgotten them as they worked.

In that same summer quiet, in an outlying quarter above the Consulate where Daville and Frayssinet were discussing business, but a little closer to the stream falling from there into the valley, Musa Krdžalija was sitting in his garden with some friends.

Everything in this steep and neglected garden was suffocating with luxuriant growth. On a patch of level ground, under a large "sugar" pear tree, a rug was spread out, with the remains of a meal, cups and a jug of chilled brandy on it. The sun had already gone from this place, only the opposite bank of the Lašva was still bathed in light. Musa the Singer and Hamza the Town-crier were lying in the grass. Murat Hodzic, known as the Reeling Hodja, was half-sitting, half-lying with his back against the slope and his feet against the pear tree. His little tamboura was leaning against the tree trunk, with a brandy glass propped on it.

He was a swarthy little man, peevish as a cockerel. His big, gloomy eyes shone in his small, sallow face, with a fixed stare and fanatical gleam. He too came from one of the better-off Travnik families and had once had some education, but brandy had prevented him from completing his studies to become an imam in Travnik, as so many of his family had been. The story went that when he was due to take his final examination, he had appeared before the muderris and the examination board so drunk that he could hardly stand, and he staggered and reeled as he walked. The muderris refused to examine him and called him the "Reeling Hodja". And the name had stuck. Hot-tempered and easily offended, the young man had then given himself up entirely to drink. And the more he drank, the more his wounded vanity and resentment grew. Cast out of the ranks of his contemporaries right at the outset, he dreamed of surpassing them all one day by some exceptional feat and so avenging himself on them all for everything. Like many unsuccessful people, small in stature but lively in spirit, he was consumed by a wild, secret ambition that he should not spend the rest of his days like this, insignificant and unknown, but would amaze the world, without himself knowing how, where or in what way. With time, inflamed by hard drinking to the point of madness, this idea took complete control of him. The lower he fell, the more he fed on lies and deceived himself with big words, daring tales and conceited dreams. This often made him the butt of humour and mockery among his friends, serious drinkers like himself.

On these fine summer days, the three of them would always start drinking in Musa's garden, and only go down to the town for more drink when it grew dark. As they waited for that darkness when large stars appeared on the narrow blue Travnik horizon, and to feel the full effect of the alcohol, they would sing softly or talk quietly, haltingly, disjointedly and without reference to what the others were saying. These were the conversations and songs of people poisoned by drink. They were a substitute for the work and movement to which they had long ago grown unaccustomed. In these conversations they travelled, performed great feats, fulfilled desires they could never have satisfied in any other way. They looked at things they could never see and listened to what they could never hear. They puffed themselves up and grew, revelling in their own greatness, they rose, flew as on wings, became all that they could never be and the kind of people they never could have been, they possessed what is nowhere to be found, what only brandy can offer, for a moment, to those who surrender entirely to its power.

Musa spoke the least. He was lying quite buried in the thick, dark green grass. He had clasped his hands under his head, bent his left leg at the knee and thrown his right leg over it, like someone sitting. He was gazing vacantly into the bright sky. Through the tangle of the grass his fingers touched the warm earth which seemed to him to be breathing in long, even breaths. At the same time he felt the hot air streaming down his sleeves and the unbuttoned leggings of his trousers. This was that barely perceptible breath of air, a special Travnik breeze, which appears in summer towards evening, creeping slowly, just above the surface of the earth, through the grass and bushes. Musa was somewhere halfway between the morning's fuddledness and the new inebriation which was coming over him. He gave himself up completely to that warmth of the soil and that slight, constant stir in the air, feeling all the time that they were lifting him up, that he was about to take off, that he was flying, not because they were strong and powerful, but because he himself was nothing but a breath of air and quivering warmth, so light and weak that he was journeying somewhere with them.

While he lay still, taking off and flying away, he seemed to hear the conversation of the other two as though in his sleep. Hamza's voice was hoarse and hard to understand, while the Reeling Hodja's was deep and sharp. He always spoke slowly and solemnly, with his eyes fixed on one spot, as though he were reading.

Three days earlier the three of them had come to the conclusion that they had run out of money. They must get some at all costs. For a long time now it had been the Reeling Hodja's turn to find money, but he always had trouble getting it, preferring to drink at others' expense.

They were talking about a loan the Reeling Hodja was supposed to be getting from an uncle, who had recently become rich.

"How come he's got money?" asked Hamza disbelievingly and caustically, like someone who was acquainted with the uncle concerned and knew that money is not easily come by.

"He made a lot on this summer's cotton."

"Carrying for the French?"

"Hell no, buying up and re-selling the cotton you 'find' in the villages."

"And is the business still going well?" asked Hamza lazily.

"They say it's thriving. You know the English have closed the sea route and Bunaparta has run out of cotton. And he's got that great army to clothe. So now he has to have cotton sent through Bosnia. From Novi Pazar to Kostajnica there's nothing but horse after horse and bale after bale, all pure cotton. The roads are jammed and the khans stuffed full. You can't get carriers for love or money. The French have hired them all and they pay good sound ducats. If anyone has a horse these days, it's worth its weight in gold. And anyone who works in cotton is a rich man in a month."

"Fine, but how do they get the cotton?"

"How? Easily. The French wouldn't sell cotton to save their lives. They wouldn't part with an oke of cotton if you offered your house for it. So, folk get thinking and start pinching it. They pinch it in the khans where the carriers unload the horses and spend the night. It's all there when they unload, but when they start loading up again the next day, they're one bale short. Then there's a to-do: who did it? Where is it? But the whole caravan can't wait because of one bale. And so off they go without it. They steal even more in the villages. The kids go out of the village, hide in the bushes by the roadside and cut a slit in one of the bales with their knives. As the road is narrow and overgrown with bushes, the cotton starts to fall out and catch on the branches on both sides of the road. As soon as the caravan has passed, the children come out, collect the cotton in baskets and hide again to wait for the next caravan. The French accuse the carriers and take it out of their pay. In some places the police go out and catch the children. But who can stop the people? Everyone's picking at Bunaparta's cotton and plucking it from the branches, as though this was Egypt, and people come from the towns to buy it up. It makes plenty of people a good living."

"And why should it be happening in Bosnia, of all places?" asked Hamza sleepily.

"It's not only Bosnia, it's right through the whole blessed Empire. Bunaparta's taken out licences in Istanbul and sent consuls and merchants with money through the whole country, and there it is. Do you know, man, that for Bunaparta's cotton my uncle…"

"You get the money," Musa broke in softly, but contemptuously, "and we won't ask if it's your uncle on your father's or your mother's side, nor where cotton grows and where steel. We need money."

Musa did not care for these stories of the Reeling Hodja's which were always long and exaggerated and supposed to show the Hodja's learning, courage and his knowledge of the ways of the world. Hamza was more patient and listened calmly, with the ready humour that never left him, not even in their most acute insolvency.

"God knows we do," Hamza joined in, like a dull echo, "desperately."

"And I'll get it, I swear to God, I'll get it now, if it kills me," the Reeling Hodja announced solemnly.

No one responded to his oaths and promises.

Silence. Their three bodies, weakened by inactivity, constantly either inflamed by alcohol or tormented by the need of it, breathed and seemed to be resting, stretched in the grass and warm shade.

"He's quite a man, this Bunaparta," the Reeling Hodja began again, in a slow drawl, as though thinking aloud, "a great man; he's beaten and conquered everything on earth. And they say he's a small, frail man; he doesn't look anything special."

"He's small, about your size, but he's got a lion's heart," said Hamza yawning.

"And they say," the Reeling Hodja went on, "he doesn't carry a sabre or a rifle. He just turns up his collar, pulls his hat down over his eyes and charges at the head of his army. And he destroys every living thing. Fire flashes from his eyes. No sabre ever cuts him down and no bullet ever hits him."

The Reeling Hodja picked his glass up from his tamboura, filled it and drank, all with his left hand, holding his right hand on his chest, inside his open shirt, his head drooping, his vacant gaze fixed on the rough bark of the pear tree. The brandy in him immediately burst into song. Barely opening his mouth, not altering his position and not shifting his gaze, he sang in his deep baritone:

"Lovely Naza has fallen sick.
Her mother's only daughter."

And he took down the glass again, filled it, drained it and put it back on the tamboura. "Ah, if only I could meet him…"

"Who?" asked Hamza, although it was the hundredth time he had heard these or similar ravings.

"Him, Bunaparta! If the two of us could only have it out, damn his infidel soul, and let the best man win."

The senseless words were lost in absolute silence. The Reeling Hodja took his glass from the tamboura again, shook himself audibly after the drink and continued in a deeper voice:

"If he gets the better of me, he can kill me. I won't give a damn. But if I knock him down I'll tie him up, but I won't do him any harm, I'll just drive him through the crowds in irons and force him to pay tribute to the Sultan, just like the lowliest Christian shepherd under Karaula mountain."

"Bunaparta's a long way off, Murat, a long way," said Hamza good-naturedly, "and he has mighty power. And what about the other infidel empires you'd have to cross, my friend?"

"Oh, I'd manage them easily," the Reeling Hodja waved him away airily. "And yes, he's a long way off when he's in his own country, but he keeps roaming the world, he's never still. He came to Vienna last year and got married there. He married the German king's daughter."

"Ah well, you might have done something near Vienna," said Hamza, smiling, "if you'd thought of it in time."

"Ah, I keep telling you, one fine day you have to get off your backside and go into the world, instead of just wasting away and rotting in this Travnik bog, and either win some glory or die once and for all. How long have I been telling you, but you two keep on: don't, not yet, later, tomorrow. And here we are…"

With these words, the Reeling Hodja took his glass from the tamboura with a resolute movement, filled it and drained it energetically.

Neither Hamza nor Musa made any further response to his fantasies. With brief movements, imperceptibly, they too drank brandy from their cups in the grass. Left to his own devices, the small Reeling Hodja sank into that proud and contemptuous silence that follows hard battles and great deeds for which there is never true recognition nor due reward. With his right hand in his open shirt, his chin on his chest, he looked sullenly in front of him with his vacant gaze.

"She was ailing for three whole years…"

His mournful baritone came suddenly again, as though someone else were singing out of him.

Hamza coughed delightedly.

"Your health, Murat, you old warrior! You'll go, with God's help, inshallah, you will, of course you will, and half the world will see and hear who and what Murat is and what he is made of."

"Your health! Here's to you!" said the Reeling Hodja painfully and emotionally, wearily raising his glass like a man weighed down by the burden of his glory.

So the time passed, while Musa lay, silent and motionless, hovering and flying with the wind and the warm earth, freed, at least for a moment, from the laws of gravity and the chains of time.

The dazzling, translucent day, all sunlight and blue sky, shimmered over the valley of Travnik.

21

At the beginning of 1812 there began to be increasingly frequent signs and rumours of the possibility of renewed war. At each of these rumours, Daville would be overcome by a slight, imperceptible dizziness, like a man who sees in store for him tribulations that have already plagued him repeatedly.

"Dear God, dear God!"

He would mutter these words indistinctly to himself in one drawn-out breath, lying stretched out in his chair, with his right hand over his eyes.

Everything was starting all over again, just as two years before at this time, and before that, in 1805 and 1806. And it would all be the same again. Unease, anxiety and suspicion of everything, and a feeling of shame and revulsion, but at the same time the base hope that it would all somehow end well, this time too – just this once more! And that this life, this inconsistent, wretched, sweet, one and only life, the life of the Empire and society, his life and that of his family, would prove constant and enduring. And that this would be the last test, that it would mark the end of this way of existence, with its constant ups and downs, like a crazy swing which left one just enough breath to be deemed alive. It would probably all end this time too with victorious bulletins, and favourable peace treaties. But who could endure a life which was becoming increasingly difficult and costly in moral terms, and who could pay the price it exacted? What was there still to give for a man who had given his all? What could his spent energies achieve? But everyone must give his all and do what he could, just to escape from this eternal warfare, to draw breath, to attain a little stability and peace, at last.

"Peace, just peace! Peace, peace!" he thought, or whispered, and the very word lulled him into a half-sleep.

But all at once, before his closed eyes, under the cold palm of his hand, the forgotten face of the forgotten von Mitterer appeared, grey and despondent, with its deep lines where a green shadow lay, with its straight, waxed moustache and black eyes with their unhealthy gleam. It was with just this expression, this time last year, that he had said, kindly and ambiguously, in this very room, that next spring "there would be a real rumpus" (yes, he had used just that barrack-room phrase). And now, here he was again, punctual and implacable, like some pedantic, humourless apparition, to show him that he had been right, that there was no peace, nor would there be. Von Mitterer's head repeated the same words as the year before, at their parting, bitterly and maliciously:

"Il y aura beaucoup de tapage."

Ugly words, a bad pronunciation, a perfidious tone underlying it all.

"…beaucoup de tapage…de tapage…de tapage…"[19]

And with this word, von Mitterer's face began to sway and to become ever paler, ever more corpse-like. Then it was no longer von Mitterer. It was that white and bloody, severed head on the sans-culotte pike he had caught sight of one morning, twenty years before, from his window in Paris.

Daville jumped up, suddenly taking his hand from his eyes, shattering his half-sleep and with it the face that had come to frighten him, helpless and weary as he was. The great wooden clock ticked monotonously in the overheated room.

That spring boded ill for Daville.

From the instructions circulated, the increasingly frequent couriers and articles in the press, he could see that momentous events

---

19 "There'll be a real rumpus."

and new campaigns were being planned, that the whole military mechanism of the Empire had been set in motion again. But there was no one he could have talked to about it, no one else's ideas to listen to, no one to explore the likely prospects with and confide his doubts and anxiety in, so as to see in the light of rational discussion how much of his anxiety was real and what was the product of his imagination, fear and weariness. For, like all lonely, weak and exhausted people whose faith in themselves is temporarily shaken, Daville wanted desperately to find confirmation and support for his own thoughts and actions in the words and eyes of others, instead of seeking them in himself. But we are always cursed with advice in abundance, except when we most need it, and no one ever wants to talk sincerely about the things that really torment us.

Von Paulich carried on his affairs, polite and cold, handsome and implacable, an Imperial Austrian machine without fault or hesitation. When they met, they would talk about Virgil or the intentions of the European courts, but in these conversations Daville never succeeded in testing a single one of his intuitions and fears. Von Paulich confined himself to general expressions about the "ties of alliance and kinship between the Austrian and French courts", about "the wisdom and far-sightedness of those who direct the fate of the European states by mutual consent", avoiding expressing himself more precisely about any aspect of the future. And Daville did not venture to ask direct questions either, for fear of giving himself away, but just gazed feverishly into those unusual, blue, dark eyes in which he always found the same implacable, off-putting restraint.

It was not worth talking to d'Avenat. Only tangible things and concrete issues existed for him. Anything that had not matured to that form simply did not exist.

All that remained were conversations with Ibrahim Pasha and the men at the Residence.

What he was able to hear from the Vizier was more or less the same thing Ibrahim Pasha had been saying for years already, endlessly repeated, ossified like himself.

It was the beginning of April. The Vizier always became restless and irritable around then because the time was approaching when he would have to despatch the army against Serbia and this exposed him to demands from Istanbul which far surpassed his energies.

"The people there don't know what they're doing," the Vizier complained to Daville, who wanted to find some relief for his own worries in this conversation, "they don't know what they're doing, that's all I can say. I am ordered to set out at the same time as the Pasha from Nis, so that we attack the rebels from two directions at once. But they don't know, they don't want to know what resources I have at my disposal here. How can my oxen keep pace with his horses? Where can I find ten thousand men and how can I feed and equip them? And you can't put three Bosnians together without them quarrelling about who is first (none of them is last, we all know that). And even if I were to manage all of that, what's the use when these Bosnian heroes refuse to fight on the other side of the Drina and Sava? Their bravery and their proverbial heroism stop there, at the Bosnian frontier."

It was obvious that the Vizier was incapable of thinking or talking about anything else at this moment. He became almost animated, if that word could be used of him, waving his hand as though he were vainly trying to drive away a tiresome fly.

"In any case, it's not worth wasting our breath on Serbia. If only the Sultan Selim were alive, everything would be different."

And once the subject of the unfortunate Selim III had been raised, it was useless to expect any other topic of conversation, at least for that day.

At about that time, Daville gave Tahir Bey, the Secretary, a special gift, just to have the opportunity of hearing his opinion.

Having got through the severe winter, more in his bed than on his feet, Tahir Bey had now suddenly come to life and become talkative and agile, almost unnaturally lively. His face was already a little tanned by the April sun, and his eyes were shining as though he were slightly drunk.

The Secretary talked, rapidly and feverishly, about Travnik, about the winters they had spent there (the fourth for him and the fifth already for Daville), about the feelings of friendship and fellow-suffering which their lengthy common stay in this little town had engendered in the Vizier and all of them towards Daville and his family, about Daville's children, about the spring, about many different things that were only apparently unconnected but were in fact very closely linked with Tahir Bey's present mood. The Secretary spoke as though he were reading, softly and with a smile, but excitedly, as though he were saying something that was being revealed to him only now, at this moment, and of which he wanted to convince both Daville and himself:

"Spring smooths everything over, and puts it right. As long as the earth blooms, again and again, and as long as there are people to observe that and enjoy it, all is well." And, with a slight movement of his brown hand, the bluish nails of which had strange ridges along their length, he demonstrated everything being smoothed over. "And there always will be people, for those who can no longer see the sun and flowers are constantly disappearing and new ones coming. As the poet says: 'In the children the river of mankind is renewed and purified.'"

Daville approved his words and smiled too as he looked at Tahir Bey's smiling face, thinking to himself: he too is saying what he needs to say at this precise moment, goodness knows for what reasons. And he immediately began to turn the conversation from spring and childhood to empires and warfare. Tahir Bey accepted every topic and talked about everything with the same calm, smiling elation, as though he were reading something new that he liked.

"Yes, we too have heard that new wars are on the horizon. We shall have to wait and see who will be with whom and against whom, but it seems there will certainly be war this summer."

"Are you sure?" asked Daville, with painful haste.

"Sure, in so far as that's what your newspapers say," replied the Secretary smiling, "and I have no reason to doubt them."

Tahir Bey bent his head slightly and looked at Daville with a bright, slightly squinting look, a look you see in weasels and martens, nimble creatures that slit throats and drink blood but do not eat the flesh of the animal they have killed.

"Sure," continued the Secretary, "in so far as I know there has been perpetual war between the Christian states for centuries."

"The non-Christian, Eastern states fight wars too," Daville interrupted him.

"They do. Only the difference is that the Islamic states make war without pretence or contradiction. They have always regarded war as an important part of their mission in the world. It was as a warring faction that Islam came to Europe and it has maintained itself there either by warfare or through the mutual warfare of the Christian nations. But as I understand it, Christian nations condemn war to such an extent that they always accuse the other side of being responsible for every war. Yet while condemning it, they never cease to wage it."

"Undoubtedly there is some truth in your account," Daville encouraged the Secretary, with the ulterior motive of drawing him into talking about the Russo-French conflict and hearing his opinion, "but do you really think that the Russian Emperor will want to bring down on himself the wrath of the greatest Christian ruler and the most powerful army in Christendom?"

The Secretary's look became even brighter and more squinting.

"I am not remotely familiar with the Emperor's intentions, my dear sir, but I make so bold as to draw your attention to one fact which I noticed long ago, and that is that there is war constantly somewhere in Christian Europe, only it shifts from one part to another, as a man shifts a hot coal he is carrying in his hand in order to burn himself as little as possible. At the moment it is somewhere on the European borders of Russia."

Daville could see that he was not going to learn anything of what interested and troubled him here either, for this man, like the Vizier, said only what he was driven to by his immediate inner need.

Nevertheless, he wanted to make one more attempt, crudely and directly: "It is well known that the main aim of Russian policy now is the liberation of its fellow-believers, including those in these regions under Ottoman rule. Consequently many people consider it more probable that its real war plans are directed against Turkey and not against West European countries."

The Secretary would not let himself be ruffled: "What can you do? The thing that looks most probable doesn't always happen. And if it were as 'many people consider', then it is not difficult to foresee the train of events, for it is no secret that all these countries have been acquired through war, they defend themselves through war and are lost through it, if they must be lost. But that doesn't change anything of what I have said."

And Tahir Bey returned persistently to his theme: "If you look carefully you will see it is true that wherever Christian Europe extends its power, with its customs and institutions, there is war, inter-Christian war. That's how it is in Africa, America, and the European regions of the Ottoman Empire which have fallen to Christian states. And should it ever happen, by the will of fate, that we lose these regions and they are conquered by some Christian country or other, as you mentioned a moment ago, it would be the same with them. So it could perhaps happen, that in the very place where you and I are now discussing the possibility of Turkish-Christian war, a hundred or two hundred years from now Christians, liberated from Ottoman domination, will be slaying one another and shedding each other's blood."

Tahir Bey laughed aloud at his vision. Daville laughed too out of politeness and in his desire to give everything a pleasant and innocent appearance, although he was disappointed with the direction the conversation was taking.

Finally, everything was given new flavour by Tahir Bey's reflecting once more on spring, on youth which is eternal, although those who are young are not eternally the same, on friendship and good neighbourliness which make even hateful places bearable.

Daville took it all with a smile behind which he endeavoured to hide his dissatisfaction.

As often happened, on his way home Daville exchanged a few words with d'Avenat.

"How does Tahir Bey seem to you?" asked Daville, just as a signal for conversation.

"He's a sick man," said d'Avenat drily and fell silent.

Their horses drew close again.

"But he seems to have made a thorough recovery this time."

"What's bad is that he keeps recovering. If he goes on making frequent recoveries, one day he will…"

"Do you think so?" Daville started in surprise.

"Why yes. Did you see his hands and eyes? That's a man who cures himself with death and lives on drugs," d'Avenat concluded in a quiet voice, sternly and firmly.

Daville said nothing in reply. Now that his attention had been drawn to it, when he thought back over all the parts of Tahir Bey's conversation, but without the Secretary's unique smile and way of talking, they did indeed seem disconnected, exaggerated and morbid.

All that, spoken in that crude and relentlessly factual manner of d'Avenat's, offended Daville like a personal unpleasantness, although he could not himself have said why. He moved his horse a length ahead of d'Avenat. This was a sign that the conversation was ended. "Strange," thought Daville looking at the broad back of the Vizier's officer, who was riding in front and making a passage for them. "Strange that there is no mercy here, none of that natural compassion we show spontaneously in the face of any other person's suffering. In these lands you have to be a beggar, someone whose home has burned down, or a cripple in the street, in order to arouse compassion. Otherwise, between equals, there is no compassion anywhere. If a man lived here for a hundred years, he would never be able to get used to this hard-heartedness, this crude directness, he would never be able to grow tough enough for it not to offend and hurt him."

Above them the voice of the muezzin from the Many-Coloured Mosque rang out, as suddenly and crisply as an explosion. That curt voice trembled and welled with a forceful, militant and angry piety which seemed to fill the muezzin's breast to overflowing. It was noon. Another muezzin was heard from an unseen mosque. His voice, excited and deep, accompanied the voice of the bazaar muezzin like a devout, zealous shadow. These voices followed them right up to the Consulate, catching each other up and vanishing in the air above Daville and his escort.

The Feast of the Annunciation marked a full year since the christening of Daville's daughter. The Consul used this as an excuse to invite von Paulich and the Dolac priest, Brother Ivo Janković, together with his chaplain, to lunch. The friars accepted the invitation, but it was immediately obvious that they had not altered their attitude in any way. Both of them were exaggeratedly polite and looked at Daville askance, not in the eye but somewhere at the level of his shoulder, their eyes lowered. Daville was familiar with this Bosnian way of looking (learned in long years of dealing with them) and he well knew that neither flattery nor force could do anything to counteract what was hidden behind it. He was familiar with the morbid and mysterious inner complexity of these Bosnians who were just as sensitive about issues that concerned themselves as they were hasty and rough about others. And he prepared for this lunch as for a difficult game he had to play, knowing in advance that he could not win.

Before lunch and during the meal, the conversation ranged over general questions, disingenuously sweet and innocent. Brother Ivo ate and drank so much that his face, in any case red, became violet, and his tongue loose. With the young chaplain the effect of the lavish meal was the opposite: the large quantity of food made him paler and even more taciturn.

As he blew out his first puff of smoke, Brother Ivo placed the large fist of his right hand, with red bristles like a bracelet round the wrist, on the table and without any introduction began to talk about relations between the Holy See and Napoleon.

Daville was surprised at how well the Friar knew the various phases of the struggle being waged between the Pope and the Emperor. He knew all the details about the national council Napoleon had summoned the previous year in Paris, about the resistance of the French bishops, just as he knew all the places where the Pope had been imprisoned and all the peripeteia of the pressures to which he had been exposed.

The Consul began to defend and explain the French actions. (His own voice sounded feeble and unconvincing even to himself.) At the same time he tried to turn the conversation to the present international situation, in order to hear what this friar, his fellow-monks and the whole Catholic population expected from the immediate future. But the friar had no intention of getting involved in general questions. He knew only what his passionate nature and fanatical conviction had taught him. For everything else he would only glance at von Paulich who was talking to Madame Daville a little way away from them. It was obvious that the friar did not care much for either the Russians or the French. In his hissing voice, which seemed strangely shrill and thin for such a sturdy man, he simply kept repeating the most ominous predictions for a nation which behaved in such a way towards the Church and its Head.

"I don't know, Monsieur le Consul, whether your army will turn against Russia or in some other direction," Brother Ivo replied to Daville's attempt to hear his opinion and learn where his sympathies would lie in that case, "but I do know for sure, and I tell you this openly, that it will find no blessing anywhere, wherever it goes, for whoever treats the Church like that…"

Here there was again a series of accusations, with quotations from the last papal bull against Napoleon, about "the new, increasingly deep wounds which were being inflicted every day on the Apostolic authorities, the rights of the Church, the holy faith and our own personal rights".

Seeing him so heavy, sullen and unshakeable, the thought occurred to Daville (not for the first time: it had been a familiar one for years already), that this man was filled to the brim with a kind of defiant anger which broke out of him in that shrill hissing with every word he spoke. And everything he thought and said, even about the Pope himself, was simply a welcome excuse for this anger and defiance to be released.

The chaplain was sitting motionless right beside the sturdy parish priest, like a silent miniature version of him, exactly the same in attitude and behaviour. He too had his right hand on the table, clenched into a fist, only that fist was small and white, with the barely perceptible beginnings of red bristles.

At the other end of the table a lively conversation was going on between Madame Daville and von Paulich. From the moment the Lieutenant-Colonel arrived in Travnik, she had been surprised and charmed by his genuine interest in everything to do with the house and housekeeping and his unusual familiarity with domestic affairs and requirements. (Just as Daville had been surprised at his familiarity with Virgil and Ovid. Just as, in his time, von Mitterer had been surprised and disconcerted by his familiarity with military questions.) And whenever they met, they easily found agreeable topics of conversation. Now they were discussing furniture, the preservation and maintenance of things in these special circumstances.

The Lieutenant-Colonel's knowledge seemed truly inexhaustible. He talked about each of these subjects as though it were the only one that interested him at that moment, and about each of them with the same cold and distant objectivity, bringing nothing personal into it. Now he was talking about the effect of damp on various kinds of wood in furniture and on seaweed and horsehair in armchairs, with confident, experienced knowledge, but also with scientific objectivity, as though they were talking of furniture in the world at large and not about himself and his personal possessions.

The Lieutenant-Colonel spoke in his slow and bookish but refined French which made such a pleasant change from the corrupted vocabulary and hurried Levantine pronunciation which had been unbearably painful with von Mitterer. Madame Daville helped him, finding words which from time to time escaped him.

She was glad that she could talk to this polite, pedantic man about the subjects that were her main preoccupation and her true life. In conversation, as in her work and her prayers, she was always the same, decisive and gentle, with no digressions or hesitations, sure of herself and full of confidence in Heaven and Earth and in everything time could bring and people were capable of doing.

Watching and listening to all these faces around him, Daville thought: they are all calm, composed, they all know, at least at this moment, exactly what they want, it is only I who am confused and alarmed at the thought of tomorrow, exhausted and unhappy and what is more, obliged to hide it and bear it secretly, not giving myself away by a single sign.

Brother Ivo interrupted him in these thoughts. He had, as always, risen abruptly, sharply reprimanding his young chaplain as though he were the reason they had sat there so long, shouting that it was late, that they had a long journey home and there was work to be done.

This introduced a still more unpleasant coldness into their encounter.

That same spring, the Metropolitan Kalinik and his attendant Bishop Joanikije came to Travnik on Orthodox Church matters. Daville invited them to lunch too in the desire to hear what they thought about imminent events.

The Metropolitan was a fat, sluggish, sickly man, he wore glasses with thick lenses (but of unequal thickness) behind which his eyes looked timidly distorted and shapeless, as though at any moment they could overflow. He had the Phanariot's sweet way of expressing himself and he spoke in an equally approving and conciliatory manner about all the great powers and about everyone. By and large, for all things and all concepts he had just a few expressions, invariably favourable, and he applied them to everything that was said to him, approximately, without much thought, without even paying attention to the topic. Among very elderly members of the clergy of all faiths, you often come across this disdainful and exaggerated politeness, a poor disguise for complete indifference to everything that people say.

Bishop Joanikije was a quite different type of man. A sturdy heavy monk, his face quite covered in a thick black beard, with a perpetual expression of anger on his face. There was something brusque and military in his whole bearing, as though he were wearing armour and heavy weapons under his habit. The Turks were very suspicious of this Bishop because of his links with the uprising in Serbia, but nothing could be proved against him.

He answered Daville's questions briefly but openly and to the point: "You would like to know whether I am for the Russians, and I tell you that I am for those who help us to keep going and with time, to gain our freedom. At least you who live here know what we have to put up with. So no one should be surprised…"

The Metropolitan turned to the Bishop, warning him with a look from his expressionless eyes, overflowing horribly behind the thick glass, but the Bishop continued, unshakeable: "The Christian states fight among themselves, instead of coming to an agreement and working together to put an end to this misfortune once and for all. It has been going on like this for centuries, and you would like to know who we are for…"

The Metropolitan turned to him again and, seeing that his look did not help, hastily broke in, in a prayerful tone: "May God save and preserve all the Christian powers, sent by God and maintained by God. We pray constantly to God…"

But now the Bishop interrupted the Metropolitan quickly and sharply: "We are for Russia, Monsieur, and for the liberation of all the Orthodox Christians from the infidel. That is what we are for, and if anyone tells you any different, don't believe him."

Here the Metropolitan broke in again, starting to say something agreeable, all sweet adjectives, which d'Avenat translated with difficulty, rapidly, inaccurately, leaving things out.

Daville looked at the sullen Bishop. His breathing was heavy, somehow constricted, and his squeaky voice did not flow steadily, but disjointedly, with occasional little sobs, like explosions of some incomprehensible, long accumulated anger which must have filled this man to the brim and kept breaking out at every word and movement.

Daville did all he could to explain the intentions of his government to the Metropolitan and the Bishop, presenting them in the most favourable possible light. But he did not himself believe that he could succeed, for nothing could drive that expression of anger from the Bishop's face. And for the Metropolitan it made no difference in any case who said what, for he listened to all human discourse as to a murmur of words without meaning, with the same agreeable inattention and indifference and the same sweet and insincere approval.

The dignitaries were accompanied to the Consulate by Pahomije, the thin, pale monk who served the Travnik Orthodox church. This sickly man, bent at the waist, with the sour, twisted face of someone with a stomach complaint, very rarely came to the Consulate. He always declined invitations, with the excuse that he was afraid of the Turks, or that he was not well. Whenever Daville met him with a friendly greeting and tried to talk to him, he would bend still lower and twist his face still more, and his look would hover (that Bosnian look Daville knew so well), directed not into Daville's eyes but somewhere low and askance, now at one of his collocutor's shoulders, now at the other. It was only with d'Avenat that he sometimes talked more freely.

That day too, when he had to come with his superiors, he sat, bent and silent, a disagreeable guest, on the edge of his chair, as though he were prepared at any moment to run away, looking straight ahead of him the whole time, without a single word. But when d'Avenat met him in the street two or three days later and initiated a conversation with him "in his way", the sallow, feeble monk came suddenly to life and began to speak, his look now sharp and direct. Little by little, the conversation became increasingly lively. D'Avenat provoked him, maintaining that every nation and every faith, all who expected something, must direct their eyes to the all-powerful French Emperor and not to Russia, which the

French would subjugate this very summer as the last European state which was not yet subordinate to them.

The monk's large mouth was usually tightly compressed. It opened wide now, and his small sickly face displayed white, regular teeth, powerful as a wolf's. On either side of this mouth there appeared new, hitherto unseen lines of some mischievous, mocking joy. The monk threw back his head and laughed unexpectedly loudly, mockingly and gaily, so that even d'Avenat was surprised. That lasted only a moment. And then Pahomije's face settled just as quickly back into its familiar furrows and became once more squat, small and screwed up. He turned away a little, glanced quickly around him, to see whether there was anyone near, brought his face up to d'Avenat's right ear and said in a strong voice which suited his smiling expression of a moment before but not this present one:

"You mark my words, neighbour: get that idea out of your head!"

Leaning towards him in this kindly, confidential way, the monk spoke as though he were donating him something of value. And saying a brief goodbye, he immediately continued on his way, choosing the side alleys as usual, avoiding the bazaar and main roads.

22

The destinies of all these foreigners, cast up and crammed into this narrow, damp valley and condemned to live in unusual conditions for an unknown length of time, now came to an abrupt maturity. The strange circumstances into which they had been thrown speeded up inner processes already at work in them, driving each of them with more relentless force in the direction of his impulses. The way these impulses developed and were manifested here was different in both degree and form than might have been the case in any other circumstances.

Even in the first months after von Paulich's arrival it was fairly clear that the relationship between the new Consul General and the interpreter, Niccolo Rotta, would be difficult, that there would inevitably be conflict and, sooner or later, rupture. For it would have been difficult to find anywhere in the world two men who were so different, so predestined for misunderstanding and confrontation.

The cold, measured, well-groomed Lieutenant-Colonel, who spread all around him an atmosphere of sharp, crystal iciness and clarity, provoked the vain, petulant interpreter by his very presence, arousing in him innumerable grievances which had been dormant or hidden in a tight knot until then. It would be wrong to say that these two men repelled each other, for in fact it was only Rotta who was repelled by the Lieutenant-Colonel as by a vast motionless iceberg. And, to make matters worse, he kept coming back, driven by some inexorable force, hurling himself at the Consul time and time again.

One would never have thought that someone so intelligent, just, and in every way cold, could have such a destructive effect on anyone.

This was the case, however. Rotta had reached such a point of inner dissolution, that a superior of this kind was bound to bring about his abrupt ruin. With his calm and almost inhuman objectivity, the Lieutenant-Colonel acted like poison on the poisoned mind of his interpreter. Had Rotta acquired a soft and lenient superior, like von Mitterer, or a hasty, moody man, subject to human passions, even the basest, he would somehow still have survived. In the first instance, he would have lived from this leniency and in the second his dark, twisted impulses would have found a springboard in conflict with similar impulses, and in that constant and friction he would have maintained some kind of balance. But Rotta flung himself against this superior like a demented man against a wall of ice or an illusory beam of light.

For Rotta, von Paulich's mere ideas, his manner and his behaviour meant a painful change for the worse. To start with, the new consul needed Rotta far less than von Mitterer for whom he had long since become indispensable. For von Mitterer, Rotta had been a kind of shelter during the most difficult and roughest conflicts in his work, a kind of glove for the most objectionable tasks. And then, the interpreter had become in many ways, and in recent years increasingly, a kind of "éminence grise". During domestic crises or conflicts in his work, von Mitterer would be beset by a temporary paralysis of the will, brought on by exhaustion and his weak liver. Whenever this occurred Rotta would be there to support him, to take "the matter" into his own hands and that in itself gave the incapacitated man a sense of relief and grateful loyalty. And Rotta would resolve "the matter" easily, for it was not actually difficult, it was just that to von Mitterer, at that moment and in that state of mind, it had appeared insoluble.

All of this, of course, was quite out of the question with his new superior. For von Paulich all his work was straight and regular as a chess-board on which he played with the calm composure of a player who thinks for a long time, but knows neither trepidation before a move nor regret afterwards, and who needs no one to advise, defend or support him.

Apart from that, von Paulich's way of working deprived the interpreter of the last satisfaction which had remained to him in his failed, arid life. For Rotta the possibility of behaving wilfully and insolently towards clients and subordinates, towards all who could do nothing to him or who depended on him, was his last, his only – admittedly wretched – pleasure in his state of inner ruin. It was a pathetic illusion of strength and a visible sign of status, for which he had given his soul, his energy and his youth in vain.

After some such scene in which, legs apart and red in the face, he would have shouted abuse at someone who dared not or did not know how to answer back, the interpreter would feel – just for a moment, but it was a wonderful moment – a profound gratification and boundless joy. He had broken something, crushed and destroyed someone, and was now standing over his silenced adversary who was sinking through the floor, while he himself was borne high above earthly creatures by his great joy, but not too high for everyone to see, and be able to measure and sense his height. But the Lieutenant-Colonel did not even allow him that brief instant of illusory joy.

His very presence rendered such behaviour impossible. Under the gaze of his cold, dark-blue eyes no illusion of any kind could be sustained. All self-deception was shattered, to fall back into the nothingness where it had originated.

In the very first weeks, on the first such occasion, von Paulich had told Rotta that there were ways of telling people things calmly and achieving what you wanted by treating them decently. Besides, he did not wish anyone from the Consulate to speak to anyone in such a manner, either in the building or in the town. The interpreter had tried then for the first and last time to influence the new Consul, to impose his attitude on him. But this proved impossible. Rotta, for whom the quick, insolent retort had become second nature, felt paralysed in the presence of this man. The corners of his lips trembled, and, with his head thrown back, his eyelids lowered still further, he clicked his heels, said curtly: "It will be as you command, Herr Oberstleutnant," and went out.

Whether because he forgot himself, or because he wanted to test the strength of his new superior's perseverance, Rotta made two further attempts to give himself airs and shout at his subordinates, despite this explicit order. The second time this happened, the Lieutenant-Colonel summoned the interpreter and told him that if it happened once more, even in the mildest form, he could expect the immediate application of the paragraph of the Regulations relating to such repeated cases of serious insubordination. On that occasion Rotta saw the Lieutenant-Colonel's blue eyes suddenly narrow and acquire in their outer corners two sharp, irate sparks which completely altered both his look and the whole expression of his face. From that moment, the interpreter withdrew, frightened, into himself and there began to nurture his hatred of his superior, imperceptibly and secretly, but with all the violent fury with which he had earlier treated his victims.

Von Paulich, who observed Rotta's case as coldly and simply as everything else in the world, saw to it that he used him as little as possible. He sent him as a courier to Brod and Kostajnica, and even expected that von Mitterer would get a new posting in which he would be able to use Rotta and that he would send for him. But he did not wish to undertake anything to remove him from Travnik. Surprisingly, Rotta himself did not consider being released from a position in which, he could see for himself, there was nothing good in store for him. Instead, he circled, as though bewitched, around his brilliant, cold employer, colliding with him constantly and with increasing vehemence, although more in his mind than in reality.

D'Avenat, who knew or at least guessed at everything that was happening in Travnik, quickly realized what Rotta's position was like at the Consulate and immediately conceived the idea that with time it would be possible to extract from it some benefit for French interests. On one occasion, in one of those idiosyncratic conversations the two interpreters used to hold, when they met somewhere in the bazaar or on the way to the Residence, d'Avenat told Rotta as a joke that he would always be able to find shelter in the French Consulate, should he ever need it. Rotta answered his joke with a joke.

After the first conflicts, there was a dull truce between von Paulich and his interpreter which lasted a whole year. Had the Lieutenant-Colonel harassed his interpreter with work and made excessive demands on him, had he shown him hatred or ill-humour, perhaps Rotta would have endured this situation and found the patience to put up with his new superior and hold out to the end. But von Paulich's cold bearing and the way in which he simply passed Rotta's person over were bound sooner or later to lead to a rift.

In the spring of 1812, things erupted at the Austrian Consulate. The little hunchbacked interpreter was unable to live so entirely ignored, confined to his basic duties, with all his wilful impulses and established habits stamped out. He lost control, attacking the servants and junior clerks in the Consulate. As he quarrelled with them, he sent unambiguous threats to his superior which brought him some relief. In the end he clashed with von Paulich himself. And when the Lieutenant-Colonel coldly announced that he would apply the Regulations and despatch the insubordinate interpreter to Brod, Rotta found the strength, for the first time, to confront him, openly and brazenly, declaring loudly that the Consul had no such power and that he, Rotta, would perhaps be despatching the Consul a little further than Travnik. Von Paulich ordered that Rotta's things be thrown out of the house and that he should be barred from entering the Consulate. At the same time he informed the Kaymakam that Niccolo Rotta was no longer in the service of the Austrian General Consulate, that he did not enjoy the protection of the Emperor and that his continued stay in Travnik was undesirable.

Rotta immediately turned to d'Avenat and through him sought the protection of the French Consulate.

There had not been a greater uproar and scandal since the arrival of the Consuls. Not even Mario Cologna's strange conversion and obscure death had aroused such unrest and so much gossip. For that incident had occurred as the integral part of a general riot, while these were peaceful times. Besides, the "Illyrian doctor" had died, falling forever silent, while Rotta was more alive and more vociferous than ever.

Rotta's desertion of his Consul was generally regarded as a great coup for d'Avenat. D'Avenat denied this, playing the restrained and rational victor. In fact, he endeavoured to exploit Rotta's position to the best possible advantage, but cautiously and without haste.

As on so many other occasions, Daville felt torn and uneasy about all that had happened. He could not, dared not disregard all the benefit to French interests which could follow from Rotta's desertion. For, driven by circumstances and borne along by his nature, the hunchbacked interpreter was sliding more and more towards complete and open treachery. Little by little he was revealing everything he knew about the work and intentions of his superiors. But, on the other hand, Daville was painfully offended that he had to use his standing to shield the conspiracy of the two interpreters, unscrupulous, base Levantines, against so honourable and intelligent a gentleman as von Paulich. For himself, he would have most liked the whole thing to subside as quickly as possible, once d'Avenat had extracted maximum benefit from it. But that was not what the two interpreters wanted, especially Rotta himself. In his battle with von Paulich he had now found a worthy aim for all his hidden passions and desires. He despatched long letters not only to the Consul but also to the Commander at Brod and the Ministry in Vienna, informing them about his case, naturally not mentioning the fact that he was in contact with the French Consulate. He went with the khavaz who served at the French Consulate up to the Austrian Consulate, asking for more of his things, provoking noisy public scenes, inventing new demands, running breathlessly through the town, calling on the Residence and the Kaymakam. In short, he revelled in his scandal like a mad, shameless woman.

While he did not lose his composure, von Paulich nevertheless made a mistake by officially requesting the Kaymakam to arrest Rotta for common theft of government files. This obliged Daville to send the Kaymakam a letter informing him that Rotta had placed himself under French protection and that consequently he could not be arrested or prosecuted. He sent a copy of this letter to von Paulich, telling him that he regretted the whole incident, but that he could not act otherwise, for Rotta, who did perhaps have an awkward temperament, but was otherwise a righteous man, had placed himself under the protection of the French Consulate and this could not be denied him.

Von Paulich replied curtly, protesting against the action of the French Consulate in taking under its protection paid informers, embezzlers and traitors. He asked Daville in future to indicate on any letter he sent him that it contained no reference to Rotta. Otherwise he would return all his letters unopened, as long as this ugly quarrel over Rotta went on.

This offended Daville and saddened him. The whole business with Rotta was becoming increasingly unpleasant.

The bad-tempered old Kaymakam, finding himself caught up in this quarrel between the two Consuls, one of whom was resolutely seeking Rotta's arrest and the other resolutely resisting it, was confused and equally exasperated with both of them, and especially with Rotta.

Several times a day he would mutter to himself, puffing through his nose: "The dogs are at each other's throats, right in my own yard."

Through one of his men he sent word to both Consuls that he would rather hand in his resignation than allow the two of them – while their Emperors were at peace – to carry on a feud in Travnik and to bring him into it, when he was already over-worked as it was. He had no desire to displease either of the Consuls for any reason, least of all because of this petulant little man who was nothing but a common hireling and errand-boy and as such should on no account be a topic of conversation between statesmen and administrators. And he sharply ordered Rotta himself to stop if he wanted to preserve what was left of his skin, because for weeks now he had been causing upset among the leading men of this town where there had hitherto reigned the peace of a place of worship, and he would never be worth that even if he had a head made of gold and the brains of a Vizier. If he wanted to live in Travnik calmly and decently, all right. But if he went on disturbing the town by running between the two Consulates, provoking scandal and dragging both the Turks and the rayah into it, then he would have to choose one of the two roads which led out of Travnik, immediately, without delay.

And Rotta really was filling the town with his dispute and dragging whoever he could into it. He rented the upper floor in the house of a certain Pero Kalajdžić, an unmarried man with a bad name. He brought gypsy blacksmiths to put iron bars on the windows and special locks on all the doors. In addition to the two good English pistols he kept under his pillow, he acquired a long musket, gunpowder and ammunition. He prepared his food himself, for fear of being poisoned, and he himself cleaned his flat, dreading robbery. The cold neglect that characterizes the dwellings of bachelors and eccentrics began to gain ground in Rotta's rooms. Rags and litter, ash and dust began to pile up. And with time this house, which was in any case unsightly, became increasingly dilapidated even on the outside.

Rotta himself changed rapidly, fading and declining. He neglected his hygiene, became disorderly in his dress. His shirts were limp, crumpled, worn for too long, his black cravat was spattered with food, his shoes scuffed and dirty. His completely white hair was tinged a greenish yellow, his nails were black, he stopped shaving regularly, he reeked of cooking and drink. And his whole bearing was no longer that of the old Rotta. He no longer walked with his head held high, stepping out and looking down, but he bustled about the town in little, busy steps, whispering confidentially to those people who were still prepared to talk to him, or abusing the Austrian Consulate in the khan, loudly and provocatively, buying glasses of brandy for those who listened and beginning to drink increasingly himself. With each day the thin veneer of his former dignity, false power and breeding was falling from him.

So Niccolo Rotta lived in Travnik, thinking that he was waging a great battle against great adversaries. Completely blinded by his morbid hatred, he did not even notice that he was rapidly changing, that he was falling, and, as he fell, going rapidly back over the whole of his long and painful rise. He did not even feel innumerable trivial circumstances coming together and carrying him, like a strong, imperceptible current, back into the life he had abandoned as a child in that poor quarter of San Giusto in Trieste. Carrying him straight back into the ugly world of poverty and vice he had been running away from with all his strength for thirty years, believing that he really had escaped.

23

Daville was secretly annoyed by his little superstitions, but he kept catching himself thinking of them. One of these was the idea that the summer months in Travnik brought bad luck and invariably unpleasant surprises. He told himself this was perfectly natural. It was in summer that all wars and uprisings began. Summer days were longer, people had more time and consequently more opportunity for the foolishness and wickedness which were their profound inner need. But after he had explained this to himself, he would catch himself just a few minutes later in the same thought: that the summer brought unpleasantness and the summer months ("those with no 'r' in them") were in every way more dangerous than the others.

This summer began with bad omens.

One day in May which had started well, with two hours' work on the verses of his Alexandriad, Daville was sitting with young Frayssinet. He had come to report to the consul in person on the difficult position of the "French khan" in Sarajevo, and all the troubles of French transit traffic through Bosnia.

The young man was sitting on the veranda among the flowers, talking in his lively, rapid Southern manner.

This was his second year in Sarajevo. During that time he had only come to Travnik on one other occasion, but he was in constant communication with the Consul General by letter. Increasing space in this correspondence was taken up with complaints about people and conditions in Sarajevo. The young man was utterly disillusioned and discouraged. He had grown haggard, his hair was thinning on top, his face had acquired an unhealthy colour. Daville noticed that his hands shook and there was a bitterness in his tone. That calm clarity with which he had planned and organized everything on his first visit, the summer before last, on this same veranda, had completely gone. (The East, thought Daville, with that unconsciously malicious human satisfaction with which we discover and observe in others traces of the sickness that torments ourselves, the East had penetrated into the blood of this young man, undermining, upsetting and souring him.)

The young man really was bitter and thoroughly discouraged. That irritable dissatisfaction with everyone and everything, which overwhelms people from the West who come to these parts on business, had evidently filled him entirely and he did not have the energy either to control it or to keep it to himself.

His proposals were radical. Everything must be liquidated, the sooner the better, and new routes must be found, through other regions where it was possible to live and work with the people.

It was clear to Daville that the young man was infected with "Oriental poison", and that he was in that phase of the illness in which, as in a fever, one could neither see reality nor judge correctly, but his every nerve, his every thought was in constant conflict with his surroundings. He was so familiar with this state of mind that in front of this young man he was able to play the role of an older, healthy man, comforting and soothing him. But the young man defended himself from every consolation, as from a personal insult.

"No," he said sourly, "in Paris they have no idea what it's like to live and work here, no one can know that. It's only by working with these people and living among them that one can perceive the degree to which these Bosnians are unreliable, arrogant, crude and deceitful. Only we can know that."

Daville seemed to be hearing his very own words which he had expressed and recorded so often. He listened to them carefully, not taking his eyes from the young man who was shaking with stifled anger and profound revulsion. ("So that's what I looked like in the eyes of Des Fossés and all those to whom I so often said these same things, in the same tone and manner," thought Daville to himself.) But at the same time, out loud, he soothed the troubled young man.

"Yes, conditions are difficult, we all know that from personal experience, but we must be patient. French reason must in the end prevail over their hastiness and arrogance. We must just…"

"We must get away from here, Monsieur le Consul Général, and as soon as possible. For, pride and reason and the energy we invest here are all lost, and nothing is gained. That is certain, at least in the work which brought me here."

"The same illness, the same symptoms," thought Daville and continued to soothe him, assuring him that they must be patient and wait, the business could not simply be abandoned. Sarajevo played an important role, unrewarding but important, in the great Imperial plan of the continental system and organization of the European economic whole. To abandon the design at any point could call the whole conception into question and damage the Emperor's plans.

"That is our bitter lot and we must accept it, however hard we find it. Even if we do not see the sense and purpose of the plan we are helping to realize, that does not mean that it will not bear fruit, if only everyone holds out in his place and does not give up. And we must constantly bear in mind that Providence has given us the greatest ruler of all time, who directs everything, including our destinies, and that we can rely blindly on his leadership. It is not by chance that the fate of the world is in his hands. His genius and his lucky star are leading everything to a satisfactory outcome. If we trust in that, we can carry out our duties with confidence despite the greatest difficulties."

As he spoke, Daville listened carefully to his calm words, hearing in some surprise the explanations he was never able to find in his daily hesitations and doubts. And he was becoming increasingly eloquent and convincing. Daville was experiencing what happens to ageing nursemaids as they lull children to sleep, telling them lengthy stories until in the end they make themselves drowsy and fall asleep beside their wakeful charges. At the end of the conversation he was satisfied and convinced, while the young man, whose life was blighted by the Sarajevo merchants and carriers, simply shook his head slowly and looked at him, with bitterly compressed lips, his face trembling, showing signs of bad digestion and bile.

At that moment d'Avenat arrived, apologizing for interrupting the conversation, and informed the Consul quietly that a messenger had arrived from Istanbul the night before bringing news of plague in Ibrahim Pasha's harem. The pestilence which had been raging through Istanbul in recent weeks had crept into the Vizier's house on the Bosphorus as well. In a short time some fifteen people had died, mostly servants, but including also the Vizier's eldest daughter and a twelve-year-old son. All the others had fled into the mountains in the interior of the country.

As he listened to this grave news, Daville felt he could see clearly the tall figure of the Vizier, comically overdressed, always bent a little to the right or left, trembling under these new blows.

On d'Avenat's advice, and in accordance with the good Oriental custom, they decided not to ask the Vizier for an audience at once, but to let a few days pass and with them the first and most painful effects of the disaster.

When he again took up his conversation with Frayssinet, Daville felt even wiser and more patient, steeled by another's misfortune. He promised the young man faithfully that he would visit Sarajevo himself the following month to see with the local authorities, on the spot, what could be done towards improving conditions for French trade.

*

Three days later, the Vizier received Daville on the upper floor, in the Summer Divan.

Coming out of the glaring summer day, the Consul stepped straight into the silent, shady ground floor of the Residence and shivered as at the entrance to a catacomb. On the upper floor there was somewhat more light, but here too, compared with the heat and glare outside, there was an abundance of cool shadow. One window was open, and luxuriant vine leaves were bursting through it into the room.

The Vizier was sitting in his usual place, without any visible sign of change. He was wearing his full formal dress, and was bent to one side like an ancient monument. Seeing him like this, Daville himself made an effort to appear ordinary and unchanged. He just thought frantically of what he should say about the disaster that had occurred, so that his words should be warm and discreet, without mentioning specifically those who had died, particularly not the women, but showing his understanding and condolence.

The Vizier's moral rigidity, which exactly suited his physical immobility, made things easier for Daville. After he had listened to Daville's words in d'Avenat's translation, motionless and without any change in his face, he turned immediately to the fate and activities of the living, not wasting words on the dead.

"Well, the plague has come to Istanbul, and to parts of it where no one can remember it having been before," said the Vizier in a ponderous voice, as though speaking through lips of stone. "It had to come, because of our sins. It must be that I am myself sinful, since it came to my house as well."

Here the Vizier fell silent, and Daville quickly asked d'Avenat to observe, as a doctor, that this was the nature of the illness and that there were very many cases of persons of saintly innocence and their families suffering through the chance transmission of the germs of this dangerous infection.

The Vizier slowly turned his head and looked at d'Avenat for the first time, as though he had only just noticed him, with that blind gaze of eyes which looked without seeing, as though made of stone, and immediately turned back to the Consul.

"No, it is sin, sin is the cause of it all. The people in the capital have lost all reason and shame. They have all lost their heads and started chasing after pleasure and luxury. And no measures are being undertaken by the government. It all stems from the fact that there is no Sultan Selim any more. As long as he was alive and in power, sin was prosecuted in the capital, drunkenness, wickedness and idleness were stamped out. But now…"

The Vizier stopped again, suddenly, like a wound-down mechanism, and Daville again made an attempt at saying something consoling to alleviate his suffering, explaining that there must eventually be a balance between sin and punishment, and that then there would presumably also be an end to expiation.

"God is one. He knows the measure," the Vizier rejected any consolation.

Through the open window came the chirping of unseen birds which made the leaves hanging over into the room tremble. On the slope blocking the view, fields of ripe corn could be made out, divided up by green boundaries or hedges. In the silence which followed the Pasha's words, the sharp, raw neighing of a stallion suddenly reverberated from somewhere on the slope.

The audience was ended with the mention of Sultan Selim, who had perished as a saint and martyr. The Vizier was moved, although this was not at all apparent from his voice or his face.

"May God grant you every joy in your children," he said to Daville as he took his leave.

Daville quickly replied that after sorrow joy would once again light up the Vizier's life too.

"As far as I am concerned, I have lost so much in my life, that what

I would most like now would be to work in my garden, dressed in rough homespun cloth, far from the world and events. God is one!"

The Vizier spoke these words like a prepared phrase, long since thought out, like a picture which was very much present in his thoughts and which had for him some special, profound significance which others could not understand.

That summer of 1812, which had begun badly, continued badly as well.

During the last war against the Fifth Coalition in the autumn of 1810, things had been in many ways easier for Daville. The struggle with von Mitterer, co-operation with Marmont and the town commanders on the Austrian frontier were difficult and tiring, as we have seen, but at least they had filled his time and focused his thoughts on real worries and tangible aims. Then, the whole campaign had progressed well, from victory to victory, and, most importantly, it had gone quickly. The early autumn had already brought the Treaty of Vienna and at least a temporary truce. Now, however, everything was remote and altogether incomprehensible, frightening in its obscurity and its gigantic proportions.

All his thoughts and his whole existence depended on the movements of an army somewhere on the plains of Russia, but he knew nothing about that army, its direction, resources or prospects. He could only keep speculating, expecting anything – even the worst – as he walked along the steep paths of the garden round the Consulate. This was how Daville lived in these summer and autumn months. And there was nothing that could have made the waiting easier for him and no one who could help him!

Couriers now passed through Travnik more frequently, but they did not bring much information about the war. Bulletins referring to the strange names of completely unknown towns – Kovno, Vilna, Vitebsk, Smolensk – could not remove the uncertainty or dissipate the anxiety. And these couriers themselves, usually full of stories and all kinds of news, were now exhausted, bad-tempered and taciturn. They did not even bring lies or guesses that could have roused a person out of all kinds of forebodings.

Work on the transport of French cotton through Bosnia was already established and progressing well, or at least it seemed so when compared to the worries and fears provoked by the large undertaking that was now unfolding somewhere far away in the North. It is true that the carriers kept putting up their prices, people stole cotton along the way, and the Turkish customs officers were disorganized, and had an insatiable appetite for bribes. Frayssinet wrote despairing letters, his strength sapped by the ailment that attacks foreigners as a result of the food, people and conditions in this land. Daville followed all the familiar symptoms of this illness and sent him wise, measured, statesman-like answers, advising him to be patient in his service of the Empire.

But at the same time, he himself kept turning about, seeking desperately for any sign of humanity that would calm him a little and give him the courage to overcome his doubts and his hidden, but constant, fear. But there was nothing a man could grasp and cling to. As always in similar circumstances, as before in the case of the young commander from Novi, Daville felt around himself a living wall of faces and eyes, cold and dumb, as though by secret agreement, or cryptic, blank and deceitful. Who could he turn to, who could know the truth and who would want to tell it to him?

The Vizier responded always with the same brief questions: "Where is your Emperor now?"

Daville would answer, quoting the place mentioned in the last bulletin, and the Vizier simply waved his hand briefly and whispered: "God grant he reach St Petersburg soon!"

At that he would glance at Daville with a look which chilled the pit of the Consul's stomach and troubled his heart still more.

The behaviour of the Austrian Consul too could only make Daville even more uneasy.

Immediately after the French army had set off against Russia, when the news came through that the Vienna government was this time on the side of Napoleon and that it was participating in the campaign with forces of more than 30,000 men, under Prince Schwarzenberg, Daville had called on von Paulich, in the desire to initiate a conversation with him about the prospects of the great war in which their courts were this time fortunately on the same side. He met with silent, icy courtesy. The Lieutenant-Colonel was more distant and alien than ever, he behaved as though he knew nothing about either the war or their alliance and left Daville to think about it alone, to rejoice in the successes and shudder at the failures. And when Daville tried to drag at least one word of agreement or disapproval out of him, he lowered his fine, blue eyes to the ground and these eyes without expression were suddenly dangerous.

After every visit to von Paulich, Daville returned home still more disheartened. In every way, the Austrian Consul was evidently endeavouring to give the Vizier and the local people the impression that in spirit he was not taking the least part in this war and that the whole enterprise was an exclusively French affair. This was confirmed also by d'Avenat's observations.

When Daville arrived home, smarting under such impressions, he would find his wife completely absorbed in preparing provisions for the winter. With the experience of previous years to guide her, she now knew exactly which vegetables kept best and longest, which kinds of local fruit were most suitable for preserving, and what were the effects of damp, cold and climatic changes. So her pickles and preserves became better, perfected from year to year, meals became more plentiful and various, and waste and loss ever less. The servants worked according to her instructions and under her gaze, and every so often she would take up the work herself.

Daville well knew (and from long experience) that it was no good interrupting her in her work, because she did not have, and could never have, any inclination for abstract discussions about the anxieties and fears which never left him. Even the least domestic worry about the children, the house or about him, was for her a far more important and worthy topic of conversation than the most complex "inner states" and moods about which he thought constantly and about which he would have so much liked to have someone to talk to. He well knew that this woman (otherwise his one, unfailing friend) was always, as now, completely dedicated to the present moment and the work before her, as though nothing else in the world existed, and as though everyone, from Napoleon to the Consul's wife in Travnik, were engaged in preparing what was needed for the winter with just as much dedication, each in his own way. For her it was clear that God's will was being carried out at every moment, everywhere and in everything. And what more was there to be said?

And again, Daville would settle into his large chair, covering his eyes with his hand and, after an inaudible sigh ("Ah, dear God, dear God!"), he would take his Delille, opening it at random, in the middle of a canto. In fact, he was looking for what cannot be found either in life or in books: a compassionate, kind-hearted friend, willing to listen to everything and able to understand everything, with whom he would converse openly and who would answer all his questions clearly and honestly. In such a conversation, as in a mirror, he would be able to see for the first time his true image, to realize the real value of his work and determine his position in the world unambiguously. There he would finally be able to recognize exactly to what extent his scruples, apprehensions and anxieties were well-founded and real, and to what extent imaginary. And in this doleful valley, where the sixth year of his solitude was now flowing by, that would have come as real salvation.

But such a friend did not come. He never does. Instead, there came only strange, unwanted guests.

In the first years too, it had sometimes happened that some French traveller or foreigner with a French passport would turn up, to stay a while in Travnik, asking favours or offering his services. But recently they had become more frequent.

Travellers would appear, dubious merchants, adventurers, tricksters who had tricked themselves and turned off the road into this impassable, destitute land. They were all passing through or running away, heading for Istanbul, Malta, Palermo, and they would see their stay in Travnik as a punishment. For Daville each of these unwanted guests meant a whole series of worries and upsets. He had got out of the habit of communicating with his fellow-countrymen and people from the West altogether. And like all easily excited people who are unsure of themselves, he found it hard to distinguish truth from falsehood and vacillated constantly between unfounded suspicion and excessive trust. Alarmed by the circulars from the Ministry which kept reminding the consuls to pay the utmost attention to the presence of English agents, who were unusually cunning and skilfully disguised, Daville saw each of these travellers as an English spy and would take a whole series of useless measures to demask them or protect himself. In fact, these travellers were for the most part people who had been shaken out of their routine, themselves unhappy and lost, their lives disrupted, shipwrecked fugitives from the tempestuous Europe which Napoleon's conquests and policies were ploughing up in all directions. It was through them that Daville was able sometimes to glimpse what the "General" had made of the world in the last four or five years.

Daville hated them also because their presence, their panic-stricken desire to get out as fast as possible, their irritation at the disorderliness, bungling, and off-hand manner of the locals, their despairing helplessness in their struggle with the country, people and circumstances, made him conscious of just where he had ended up and in what sort of land the best years of his life were passing.

Each one of these unwanted guests was a trial and an inconvenience for Daville. He felt they were breathing down his neck, embarrassing him in front of the whole of Travnik; and he endeavoured in every way, with money, concessions, persuasion, to get them out of Bosnia as quickly as possible, so as not to have to look at the embodiment of his own fate, or at least so as not to have witnesses to his failure.

There had been incidental travellers like these earlier too, but never as many as this year when the campaign against Russia began, and never as eccentric, suspect and iniquitous as these. Fortunately, d'Avenat never lost his sense of reality – not even in these circumstances – his coldly insolent composure and his disregard for everything and everyone resolved even the most complex situations.

One wet May afternoon, some travellers arrived in front of the main khan. At once innumerable children and the bazaar layabouts gathered round them. Three figures in European clothes emerged from their blankets and scarves. A small, brisk man. A tall, strong woman, wearing rouge and white face-powder, with dyed hair, like an actress. And a little girl of about twelve. They were all exhausted by the difficult journey and long ride, hungry, irritated with each other and everything around them. They argued ceaselessly with the carriers and the inn-keeper. The small man with yellow skin and black hair moved about with the alacrity of a man from the South, shouting, giving orders, yelling at his wife and child. At last their boxes were unloaded and piled in front of the khan. The restless man lifted up his plump daughter, holding her under both arms and placed her on the topmost trunk, commanding her to sit there without stirring.

Then he set off to look for the French Consulate.

He came back with d'Avenat who scrutinized him disdainfully, while the little man explained that his name was Lorenzo Gambini, that he came from Palermo, that he had lived until now in Romania as a merchant and that he was returning to Italy, for he could no longer endure life in the Levant. He had been cheated and robbed, his health ruined. He needed a visa to get back to Milan. He had been told that he could obtain one here in Travnik. He had an outdated passport from the Cisalpine Republic. He wanted to leave immediately, immediately, for he was going mad, he said, with every day he had to spend among these people and he would not be able to answer for himself or his actions if he had to stay here any longer.

Without listening to the traveller's gabbling, d'Avenat intervened on their behalf with the inn-keeper, asking him to find rooms and prepare food.

The woman joined in the conversation as well, with the tearful, weary voice of an actress who realizes she is ageing and cannot for a moment forget the fact or reconcile herself to it. From the top of the trunks the little girl was shouting that she was hungry. They were all talking at once. They wanted to find rooms, to eat, to rest, to get their visa, to leave Travnik and get out of Bosnia as soon as possible. But nevertheless, it seemed as though what they most wanted was to talk and quarrel. No one was listening to anyone else or following what they were saying.

Forgetting the inn-keeper and turning his back on d'Avenat, the tiny Italian shouted at his wife who was twice his height: "Don't you butt in. Just don't you speak to me. Damn the day you first spoke and I first heard you. This is all your doing."

"Mine? Mine? Ah!" shrieked the woman, turning to the sky and all present as her witness, "ah, my youth, my talent, I gave him everything, everything! Ah! And now: it's all my fault!"

"Your fault, my precious, yes, yours, damn your eyes! . . . You're the one who's made me suffer and waste my life, and you're the reason I'm going to kill myself, right here."

And with a habitual movement, the little man took a large pistol from his outsize travelling cloak and put it to his forehead. The woman screamed, rushed up to the man who had not even dreamed of pulling the trigger, and began hugging him and murmuring tenderly to him.

The plump girl was sitting high up on the boxes, calmly munching a yellow Albanian cake someone had given her. D'Avenat was scratching behind his ear. The little man had already forgotten about both his wife and his threat of suicide. He explained with passion to d'Avenat that he must have the visa by the following morning, waved some sort of crumpled passport that was falling apart and scolded the girl for climbing onto the boxes and not helping her mother.

Having arranged things with the inn-keeper and promised to give the traveller an answer early the next morning, d'Avenat set off for the Consulate without looking at the strange family or making any further response to the Italian's passionate pleas and assurances.

A crowd of inquisitive people remained in front of the khan, looking in bewildered amazement at the foreigners, their clothes and unusual behaviour, as though it were a theatre or circus. The Turks in their shop-fronts and people going about their business glanced at them with a scowl, out of the corner of their eye, and immediately turned their heads away.

D'Avenat had only just got back and managed to tell the Consul what extraordinary visitors they had and shown him Gambini's passport of fantastic origin, full of visas and recommendations, stitched and restitched and with bits added, when there was a banging and shouting at the gate. Lorenzo Gambini had come in person to ask to be allowed to talk to the Consul in private. The khavaz was driving him away from the gate. The bazaar children had followed him at a distance, for they felt that wherever this foreigner went there must be trouble, noise and excitement. D'Avenat went out and shouted something sharply to the fussing man, who assured him that he had done French interests good service, that he would have things to say in both Milan and Paris. In the end he gave in and went back to the khan, proclaiming that he would kill himself on the threshold of the Consulate if he did not get his passport by the following day.

Daville was alarmed, disgusted and annoyed. He instructed d'Avenat to complete the business as quickly as possible, so that the bazaar people should not witness such scenes and so as to avoid any even worse ones. D'Avenat, completely insensitive to such considerations and accustomed to seeing quarrels as a regular phenomenon accompanying every transaction in the East, soothed the Consul in a dry and matter of fact way:

"He's never going to kill himself. And when he sees that we aren't going to give him anything, he'll go off the way he came."

And that was what actually happened. Two days later the whole family left Travnik, after a noisy argument between d'Avenat and Lorenzo in which the Italian threatened at one minute that he would kill himself on the spot, and the next that he would take his complaints about the French Consul in Travnik directly to Napoleon, while his tall wife flashed at d'Avenat the dangerous glances of a former beauty.

Daville, constantly worried about the reputation of his country and the Consulate, sighed with relief. But three weeks later another unwelcome guest materialized in Travnik.

A Turk had taken a room at the main khan. He was strikingly well dressed. He was on his way from Istanbul and immediately sought out d'Avenat. He called himself Ismail Raif, but he was actually an Alsatian Jew named Mendelsheim who had converted to Islam. He too wanted to talk to the Consul in person and maintained that he had important information for the French Government. He boasted that he had extensive connections in Turkey, France and Germany, that he was a member of the first Freemasons' lodge in France and that he knew many of Napoleon's enemies' plans. He was athletically built and strong, red-haired and ruddy-faced. He behaved arrogantly and talked a lot. His eyes had a drunken gleam. D'Avenat got rid of him by using a trick he often employed. In a serious tone he advised him to continue his journey immediately, without wasting a moment and to convey all he had to say to the military commander in Split, for he was the only person competent to deal with these matters. The Jew protested, complaining that French consuls never had any understanding of such things, while the English or Austrian consul would have grasped them with both hands and paid for them in pure gold. But nevertheless he set off a few days later.

The day after his departure d'Avenat discovered that, before he left, he had gone to von Paulich and offered him his services against Napoleon. D'Avenat immediately informed the commander in Split about this.

No more than ten days had passed when Daville received a lengthy letter from Bugojno. That same Ismail Raif was writing to inform him that he had stopped in Bugojno and entered the service of Mustapha Pasha Suleimanpašić. He was writing on Mustapha Pasha's instructions to ask in his name that he be sent at least two bottles of cognac, calvados, or any other French drink, "as long as it was strong".

Mustapha Pasha was the eldest son of Suleiman Pasha Skopljak, a spoiled and worthless young swell, inclined to many vices, but particularly to alcohol, not in the least like his father, a cunning and deceitful, but courageous, upright and hard-working man. The young Pasha lived an empty, extravagant life, harassing the peasant women, drinking with idlers and riding horses over the plain of Kupres. Old Suleiman Pasha, stern and skilful in handling others, was indulgent with this son, always finding excuses for his idleness and infamous exploits.

D'Avenat immediately understood the connection between these two men. With the Consul's approval, he replied directly to the young Pasha that he would send the drink on another occasion, but advising him not to place any confidence in this Ismail who was an adventurer and in all probability an Austrian spy.

Ismail Raif replied with a long letter in which he defended and justified himself, insisting that he was no one's spy, but a good Frenchman and citizen of the world, an unhappy man, a wanderer. The letter, inspired by Kupres brandy, ended with some obscure verses in which he bewailed his own fate:

O, ma vie! O vain songe! O rapide existence!
Qu'amusent les désirs, qu'abuse l'espérance.
Tel est donc des humains l'inévitable sort!
Des projets, des erreurs, la douleur et la mort![20]

Ismail wrote in the same vein several more times, justifying and explaining himself in alcoholic prose adorned with verses and signing with his former name and ostensibly masonic rank Cerf Mendelsheim, Chev˙*˙ d'or*˙*, until he too was swept out of Bosnia by drink, events and his wandering spirit.

As though they had arranged to change places, no sooner had the Jew ceased to write than another French traveller arrived. This was a certain Pépin, a meticulously dressed little man, perfumed and powdered, with a thin voice and lively movements. He explained to d'Avenat that he was on his way from Warsaw, where he ran a dancing school, that he had stopped here because he had been robbed on the way, that he was returning to Istanbul where he had once lived and where he had some creditors. (How he had strayed

---

20 "Oh, my life! Oh vain dream! Oh brief existence!/Which desires amuse, which hope abuses./Such then is the inevitable fate of humans!/Plans, mistakes, pain and death!"

into Travnik, which was not conceivably on the road from Warsaw to Istanbul, he never explained.)

This little man was as brazen as a whore. Running out in front of Daville's horse and stopping him as he was riding through the bazaar, he asked the consul ceremoniously to receive him. So as not to provoke a public scandal, Daville concurred. But once home, trembling with indignation, he immediately sought out d'Avenat and begged him to rid him of this importunate man.

The Consul, used to seeing English spies even in his dreams, insisted that this man had an English accent. D'Avenat, always unshakeably calm, without any imagination and without the capacity to see what was not there or to glamorize what he did see, was already quite clear about this traveller.

"Please watch that man carefully," said the Consul in some agitation to d'Avenat. "Get rid of him for me, please, because he is a spy, evidently sent to compromise the Consulate or for some similar purpose. He is an agent provocateur…"

"No he's not," answered d'Avenat drily.

"How do you mean, he's not?"

"He's a homosexual."

"A what?"

"A homosexual, Monsieur le Consul Général."

Daville clasped his head.

"Oh, o-o-o-oh whatever will this Consulate have to cope with next. So, that's it, you say? O-o-oh!"

D'Avenat soothed his superior and rid Travnik of Monsieur Pépin the very next day. Without saying anything to anyone, he had driven this "deviant" into a corner of his room, grasped him by his faultless jabot, shaken him soundly and threatened that he would be beaten in the centre of the bazaar the next day and thrown into the fortress by the Turkish authorities if he did not continue his journey immediately. The dancing-master obeyed.

Daville was glad to be rid of that vagrant, but he was already secretly trembling, wondering what other social riff-raff and outcasts would be swept by the obscure, foolish game of chance into this valley where it was already hard enough to live without them.

And this sixth autumn of Daville's in Travnik was ripening and moving rapidly towards its climax, like a play.

Towards the end of September, news came of the capture but also of the burning of Moscow. No one came to congratulate Daville. With shameless calm, von Paulich continued to maintain that he had no information about the war and avoided all discussion of it. D'Avenat discovered that his men all took the same line in conversation with the local people, behaving as though they knew nothing whatever of the fact that the Austrian Empire was at war with Russia.

Daville deliberately visited the Residence more frequently and met people in the town, but, as though by agreement, they all avoided talking about the campaign against Russia, hiding behind general, meaningless phrases and non-committal kindnesses. At times Daville felt they were all looking at him with alarm and wonder, as at a sleepwalker crossing dangerous heights, and that they were all trying not to wake him with a careless word.

But nevertheless, the truth was coming slowly to light. On that rainy day, when the Vizier as usual asked Daville what news he had from Russia and when Daville informed him of the bulletin about the capture of Moscow, the Vizier was glad, although he had actually heard this news already, and he congratulated him, expressing the hope that Napoleon would advance as Cyrus, the righteous conqueror, once had.

"But why is your Emperor going north now, as winter sets in? That's dangerous. Dangerous. I would like to see him a little further south," said Ibrahim Pasha looking anxiously through the window, into the distance, as though he were looking out at dangerous Russia itself.

The Vizier said this in the same tone in which he had uttered his good wishes and the comparison with Cyrus, and d'Avenat translated it in the same way as he translated everything that was said to him, drily and simplifying it, but Daville felt a slight nausea. ("There, that's what I suspected, that's what all these people think, but no one will ever say," thought Daville, waiting tensely to hear the Vizier's next words.) But Ibrahim Pasha was silent. ("Even he won't say," thought Daville painfully.) And it was only after quite a long silence that the Vizier spoke again, but now about something else. He told Daville that Ghisari Chelebi Khan had once marched against Russia. He had crushed the enemy army several times as it retreated steadily further and further, to the north. Then winter had taken the victorious Khan by surprise. His hitherto triumphant army was confused and frightened, while the wild infidels, shaggy men accustomed to icy weather, began to attack from all sides. It was then that Ghisari Chelebi Khan spoke his famous words:

"When a man is abandoned by the sun of his homeland,
Who will illuminate the path of his return?"

(Daville was always irritated by this Turkish habit of quoting lines of verse in the middle of a conversation, as though they were something especially important and significant. He could never see the real point of the lines quoted or what their connection was with the subject under discussion, but he always felt that the Turks attributed to them an importance and significance which eluded him.)

The young Khan was furious with the astrologers he had brought with him for this express purpose, who had predicted a later onset of winter. So he ordered these wise men, who had shown themselves so ignorant, to be bound, and driven, barefoot and lightly dressed, in front of the first ranks of the army, so as to feel on their own bodies the consequences of their error. But, then it was seen that these lean scholars, shrivelled, sapless men, could, like lice, withstand the cold better than the soldiers. While they survived, the young full-blooded warriors' hearts burst in their breasts, like sound beech wood in the frost. You could not touch steel, they say, because it burned as though red hot and the skin of your hands stuck to it. That was the plight of Ghisari Chelebi Khan, who lost his magnificent army and only just escaped with his life.

The conversation ended with blessings and best wishes for the success of Napoleon's undertaking and the defeat of the Muscovites, who were known as bad neighbours who did not like peace and did not keep their word.

Of course the stories of Cyrus and Ghisari Chelebi Khan did not spring from the Vizier's head, but from Tahir Bey's. He had related them while they were talking in the Residence about the capture of Moscow and the further prospects for Napoleon's campaign against Russia. D'Avenat, who discovered everything, found that out too, and also the true opinion of the Residence about the French army's position in Russia.

Tahir Bey explained to the Vizier and the others that the French had already gone too far and that they would not be able to withdraw without great loss.

"And if Napoleon's soldiers stay where they are for a few more weeks," said the Secretary, "I can already see them as mounds, shrouded in Russian snow."

An informer repeated these words to d'Avenat exactly, and he passed them coldly on to Daville.

"In the end, all our fears come true." Daville said this to himself, out loud and quite calmly, when he woke up one winter morning.

It was an exceptionally cold December morning. He had woken abruptly, feeling his own hair on the crown of his head like someone else's cold hand. Opening his eyes, he uttered these words as though they were a message from somewhere.

He repeated these same words to himself a few days later, when d'Avenat came and informed him that people in the Residence were talking a lot about Napoleon's defeat in Russia and the total disintegration of the French army. The most recent Russian bulletin was being passed round the town, with all the details of the French defeat. Everything pointed to the suspicion that the Austrian Consulate had acquired and spread the Russian bulletins, indirectly of course. In any case, Tahir Bey had that last communiqué and he had shown it to the Vizier.

"Everything comes true…" Daville repeated to himself, as he listened to d'Avenat's words. Eventually he pulled himself together and instructed d'Avenat calmly to find some excuse to go to Tahir Bey and, in the course of conversation, to ask him for the Russian bulletin. At the same time he sent for his other interpreter, Rafo Atijas, and instructed him, as well as d'Avenat, to crush these negative rumours in the town and assure people of the invincibility of Napoleon's army despite the momentary difficulties, caused by the winter and the distance, and not by Russian victories.

D'Avenat succeeded in seeing Tahir Bey. He asked him for the Russian bulletin, but the Secretary did not want to give it to him.

"If I give it to you, you will have to show it to Monsieur Daville, and I don't want that. These words are too unfavourable for him and his country, and I respect him too much to want him to hear such news from me. Tell him that my good wishes are always with him."

D'Avenat repeated all this to Daville in his mercilessly accurate and tranquil way and went straight out. Daville was left alone with his thoughts and Tahir Bey's Eastern considerateness which made his flesh creep.

"Anyone the Ottomans treat with such care is either dead or the most unfortunate of men," Daville was thinking as he leant on the window-sill, looking out at the winter twilight.

In the narrow, dark-blue sky above Vilenica mountain a young moon had appeared unnoticed, sharp and cold, like a metal cipher.

No, this time the affair was not going to end as before, with triumphal communiqués and victorious peace treaties!

What had long been a hidden foreboding, now stood before him as a clear realization. In the icy, alien night, under the mean young moon, he was obliged to think what total collapse and definitive defeat would mean for him and his family. And he forced himself to think about this, although he felt it required more strength and more courage than he had that evening.

No, this time it had not ended, as always before, with a victorious bulletin or peace treaty that would bring France territories and the Imperial army new laurels. On the contrary, it had ended with retreat and disintegration. Silence had fallen over the whole world, in numb anticipation of certain, terrible collapse. At least that is how it seemed to Daville.

During those months, Daville was left entirely without news, virtually without any contact with the outside world to which all his thoughts and fears were directed and with which his fate was linked.

Travnik and the whole region was shackled by a vicious, long and unusually harsh winter, the worst of all the winters Daville had spent there.

People talked about a similar winter twenty-one years before, but, as is always the case, this one seemed even fiercer. As early as November, cold had begun to grip everything, to change the face of the earth and the appearance of the people. And then it had descended on this valley, unifying everything and settling in like a deathly wasteland without hope of change. It had emptied the barns and closed the roads. Birds fell dead out of the air, like ghostly fruit from invisible branches. Wild animals swarmed down the steep hillsides and appeared in the town, forgetting their fear of humans for fear of the cold. In the eyes of the poor and homeless you could glimpse a silent fear of death without defence. People froze on the roads in search of bread or warm shelter. The sick died, for there was no cure for cold. In the icy night one could hear boards in the roof of the Consulate cracking with the cold, and wolves howling on the mountains.

Fire was kept burning in the earthenware stoves all night, for Madame Daville was fearful for the children, thinking always of the little boy she had lost four years before.

On these nights, Daville and his wife would sit after dinner, she fighting sleep and fatigue from the day's chores, and he his insomnia and anxieties without end. She was drowsy, but he wanted to talk. She found all this talk about cold and poverty unpleasantly alien, for she spent her whole day fighting them, frail as she was, completely wrapped in shawls, but sprightly and always on the move. He, on the other hand, found in it his only respite, at least for a moment. She listened to him, although she had long been tormented by a desire for sleep. So she carried out her duty towards him, as she did towards everyone, always.

And Daville said whatever came into his head in connection with this disastrous winter, the general misery and his hidden fears.

He had seen and experienced, he said, many of the evils that afflict a man in his relationship with the elements, the elements which surround him as well as those which live in him or are born of human conflict. He had known hunger and every kind of shortage during the terror, twenty years before, in Paris. Then, violence and chaos were, it seemed, the only prospect for the whole people. Greasy, torn banknotes, thousands and thousands of francs were worth nothing, and for a scrap of bacon or a handful of flour, people would go to the remote quarters at night and bargain with dubious individuals, in dark cellars. Day and night people rushed to and fro, concerned only with maintaining life which was in any case not worth much and could be lost at any moment on someone's denunciation, through a mistake by the police or simply by the whim of chance.

He remembered fighting in Spain as well. For weeks and months he had worn one single shirt which became mouldy with sweat and dust, but he did not dare take it off and wash it for at the least touch it would tear into ribbons. Apart from his rifle, bayonet and a little gunpowder and shot, his one and only possession was a knapsack of untanned leather. Even that he had taken from a dead Aragon peasant who had set out for the love of God to kill the French intruders and Jacobins. There was never anything in this knapsack except, on exceptionally lucky days, a small piece of hard barley bread seized from an abandoned house. Then too there had been violent snowstorms which better clothes and stronger footwear could have done nothing to protect one from, which made one forget everything, and simply search for shelter.

He had known all of this in his life, but he had never yet experienced the strength and horror of cold, as a dumb, destructive force. He had had no inkling that there could be such a thing as this Eastern poverty and deprivation, this absolute paralysis which accompanied the endless, harsh winter, and which oppressed this whole hilly, destitute and unhappy land, like a punishment from God. He had only discovered this here in Travnik, and not until this winter.

Madame Daville did not care at all for reminiscences, and like all active, truly religious people she shrank from reflections which did not lead anywhere but just made people sorry for themselves and weak in the face of the hard facts of life, often distracting their thoughts along false paths. Up until then she had listened with an effort and out of kindness, but at this point she rose, overcome by weariness, and announced that it was time for bed.

Daville remained in the large room which was becoming increasingly cold. He sat on for a long time, alone, with no one to talk to, "listening" to the intense cold entering into everything and breaking everything up from inside. And as far as his thoughts could reach: whether he was thinking of the East and the Turks and their way of life without order or stability, therefore without sense or value; or whether he was trying to guess what was going on in France; and what was happening to Napoleon's army, returning defeated from Russia – everywhere he came up against suffering, misery and dire uncertainty.

So the days and nights of this winter passed. It seemed to have no end and there was no relief anywhere.

When it happened that the cold abated a little for a day or two, heavy snow would fall, lying on the heaps of old snow where a hard, icy crust had formed, like the new face of the earth. And it would be followed immediately by a still fiercer frost. The breath froze, water turned to ice, the sun went dark. People's thoughts became petrified, confined to defence from the cold. It required a great effort to remember that somewhere deep down was the earth, the living, warm source of nourishment, which blossomed and brought forth fruits. Between these fruits and mankind an icy, white, impassable element had fallen.

The prices of everything, especially wheat, had been soaring since the first months of winter; now wheat had disappeared altogether. Hunger raged in the villages, in the towns painful shortages. In the streets one could see gaunt villagers with an uneasy look, carrying empty sacks over their arms, searching for wheat. Beggars would assault one at street corners, blue with cold and wrapped in rags. Neighbours counted each other's mouthfuls.

Both Consulates endeavoured to help the people and alleviate the troubles caused by hunger and cold. Madame Daville and von Paulich competed in giving help in food and money. Hungry people, mostly children, would gather at the gates of the Consulates. At the beginning these were only gypsies and an occasional Christian child, but as the winter intensified and with it the deprivation, poor Turkish children began to be seen as well, wandering in from the outskirts of the town. For the first few days they were met in the bazaar by Turkish children from the town houses, throwing snowballs and laughing at them for begging and eating infidel food, and shouting: "Gluttons! Unbelievers! Stuffing yourselves with pork, eh? Gluttons!"

But later such intense cold gripped them all that the town children could not venture out of their houses. And in front of the Consulates a crowd of frozen children and beggars shivered, hopping about with cold, so chilled through and wrapped in all kinds of rags that one could not make out what faith they were or where they were from.

The Consuls distributed so much that they began to run short themselves. But as soon as the cold let up enough to enable carriers to get through from Brod, von Paulich organized, efficiently and decisively, a constant supply of flour and food both for his Consulate and for Daville's.

The French consignments of cotton through Bosnia had stopped at the very beginning of the winter. Frayssinet continued to write despairing letters and kept preparing to abandon everything. But despite that, there was a unanimous opinion among the people that the high prices the French paid their carriers were responsible not only for the expense of everything, but also for the shortages, because the peasants had been taken away from work in the fields. Altogether, "Bunaparta's war" was to blame for everything. As so many times in history, the people made their oppressor their victim who would have to bear on his shoulders everyone's sins and crimes. And there was an ever increasing number of those who, without themselves knowing why, began to see salvation in the defeat of that "Bunaparta", about whom they knew nothing, except that he had "become a burden to the earth", for he brought war, unrest, high prices, illness and shortages wherever he went.

Beyond the Sava, in the Austrian lands, where people were oppressed by taxation and financial crises, military service and bloody losses on the battlefields, "Bunaparta" had already entered into songs and stories as the cause of it all and a hindrance to the personal happiness of every individual. In Slavonia, the girls without husbands sang:

Oh Frenchman, mighty Emperor,
Let the lads go, the girls are alone,
The quinces and apples have rotted,
As have the gold-threaded shirts.

This song crossed the Sava, was sung in Bosnia and reached Travnik.

Daville knew quite well how these general ideas sprang up in such regions, how they spread and took root, and how difficult and hopeless it was to fight them. But nevertheless he waged the battle now as before, only with a paralysed will and depleted energy. He wrote the same reports, gave the same instructions to his staff and associates, endeavouring to gather as much information as possible, to exert as much influence as he could on the Vizier and every individual at the Residence. This was all the same as before, but he, Daville, was not the same.

The Consul held himself upright, behaved calmly and confidently. Everything was apparently the same. But in fact much was changed.

If it were possible for someone to measure the strength of a man's will, the current of his thoughts, the energy of his inner impulses and outward movements, he would have discovered that all Daville's actions were now far closer to the rhythm with which this Bosnian town breathed, lived and worked, than to the one he had moved by when he came here, more than six years earlier.

All these changes had taken place gradually and imperceptibly, but relentlessly. Daville shrank from the written word and swift, clear decisions, he was afraid of news and visitors, he was worried by change and the prospect of change. He preferred the predictable minute of calm and rest to the years which were to come, bringing no one knew what.

But even the outward changes could not be concealed. People who live in cramped surroundings such as these, constantly before each other's eyes, hardly notice that they are ageing and changing. Nevertheless, particularly in the last few months, the Consul had lost weight and aged visibly.

That wave of unruly hair above his brow had flattened out and taken on the dull colour of blond hair beginning suddenly to go grey. His face was still ruddy, but his skin was drier and beginning to sag and lose its freshness around his chin. That winter he suffered from acute toothache, and he was beginning to lose his teeth.

These were the visible traces left on Daville, over the years, by the Travnik frosts, rains and damp winds, trivial and major domestic anxieties, his innumerable consular duties, and particularly his inner struggles provoked by the most recent events in the world and in France.

This was Daville's situation at the end of his sixth year of uninterrupted living in Travnik and at the start of the events which followed Napoleon's return from Russia.

24

In the middle of March, when the bitter cold finally eased and the ice which had seemed eternal began to melt, the town was left silent and fearful, as though after a plague. The streets had been eroded, the houses were dilapidated, the trees bare and the people exhausted and careworn. It seemed as though they had survived the cold in order to endure still greater torments over food, seed and hopeless, stifling debts.

It was on such a March morning, in that deep, surly voice in which d'Avenat had for years been monotonously announcing both pleasant and unpleasant, important and insignificant news, that he informed Daville that Ibrahim Pasha had been replaced, without any new posting. The decree ordered him to leave Travnik and await further instructions in Gallipoli.

When he had been told, in the same way, of Mehmed Pasha's transfer five years earlier, Daville had been upset and felt the need to move, to talk, to take steps to oppose such a decision. Now too the news saddened him, signifying, in times like these, an incalculable loss. But he no longer found in himself the strength to resist. Ever since the last winter, since the Moscow catastrophe, he was oppressed by the constant feeling that everything was disintegrating and falling apart. And every loss, wherever it originated, found its meaning and justification in that feeling.

Everything was disintegrating – emperors, armies, institutions, wealth and enthusiasm that used to reach to the sky. So how could it be that this ossified, unhappy Vizier, who had sat for years perpetually bent to the left or right, should not one day fall too?

Everyone knew what "to await further instructions in Gallipoli" meant. This was exile, sorrow, and semi-poverty, without a word of complaint and with no possibility of anything being explained or put right.

It was only after this that Daville began to think that he would be losing a long-standing friend and support, at a time when it could have been most vital to him. But he did not find any trace of his former dismay and zeal and the urge to write, remind, rebuke and call for help, as once at the departure of Mehmed Pasha. Everything was disintegrating, including his friends and their support. And no one would achieve anything at all by getting agitated and trying to save either himself or others. So, the perpetually bent Vizier was collapsing, like everything else. All you could do was regret it.

While he was still thinking like this, incapable of reaching any decision, a message arrived from the Residence that the Vizier had invited him to come and talk.

There was a sense of confused bustling at the Residence, but no sign of any change in the Vizier. He spoke about his replacement as about something entirely understandable in the series of misfortunes that had beset him over the years. As though he himself wished this series to be completed as quickly as possible, the Vizier was resolved not to drag out his departure but to be on the road within ten days, that is by the beginning of April. He had learned that his successor had already set out and he did not wish on any account to be in Travnik when he arrived.

Just as Mehmed Pasha had once done, the Vizier maintained that he was the victim of his affection for France. (Daville knew quite well that this was one of those Oriental lies or half-truths that circulate among genuine human relations and favours, like forged coins among real ones.)

"Yes, yes. As long as France was winning, they kept me on and did not dare touch me, but now that her luck has turned, they are replacing me, removing me from contact and co-operation with the French."

(Suddenly the false coin became real and Daville, forgetting the Vizier's inaccurate premise, felt the reality of the French defeat. That cold, painful contraction, now strong, now weak, that had so often gripped his stomach in this Residence, tormented him now again, as he listened calmly to the Vizier's speech shifting from false courtesy to bitter reality.)

Lies are mixed with truth, thought Daville, letting the interpreter translate the words he understood quite well himself. Everything is mixed up so that no one can tell the difference, but one thing is certain: everything is disintegrating.

Now the Vizier had already turned from France to his attitude to the Bosnians and to Daville personally: "Believe me, these people need a more rigorous, more ruthless Vizier. It is true, they say the poor throughout the country bless me. And that is all I want. The rich and powerful hate me. They gave me false information about you at the beginning, but I got to know you and soon saw that you were my only friend. Glory to the one God! But, in truth, I have myself asked the Sultan to recall me several times. I do not need anything. What I would most like would be to cultivate my own plot like an ordinary gardener and thus spend my last days in peace."

At Daville's words of reassurance and good wishes for a better future, the Vizier responded, rejecting all solace: "No, no! I see what is in store for me. I know that, as so often in the past, they will endeavour to slander me, to seize my property and kill me. I feel I can hear them, in high places, undermining me and breaking me. But what can I do? God is one. And since I lost my dearest children and so much of my family, I am prepared for all other ills. If Sultan Selim were alive, everything would be different…"

Daville knew the mechanism of what was to come next. And d'Avenat translated from memory, like the text of some familiar ritual.

As he left the Residence, Daville was able to observe an uneasy haste mounting with every minute. The Vizier's colourful, complex household, which had grown during these five years, put down roots and become part of the building and its surroundings, had been suddenly shaken up as though it were all collapsing.

From all the apartments and courtyards came the sound of voices, the clatter of footsteps, the clang of hammers and the banging of packing cases and boxes. Everyone was trying to escape and to provide for himself. This large, discordant but connected family was setting off into complete uncertainty, and it was creaking in all its joints. The only person to remain coldly motionless in this jostling and bustling, was the Vizier. He sat in his place, a little bent to one side and immobile, like a garish stone idol, borne along in the centre of the turbulent, frightened crowd.

The following day, the Vizier's servants brought to the French Consulate a whole procession of domestic or tamed animals, angora cats, greyhounds, foxes and white rabbits. Daville received them solemnly in the courtyard. The attendant who had accompanied the procession stood in the middle of the yard and announced in a solemn tone that all these creatures of God's had been friends of the Vizier's home, and that the Vizier was now leaving them to a friendly house.

"He loved them and can leave them only to someone he loves."

The attendant and the servants were rewarded, and the animals put away in the yard behind the house, to Madame Daville's great inconvenience and the children's exceptional delight.

A few days later the Vizier summoned Daville once again, to take his leave of him alone, informally, as a friend.

This time the Vizier was really moved. There were none of those false coins, half-truths or courtesies which both are and are not what they seem.

"One has to part with everything in time, and now our turn has come. We found one another as two exiles, imprisoned and shut in among these terrible people. It was here long ago that we became friends and we shall be friends always, should we ever meet again in some better place."

And then there occurred something quite new, unknown in the five years of ceremonial at the Residence. Attendants rushed up to the Vizier and helped him to rise. He stood up with his familiar sudden, sharp movement and it was only then that one could see how tall and strong he was. And then he set off across the room slowly and heavily, with the minimum of movement, on unseen legs as though he had wheels under his long, heavy robe. They all moved together into the courtyard. There stood the black carriage, cleaned and polished, the former gift of von Mitterer, and a little way from it, a beautiful thoroughbred sorrel horse, with a pink and white muzzle, saddled and fully harnessed.

The Vizier stopped beside the carriage and whispered something like a prayer. Then he turned to Daville:

"As I leave this sorrowful land, I bequeath you this means for you yourself to leave it as soon as possible…"

Then they led the horse up and the Vizier turned to Daville again:

"…and this noble creature, to carry you towards all that is good."

Deeply moved, Daville wanted to say something, but the Vizier went on, completing the planned ceremonial solemnly.

"The carriage is a sign of peace and the horse a symbol of happiness. These are my wishes for you and your family."

It was only then that Daville managed to express his gratitude and offer his good wishes for the Vizier's journey and his future.

While they were still at the Residence, d'Avenat discovered from someone that the Vizier was not giving von Paulich anything and that he had taken his leave of him briefly and coldly.

Caravans of horses and carriers were camped in front of the Residence, loading and reloading, waiting, and calling to each other. Footsteps, orders and arguments echoed through the empty building. Baki's shrill voice out-shouted it all.

He was miserable and sick at the very thought of having to travel in this cold weather (there was still snow on the mountains) and on these terrible roads. And the expense and impossibility of taking everything with them drove him to despair. He ran from room to room to see whether anything had been left behind, urging that things should not be thrown about and broken, threatening, begging. He was angry with Behdjet because of the constant smile with which he surveyed this whirlwind. ("With those brains in my head, I would do nothing but smile as well, of course!") He was offended by Tahir Bey's unconcern and frivolity. ("He's ruined himself, so why not ruin everything else as well!") The gifts which the Vizier intended for Daville upset him so much that he forgot the packing cases and the carriers. He ran from one person to another, went to the Vizier himself, imploring him, begging him at least not to give away the horse. And when nothing helped, he sat down on the bare sofa and sobbed as he informed everyone that Rotta had told him in confidence that when von Mitterer was transferred from Travnik he had taken 50,000 thalers with him, saved in under four years.

"Fifty thousand thalers! Fif-ty thou-sand! And that German swine too! And in four years!" shouted Baki, asking out loud how much this Frenchman was likely to save, then slapping himself in helpless rage on his silk coat, somewhere where his thigh must have been.

And at the end of the week, in cold rain which turned to wet snow on the hills, Ibrahim Pasha and his retinue set out.

Both Consuls escorted him, with their khavazes. There were quite a few Travnik beys on horseback as well and people who went some of the way on foot, for Ibrahim Pasha was not leaving under cover and amid general hatred as Mehmed Pasha had done.

During the first and second years of his rule there had been riots and intrigues among the ayans, directed against him, as there had been against the majority of his predecessors, but as time went on these were increasingly rare. The Vizier's complete rigidity, his uprightness in financial matters, and Tahir Bey's skill, restraint and generosity in administering the country, had with time created a tolerable situation and cool but calm relations between the Residence and the beys. They criticized the Vizier for not doing anything for the country and not undertaking any measures against Serbia. But the beys made these criticisms more to ease their own consciences and emphasize their zeal, than because they really wanted to break the barren but agreeable "silence" that had settled in during Ibrahim Pasha's long term of office. (For his part, the Vizier complained with much justification that the reason he could not despatch his army against Serbia was the indolence, disorder and dissension among the Bosnians.) And as, from year to year, the Vizier began increasingly to resemble a corpse, so judgements of him became increasingly mild and opinions of his administration increasingly favourable.

Little by little, the procession accompanying the Vizier began to dwindle. First of all those on foot dropped back, then individual horsemen. Finally, only the ulema, some ayans and both the Consuls with their escorts were left. The Consuls took their leave of the Vizier by that same little inn where Daville had once bid farewell to Mehmed Pasha.

The dilapidated bower still stood in front of the inn, in a pool of water, black with rain. Here the Vizier halted his retinue and took his leave of the Consuls with a few indistinct words which no one even translated. D'Avenat loudly repeated his master's good wishes and greetings, while von Paulich himself responded in Turkish.

There was a cold drizzle. The Vizier was riding his strong, broad horse, nicknamed "the cow" at the Residence. He was wearing a large coat of heavy fur and dark red cloth whose cheerful colour stood out strangely in the wet, mournful landscape. Behind the Vizier one could see Tahir Bey's sallow face with its brilliant eyes, the long, huntsman's figure of Eshref Effendi the doctor, and the round, inflated mass of clothes out of which Baki's blue eyes peered, furious and ready to weep.

Everyone was in a hurry to get away from this boggy ravine, as though from a formal funeral.

Daville went back with von Paulich. It was after midday. The rain had stopped and there was an indirect glow of sun from somewhere, feeble and without warmth. Thoughts and memories broke through their perfunctory conversation. The closer they came to the town, the narrower the gorge became. Young grass was poking through on the steep slopes and blue, rainy shadows lay over it. At one point Daville caught sight of the half-open flowers of yellow primroses and immediately felt the full desolation of his seventh Bosnian spring, and with such force that he was barely able to reply in polite monosyllables to some tranquil exposition of von Paulich's.

Daville was surprised to receive his first news of the Vizier some ten days after his departure. In Novi Pazar, Ibrahim Pasha had met up with the Siliktar Ali Pasha, his successor in the post of Bosnian Vizier, and they had spent a few days there. The French courier from Istanbul had turned up at the same time, and through him Ibrahim Pasha sent his friend his first greetings from the journey. His letter was full of friendly recollections and good wishes. In passing, Ibrahim Pasha had also added a few words about the new Vizier. "I would like to describe my successor to you, respected friend, but

I find it quite impossible. I can only say: may God have mercy on the poor, and on all who have no protection. Now the Bosnians will see…"

What Daville learned from the courier and then from Frayssinet's letters conformed entirely with Ibrahim Pasha's impressions.

The new Vizier was coming without many officials, without attendants or harem, "naked and alone like a bandit in the woods", but with twelve hundred well-armed Albanians "of dangerous appearance" and two large fieldpieces. Before him went the reputation of a cold-blooded murderer and the cruellest Vizier in the Empire.

Somewhere on the road between Pljevlje and Priboj, one of the Vizier's cannon had got stuck in the mud, for the roads were always hard to pass, especially at this time of year. As a result, when he reached Priboj, the Vizier had executed all the state officials, without discrimination (fortunately, there were only three of them) and two of the most prominent men in the bazaar. A messenger was sent ahead of him with strict orders that the roads should be repaired. But the order was superfluous. The Priboj example had achieved its purpose. Labourers and craftsmen thronged the whole road from Priboj to Sarajevo, the puddles and holes were filled in, the wooden bridges mended. Terror levelled the road for the Vizier to pass.

Ali Pasha travelled slowly, stopping for a while in every town, and immediately establishing his kind of order: he brought in taxes, executed the insubordinate Turks, arrested the prominent people and Jews without distinction.

In Sarajevo, according to the exhaustive and colourful report sent by Frayssinet, fear reached such a pitch that the most prominent beys and bazaar people went out beyond the Goats' Bridge to greet the Vizier and take him their first gifts. Ali Pasha, who knew that the Sarajevo beys were renowned for always receiving the Viziers on their way from Istanbul to Travnik coldly and defiantly, now rudely refused to receive their deputation, shouting aloud from his tent that they should get out of his way immediately, he would find anyone he needed in his own home.

And the next day all the richer Jews in Sarajevo were arrested, as well as a few of the most prominent beys. One of them, who had simply dared ask why he was being arrested, was beaten in the presence of the Vizier.

News of all of this reached Travnik, and the new Vizier had already grown into a monster in the people's tales. But his actual arrival in Travnik, the way he received the ayans and held his first Divan with them, surpassed the reputation that had preceded him.

It was a detachment of three hundred of the Vizier's Albanians that entered Travnik first on that spring day. In wide, regular lines, in perfect order, they all looked alike and as beautiful as girls. They carried short rifles and stepped stiffly, looking straight ahead of them. Then came the Vizier, with a small retinue and a detachment of cavalry. They too rode at a funereal pace, without any noise. In front of the Vizier's horse, at the head of the procession, walked an enormous fellow holding a large, bare sword in front of him in both hands. Not even the most ferocious Bashi-Bazouk, nor hordes of wild Caucasians yelling and shooting, could have terrified the people as much as this slow, silent procession.

The very same evening, Ali Pasha's customary arrest of Jews and prominent people took place, according to the principle that "one talks in a different way to a man who has spent a night in gaol". If any of their relations or friends began to weep and complain or wanted to give something or help those under arrest in any way, they were beaten. All the heads of the Jewish households were arrested, for Ali Pasha had an exact list and held the view that no one paid so much in order to secure their release and no one spread fear through the town afterwards as did the Jews. And the people of Travnik, who remember all kinds of things, witnessed, among other amazing and scandalous scenes, seven members of the Atijas family being led past on one chain.

That same night, the Dolac parish priest, Brother Ivo Janković, guardian of the monastery at Guča Gora, and the Abbot Pahomije were led away, and thrown into the fortress.

At the break of day the following morning all who had been imprisoned earlier for murder or serious theft were led out of the fortress, where they had been waiting for the verdict of Ibrahim Pasha's justice, which was slow and circumspect. At sunrise they were all hanged at the crossroads into the town. And at noon the ayans gathered at the Residence for the first Divan.

This Divan had witnessed many stormy and spine-chilling meetings, heard many harsh words, important decisions and death sentences. But there had never been such a silence as this which stopped the breath and gripped the stomach. Ali Pasha's skill lay in being able to create, sustain and spread just such an atmosphere of fear, which overwhelmed and broke even those who were afraid of nothing, not even death.

After reading the Sultan's decree, the first thing the Vizier relayed to the ayans gathered there was the sentence of death on the Travnik Kaymakam, Resim Bey. Ali Pasha's blows were particularly horrifying because they were unexpected and incredible.

When Ibrahim Pasha left Travnik three weeks earlier, Suleiman Pasha Skopljak had been somewhere on the Drina again with the army, and had found a good excuse for declining to return to stand in for the Vizier until the new one's arrival. That was how old Resim Bey had been left as the highest authority in Travnik.

This man had already been arrested, said the Vizier, and he would be executed on Friday, because during the time he had been deputizing for the Vizier he had run things in such a lax and disorderly manner that he had deserved to die twice over. This was just the beginning. He would be followed by everyone who took

Imperial affairs and state concerns on himself and did not manage them properly, or resisted them either publicly or in secret.

At this news, coffee, tobacco and sherbet were served.

After the coffee, Hamdi Bey Teskeredžić, as the oldest of the beys, spoke a few words in defence of the unfortunate Kaymakam. While he was still speaking, one of the servants, having served the Vizier, withdrew towards the right-hand door, backwards. Here he bumped lightly into one of the Pipemasters, knocking a small pipe out of his hand. With flashing eyes, as though he had been waiting for this, the Vizier leaned to one side, stretched out his body and hurled a large knife he kept near him at the petrified lad. The servants hurried to carry out the unfortunate boy, covered in blood, and the ayans and beys froze, each staring straight ahead, at his coffee cup, forgetting the chibouks smoking in front of them.

Only Hamdi Bey retained his calm and composure, completing his defence of the old Kaymakam, asking the Vizier to take account of his age and his earlier merit and not his present mistakes.

In a loud, clear voice, the Vizier retorted curtly that under his administration everyone was going to get what was coming to him, rewards and recognition for the deserving and obedient death or a beating for the villainous and insubordinate.

"I did not come for us to tell one another lies and kiss through our pipes, or so that I could sleep on this cushion," the Vizier concluded, "but to bring order into this land which is renowned all the way to Istanbul for taking pride in disorder. There is a sabre for even the hardest heads. The heads are on your shoulders, the sabre is in my hand and the Imperial decree is under my pillow. Therefore, let all those who wish to eat their daily bread and get their fill of sunshine behave accordingly. You yourselves remember that, and explain it to the people, so that we may work together to carry out what the Sultan asks of us."

The beys and ayans rose and took their leave silently, glad to be alive and as perplexed as though they had witnessed a conjurer's performance.

The following day, the new Vizier received Daville to a solemn audience.

The Vizier's Albanians came for Daville, in ceremonial dress, on fine horses. They rode through the empty streets and virtually deserted bazaar. No doors were opened, no windows raised and not a single head peered out.

The audience followed its set pattern. The Vizier presented the Consul and d'Avenat with fine furs. It was noticeable that the rooms and corridors of the Residence were empty, without any furnishings or decorations. And the number of dignitaries and servants was unusually small. After the bustle which had reigned in the Residence under Ibrahim Pasha, everything now looked bare and deserted.

Uneasy and inquisitive, Daville was surprised when he saw the new Vizier. He was tall and strong, but had small bones, and he took brisk, swift steps, without that sluggish dignity that prominent Turkish personages display. His face was swarthy, his eyes large and green, and his beard and moustache completely white and trimmed into an unusual shape.

The Vizier spoke easily and freely, laughing often and unusually loudly for a Turkish dignitary.

Daville wondered whether this really was that same Vizier about whom he had heard all those terrible things and who had only yesterday sentenced the old Kaymakam to death and thrown a knife at one of his servants in this same Divan.

The Vizier laughed and talked about his plans for organizing the country and leading the army resolutely against Serbia. He encouraged the Consul to continue to work as he had up to then, assuring him of his readiness to show him every attention and protection.

For his part, Daville did not spare courtesies and assurances, but he could see at once that the Vizier's store of fine words and pleasant grimaces was very meagre, for as soon as he stopped smiling and speaking for a moment, his face became dark and his eyes restless, as though he were trying to see where he should deliver his next blow. The cold smouldering of those eyes was unbearable and in curious contrast with his loud laughter.

"These Bosnian beys have already told you about me and my method of administration. Don't let that disturb you in the least. I believe that they do not find me agreeable. But I have not come in order for them to like me. They are fools who seek to live on their empty nobility and big, insolent words. But that cannot be. The time has come when they too must come to their senses. Only, it is not through their heads that people learn reason, but from the other end, from the soles of their feet. I have yet to meet anyone who has had a good beating on the soles of his feet and forgotten it, but I have seen a hundred times that people forget even the finest instruction or advice."

The Vizier laughed aloud, a youthful, mischievous expression playing around his mouth and his trimmed beard and moustache.

"Let them say what they like," the Vizier continued, "but believe me, I shall drive discipline and order into these people's bones. And you take no notice of any of it, but if you need anything come straight to me. It is my wish that you should be untroubled and content."

This was the first time that Daville had before him one of those completely uneducated, crude and bloodthirsty Ottoman administrators he had known about till then only from books and other people's tales.

There now began a period when everyone endeavoured to be invisible, everyone sought shelter and a hiding place, so that now people in the bazaar were saying that "even a mousehole was worth 1,000 ducats". Fear lay over Travnik like a fog, weighing on everything that breathed and thought.

This was that great fear, unseen and immeasurable, but all-powerful, which comes over human communities from time to time, bowing or severing heads. At such times many people, blinded and maddened, forget there are such things as reason and courage, that everything in life passes and that human life, like everything else, has its value, but that value is not unlimited. And so, deluded by the temporary magic of fear, they pay far more dearly for their bare life than it is worth, doing base, contemptible things, humiliating and shaming themselves, and when the moment of fear passes, they see that they have bought this life of theirs at too high a price or even that they were not actually under threat, but had just succumbed to the irresistible delusion of fear.

The Sofa at Lutvo's café was deserted, although spring had come and the lime tree above it had begun to turn green. All that the Travnik beys dared was to humbly beg the Vizier to pardon the Kaymakam for his mistakes (although no one knew what they were) and, in view of his age and earlier merit, grant him his life.

All the other prisoners from the fortress, gamblers, horse-thieves and arsonists, were summarily tried and executed and their heads stuck on stakes.

The Austrian Consul immediately intervened on behalf of the imprisoned friars. Daville did not wish to lag behind. Only, he mentioned the Jews as well as the friars. The friars were the first to be released. Then, one by one, the Jews were let out and they immediately organized a levy and placed such a ransom in the Residence that all the Jewish coffers were emptied down to the last coin, the last coin of the sum set aside for bribes, that is. The longest to remain in the fortress was the Abbot Pahomije, as no one took his part. Finally, he too was redeemed by his few, impoverished parishioners with a round sum of 3,000 groschen, of which over

2,000 was given by the two Fufić brothers, Petar and Jovan. Of the beys from Travnik and other places, some were released and others arrested, so that there were always some ten to fifteen in the fortress.

This was how Ali Pasha began to rule in Travnik, and swiftly to prepare the army against Serbia.

25

The troubles that beset Travnik with the arrival of the new Vizier were hard for the whole town, and they seemed as vast as the universe to each individual they touched directly. But of course they remained buried in the mountain chain that surrounds the town, and in the reports of the two Travnik Consuls which no one, either in Vienna or in Paris, managed to read attentively at this time. The whole world was now taken up with news of the great European drama of Napoleon's downfall.

Daville spent Christmas and the New Year in horrified expectation and the panic-stricken feeling that all was lost. But as soon as it was known that Napoleon had returned to Paris, things took a milder turn. Reassuring commentaries, orders and circulars began to arrive from Paris about the training of new armies and decisive measures by the government in all areas.

Daville was once again ashamed of his faintheartedness. But that same faintheartedness now drove him to surrender once more to an undefined hope. The weak have a pressing need to delude themselves like this and a limitless capacity for being deceived.

And so this crazy, painful swing on which Daville had been inwardly rising and falling for years, began once again to sway from daring hopes to profound despair. Only, at every swing, his hope spent itself and was diminished.

At the end of May bulletins arrived with news of Napoleon's victories in Prussia at Lutzen and Bauzen. The old game was continuing.

But in Travnik at that time there were such shortages, such

oppression and such fear of the new Vizier and his Albanians, that there was no one he could tell about these triumphant bulletins.

It was at just this time that Ali Pasha set out against Serbia, after he had first driven "fear and discipline" into every single being. In this too he proceeded differently from all his predecessors. Formerly these "expeditions against Serbia" had been a public festivity. For days and weeks commanders from the towns in the interior of Bosnia would gather on the plain of Travnik. They would arrive slowly and arbitrarily, bringing with them an army of whatever kind and size they wished. And once they reached Travnik, they would settle there, negotiating with the Vizier and the authorities, making demands, imposing conditions, asking for food, equipment and funds. And this was all concealed under the guise of enthusiastic demonstrations and military ceremonial.

During those days strangers would roam through Travnik, armed, suspect and idle. The colourful, noisy fair on the plain of Travnik would go on for weeks. Fires were lit and tents put up. In the centre a lance was driven into the ground with three horses' tails tied to it, spattered with the blood of rams slaughtered to ensure a successful campaign. Drums were beaten and bugles blared. Prayers were read. In short, everything was done to delay leaving. And often the focal point of the whole thing was the moment of departure and the festivities that accompanied it, with the result that the majority of the warriors never even saw the battlefield.

This time, under Ali Pasha's hand, everything was carried out in strict silence and great fear, with no special festivities, and no negotiation. There was no food anywhere. People lived on meagre rations from the Vizier's storerooms. No one felt like singing or playing music. When the Vizier came out onto the plain in person, he had his executioner slay the Cazin Commander, for having brought nine fewer men than he promised. The Vizier immediately selected a new commander from among the horrified Cazir detachment.

That was how they set off this time to Serbia, where Suleiman Pasha was already waiting with his unit.

The old Kaymakam, Resim Bey, whom Ali Pasha had condemned to death as soon as he arrived in Travnik, and whose life had barely been saved by the beys, was left once again as the highest authority in the town. The terror which the Kaymakam had been through was the Vizier's best guarantee that he would carry out his duties strictly according to the Vizier's wishes.

What would be the point, Daville thought now, of informing this unfortunate old man about the bulletins on Napoleon's victories? And who else was it worth informing?

The Vizier had gone off with the army and his Albanians, but he had left behind him fear, as icy, solid and enduring as the hardest wall, and the prospect of his return, which was more effective than any threat and more terrible than any punishment.

The town was left deaf and dumb; empty, impoverished and hungry as never before in the previous twenty years. The days were already sunny and long, so less time was spent in sleeping, and people grew hungry more quickly than during the short days of winter. A few thin, scabby children roamed the streets searching for wholesome food that was not there. People went as far as the Sava for wheat, or at least for seed.

Market days did not differ from ordinary days. Many shops did not even open. The shopkeepers, sitting on their raised shop-fronts, were sullen and dispirited. There had not been any coffee or other goods from overseas since the autumn. Food supplies were running out. There were only customers who would have liked to buy things that did not exist. The new Vizier had placed such heavy taxes on the bazaar that many had to borrow in order to pay them. And their fear was such that no one dared complain, even at home, within their own four walls.

In the houses and shops there was talk of six Christian Emperors attacking Bunaparta, all of them sending every male creature in their land to the army. It was said there would be no ploughing or digging or sowing or harvesting until Bunaparta was defeated and destroyed.

Now even the Jews avoided being seen near the French Consulate. Frayssinet, who had already begun the gradual liquidation of the French agency in Sarajevo, wrote that the Jews there had suddenly submitted all their promissory notes and all other claims, so that he was not in a position to meet his obligations. No one in Paris replied to a single question any more. It was already three months since any funds had been received for the Consulate expenses and salaries.

At this time when the Viziers were changing in Travnik and momentous events were taking place in Europe, in the Consul's little world things were following their natural course: new beings were coming into the world, while old ones were becoming exhausted and broken.

Madame Daville was in the last months of a pregnancy which she was taking as easily and imperceptibly as the one of two years before. She would spend the whole day in the garden, with the workmen. Thanks to von Paulich, she had succeeded in acquiring the seed she wanted from Austria this year as well, and she was expecting a great deal from her crops, although her confinement fell at an awkward time, when her presence in the garden was most needed.

At the end of May, a fifth child was born to Daville, a boy this time. The child was weak and was therefore christened immediately and entered in the register of births in the Dolac parish as Auguste-François Gérard.

Everything that happened around Madame Daville's delivery was just as it had been the time before: discussions and lively interest among all Travnik's womenfolk, visits, enquiries and good wishes from all sides; even presents, despite the shortages and general poverty. Only the gift from the Residence was lacking this time, as the Vizier had already left with the army for the Drina.

Everything had changed in those two years: relations between countries, and conditions in Bosnia. But the general attitude towards family life remained unaltered and everything that related to it linked these people as firmly and immutably as a sacred bond whose value was general, lasting and independent of changes in the world. For, in places like this, life was focused on the family as the most perfect form of a closed circle. And these circles, although they were strictly separate, had somewhere an invisible common centre and rested a part of their weight on it. That was why nothing that occurred in one family here could be entirely irrelevant to others and why everyone took part in all family events – births, weddings, deaths. And they did so unreservedly, with instinctive verve and sincerity.

Somewhere around this time, the former interpreter of the Austrian Consulate, Niccolo Rotta, waged his last, senseless, and desperate battle with his destiny.

An old Hungarian cook had served in the von Mitterer family for years, barely able to move from overweight and rheumatism in her legs. She was a superb cook, a sincere friend of the family, but at the same time she tyrannized everyone in the house intolerably. For fifteen full years, Anna Maria had quarrelled and made peace with her. As she had become quite immobilized by weight in recent years, they had taken on a younger woman from Dolac to help her. Her name was Lucia and she was strong, sprightly and hard-working. She was so good at adapting to the moods of the old cook that she was able to learn cooking and other household chores from her. And when the von Mitterer family left Travnik, taking with them, of course, their family dragon (as Anna Maria called the old cook), Lucia had stayed on as cook for von Paulich.

This Lucia had a sister, Andja, who was the misfortune of her family and the shame of the whole Dolac community. While still a girl she had set out on the wrong road, been cursed from the altar and thrown out of Dolac. Now she ran a café beside the highway in Kalibunar. Lucia had suffered a great deal, as had all her family, on account of this sister of whom she was exceptionally fond and with whom, despite everything, she had never completely broken. She would go to see her surreptitiously from time to time, even though these meetings made her suffer more than her previous yearning for her sister. Andja remained stubbornly on her chosen path, while Lucia, after vain entreaties, would weep over her each time as though she were dead. Nevertheless, they never stopped seeing each other altogether.

As he wandered through Travnik and its surroundings, with nothing to do but make himself seem important and busy, Rotta would often go to Andja's café. Bit by bit he formed a bond with this dissolute woman who had, like him, been thrown out of her community, and was beginning to age prematurely and give herself up to drink.

Some time just before Easter, Andja found a way of seeing her sister. In conversation, she proposed bluntly that they should poison the Austrian Consul. She had even brought poison.

The plan was of a kind that could only have been conceived at night, in an ill-famed café, by two sick, unhappy creatures, under the influence of brandy, ignorance, and hatred. Entirely under Rotta's spell, Andja assured her sister that the poison was of a kind that would make the Consul decline slowly and imperceptibly, as from a natural illness. She promised an enormous reward and a lordly life with Rotta, whom she was going to marry and who would take up an important position again after the Consul's death. There was ready cash as well, in ducats. In short, they could all be provided for and happy for the rest of their lives.

Lucia felt faint with fear and shame when she heard what her sister was suggesting. She immediately took the two white bottles and hid them quickly in the pockets of her shalwars. Then she grasped the wretched woman by the shoulders and began shaking her as though trying to wake her from a morbid dream, begging her on their mother's grave and all the saints to come to her senses and get such ideas out of her head. In order to convince and shame her sister, Lucia talked of how good the Consul had been to her, of the sin and horror of the very thought of repaying his goodness in such a way. She advised her to break off with Rotta at once, not only this business, but all contact altogether.

Surprised by the resistance and disapproval she was meeting with, Andja apparently abandoned her infamous intentions and asked her sister to return the bottles. But Lucia would not hear of it. So they parted – Lucia devastated, in tears, and Andja, silent, with an obscure, sinister expression on her red face. Lucia did not shut her eyes the whole night, struggling to make up her mind. And when morning broke, she went unnoticed to Dolac and confided the whole thing in the parish priest, Brother Ivo Janković, handed him the little bottles and asked him to do whatever he felt appropriate to redeem the sin.

That same morning, without wasting a moment, Brother Ivo called on von Paulich, told him of the whole affair and handed over the poison. The Lieutenant-Colonel immediately wrote Daville a letter informing him that his protégé Rotta had tried to poison him. He had both proof and witnesses. The wretch had not succeeded, nor would he, but he, von Paulich, left it to Daville and his judgement to decide whether he should continue to extend the protection of the French Consulate to such a man. In a similar letter he also informed the Kaymakam about the whole matter. When he had done this, the Lieutenant-Colonel continued to work and live calmly as he had up to now, eating the same meals, with the same servants and the same cook. But there was great agitation among everyone else: the Kaymakam, the friars, and particularly Daville. It was d'Avenat's task to give Rotta the choice: either to get out of Travnik immediately or to lose the protection of the French Consulate and be arrested by the Turkish authorities for the proven attempted poisoning.

That same night, Rotta vanished from Travnik, together with Andja from the café in Kalibunar. D'Avenat helped him escape to Split. But at the same time Daville informed the French authorities there about Rotta's latest exploits and advised them, as he was a dangerous man, not to use him in any way but to despatch him further into the Levant and leave him to his fate.

26

This time the summer months brought at least a little respite. The fruit arrived, the grain ripened and the people began to fill out and relax a little. But there was no end to the talk of wars, of the settling of great scores and of Napoleon's inevitable collapse before the autumn. It was particularly the friars who spread that whispered rumour among the people. And they did it with such insidious zeal that Daville was unable either to catch them at it or stop them effectively.

On one of the first days of September, von Paulich called on his French colleague with a larger retinue than usual.

Throughout the summer, while the most incredible news and disturbing rumours against France were spread about, von Paulich was serene, always identical in his relations with everyone. Every week he sent Madame Daville his samples of the flowers and vegetables from the seeds they had acquired together. During his rare visits to Daville he would announce that he did not believe in general war and that there were no signs that Austria would be able to abandon its neutrality. He quoted Ovid and Virgil. He explained the causes of the shortages in Travnik and put forward a scheme whereby this misfortune could be eliminated. As always, he spoke about all of this as though it were a question of war on another planet and famine in some other part of the world.

Now, at precisely noon on that tranquil September day, in Daville's ground-floor study, von Paulich was sitting opposite Daville, more formal than usual, but calm and cold as ever.

He had come, he said, on account of the increasingly frequent stories circulating among the local people about impending war between Austria and France. As far as he knew, the stories were inaccurate, but he wished to assure Daville of this as well. And he wanted nevertheless to tell him how he envisaged their relations in the event of war actually breaking out.

And the Lieutenant-Colonel calmly stated his views, looking at his folded white hands: "In all matters which have no bearing on politics and war our relations should, in my opinion, remain as hitherto. In any case, as two honourable men and Europeans, who have been flung into this country in the course of carrying out their duties and obliged to live in exceptional circumstances, I believe that we should not quarrel or slander one another in front of these barbarians, as perhaps happened in the past. I considered it my duty to say this to you, on the occasion of the disturbing news which I believe to be unfounded, and to ask you for your opinion."

Something trembled in Daville's throat.

Judging by the agitation among the French authorities in Dalmatia, he had seen over the last few days that they were preparing for something, but he had no other information, although he did not want to let von Paulich know that.

Composing himself a little, he thanked von Paulich in a voice hoarse with emotion, adding immediately that he entirely endorsed his views, that this had always been his attitude and that he was not to blame if things had once been different with von Paulich's predecessor. Daville wanted to go even a step further: "I hope, dear sir, that war will be avoided, but that if it must come it will be waged without hatred and will not last long. I believe, should it come to this, that the tender and exalted ties of kinship linking our two courts will soften its virulence and hasten reconciliation."

Here von Paulich, who had so far been looking straight ahead suddenly lowered his eyes and his face became stern and obdurate.

That is how they parted.

A week later special couriers arrived, an Austrian one from Brod and then a French one from Split, and both Consuls were informed almost simultaneously that war had been declared. The very next day Daville received a letter from von Paulich in which he informed him that their two countries were in a state of war and repeated all that they had affirmed verbally about their mutual relations during the course of the war. At the end he assured Madame Daville of his enduring respect and his readiness for any service of a private nature.

Daville replied at once, reiterating that he and his staff would hold to what they had agreed since "all citizens of Western countries, without exception, comprised one family here in the East, whatever disagreements there might otherwise be between them in Europe". He added that Madame Daville thanked him for remembering her and regretted that she would be losing the Lieutenant-Colonel's company for a while.

So, in the autumn of 1813, the Consulates entered into war and into the last of the "days of the Consuls".

The steep tracks in the large garden round the French Consulate were full of yellow leaves which poured in dry, rustling streams towards the cultivated terrace. On these steep paths, under the bending trees now bare of fruit, it was warm and peaceful, as it can be only on days when a brief truce reigns in the whole of nature – that strange pause between summer and autumn.

Here Daville, hidden from sight, with a restricted view of the neighbouring hill before his eyes, was taking stock of his whole life, his enthusiasms, plans and convictions.

Here, in the last days of October, he learned from d'Avenat of the outcome of the battle at Leipzig. Here he learned from a courier in transit of the French defeats in Spain. For he spent the whole day in this garden, until the weather became really cold and until the icy rains turned the rustling yellow leaves into a slimy mass of shapeless mud.

One Sunday morning (it was 1 November 1813), a cannon fired from the Travnik fortress, shattering the damp silence between the steep, barren hills. The townspeople raised their heads, counted the cannon shots, looking at each other at the same time with silent, questioning glances. Twenty-one salvoes were fired. The white smoke dispersed over the fortress and silence settled in once more, to be rent again a little later.

In the middle of the bazaar the town-crier was shouting – asthmatic, goitrous Hamza, who was steadily losing his voice and his cheerful, brazen wit. Nevertheless he made an effort to shout as loudly as he could, using gestures to reinforce the voice he no longer had.

So, hardly breathing from his winter attacks of asthma, he announced that God had blessed Islamic arms with a great and just victory over the rebellious infidel, that Belgrade had fallen into Turkish hands and that the very last traces of the unbelievers' rising in Serbia had been wiped out forever.

The news spread rapidly from one end of the town to the other.

That same afternoon, d'Avenat went into town to see what effect this news had had on the people.

The beys and the bazaar people would not have been what they were – Travnik gentlemen – had they rejoiced sincerely and openly about anything, even the victory of Turkish arms. With restrained dignity, they all simply muttered meaningless, monosyllabic words, and they did not consider it worthwhile pronouncing even these out loud. In fact, they did not feel entirely easy in themselves. For, however good it was that Serbia should be pacified, it was just as disturbing that Ali Pasha would be returning as a victor and would be, in all likelihood, more of a trial and burden to them than ever. Besides, they had heard many town-criers and known of many victories in their long lives but none of them remembered that any new year was better than the one just past.

This was how d'Avenat "read" them, although no one deigned with so much as a glance to answer his importunate curiosity.

He went to Dolac as well, to hear what the friars were saying. But Brother Ivo made the excuse that he had church business, and drew out the evening mass as never before, not stirring from the altar until d'Avenat grew tired of waiting and went back to Travnik.

He sought out the Abbot Pahomije at his house and found him lying like a log in a cold, empty room, fully dressed, with an ashen face. D'Avenat offered his services as a doctor, not asking him anything about the day's news, but the Abbot refused to take medicine, assuring him that he was well and did not need anything.

The next day, Daville and von Paulich made an official visit to the Deputy to congratulate him on the victory, managing things so that they did not meet at the Residence either on their arrival or as they left.

Ali Pasha returned with the first deep snow. As he entered the town cannon were fired from the fortress, trumpets blared, children ran about. And the Travnik beys' tongues were loosened. Most of them glorified the victory and the victor, with dignified and measured words, but spoken out loud and in public.

On the very first day, Daville sent d'Avenat to the Residence to express his good wishes and convey a gift to the victorious Vizier.

Some ten years earlier, while acting as chargé d'affaires to the Maltese Order in Naples, Daville had bought a heavy, engraved gold ring. It had no stone, but a finely wrought wreath of laurel leaves where a stone would normally have been. Daville had bought it from among the possessions of one of the Knights of Malta who had left a large number of debts and no heirs. It was said that this ring had once served as a prize for the victor in the chivalric games of the members of the Maltese Order.

(In recent times, since things had been irrevocably heading towards defeat, and since he had found himself without any direction of his own, in his distressing uncertainty about his country, his family and his own future, Daville had made gifts more easily and frequently. He found previously unknown satisfaction in giving to others objects he had loved and kept jealously up to then. In giving away these cherished objects, which he had thought till then were an integral part of his personal life, he was unconsciously bribing a fate that had now turned completely against him and his country. And at the same time, as he did so, he felt a sincere and profound joy, quite similar to that he had once experienced when he had acquired these things for himself.)

D'Avenat was not allowed in to the Vizier, but he gave the gift to the Secretary, explaining to him that for hundreds of years this precious object had been bestowed on whoever had succeeded in coming first in the contest and that now the Consul was sending it to the happy victor, with his congratulations and good wishes.

Ali Pasha's Secretary was a certain Asim Effendi, known as The Stammerer. He was pale and thin, the shadow of a man, with a stutter, and eyes of different colours. He always looked terribly frightened and so filled every visitor in advance with dread of the Vizier.

Two days later, the Consuls were received, first the Austrian, then the French. The days of French precedence were over.

Ali Pasha was exhausted, but satisfied. In the light of the snowy winter day, Daville noticed for the first time that the pupils of his eyes sometimes shifted momentarily up and down. As soon as the Vizier's eyes stopped moving and his glance was focused, this strange flickering of his pupils would begin. It seemed that he himself knew this and disliked it, so he kept moving his eyes and shifting his gaze, which gave his whole face a disagreeable, slightly puzzled expression.

Ali Pasha, who had put the ring on the middle finger of his right hand for the occasion, thanked him for the gift and his congratulations. He spoke very little about the campaign against Serbia or his successes, with that false modesty of vain and sensitive natures who say nothing, because they consider that any words would be inadequate. Their silence seems to scorn whoever they are talking to and so magnifies their success, making it something indescribable and difficult for average people to comprehend. Such victors continue, even years later, to vanquish everyone who talks to them about their victory.

The conversation was stilted. Every few moments there would be a pause in which Daville would search for new, stronger words to praise Ali Pasha's success. The Vizier left him to think while his eyes roved about the room, with an expression of restless boredom on his face and the silent conviction that he would never be able to find the right, entirely apt phrase.

And, as so often happens in similar situations, the desire to demonstrate the liveliest involvement and the most sincere delight made Daville unwittingly offend the sensibility of the victorious Vizier: "Does anyone know where the leader of the rebels, Black George, is now?" asked Daville, doing so just because he had heard that Karadjordje had escaped into Austria.

"Who knows and who cares a jot where that creature may be," replied the Vizier contemptuously.

"But is there not a danger that some state will offer him hospitality and assistance, and that he will return to Serbia?"

The muscles in the corners of the Vizier's mouth twitched angrily and then settled into a smile. "He won't go back. Besides, there'd be nowhere for him to go. For Serbia is laid waste to such an extent that neither that cur nor anyone else will dream of raising rebellions there for many a year."

Daville had even less success in trying to steer the conversation to the position of France and the war plans of the allies who were already preparing to cross the Rhine.

While he was travelling back to Travnik, the Vizier had received a special courier sent by von Paulich to meet him on the way. In addition to von Paulich's congratulations, this messenger had handed him a lengthy written report about the position on the European battleground. Von Paulich had written to the Vizier that "God had finally scourged the intolerable arrogance of France, and that the combined efforts of the European nations had borne fruit." He described in detail the battle at Leipzig, Napoleon's defeat and retreat across the Rhine, the inexorable advance of the allies and the preparations being made for crossing the Rhine and final victory. He quoted the exact number of French losses in dead, wounded and captured arms, and listed all the armies of subjugated peoples who had abandoned Napoleon.

When he reached Travnik, Ali Pasha found further information which confirmed what von Paulich had written to him. That was why he was talking to Daville like this now, not mentioning by so much as one word the name of his ruler or nation, as though he were speaking with the representative of a nameless country in the air which had no real form, as though he were carefully avoiding, even by a thought, touching those whom fate had set upon and who had long since passed onto the side of the defeated.

Daville cast one more glance at his ring on the Vizier's hand, and then took his leave with an expression of forced cheerfulness in which he was becoming increasingly skilled the more difficult and unclear his position grew.

When they emerged from the Residence it was already dark in the covered courtyard, but when they rode out of the gate Daville was dazzled by the whiteness of the soft, wet snow weighing down all the houses and filling the streets. It was about four o'clock in the afternoon. Blue shadows lay over the snow. As always on the shortest days, it grew dark early and cheerlessly among these mountains. Running water could still be heard under the heavy snow. Everything exuded damp. The wooden bridge echoed dully under the horses' hooves.

As usual when he left the Residence, Daville felt a momentary relief. For a while he forgot who was the victor and who defeated, concentrating on riding calmly and with dignity through the town. A shudder ran through him, from tension, from the overheated Residence and from the evening damp in the air. He tried not to shiver. That reminded him of the February day when he had ridden through this same bazaar for the first time, accompanied by the cursing and spitting and the contemptuous silence of the fanatical people, as he went to his first reception with Husref Mehmed Pasha. And suddenly he felt that as long as he could remember he had been doing nothing except ride along this same road, with the same escort, thinking the same thoughts.

Gradually over these last seven years he had of necessity grown used to many difficult, unpleasant things, but he always went to the Residence with the same uncomfortable sense of apprehension. Even in the happiest times and under the most favourable conditions, he had avoided visiting the Residence whenever possible and sought to get things done through d'Avenat. But when some matter did require a visit to the Vizier and there was really no other way of doing it, he would prepare himself as for a difficult campaign. He would sleep badly and eat little the whole of the previous day. He would rehearse what he was going to say and how he would say it, anticipating the other's replies and stratagems, and so tire himself out in advance. Then in order to have some kind of rest, to calm and comfort himself, he would think, when he was in bed: "Ah, this time tomorrow I shall be in this same place, and those two painful and unpleasant hours will be far behind me."

The painful game would begin first thing in the morning.

Horses' hooves rang out in the courtyard in front of the Consulate and servants ran to and fro. Then, at the appointed time, d'Avenat arrived, with his grim face which was enough to discourage the angels in heaven let alone a mortal, anxious, man. This was the signal for the agony to begin.

It was obvious from the way the children and idlers were hanging about in the town that one of the Consuls was going to pass by on his way to the Residence. Then, round the turning at the top of the bazaar, Daville's procession appeared, always the same. In front rode the Vizier's outrider, who had each time to meet the Consul and accompany him home. Behind him came the Consul on his black horse, absolutely composed and dignified, two paces behind him and a little to the left came d'Avenat on his skittish dappled mare, which the Travnik Turks hated as much as d'Avenat himself. And behind the two of them, the Consul's khavazes on good Bosnian horses, armed with pistols and knives.

He had to ride like this every time, sitting upright on his horse, looking neither to left nor right, not too high, nor down between the horse's ears, neither vacantly nor anxiously, not smiling or frowning, but serious, attentive and calm, with roughly that slightly unnatural expression with which military commanders are shown in portraits gazing above the battle into the distance, somewhere between the road and the line of the horizon from where at the critical moment planned reinforcements are certain to come.

He himself did not know how many hundreds of times in the course of the years he had ridden this same road, but he knew that it was always, at all times and under all the Viziers, as difficult as going to be tortured. He used to dream of this same road and suffer agonies in his dream: he would be riding with a ghostly escort through two rows of threats and potential ambush, towards the Residence which was always out of reach. And, as he recalled all of this, he really was riding through the dusk of the snow-filled bazaar.

Most of the shops were already shut. There were few passers-by and they walked, bent and slow, as though dragging chains, through the deep, heavy snow, with their hands thrust into their sashes and their ears wrapped in scarves.

When they reached the Consulate, d'Avenat asked Daville to receive him for a few minutes, and he told him some news he had heard from the Vizier's household.

A traveller from Istanbul had brought word of Ibrahim Halimi Pasha.

After spending two months in Gallipoli and after all his possessions in Istanbul and its surroundings had been confiscated, the former Vizier had been exiled to a small town in Asia Minor. His retinue had gradually declined; they had all gone in search of a livelihood, each following his own destiny. Ibrahim Pasha had set off into exile virtually alone. And as he travelled to the distant provincial town where the earth was bare, parched and rugged – a steep rocky expanse without a blade of grass and without a drop of running water – he kept repeating, ceaselessly, his constant idea of how, withdrawn from the world and dressed in simple gardener's clothes, he would cultivate his little plot of land, in solitude and silence.

A few days before his departure into exile, the former Vizier's Secretary, Tahir Bey, had suddenly died, of heart failure people said. This was a heavy blow for Ibrahim Pasha, from which he recovered only with the forgetfulness of old age, as he lived out his last days in that rocky, waterless place.

Daville dismissed d'Avenat and was left alone in the snowy twilight. Damp rolled up from the valley in great waves. The deep, soft snow muffled every sound. At the limit of his vision he could just make out Abdullah Pasha's tomb, covered in snow. A feeble light from the taper burning in the mausoleum over the grave reached his window.

The Consul shuddered. He felt weak and feverish. The news and his emotions were seething in him.

As often happens with people who are very anxious and overtired, for a moment Daville forgot everything he had heard and experienced that day, all the difficulties and unpleasantness that were in store for him the following day and in the future. He thought only about what he could see immediately in front of him.

He thought about the octagonal stone tomb, which he had been passing for years; about the flame of the candle which this evening could scarcely penetrate the mist, but which he and Des Fossés had once named "the perpetual light"; about the origin of the tomb and the story of Abdullah Pasha who rested in it. He thought about the low stone sarcophagus covered in green cloth, with the words: "May the Almighty illuminate his grave!" embroidered on it; the thick wax candle in its tall wooden holder burning day and night above the dark grave, in a powerless effort to achieve what that inscription asked of God, and which God, it seemed, was not going to fulfil; about the Pasha who had gained a high position while still a young man and had happened to come to his native land to die. Yes, he remembered everything, as though it were everyone's destiny, including his own. He remembered that before he left, Des Fossés had after all succeeded in reading Abdullah Pasha's testament, and how vividly he had talked about it.

Knowing how little light there was in this valley, the Pasha had given over his houses and serfs and left some ready money in addition, simply in order that at least this one large wax candle should burn over his grave until the end of time. And he had seen to all the formalities during his lifetime, and specified, in writing, in the presence of the Cadi and before witnesses: the kind of wax, the weight of the candle and the wages of the man who would change and light it, so that none of his descendants nor any stranger could ever deny or betray his intentions. Yes, this Pasha had known what dark evenings and foggy days there were in this gorge, where it was his lot to lie until Judgment Day. He knew too how quickly people forget both the living and the dead, how they neglect their obligations and break their promises. And while he lay ill in one of these houses, with no prospect of recovery, without hope that his eyes, which had seen so much of the world, would ever see a broader view than this one, the only thing that could give him a little comfort in his boundless anguish at his premature death and all that he had missed in life, was the thought of the pure beeswax candle which would burn over his grave with a steady, noiseless flame, without smoke or debris. That was the reason he had given everything he had acquired in his short life with great effort, courage and intelligence, for this little flame burning over his powerless remains. In his restless life, seeing countless countries and peoples, he had observed that fire was the foundation of the created world; it set life in motion and destroyed it, visibly or invisibly, in innumerable forms and varying degrees. That was why his last thoughts were of fire. Of course, this little shred of flame was not much, not reliable, and it would probably not last forever, but it was all that could be done: to illuminate continuously one point of a dark and icy land. Which meant to light up, even with just one small beam, the eyes of all who would ever pass this way.

Yes, strange vows and strange people! But anyone who lived a few years here and spent his nights like this by the window would easily understand it all.

With difficulty he tore his eyes away from the feeble flame which was sinking increasingly into the darkness and damp vapours. But then all at once there sprang up before him recollections of the past day, of his awkward conversation with the Vizier, of Ibrahim Halimi Pasha and Tahir Bey the former secretary, whose death he had learned about this evening.

More alive than when he had lived in Travnik, the Secretary now stood before him. Bent at the waist, with shining eyes, squinting a little in the sharp glare, the Secretary said, as he had once before, on just such a cold evening: "Yes, monsieur, everyone sees the victor in a bright light, or, as the Persian poet says: 'The face of the victor is like a rose.'"

"Yes, the face of the victor is like a rose, but the face of the vanquished is like the earth of the grave, which everyone runs from, turning away his head."

Daville spoke aloud this reply he had long owed the living Secretary.

And only then did he realize that he was talking to a dead man. Again he felt a cold shudder run through his whole body, and he rang for candles to be brought in.

But even after this Daville went frequently to the window, looking out at the glow of the taper from Abdullah Pasha's tomb and the little, dim lights in the Travnik houses, and reflecting about fire in the world, about the fate of the defeated and the victorious, remembering the living and the dead, until the lights in the windows went out one by one, including the one in the Austrian Consulate. (The victorious go to bed early and sleep well!) There remained only the sad wax candle by the tomb and, on the opposite side of town, one other fire, larger and quite different. This came from a shed where brandy was being distilled, as every year at this time.

On the other side of the damp, snow-filled Travnik gorge, the first brandy still had been set up in Petar Fufić's shed and the distilling had begun. The shed was outside town, just above the Lašva, below the road leading to Kalibunar.

The valley was full of icy draughts. In the shed just above the water, the "witch" was playing her music, hissing all night long under the roof, sending smoke up through the opening.

The green logs whined under the brandy still around which frozen people were milling, wrapped up, spattered with soot, swathed in red scarves, as they struggled with the smoke and sparks, the wind and the draught and the strong tobacco which, on top of everything else, kept burning their lips and stinging their eyes.

Here was Tanasije, the famed expert in distilling brandy. During the summer he would find work where he could. But as soon as the first plum fell, he would go from house to house, through the little towns of the Travnik district and even further afield. No one knew better how to soak the plums, to gauge when the marc had fermented, to distil and decant the brandy. He was a grim-faced man, who spent his whole life in cold, smoke-filled distilling sheds, always pale and unshaven, sleepy and frowning. Like all good craftsmen he was always dissatisfied both with his work and with the people helping him. His whole conversation consisted of irritable mumbling and all his directions were negative: "Not like that...Don't let it boil away...Don't add anything...Don't touch it again...Leave it, that's enough...Stop it!...Get out of the way!"

And after these irritable, indistinct mutterings, which both he and his assistants understood quite well, out of Tanasije's soot-stained, chapped hands, out of the mud, smoke and apparent disorder, finally, the perfect, honest piece of work emerged: good, pure brandy, divided into the "first running", "strong", "mild" and "second running"; a shining, fiery liquid, clear and healing, without a single speck of dust or soot in it, with no trace of the effort and dirt out of which it was created. There was no taste of smoke or decay: it smelled of plums and orchards as it was poured into containers, precious and pure as the soul. Right up to then Tanasije hovered over it, as over a tender newborn infant. Towards the end he would forget his complaints and just his lips would move, as though he were whispering or casting a spell, watching with an unfailing eye as the brandy was poured out, and, without trying it on his tongue, gauging from the way it poured its strength, worth and quality.

There were always guests around the fire burning under the still, people from the town. And they always included some unexpected guest or idler, a gusle[21] player or storyteller, because it is good to eat, drink and chat by a still, despite the fact that the smoke stings the eyes and icy cold beats down from behind. But for Tanasije, these people did not exist. He worked and mumbled, gave instructions, saying always what should not be done, and in doing so passed over the people who had sat down around the fire, as though they were made of air. It seemed that as far as he was concerned these idle people formed an integral part of the still. Certainly, he neither invited them nor chased them away, and nor did he notice them.

For forty years Tanasije had been distilling brandy like this in the towns, villages and monasteries. And he was still the same. Only, one could see that he had declined and grown old. His mumbling was quieter than it once had been and it would often turn into the coughing and rasping of an old man. His thick, bushy eyebrows had grown grey, and, like his whole face, were always spattered with soot and the clay that coated the still. And under these tangled brows one could just make out his eyes like two unequal glassy glints, flashing brightly one minute and the next completely extinguished.

There was quite a large gathering around the fire this evening. The landlord himself, Pero Fufić, with two other Travnik Serbs; merchants, a gusle player and a certain Marko from Džimrije: a holy man and soothsayer, who spent his time travelling through Bosnia and sometimes came to Travnik, but he never went further than this shed, nor into the town or bazaar.

This Marko was a greying peasant from Eastern Bosnia, small, lively, neat, altogether spruce and adroit.

He was well-known as a prophet and soothsayer. In his village he had grown-up sons and married daughters, a house and land. But since he became a widower, he had begun to say prayers and

---

21 A single-stringed instrument, played with a bow, used to accompany epic songs.

foretell the future. He was not avaricious: he would not always make prophecies and not for everyone. He was sharp-tongued and uncompromising with sinners. Even the Turks knew him and permitted him to carry on with his prophecies.

When Marko came to a place, he would not go into the wealthy houses, but perched in some distilling shed or peasant house, beside the fire. He would chat with the men and women gathered there. Then, at a certain time, he would go out into the night and stay there for perhaps an hour, sometimes two. And when he came back, damp with dew or rain, he would sit down by the fire, where his audience was still waiting, and, gazing at his little thin yew board, begin to speak. But frequently even before that he would turn to one of those present, reprimand him or her sharply for some sin and suggest that they leave the company. More often than not this was a woman.

He would stare sternly at her for a long time and then say calmly but decisively: "My girl, your arms are in flames up to the elbows. Go and put the fire out and take the sin from yourself. You know what kind of sin you are living under."

Ashamed, the woman would leave, and then Marko began to prophesy general things for all the people gathered there.

Tonight too, Marko had gone out, despite the penetrating wind and icy sleet. Now he was looking at his board, tapping it lightly with the index finger of his left hand.

He stared at it for a long time and then began slowly: "A fire is smouldering in this town, smouldering in many places. It can't be seen, for the people carry it within them, but one day it will flare up and engulf guilty and innocent alike. Whoever is righteous will not be in town that day, but outside. Far outside. And let everyone pray that he may be among them."

Then he turned slowly to Petar Fufić. "Master Pero, there is some grief in your house as well. It is great and it will grow still greater, but it will turn to good. It is turning to good. But don't you neglect the church and don't forget the poor. Don't let the lamp go out in front of the icon of St Demetrius."

As the old man spoke, Pero, otherwise a proud, irascible man, bowed his head and lowered his eyes to his sash. Silence and embarrassment reigned, until Marko looked again at his little board and began tapping it thoughtfully with his nail. His soft, firm voice began imperceptibly to be distinguished from that dry sound. At first just a few incomprehensible words and then increasingly clearly. "Ah, poor Christians, poor Christians!"

This was one of those general prophecies which Marko would utter from time to time and which were later spread from person to person among the Serbs: "They have trodden in blood. There is blood to their ankles, and it is still rising. There will be blood, from today, for one hundred years; and half another hundred. So much I see. Six generations passing down to each other handfuls of blood. All Christian blood. There will come a time when every child will know how to read and write; people will speak to each other from one end of the world to the other and they will hear every word, but they will be unable to understand one another. Some will grow arrogant and acquire treasure such as no one has ever known, but their riches will vanish in blood and neither speed nor skill will help them. Others will grow poor and hungry, so that they will eat their own tongues for hunger and call on death to despatch them, but death will be deaf and slow. And whatever the earth brings forth, all nourishment will grow sickly with blood. The cross will turn black. Then a man will come, naked and barefoot, with no staff or bag, and he will dazzle everyone's eyes with his wisdom, strength and beauty, and he will save mankind from blood and violence and bring comfort to every soul. And the third of the Three shall reign."

Towards the end of this speech, the old man's words became increasingly quiet and incomprehensible until they vanished completely in an indistinct murmur and the quiet, even tapping of his nail on the dry, thin yew board.

They were all looking at the fire, under the effect of these words which they did not understand, but whose vague meaning oppressed them, filling them with that indistinct thrill with which simple people greet any prophecy.

Tanasije stood up to check the still. Then one of the merchants asked Marko whether a Russian Consul would be coming to Travnik.

There was a silence in which everyone felt that this question was out of place. The old man replied curtly: "Neither he nor any others will be coming, and those who have been here up to now will soon be leaving. Years are on their way when the main road will turn away from this town. You will be eager to see a traveller or a merchant, but they will go elsewhere, and you will sell to each other and buy from each other. One and the same coin will go from hand to hand, but it will never get warm or bear fruit."

The merchants looked at one another. There was an unpleasant silence, but only for a moment, for it was immediately broken by a quarrel between Tanasije and the servants helping him. The merchants began to talk too. And the old man once again resumed his habitual, humble and smiling expression. He opened his worn-out leather bag and took from it a piece of maize bread and some onions. The servants put chunks of beef on the hot coals where it sizzled and gave off a strong smell. They did not offer any to the old man, for it was known that he would not eat in anyone's house and that he lived on the bread and onions he carried in his little bag. He ate slowly and with relish, and then he went to one side of the shed, where the smoke of the fire and smell of the roast meat did not reach, and, curled up there as meekly as a schoolboy, he fell asleep with his right hand under his cheek.

Brandy enlivened the conversation among the merchants, but they kept glancing at the corner where the old man was sleeping and then lowering their voices. His presence filled them with unease and a kind of solemn seriousness which they enjoyed.

And Tanasije kept feeding the fire with beech logs, drowsy and sullen as ever, patient and imperturbable as nature itself, without thinking for a moment that from the other side of Travnik some French Consul was looking at the red glow of his fire; without even guessing, in his simplicity, that there were in the world such things as consuls and living people who did not feel like sleeping.

27

Daville spent the first months of 1814 – his last in Travnik – entirely alone, "ready for anything". He had no instructions, no information of any kind from Paris or Istanbul. He had to pay the khavazes and servants out of his own money. There was confusion among the French authorities in Dalmatia. Even French travellers and couriers had disappeared. The news from Austrian sources, which reached Travnik slowly and uncertainly, was increasingly unfavourable. He stopped going to the Residence, for the Vizier received him with ever less regard, with a kind of absent-minded and insulting affability, which hurt more than any rudeness or insult. Besides, with each day, the Vizier was becoming increasingly oppressive to the whole country. His Albanian units lived in Bosnia as in a conquered land, taking from both Turks and Christians. Dissatisfaction was becoming increasingly acute among the Muslim population. Not the kind of loud dissatisfaction that finds its outlet in trivial disturbances in the town, but the kind that smoulders for a long time, suppressed, insidious, and, when it does break out, entails blood and massacre. The Vizier was intoxicated with his victory in Serbia. In truth, later on, in the accounts of witnesses and those who knew, this victory proved to be questionable and Ali Pasha's part in it insignificant, but that only made it all the greater and more momentous for Ali Pasha himself. In his own eyes, he grew in stature as a victor with each day. With each day, his imperious attacks on the beys and most prominent Turks grew more frequent. But that was precisely what weakened his own position. For violence may be used to carry out surprise attacks and achieve useful changes, but no one can govern like that forever. As a means of government terror soon grows blunt. Everyone knows this, apart from those who are obliged by circumstance or their own instinct to rely on it. And the Vizier knew no other methods. He did not even notice that fear had already "died out" among the beys and ayans and that his attacks, which had at first really provoked panic, now no longer frightened anyone, just as they were ever less able to encourage him himself. Formerly, the beys had trembled with fear, but now they had "grown numb and cooled", while he, on the other hand, shook with fury at every least sign of disobedience or resistance, and even at their silence. The town commanders wrote to one another, the beys whispered among themselves, and in all the towns the bazaars were ominously silent. With the warmer weather an open movement against Ali Pasha's rule could be expected. D'Avenat foresaw this with certainty.

The friars avoided the French Consulate, although they continued to receive Madame Daville courteously on Sundays and holy days, when she came to Mass in the Dolac church.

The khavazes enquired of d'Avenat how much longer they could expect to remain in French service. Rafo Atijas looked for another position as an interpreter or agent, because he did not feel like going back to his uncle's warehouse. Through the unseen but constant activity of the Austrian Consulate, news of the allied victories and of Bonaparte's end which was now only a question of days, reached down to the very last man in the town. And the opinion was growing stronger that the time of the French was over and the Consulate's days in Travnik were numbered.

Von Paulich himself did not appear anywhere and did not say anything to anyone. Daville had not seen him for six months, ever since Austria entered the war, but he was conscious of his existence at every moment. He thought of him with a special feeling which was neither fear nor envy, but in which there was an element of each. He felt he could see him calmly running his affairs in the large building on the other side of the Lašva, cold, fully aware of everything, always in the right, never doubtful or hesitant, upright but wily, honest but inhuman. The complete reverse of the sick, insane victor from the Residence, he was in fact the sole victor in the game that had been going on for years in this Travnik valley. He was only waiting, immovable and serene, for the cornered victim to fall and thus proclaim his victory.

And that moment came. And here too von Paulich behaved like a man participating in some ancient, solemn game, the rules of which were inexorable and harsh, but logical, just and honourable for both vanquished and victors.

One April day, the Austrian khavaz came to the French Consulate, for the first time in seven months, bringing a letter for the Consul.

Daville recognized the handwriting, all clean, straight lines as though made by steel arrows, all equally sharp and all going in the same direction. He recognized the calligraphy, guessed at the purpose of the letter, but was surprised by its contents.

Von Paulich wrote that he had just received news that the war between the allies and the French had been happily concluded. Napoleon had abdicated. The lawful ruler had been summoned to the throne of France. The Senate had proclaimed a new constitution and a new government had been formed with Talleyrand, Prince of Benevento, at its head. On the assumption that this news, which concerned the fate of his homeland, would interest him, he was passing it on to Daville, glad that the end of the war had enabled them once again to renew their mutual contacts, he asked him to convey his respects to Madame Daville, as ever, etc., etc.

Daville's surprise was so great that the true sense and full significance of what he had learned were quite unable to penetrate his consciousness. At first he left the letter and got up from the table, as though he had received a message he had long been expecting from von Paulich.

For a long time, but particularly since December of the previous year, and the defeat in Russia, Daville had been considering the possibility of such an outcome, pondering over it and determining his attitude to it.

So he had been slowly and imperceptibly coming to terms with the possibility of the fall of the Empire. With each day and with each occurrence, that distant, long-standing threat had been coming nearer, entering unnoticed into the reality he knew, and gradually replacing it. And now, beyond the Emperor and the Empire life could be glimpsed, eternal, omnipotent, unbounded life, with its innumerable possibilities.

He did not himself know when it was that he had begun to get used to thinking about events and things in this world without Napoleon as the basic assumption. At first it had been hard and painful, like a kind of inner faintness. He had stumbled inwardly like a man with the earth shifting beneath his feet. After that he had felt only a great emptiness, the absence of any elation or anything firm and stable, nothing but dry, arid life, with no prospects or any of those distant visions which may be unreal but which give us strength and a true dignity to our step. Finally, he had thought about it so much and given himself up to that feeling so frequently that he had begun increasingly often to start from that imaginary point in his assessment of the world, France, his own fate and that of his family.

All that time, as hitherto, Daville carried out his duties conscientiously, reading circulars and articles in the *Moniteur*, listening to couriers and travellers as they talked about Napoleon's plans for the defence of inner France or the prospects of achieving peace with the coalition powers. But immediately afterwards, his thoughts would return to the question of what would happen when the Emperor and the Empire were no more, and he dwelt increasingly long on these thoughts.

In short, he was sharing the experience of thousands of French people at that time, exhausted in the service of a régime which had in fact been defeated long ago because it had been obliged to ask of people more than they could give.

And when a person becomes accustomed to something and reconciled to it in his thoughts, he begins sooner or later to find confirmation of it in reality as well. And he does so all the more easily when reality has been going in the same direction as his thoughts, often even overtaking them.

In recent times, Daville had been able to see, with some surprise, that he had already covered an enormous amount of ground in that direction. Forgetting the numerous and lengthy battles he had waged in himself in the course of the last year, it seemed that he had come easily and all at once to the point where he now found himself. In any case, he had felt for a long time now like a man who was "ready for anything", which actually meant that he had already, inwardly, completely broken with the order that was now disintegrating in France, and was willing to accept whatever was to come after it, no matter what it was.

But nevertheless, now, at the moment when all this appeared before him as reality, Daville reeled, as though from a hard and unexpected blow. He walked about the room, and the meaning of what he had read in von Paulich's letter began to come clear, provoking ever new waves of mixed emotions: surprise, fear, pity, then a pathetic satisfaction that he and his family had been spared and were alive amid such ruin and upheaval, and then again, uncertainty and alarm. From somewhere he remembered the Old Testament saying that the Lord is great in all his deeds, And these words returned to him constantly like a melody he could not shake off, although he would not have been able to say what those deeds were or what their greatness consisted of, nor what all of this had to do with the Lord of the Bible.

He walked about the cold room for a long time, but he could not stop on one thought, and still less put what he had heard into some order in his mind. He felt that he was going to need a lot of time for that.

He could see that all his reflections, forethought and his easy mental reconciliation were not worth much and did not help at the moment when the blow fell. For, it is one thing to project your fears in your imagination, to foresee the worst, to work out your attitude and your defence, and at the same time to feel the satisfaction that all is still in order and in its place. It is quite another to find yourself facing an actual breakdown which demands urgent decisions and concrete actions. It is one thing to listen to your tipsy, quick-tempered colleague from the Admiralty saying, with burning eyes: "The Emperor is mad! All of us, him included, are careering into the disaster waiting for us at the end of all our victories." But it is quite another to grasp and accept as reality the fact that the Empire has been beaten and destroyed, that Napoleon no longer exists, but is nothing but a deposed usurper, worth less than if he had perished in one of his victories. It is one thing to doubt the value of victory and the permanence of military successes, as he had begun increasingly to do in recent years, and to reflect on what would become of him and his family "in the event that…" But it is quite another to realize suddenly that everything had vanished overnight – not only the Revolution and all that it had brought, but "The General" and that irresistible magic of his victorious genius and the whole order which had rested on him – as though they had never existed, and that now everything had all at once to return to the state it was in when he, Daville, as a boy, on the square of his native town, carried away by "the King's goodness", had cheered Louis XVI.

That would be a lot, even in a dream.

Incapable of pulling himself together, of penetrating the sense of what was happening and making out the future, Daville latched onto the fact that his old protector Talleyrand was at the head of the new government. That appeared to him as the only sign of salvation, as a special blessing of fate bestowed on him personally, in the general chaos and destruction.

As with "The General", Daville had only spoken to Talleyrand once in his life, and that was more than eighteen years ago, when he was not yet famous and did not hold the title of Prince of Benevento. In the old Ministry of Foreign Affairs, where total disorder had reigned at that time – not only in its work and staff, but even in the furniture and its arrangement – he had been received for a few minutes in an improvised reception room by Talleyrand, who had wanted to see him because he had noticed his articles in the *Moniteur*. And their short conversation had been characterized by a similar disorder.

A robust man, who had received him standing and remained on his feet throughout their whole conversation, he had an all-embracing, impudently serene gaze which simply brushed superficially over the young man, as though it were seeking the real object of its attention somewhere over his shoulder. And he spoke absent-mindedly and superficially too, as though he regretted showing interest in those articles and voicing the wish to see the young man. He told him "he must carry on" and that he would always support him in his work and career. That was, in fact, all that Daville had seen and heard of his protector. But nevertheless, throughout these last eighteen years, for Daville himself and for all the officials at the Ministry, it was an acknowledged fact that Daville was Talleyrand's protégé and that the course of his career was linked to Talleyrand's star. And whenever Talleyrand had been in power and in government, he really had supported him. It often happens that the powerful drag persistently behind them a crowd of protégés, not for the sake of them, whom they do not know or value, but for themselves, because the support and protection they offer these people is a visible sign of their own power and worth.

I shall turn to the Prince, said Daville to himself, not yet knowing how or why. I shall turn to the Prince, he repeated to himself that whole night, unable to devise anything else and with a sinking feeling that there was no one he could consult. And the following day found him exhausted and confused, but just as undecided as the day before.

Watching his wife walking round the house, organizing the work to be done in the garden, with no inkling of what was going on, as though she would be living in Travnik for ever and a day, he saw himself as a cursed being who knew what other mortals did not and was therefore above them and unhappier than they were.

The arrival of a courier from Istanbul shook him out of his indecision. The courier bore the congratulations of the Ambassador and his staff to the new government and expressions of their loyalty to the legitimate ruler, Louis XVIII and the Bourbon dynasty. He also brought an order for Daville that the Vizier and local authorities be informed of the changes in France and told that as of now the Consul was in Travnik as the representative of Louis XVIII, King of France and Navarre.

As though he were working according to a plan made long ago, or an inaudible command, Daville wrote in the course of that day, without hesitation or second thought, all that Paris required.

"I have learned from the Austrian Consul here of the fortunate turn of events which has restored to the throne the descendant of Henry the Great, and to France peace and the prospect of a better future. As long as I live I shall regret that I was not in Paris on that occasion to add my voice to the cheers of the delighted people."

So began Daville's letter in which he placed his services at the disposal of the new government, begging that "expressions of his devotion and loyalty should be laid at the foot of the throne" and stressing modestly that he was "an ordinary citizen, one of those 20,000 Parisians who had signed the famous petition in defence of the martyr king, Louis XVI and the Royal Family".

He ended his letter with the hope that "after the Iron Age, a Golden Age was dawning".

At the same time he sent Talleyrand congratulations in verse, as he had often done on previous occasions while Talleyrand was in power. The congratulations began:

Des peuples et des Rois heureux modérateur,
Talleyrand, tu deviens notre libérateur![22]

And as he did not have time to complete it, because of the courier, he designated these two dozen feeble lines a "fragment".

At the same time, Daville proposed that the Consulate in Travnik be closed, because there was no need for its further maintenance in the completely altered circumstances. He asked to be permitted to leave Travnik with his family in the course of the month, and to entrust d'Avenat, whose loyalty had been tried and proved many times, with running the Consulate until its closure. In view of the exceptional circumstances, if he did not receive any contrary instructions by the end of the month, he would set out for Paris with his family.

Daville spent the whole night writing these congratulations, requests and letters. He slept for just two hours, but he rose fresh and strengthened and accompanied the courier on his way.

From the terrace, on which the still closed tulips were bent under a heavy dew, Daville watched the courier and his companion going down the steep road to the highway in the valley. Their horses were stepping up to their knees through a low, dense mist, red with the unseen sun, and sinking ever deeper into it as they disappeared from view.

Then he returned to his study on the ground floor. Everywhere there were visible signs of the previous night spent working and writing: crooked, burned-down candles, scattered papers, broken

---

22 "Happy appeaser of peoples and Kings,/Talleyrand, you have become our liberator!"

sealing wax. Without touching anything, Daville sat down among the drafts and torn-up papers. He felt a heavy weariness, but also a great relief that it was all done and despatched to the appropriate people, decisively and irreversibly, and that there could no longer be any doubt or reflection about it. He sat down at his desk and rested his sleepy head on his crossed arms.

Nevertheless, it was difficult not to think, not to remember, not to see. He had spent twenty-five years looking for "the middle way" which would bring peace of mind and give a person the dignity he could not live without. For twenty-five years he had been moving from one "elation" to another, seeking and finding, losing and gaining, and now he had arrived, exhausted, inwardly rent, worn out, back at the point from which he had set out when he was eighteen years old. This meant that all the paths were only apparently going forward, but were in fact leading in a circle, like the deceptive labyrinths of oriental tales, and so they had brought him, tired and faint-hearted, to this place, among the torn papers and jumbled copies, to the point where the circle began again, as from every other point. This meant there could be no middle path, that true path leading forward, into stability, peace and dignity, but that we were all travelling in a circle, always along the same, deceptive path, and only the people and the generations change as they travel, constantly deceived. This meant, the tired man concluded his false, weary reasoning, that there was no path at all. And this one along which he was now to be taken by his stumbling, lame protector, the powerful Prince of Benevento, was only a part of that circle which was nothing but a false path. One just travels. And the road has meaning and dignity only in so far as we are able to find those qualities in ourselves. There is no path or purpose. One just travels. Travels and exhausts oneself.

Yes, this was how he was travelling now, without pause or rest. His head drooped, his eyes closed of their own accord, and before him a red mist grew, with a succession of horses taking small steps, sinking ever deeper into that mist and disappearing in it, together with their riders. Ever new ones, innumerable horses and horsemen appeared and sank in the endless mist, where a man would fall from weariness and the desire for sleep.

Lowering his head onto his folded arms, overcome with fatigue and inextricable thoughts, Daville fell asleep on his desk, among the papers and burned-out candles of the night before.

If only he could be left to sleep, not to raise his head or open his eyes, even in this damp, red mist among the ever denser waves of horsemen. But they would not leave him. One of these horsemen stopped behind him and kept placing a cold hand mercilessly on Daville's neck, repeating incomprehensible words to him. He bowed his head ever lower, but the horsemen kept waking him ever more persistently.

When he raised his head and opened his eyes, he saw his wife's smiling, disapproving face. Madame Daville was reproaching him for over-tiring himself and trying to persuade him to undress, lie down and rest. Now that he was quite awake, the very idea of being left alone in bed with his thoughts seemed intolerable. He began to organize his desk and to talk to his wife as he did so. Until now he had avoided telling her clearly what changes had taken place in the world and in France and what they meant for them. Now, all at once, it seemed simple.

When she heard, definitively, that everything was fundamentally altered, including their situation, and that the end of their stay in Travnik had really arrived, for a moment Madame Daville was stunned. But only for a moment, until she had fully taken in what it meant for her family and what concrete tasks it placed before her personally. As soon as she grasped this, she grew calm. And they began immediately to discuss the journey, the transport of their belongings, their future life in France.

28

Madame Daville set to work.

In just the same way as she had once arranged and furnished this same house for them to live in, now she prepared to move out: calmly, painstakingly and tirelessly, not sparing herself and not asking anyone's advice. The household she had created in the course of these seven years began systematically to be dismantled. Everything was marked, carefully wrapped and prepared for the journey. The terrace, with its flowers and the large garden with its beds of vegetables, were the most painful part for Madame Daville.

The white hyacinths which Frau von Mitterer had once christened "Wedding Bliss" or "The Imperial Bridegroom", were still strong and full, but the centre of the terrace had been taken over by Dutch tulips which Madame Daville had managed in recent years to acquire in large numbers and varied colours. The year before they had still been feeble and uneven, but this year they had done well and had just finished blooming consistently, so that they had looked like rows of schoolchildren in a church procession.

The peas were already flowering in the garden. She had acquired the seed from von Paulich the previous year, a few weeks before the declaration of war. Now the deaf and dumb Munib, the "Mumbler", was hoeing round them.

Munib was working now, as every spring. He knew nothing of events in the world, nor of the change in the fortunes of these people. For him this year was like any other. Constantly bent, he crumbled the soil with his hands lump by lump, fertilized, transplanted and watered, smiling at Jean-Paul or little Eugénie when the maid brought her out onto the terrace. With swift, delicate movements of his muddy fingers, he explained to Madame Daville that these same peas had grown taller and were flowering more abundantly in von Paulich's garden, but that did not mean anything, for it was no guide to the true crop. That would not be seen until the pods began to form.

Madame Daville looked at him. She signalled that she had understood everything and went into the house to continue packing. It was only there that she realized that in a few days she would have to leave everything, the house and the garden, and that neither she nor her family would see the mature fruit of these peas. Her eyes filled with tears.

So the people in the French Consulate were preparing calmly for their departure. However, there was one question confronting Daville. This was the question of money. What little they had in the way of savings, Daville had despatched earlier to France. For months now no salaries had been arriving. The Sarajevo Jews who had worked with Frayssinet and often given loans to the Consulate as well, were now distrustful. D'Avenat had some money saved, but he was being left in an indeterminate role and complete uncertainty here in Travnik. It would not have been right to deprive him of what he had and ask him to lend to the state, and with no guarantees.

Both interpreters, d'Avenat and Rafo Atijas, well knew the position Daville was in. And as he tormented himself, trying to think where he might turn, one day Rafo's uncle, old Salomon Atijas, arrived. He was the most eminent of the brothers and the head of the whole numerous tribe of Travnik Atijases.

Stocky, overweight and bandy-legged, in a greasy coat, his head set directly between his narrow shoulders as though he had no neck, he had large bulging eyes, like those of people suffering from a heart complaint. He was covered in sweat and out of breath from the warm May day and his unaccustomed walk up the steep hill. He closed the door timidly behind him and fell panting onto a chair. He gave off a smell of garlic and untanned skins. He held his black, hairy fists clenched in his lap, and on every hair there glistened a tiny drop of sweat.

They exchanged greetings several times, repeating the same meaningless expressions of politeness. Daville did not wish to admit that he and his family were leaving Travnik forever, and nor was the breathless, heavy Master Salomon able to say why he had come. In the end, the Jew did after all begin, in his rasping, guttural voice which always reminded Daville of Spain, assuring the Consul that he understood the unexpected changes and great needs of the state and state employees, that times were hard for everyone and even for a merchant who simply got on with his own business and – finally, there, finally – if the state money should not reach Monsieur le Consul in time, and a journey was a journey, and official requirements could not wait, he, Salomon Atijas, was always at the service of the French Imperial...that is, the Royal Consulate and Monsieur le Consul personally, and at his disposal with what little he had and could offer.

Daville, who had at first thought that Atijas had come to ask him for something, was surprised and touched. His voice was unsteady with emotion. His facial muscles twitched visibly between his mouth and chin, where his ruddy skin was beginning to fade, wrinkle and sag.

There followed an embarrassed process of offering and thanking. In the end they arranged that Atijas would lend the Consulate 25 Imperial ducats against a promissory note.

Salomon's large, protruding eyes were moist, which gave them an unusual brilliance, despite their yellowish, bloodshot whites. Tears of emotion – a constant state with him these days – shone in Daville's eyes too. Now they talked more easily and freely.

Daville sought carefully chosen words to express his gratitude. He spoke of his affection and understanding for the Jews, of compassion and the need for people to comprehend and help one another without discrimination. He confined himself to general, vague expressions, for he could no longer talk about Napoleon, whose name had a powerful attraction and special meaning for the Jews, and still less did he dare mention his new government and the new ruler by name. Salomon watched him with his large eyes, constantly perspiring and breathing heavily, as though this was all quite clear to him too, and difficult, just as difficult or even more so than for Daville, as though he fully understood what a torment and a danger all these emperors and kings, viziers and ministers were, whose departures and arrivals did not depend on us in the slightest, but who nevertheless raised us up and cast us down, us and our families, and everything we were and possessed. It seemed he was altogether unhappy that he had had to leave his gloomy warehouse and its piles of hides, to clamber up to this high, sunny place and to sit with gentlemen, on unaccustomed chairs, in luxurious rooms.

Glad that the question of money for the journey had been resolved so unexpectedly easily and in order to give the whole conversation at least a slightly more cheerful tone, Daville said half-jokingly: "I am grateful to you, and I shall never forget that despite all your other worries you managed to spare a thought for the fate of the representative of France. And, if I may say so, after all that has happened here, after all the fines you have paid, I admire you for being in a position to lend anything to anyone. For the Vizier boasted that he had drained your coffers quite dry."

At the mention of the persecution and fines the Jews had had to suffer from Ali Pasha, Salomon's eyes took on a fixed and anxious, sorrowful expression, like an animal's.

"It cost us a great deal and took a lot from us and it really did drain our coffers dry, but I can tell you and you should know…"

Here Salomon glanced in embarrassment at his sweaty hands on his knees and after a short silence continued in a different, thinner voice, altered, as though he were suddenly talking from some other part of the room: "Yes, it frightened us and cost us a lot. Yes. And the Vizier is really a severe, a severe and hard gentleman. But he has only to deal with the Jews once, and we have endured dozens and dozens of viziers. Viziers are replaced and leave. (It's true that each one takes something with him.) The viziers go, forgetting what they did and how they behaved, new ones come and each starts all over again. But we remain, we remember, we record everything we have suffered, how we defended ourselves and we pass this dearly bought experience on from father to son. That is why our coffers have two bottoms. The Vizier's hand reaches one, taking everything, but below that there is always something left for us and our children, to save our souls, to help our families and a friend in distress."

Here Salomon glanced straight at Daville, no longer with his comically timid and sad eyes, but with a new, direct and courageous look.

Daville laughed heartily. "Oh, that's good. I like that. And the Vizier thought that he was extraordinarily cunning and skilful."

Salomon immediately interrupted him in a quieter voice, as though he wanted to impose a lower tone on him as well: "No, I don't mean he isn't. Oh yes, those are powerful gentlemen, wise and skilful. Only you know how it is, the gentlemen are wise, they are powerful, like dragons, these gentlemen of ours, but the gentlemen wage wars, the gentlemen quarrel, spend money. For you know what our people say: great power is like a great wind, it blows, lashes about, and subsides. And we sit still and work, make money. And that is why it lasts longer with us and can always be found."

"Ah, that's good, that's good," Daville nodded his approval, laughing all the time and encouraging Salomon to continue.

But it was just this laugh that made the Jew suddenly stop and look a little more closely at the Consul's face, with that first anxious and fearful look again. He was afraid he had gone too far and said more than he should. He could see that what he had said was not what he had wanted to say. He did not know himself what that should have been. But something was driving him to speak, complain, boast, explain, like a man who has been given a unique opportunity, just a few precious minutes, for an important and urgent message. Once he had left his warehouse, climbed up the steep slope he never went up otherwise, and sat down in this bright room, in a splendour and cleanliness he was not accustomed to, it had seemed to him very important that he could talk with this foreigner, who would be leaving the town in a few days, and that he should talk in a way he would perhaps never be able or dare to again with anyone.

Forgetting his original embarrassment and acute awkwardness, he felt increasingly strongly the need to say something else to this foreigner, about himself and his people, something urgent and secret, from this Travnik pit, from his damp warehouse, where life was hard, where there was no honour or justice, no splendour or order, no judge or witness, something that would be a message directed he did not himself know to whom, to some better, more orderly and enlightened world out there, to which the consul was returning. For once, to say something that was not simply cunning and caution, that had nothing to do with acquiring and saving, with everyday calculation and bargaining, but on the contrary, with giving, with generous pride and sincerity.

But it was precisely this strong desire, which had suddenly come over him, to communicate and pass on something general and weighty about his existence in the world, about the torments of all the Travnik Atijases through the ages, that prevented him from finding the right way and the words he needed to express briefly but adequately what was now stifling him and sending the blood rushing to his head. That is why he spoke haltingly, saying not what was filling him completely and what he so much wished to express – how they fought and how they succeeded in preserving their unseen strength and dignity – but just the broken words that happened to come onto his tongue:

"There…that is how we keep going, and manage to acquire, and do not regret…for friends, for justice, for the kindness that is shown us. For we…for we too…"

Here his eyes suddenly clouded over and his voice broke off. He stood up in confusion. Daville stood up as well, moved by a vague emotion and friendship, and offered him his hand. Salomon took that hand quickly, with an unaccustomed, clumsy movement, mumbling a few more words, asking him not to forget them and to say where he could, to the right people, that they were living here, that they were struggling and redeeming themselves through their struggle. These were just indistinct and unconnected words which merged with Daville's expressions of gratitude.

It will never be possible to say what it was that was stifling Salomon Atijas at that moment, what was driving tears to his eyes and an agitated trembling through his whole body. Had he known how, had he been able to speak at all, this is roughly what he would have said:

"Monsieur, you have been here among us for more than seven years, and during that time you have shown us Jews an attention we have never experienced, either from the Turks or from foreigners. You have acknowledged us as human beings, not distinguishing us from others. Perhaps you yourself don't even know how much kindness you showed us in so doing. Now you are going away. Your Empire has been obliged to retreat in the face of all-powerful enemies. Painful things and great upsets have taken place in your country. But it is a noble and powerful country and it must all change for the better. And you will find your way in your homeland. It is we who remain here who are to be pitied, this handful of Travnik Sephardic Jews of whom two-thirds are Atijases, for you have been like a little light for our eyes. You have seen the life we lead, and you have done us every kind of good a man may do a man. And whoever does good leads people to expect still more good from him. That is why we dare to ask also this of you: to be our witness in the West from where we ourselves once came and where people ought to know what has been done to us. For, it seems to me, if we were sure that someone knew and acknowledged that we are not what we seem, that we are not as we live, then everything we have to endure would be easier.

"More than three hundred years ago we were lifted out of our homeland, our one and only Andalusia, by a terrible, senseless, fratricidal whirlwind, which we still cannot understand today, and which has yet to understand itself. It hurled us all over the world, making us beggars whom not even gold can help. It cast us here, into the East, and life in the East is not easy or blessed for us, and the further a man goes and the nearer he gets to the sun's origin, the worse it is, for the earth is ever younger and more raw and the people are of the earth. And our torment lies in the fact that we were unable either completely to come to love this land to which we owe the fact that it took us in and gave us refuge, nor were we able to come to hate the one that drove us unjustly away, exiling us like unworthy sons. We do not know whether it is harder for us to be here or not to be there. Wherever we were outside Spain, we would suffer, for we would always have two homelands, I know that, but here life has confined and belittled us too much. I know that we were changed long ago, we no longer remember what we were like, but we do remember that we were different. We set off long ago and we travelled with difficulty and unluckily for us we happened to stop in this place, and that is why we are no longer even a shadow of what we once were. Like the bloom on a fruit which goes from hand to hand, a man loses first what is finest about him. That is why we are as we are. But you know us, us and our life, if this may be called 'life'. We live between the Turks and the rayah, the wretched rayah and the dreadful Turks. Cut off completely from our own people and those close to us, we endeavour to preserve what is Spanish – songs and food and customs – but we feel everything in us changing, being spoiled and forgotten. We remember the language of our country, as we brought it with us three centuries ago and as it is no longer spoken even there, and we stutter comically in the language of the rayah with whom we suffer and of the Turks who rule us. So that the day is perhaps not far off when we shall be able to express ourselves purely and humanly only in a prayer which does not in fact require words. Isolated and few in number as we are, we inter-marry and watch our blood grow thin and pale. We bow down and get out of everyone's way, we toil, but we get along, as they say: we light fires on ice, we work, we make money, we save, and not only for ourselves and our children, but for all those who are stronger and more brazen than we are and who assault our lives, our honour and our purses.

"That is how we have preserved the faith which caused us to abandon our lovely country, but we have lost virtually everything else. Fortunately, and distressingly for us, we have not lost from memory the image of that dear land of ours, as it once was, before it drove us out like a step-mother; neither will our desire for a better world ever fade, a world of order and compassion in which one can walk upright, look calmly and speak openly. We cannot free ourselves of this, nor of the feeling that, despite everything, we belong to such a world, although we live, persecuted and miserable, in its opposite.

"There, that is what we should like known, *over there*. That our name should not perish in that brighter, higher world which is constantly darkened and disrupted, constantly shifting and changing, but is never destroyed and always exists somewhere for someone. That this world should know that we carry it in our hearts, that we serve it even here, in our way, and that we feel at one with it, although we are forever hopelessly separated from it.

"And this is not vanity or an empty wish, but a real need and a sincere appeal."

That, roughly, is what Salomon Atijas would have said at that moment when the French Consul was preparing to leave Travnik forever, as he gave him the ducats, saved with difficulty, to enable him to travel. That or something like it is what he would have said. But all of that was far from being completely clear and precise in his consciousness, and still less ripe for expression. It lay in him, vivid and heavy, but unspoken and inexpressible. And who does ever succeed in expressing his finest feelings and best impulses? No one, virtually no one. So how could it be done by a Travnik hide merchant, a Spanish Jew, who did not know a single one of this world's languages properly, and if he had known them all it would not have done him any good, because he was not permitted to cry out loud even in his cradle, let alone speak freely and clearly in his lifetime. But that was the cause and the barely intelligible sense of his stuttering and trembling at his parting with the French Consul.

While creating a home is as difficult and slow as going uphill, the dismantling of an institution or a household goes as quickly and easily as a downhill path.

Daville received a reply from Paris sooner than he could have hoped. He had been granted three months' leave, so that he could bring his family immediately, leaving d'Avenat in charge of the Consulate. During his stay in Paris the question of the liquidation of the Travnik General Consulate would be decided.

Daville sought an audience with the Vizier to inform him of his departure.

Ali Pasha had the appearance of a sick man now. He was exceptionally affable with Daville. It was obvious that he had been informed that the closure of the Consulate was imminent. Daville made the Vizier a gift of a hunting rifle, while the Vizier gave him a greatcoat lined with fur, which meant he believed Daville was leaving for good. They parted like two men who did not have much to say to each other, for each was too preoccupied and weighed down by his own worries.

The same day Daville sent von Paulich a gift of a rifle, a valuable carbine of German make, and a few bottles of Martinique. In quite a long letter he informed him that he and his family would be leaving Travnik during the next few days for "a long leave which will be, God willing, for good". Daville asked to be given visas and letters of recommendation for the Austrian border authorities and for the officer in charge of quarantine in Kostajnica.

"It is my wish", Daville continued, "that the agreements that are now being drawn up in Paris will bring the world a lasting peace, as enduring and wise as that of Westphalia, and that they will ensure the present generation long respite. I hope that our great European family, reconciled and united, will never again offer the world the pitiful spectacle of disunity and disagreement. I hope and fervently wish that it may be so. You know that these were my principles before the recent war, during the war, and that they remain even more than ever so, today.

"Wherever I am," wrote Daville, "and wherever fate bears me, I shall never forget that in the barbaric land where I was condemned to live, I found the most enlightened and decent man in Europe."

And as he ended his letter in this way, Daville was resolved to depart without taking his leave of von Paulich personally. He felt that, of all the difficulties he had to endure, the worst would be the tranquil, victorious face of the Lieutenant-Colonel.

Informing the Court Chancery of the imminent closure of the French General Consulate in Travnik, von Paulich proposed the immediate closure of the Austrian General Consulate as well.

This Consulate was becoming redundant not only because there would no longer be any French activity in these regions, but also because, by all accounts, one could expect internal upheaval in Bosnia and open conflict between the Vizier and the beys. All energies and attention would be focused on that conflict and consequently one could not expect in the foreseeable future that any measures would be taken against the Austrian frontier. And Vienna could always be kept informed about these internal Bosnian matters through the friars or special agents.

With this proposal, von Paulich also sent a copy of Daville's letter. At the end, where Daville spoke flatteringly about him personally, he added in his own hand: "I have already several times had occasion to draw your attention to Monsieur Daville's fertile imagination and his tendency to exaggerate."

Daville spent the whole summer afternoon with d'Avenat, organizing papers and giving him instructions.

D'Avenat was grim-faced as ever, his tense jaw muscles twitching. It had been decided that his son should be appointed to work at the Embassy in Istanbul. Daville had promised that he would look into the matter at the Ministry, where it had been held up because of the upheaval in France, and see that the appointment was made. Thinking only of his son, a handsome, clever young man of twenty-two, d'Avenat assured Daville that he would carry out the liquidation properly and remove everything down to the last pen and smallest scrap of paper, even if they were to cut him to pieces. As they did not manage to finish, they continued the work after dinner. It was not until about ten o'clock that d'Avenat left.

When he was left alone, Daville looked round the half-empty room where one candle was burning and darkness was gathering. There were no curtains at the windows. On the white walls lighter places stood out where there had been pictures until the day before. Through the open window came the sound of water.

Both clock towers struck some Turkish hour, first the one in the neighbourhood and then the further one in the Lower Bazaar, as though it were imitating the first one.

The Consul was exhausted, but tense, which kept him alert, giving him a kind of energy, and he went on organizing his personal papers.

In cardboard covers, tied with green ribbons, lay the manuscript of his epic about Alexander the Great. Of the twenty-four proposed cantos, seventeen were written, and even they were not complete. Earlier, as he wrote about Alexander's campaigns, he had always had "The General" before his eyes, but now that he had been experiencing, for more than a year, the downfall of the living conqueror as his own personal destiny, he no longer knew what to say about the rise and fall of the long dead hero of his epic. And so now this unfinished work lay before him, like a logical and temporal absurdity: Napoleon had followed the great arch of his rise and fall, and had once again touched the ground, while Alexander was still somewhere in flight, conquering "the Syrian gorges" near Isos and not dreaming of his fall. Daville had often struggled to move further, but each time he had seen clearly that his poetry always fell silent in the face of real events.

Here too lay the beginning of a tragedy about Selim III which he had wanted to write the previous year, after Ibrahim Pasha's departure, recalling his long conversations with the Vizier about the unfortunate, enlightened Sultan.

Here were all those felicitations and missives in verse, on the occasion of various solemn events, and celebrations of different people and regimes. Poor lines, dedicated to lost causes or personalities who today meant less than the dead. Finally there were bundles of bills and personal letters tied up with string, yellowed and torn at the edges. As soon as he broke the string these papers fell apart. Some were more than twenty years old. Daville recognized some of the letters at the very first glance. He saw the regular, firm handwriting of one of his best friends, Jean Villeneuve, who had died suddenly the year before, on a ship outside Naples. The letter was dated 1808, written in answer to some anxious letter of Daville's:

"…Believe me, my dear friend, your anxieties and black thoughts are quite unfounded. Today less than ever. The great and exceptional man who is now directing the destiny of the world, is creating the foundations for a better and more lasting order for the most distant times. That is why we may rely completely on him. In him lies the best guarantee of a happy future, not only for each of us, but also for each of our children and our children's children. Therefore be tranquil, my dear friend, as I am tranquil, for my peace of mind rests on the clear realization I have outlined above…"

Daville raised his eyes from the letter and gazed at the open window, through which moths were flying, attracted by the light in the room. Then, from the neighbouring quarter, a song began to be heard, feebly at first, then ever more loudly. This was Musa the Singer going home. His voice had become hoarse and weak, and his singing was disjointed, but drink had not yet finished him off, he was still alive and so was what von Mitterer had once called the "Urjammer" in him. Now Musa had turned the corner into his quarter, for his voice came ever more weakly, with ever longer pauses, like the calling of a drowning person sinking, coming to the surface again to call once more, and then sinking again, still deeper.

Now the singer had staggered into his courtyard. His voice could no longer be heard. Silence reigned once more, undisturbed by the sound of the water in the night, which only made it more uniform and complete.

So everything sinks. That is how "The General" had sunk, and, before him, so many powerful people and great movements!

Left again in the untroubled night silence, as though wrapped in it, Daville sat for a moment longer, his arms folded and his gaze vacant. He was tense and anxious, but not afraid or lonely. Despite all the uncertainty and all the difficulties that awaited him, it seemed – for the first time since he had been in Travnik – as though a small part of the path before him was clearing a little.

Ever since that February day, more than seven years before, when, after the first Divan with Mehmed Husref Pasha, he had come, humiliated and upset, into Baruh's room on the ground floor and collapsed onto the hard settee, all his work and efforts in connection with Bosnia and the Turks had been dragging him down towards the earth, restricting and weakening him. From year to year, he had been increasingly affected and corroded by the "oriental poison" that clouds the eyes and undermines the will, and with which this country had begun to infect him from the very first day. Neither the proximity of the French army in Dalmatia, nor all the brilliance of its great victories could alter this. And now, in defeat, when he was preparing to leave it all and set off into uncertainty, he felt a strength and will he had not known in these seven years. His worries were greater than ever, but, strangely, they did not drive him to distraction as they had once, but rather sharpened his thoughts and broadened his perspective. Instead of ambushing him, like a curse or calamity, they flowed along with the rest of life.

Something could now be heard rustling and scratching in the next room, like a mouse in the skirting. That was his wife, tireless and composed as ever, wrapping up the last things. In this same house his children were sleeping. They too would one day grow up (he would do all he could to ensure that they grew up well and happily) and set off to find the road he had been unable to find. And, even if they did not find it, they would, presumably, look for it with more energy and dignity than he had been able to summon.

They were growing now, as they slept. Yes, life went on in this house as in the world outside, where new vistas were opening up and new possibilities coming to fruition. As though he had left Travnik long ago, he no longer thought of Bosnia, of what it had given him or how much it had taken from him. He felt only that an energy was coming to him from somewhere, together with patience and the determination to save himself and his family. And he went on organizing his yellowed papers, tearing up what was out of date and superfluous, and making piles of what he might need for his future life, in altered circumstances, in France.

But this mechanical task was accompanied, as by an insistent melody, by the vague but constant thought: that, nevertheless, there must somewhere be that "right path" he had been seeking his whole life in vain; that it existed and that someone would find it, sooner or later, and open it up for everyone. He did not himself know how, when or where, but it would be found some day, by his children, his children's children, or his still more distant descendants.

Like an inaudible inner melody, this made his work easier.

Epilogue

It was already the third week that the weather had been settled. As every year, the beys had begun to come out to talk together on the Sofa at Lutvo's. But their conversations were restrained and sombre. A silent agreement to rebel against the intolerable government of Ali Pasha was being reached throughout the whole country. This matter had been quite decided in people's hearts and now it was maturing of its own accord. Ali Pasha himself speeded up this maturing process by his actions.

It was the last Friday of May, 1814. All the beys were present and the discussion was lively and serious. They had all heard the news of the defeats of Napoleon's armies and his abdication; now they were simply exchanging, comparing and extending their information. One of the beys, who had been speaking with people from the Residence that morning, said that everything was arranged for the departure of the French Consul and his family, and it was known for certain that the Austrian Consul would soon be following him, since he was in Travnik solely on account of the French. So it could be safely estimated that by the autumn the Consuls and Consulates and all that they had brought with them would disappear from Travnik.

They all received this news like the announcement of a victory. For, although over the years they had become to a large extent accustomed to the presence of the foreign Consuls, they were all nevertheless glad that these foreigners were going, with their different and unusual way of life, and their brazen meddling in Bosnian affairs. They were discussing the question of who would take over the "Dubrovnik Khan" where the French Consulate was now, and what would happen to Hafzadć's big house when the Austrian Consul left Travnik too. They were all speaking a little more loudly than usual, so that Hamdi Bey Teskeredžić, who was sitting in his place, would be able to hear what was going on. He had grown very old and decrepit, collapsed into himself like a dilapidated building. His hearing was giving out. He could not raise his eyelids, which were even heavier now; instead he had to throw his head back if he wanted to see someone better. His lips were blue and they stuck together as he spoke. The old man raised his head and asked the person who had last spoken: "When was it that those...consuls came?"

People began to look at one another and make guesses. Some replied that it was six years ago. Some that it was more. After a brief argument and calculation they agreed that the first consul had arrived more than seven years earlier, three days before the Ramadan Bairam.

"Seven years," said Hamdi Bey thoughtfully, drawing out the words, "seven years! And do you remember how much noise and excitement there was because of those consuls and that...that... Bunaparta? Bunaparta this, and Bunaparta that. He's going to do this, he won't do that...The world is too small for him; there's no limit to his power. And our Christian pigs had raised their heads like barren corn. Some were hanging on to the French Consul's coat-tails, others clung to the Austrian, while yet others were waiting for the one from Moscow. Our rayah quite lost their wits. And – it came and it passed. The Emperors rose up and they smashed Bunaparta. The consuls will clear out of Travnik. People will refer to them for another year or so. The children will play consuls and khavazes on the river bank, riding on sticks, and then they too will be forgotten as though they had never existed. And everything will be as it always has been, by God's will."

Hamdi Bey stopped, for his breath had given out, and the others said nothing in anticipation of what else the old man might say. And as they smoked they all savoured the good, triumphant silence.

Glossary of Turkish Words

N.B. As was the common practice in nineteenth-century Bosnia, the words "Turk" and "Turkish" in the text are frequently used to denote Bosnian Muslims, i.e. Slavs converted to Islam.

Aga	Originally an officer, later used to denote a gentleman, landowner
Ayan	Notable, prominent, distinguished person
Bairam	Muslim festival at the end of the Ramadan fast
Bashi-Bazouk	Irregular auxiliary soldier
Bey	High-ranking official in provincial service, administrator of a province
Cadi	Civil judge of Islamic and Ottoman law
Caliph	The chief civil and religious ruler in Muslim countries, successor of Mohammed
Chibouk	Long tobacco-pipe, with long stem and bowl of baked clay
Defterdar	Tax officer, Minister of Finance, Secretary
Dervish	Member of Islamic religious fraternity
Devlet Musahfir	Guest of the state
Divan	Council, chamber where council meets
Effendi	Title of respect, used initially for government officials and members of learned professions
Emin	Commissioner
Feredjee	Women's ankle-length coat worn outside the house
Giaour	Turkish derogatory name for non-Muslim; infidel
Hafiz	Honourable title, earned by one who knows the Koran by heart

Hamam	Steam bath
Hodja	Muslim man of religion; teacher
"Inshallah"	"With God's help"
Kapidji Bashi	Head of guards
Katil-Ferman	Death warrant
Kaymakam	Deputy for the Vizier in his absence
Khan	Caravanserai, inn, lodging place, warehouse
Khavaz	Courier, bodyguard
Mahal	District, quarter of a town
Mameluke	Member of a body of warriors, originally brought to Egypt as slaves to act as bodyguard for the caliphs
Medrese	Islamic university, theological school
Merhaba	"Good day"
Mubassir	Envoy, agent bearing orders
Muderris	High-ranking teacher in Islamic college, medrese
Muezzin	One who proclaims the hour of prayer from the minaret or highest point of a mosque
Mullah	Ottoman specialist in theology and Islamic law
Muteselim	Lieutenant-governor in a province, in charge of local tax-collection
Pasha	The highest civilian and military rank under the Turkish Sultan (higher than Bey or Effendi)
Pashalik	Area administered by Pasha
Porte	Ottoman court at Constantinople
Rahmet	"Peace to his soul"
Ramadan	Ninth month of Muslim year, rigidly observed as 30 days' fast during the hours of daylight

Rayah	Tax-paying subjects of the Ottoman Government – in Bosnia used to denote the non-Muslim subject-people
Seraglio	Harem
Shalwars	Wide oriental trousers (worn by men and women)
Sherbet	Drink of water, sweetened with sugar or honey
Softa	Student in Islamic university
Spahi	Trained auxiliary member of the Turkish cavalry, usually a landowner whose duty was to serve on horseback
Sultan	One of the titles of the ruler of the Ottoman Empire
Surah	A prayer for the dead
Tekke	Monastery belonging to a Dervish order, or Islamic fraternity
Ulema	Doctors of Islamic sacred law
Vizier	High administrative official
Yamak	Officer of the provincial infantry

(I am grateful to Bogdan Rakić, Dr Margaret Bainbridge of SOAS, and Dr Leslie Collins of SSEES for their help in the preparation of this glossary. C. H.)

More from Apollo

THE LOST EUROPEANS
Emanuel Litvinoff

Coming back was worse, much worse, than Martin Stone had anticipated.

Martin Stone returns to the city from which his family was driven in 1938. He has concealed his destination from his father, and hopes to win some form of restitution for the depressed old man living in exile in London. *The Lost Europeans* portrays a tense, ruined yet flourishing Berlin where nothing is quite what it seems.

MY SON, MY SON
Howard Spring

What a place it was, that dark little house that was two rooms up and two down, with just the scullery thrown in! I don't remember to this day where we all slept, though there was a funeral now and then to thin us out.

This is the powerful story of two hard-driven men – one a celebrated English novelist, the other a successful Irish entrepreneur – and of their sons, in whom are invested their fathers' hopes and ambitions. Oliver Essex and Rory O'Riorden grow up as friends, but their fathers' lofty plans have unexpected consequences as the violence of the Irish Revolution sweeps them all into uncharted territory.

THE MAN WHO LOVED CHILDREN
Christina Stead

> All the June Saturday afternoon Sam Pollit's children were on the lookout for him as they skated round the dirt sidewalks and seamed old asphalt of R Street and Reservoir Road that bounded the deep-grassed acres of Tohoga House, their home.

Sam and Henny Pollit have too many children, too little money and too much loathing for each other. As Sam uses the children's adoration to feed his own voracious ego, Henny becomes a geyser of rage against her improvident husband.

NOW IN NOVEMBER
Josephine Johnson

> Now in November I can see our years as a whole. This autumn is like both an end and a beginning to our lives, and those days which seemed confused with the blur of all things too near and too familiar are clear and strange now.

Forced out of the city by the Depression, Arnold Haldmarne moves his wife and three daughters to the country and tries to scratch a living from the land. After years of unrelenting hard work, the hiring of a young man from a neighbouring farm upsets the fragile balance of their lives. And in the summer, the rains fail to come.

DELTA WEDDING
Eudora Welty

The nickname of the train was the Yellow Dog. Its real name was the Yazoo-Delta. It was a mixed train. The day was the 10th of September, 1923 – afternoon. Laura McRaven, who was nine years old, was on her first journey alone.

Laura McRaven travels down the Delta to attend her cousin Dabney's wedding. At the Fairchild plantation her family envelop her in a tidal wave of warmth, teases and comfort. As the big day approaches, tensions inevitably rise to the surface.

THE DAY OF JUDGMENT
Salvatore Satta

At precisely nine o'clock, as he did every evening, Don Sebastiano Sanna Carboni pushed back his armchair, carefully folded the newspaper which he had read through to the very last line, tidied up the little things on his desk, and prepared to go down to the ground floor...

Around the turn of the twentieth century, in the isolated Sardinian town of Nuoro, the aristocratic notary Don Sebastiano Sanna reflects on his life, his family's history and the fortunes of this provincial backwater where he has lived out his days. Written over the course of a lifetime and published posthumously, *The Day of Judgment* is a classic of Italian, and world, literature.

THE AUTHENTIC DEATH OF HENDRY JONES
Charles Neider

> *Nowadays, I understand, the tourists come for miles to see Hendry Jones'*
> *grave out on the Punta del Diablo and to debate whether his bones are*
> *there or not; and some of them claim his trigger finger is not there, and*
> *others his skull...*

A stark and violent depiction of one of America's most alluring folk heroes, the mythical, doomed gunslinger. Set on the majestic coast of southern California, Doc Baker narrates his tale of the Kid's capture, trial, escape and eventual murder. Written in spare and subtle prose, this is one of the great literary treatments of America's obsession with the rule of the gun.